THE

Consequence

OF

C H A N C E

(A   J U X T A P O S I T I O N)

The Consequence of Chance
Published by The Late Bloom, LLC
Copyright © 2015 by L. Lamont

Please send your comments to the address below.
Thank you in advance.

L. Lamont c/o
www.thelatebloom.com
info@thelatebloom.com

This book is available at quantity discounts for bulk purchases.

Printed in the United States of America.

ISBN: 978 -0-9966569-0-0

Requests for information should be addressed
to the above address.

For Pam, Rita, and all who hope for better days.

THE DAY IT ALL TURNED AROUND [1]

For all the hustle and bustle of 5:30 mornings, motivated by debt and driving through traffic for a career I loved and a job I hated. For all the student loans, credit cards, and car payments meant to enslave me. For living by "faith" every two weeks like a mouse stuck on the wheel of perpetuity. For this self-inflicted insanity, my "exodus" had finally come. On Saturday, October 16, 2010, I looked desperation and generational poverty in the eyes, and screamed, "Fuck you!" The Mega-ball, multi-state lottery drawing of $325 million had become my early birthday gift.

If you would ask me what memorable thing happened the day before, whether the line was long, or if my palm itched, signifying good luck, I'd be at a loss. That day wasn't any different nor the sun shining any brighter than usual, and there wasn't any magical or spiritual indication of things to come. Simply put, I bought a lottery ticket late in the evening on the 15th, along with my customary bag of hot Cheetos, pack of mini cigars, and cranberry juice. Unaware, broke, and optimistic, I was a 36-year-old, single man, about to become one of the luckiest bastards I'd ever known.

Prior to that, most of my days were a struggle in mediocrity, maintaining an existence rather than defining one. Every day of every week seemed to blend into a glob of nothingness in apartment 713, a holding cell for my dreams. Blinded by the ambition of wealth like most people, I nurtured a false sense of optimism; *if I could just win ...* my salvation and resurrection.

Habitually, I'd buy a ticket a day before the draw, playing the same numbers for years. That faithful Friday afternoon was like any other, aside from the special happy hour get together with a co-worker. "M" as we'll call her, agreed to meet at five, but of course she was late and I, disappointed with passing 1,000 convenience stores to change my shirt and spray on cologne, hoping to impress her.

When she finally arrived at Pappadeaux's, she walked in with that seductive high-heeled strut and Georgia peach ass. For a second, I disregarded all things Mega-Ball. Part of me said, *fuck the ticket and let the night take its course*, while the other part said, *you have until 9:45 p.m. before they shut down the system; give this a good two, two and a half hours tops and get the fuck outta there.* Okay, I could do that.

When she spotted me sitting at the bar, she tilted her head to the side with a warm, familiar grin. Other guys noticed her; they admired the very characteristics that made me alter my plans to begin with. Two Swamp Things and an order of seafood fondue, along with her arrival made it worth it all.

"Hey there," I said.

"Hey there, Moore," she replied.

Submitting to the enchantment of her smell and the liberty of our friendly embrace, how dare I have the audacity of being upset?

"Sorry I'm late. I took care of some things for my daughter ... school project."

"Oh, that's cool. I understand ... glad you made it."

"Been here long?" she asked.

I was stuck between hyperbole and compassion.

"Oh, I've only been here a few minutes ... was running late myself, hoping you wouldn't beat me," I lied.

"Okay, well I'll get the next round ..."

"After I buy yours first. You're good ... trust me."

My thirst-o-meter was on 1000, but this was "M," the most desired amongst all male staff and even the gay female staff at our place of employment.

For the first 20 minutes, it was small talk about work. We both were teachers at Winston Perkins Middle School. Sadly, my erection and buzz had succumbed to discussing the standing gossip and drama of the day; I had to change gears.

"So, tell me something I don't know about you?" I asked.

My frankness, fueled by alcohol, was objectified; *this conversation is boring, are we having sex?* Otherwise I had a ticket to buy.

"Well, okay let's see ... I'm into a lot of things; first and foremost, I love the Lord."

My face began to crack from the fabricated smile I held as I pretended to care.

"That's good ... loving the Lord." A momentary resort to thirsty tactics.

"Oh, you're a church going man?"

Her response inferred hope for my cause, possibly the stars would align; *we fucking*?

"Indeed, sister."

"Amen, brother," she replied, with a slight chuckle.

"We need to get you that drink, what will you have?"

"Oh, just give me a Mai Thai."

The evening went on, with peaks and valleys in the conversation. The ambiguity was torturous, especially her "Baby Daddy" talk.

"It's all good though, I've moved on," a familiar phrase of countless single women. At that time, it was 6:57 p.m. I figured if we ordered food, the evening would move along. I asked for two menus from the bartender.

"I don't know what I want, I mean I'm hungry, I don't know what I want though," she repeated. *Shit*. I knew exactly what I wanted; fried catfish platter with another Swamp Thing.

"Try the gumbo, it's pretty good for a restaurant," I offered.

"Yeah, that sounds good ..."

"Sir, we're ready," I interrupted.

In my haste, the realization of another routine was unfolding. Here I was, anticipating a sexual encounter and the possibility of purchasing the winning lottery ticket, fully aware that neither would take place. I'd been down this road before, fantasizing my way through life, being unfulfilled in the process.

The fact that she found reason enough to dine with me, as attractive as she was, should have been enough. And as far as the lottery ticket, if time permitted, I'd buy it. If not, I'd only hope that no one else won, for a chance next Tuesday.

"Do you mind if I call for a toast?" I asked.

"A toast? ... Okay, for what?"

"Good food, good conversation, the beautiful woman sitting across from me, and this Swamp Thing in my hand." She appreciated the humor with a charming smirk. After we finished, we walked to her car, exchanging pleasantries. It was 9:05 p.m., still enough time but no rush. I thanked her for a lovely evening and proceeded to the corner store near the crib, buying my ticket before 9:45 p.m. It was a good night.

The next day, after a late afternoon session of fooling myself at the gym, I arrived at home, checked voice mails, emails, walked Buddy Boy my pug, and fixed a bowl of cereal. After that, came a long hot shower and a nap, along with a slight headache. Later, I called Mom, and afterward played my season of Madden for three or four games. Around 6:30 that evening, it was laundry time and the weekend news played in the background.

"Someone hit it big on Mega-Ball in our very own back yard, stay tuned for details," the announcer said before going to a commercial break.

A flutter of excitement hit me, similar to a moment of wishful thinking like the last time, but it ended up being some old motherfucker in Conroe. *Calm it down…be real*, I told myself.

"Someone has 325 million reasons to be happy today; that's right Jane, the winning Mega-Ball lottery ticket was purchased right here in Houston, Texas … "

I stopped folding clothes, ran into the living room, and stood right in front of the TV.

"According to the Mega-Ball offices out of Austin, the winning ticket was purchased at this Ready Mart, at the corner of Bradley & Hurst … "

My stomach did some weird gravity pull. *"My"* store flashed on the screen. *Please don't fuck with me.* Silence ensued from that moment on. I zoned out on possibility, fearful with believing the unthinkable. A bit numb, I sat on the couch staring at the TV until my next nap.

When I woke up an hour later, the newscast replayed in my mind. The burden of checking my numbers dreadfully remained. Getting my hopes up was emotional suicide, a regrettable feeling; *but what if I won?* I mustered the nerve to go to the lottery website. Matching a few numbers, winning a couple hundred bucks, was fine enough, let alone matching five of the six numbers for the $250,000 prize.

Scrolling down the screen, with ticket in hand, my nerves caused trembling and sweaty crack-like behavior. *God, let me have this, please.* My attention juxtaposed ticket and screen, meticulously. "My" numbers were the following: *5* for the month of my mother's birthday; *6* for the day of my birthday; *11* for the month of my birthday; *37*, for the year I was born, but in reverse, 1973; *52*, the year of my mother's birth; and finally, *10*, the day she was born.

The ticket started with **5**, a cause for slight celebration, but randomly probable. So I glanced at the next number, **6**. I tensed up having two in a row; **10**, *oh my God, I have three numbers in a row*. That was enough for the $500 prize, but I continued on. The next number was **11**. When I saw 11, I paused in anxious disbelief, and put the ticket down. My hands were visibly trembling, almost violently. For a minute I stood to collect myself and get a glass of water. Buddy Boy ran around the apartment while I focused on him, ignoring the ticket. Then I sat patiently, deciding to continue. When I saw the remaining two numbers, **37** and **52**, my body was immediately flush with heat.

Realizing what was in my hand, I sat there, frozen, removed from time, and aligned with the universe, void of any sensibility. Emotionally paralyzed, I wanted to cry, but a single tear wouldn't fall. Slowly standing, I dropped the ticket to the floor, looked around the living room, holding my head, overwhelmed with 325 million thoughts. *What the fuck just happened?*

In a T-shirt and sweats I was instantly a multimillionaire, living in an apartment complex where the average income was no more than $40k a year. *This can't be real, I've gotta check the numbers again.* Once more, a third time, and a fourth, it was real. "I'm rich, bitch!" I screamed. I sat on the edge of my couch for another hour, and stared at the ticket. My cell phone rang. Startled, I looked at the unrecognizable number, assured that it was a bill collector.

"Hello?" I answered.

"Yes, is this Mr. Douglas Moore?" the lady asked.

"Yes, whom might I be speaking with?" I asked, fully aware that it was a bill collector.

"I'm calling on behalf of Anderson Furnishings & Electronics regarding your September payment."

"Don't even worry about it … I'll pay that whole thing off in a few days," I smugly replied.

"Sir, the remaining balance is $4,670. …" she countered in condescension.

"Ma'am … are you implying something?" I interrupted, fucking with her.

"Well sir, I just wanted to clarify the amount you're intending to pay off."

"$4,670, right?"

"I didn't mean to be rude sir. …"

"You think I don't have the money?"

I was trying to contain my laughter while keeping a serious tone with her.

"Well, sir, that's good. So… when will you have this payment?"

"Let me say it again … I-am-going-to-pay-the-entire-account-off-in-a-few-days."

"Okay sir, I'll just put that in my notes; you'll pay the balance of $4,670, in its entirety, in a few days. But do you have a date in mind?"

"The first of when I pay it."

I was done with the conversation and politely hung up.

Before the money, I'd been with the district as a middle school social studies teacher for 11 years, with good friends and a supportive family. Even with all my debt, the kid could still splurge, like the 50 inch flat screen TV, PlayStation 3 and surround sound system I was late paying on. In reality, my financial rut was caused by chasing happiness at the swipe of a card.

The lottery was my religion. I "tithed" my money away with no real expectation other than an addiction to "faith." It was like a drug for that "what if?" feeling. But with every loss of a dollar, I loathed the lottery, surmising it to be a racket. Most winners came from small, backwoods, bum-fuck towns anyway.

So when it happened to me, it was the surrealistic death of my old self. The new Douglas Moore couldn't care less about being 30 days past due or a fucking FICO score; the shackles of debt were unlocked. This was my "phoenix rising," a man about town, a man with matters, an itinerary, a life, Douglas Moore, world traveler and philanthropist. But first, I had to tell my mother.

The call to the Mega-Ball office would follow next Monday morning. It would be the most nerve wrecking 24 hours in life. It hadn't settled that this wasn't a fluke, even after checking the numbers a trillion times online.

To clear my head and regain my composure, Buddy and I went outside, and walked around the complex, with every step better than the next. Anonymity came to mind. *Did I really want people knowing about the money?* The freedoms of everyday life like grocery shopping or going to the International Festival in Tranquility Park weren't expendable.

Later in the evening I did a web search, *what to do when you win the lottery*. A myriad of information from tax havens and offshore accounts to creating a charity fund popped up. It was dizzying. One term stood out most, prompting me to do more research: "Blind Trust." A blind trust allowed someone in my situation to receive a massive amount of money anonymously. It made perfect sense.

The thought of saying, "I've won $325 million," was mind-blowing. Just then, the evening rerun of the news announced that the winning ticket was sold in Houston. My heart jumped into my throat. *They're talking about me. Fuck, I'm the winner. Maybe I should call a lawyer.*

NEW YORK, NEW YORK [2]

On Monday morning after calling in "sick," the hunt continued, and I searched the web for firms in New York City, Los Angeles, Boston, and Washington, D.C. For some reason, this firm in New York, *Berber, Morrison & McDouglas*, stood out. Maybe because my name is Douglas. It was really random. When I called, I had no script, no rhyme, or reason.

"Yes, I'd like to speak with someone regarding a blind trust?" I announced.

"One moment please," the guy on the other end said. I sat there, nervously, trying to formulate the words for financial advice in a professional, educated voice. The wait was a minute or less, but felt like five. I hurriedly turned the TV down from the thunderous applause of the Maury Povich audience in response to the "baby daddy" test results.

"Law offices of Berber, Morrison & McDouglas, Frankie Collins speaking. How may I help you?"

"Yes, hi. I am interested in getting information about creating a blind trust. I understand your firm provides those services."

"Indeed we do, sir. May I have your name?"

"Yes, I'm Douglas Moore," I said still in my professional, educated voice.

"Mr. Moore, it would be my pleasure to assist you. Could you give me some information as to how this blind trust could best serve your needs? I'll jot it down and present it to our counselors for further review."

"Well Ms. Collins ..."

"Frankie is fine," she interrupted.

9

"Okay, uh, Frankie … I've recently come into a large amount of money, but I'd like to maintain my privacy," I replied.

"Well first, let me begin by saying congratulations, and that our attorneys are well equipped to provide you legal representation. May I ask whether this was an inheritance or a …" I interrupted her, eager to finally tell someone this secret that burned inside. Yeah, I hadn't told my mother, but damn, someone needed to know.

"I, uh … I won the Mega-Ball multi-state lottery jackpot." For ten seconds the conversation paused.

"Are you serious, sir?" she asked, in a cynical tone.

I giggled as if a dirty joke was told; spilling the beans felt therapeutic, marking the first time I'd ever officially told anyone.

After talking with Frankie for a few minutes more, we ended the conversation optimistically. Wearing my favorite raggedy gray T-shirt and 10-year-old sweats, it dawned on me that I was becoming a fugitive. The time had come to emerge from obscurity and go somewhere public. *Let me check the fridge, the supermarket sounds good.* I hopped in the shower, dressed, jumped in my 98 Ford Explorer Sport, with its tricky driver side door handle and fucked up radio knob. It wouldn't allow the volume to be turned up or down unless you turned off the radio and turned it back on, while turning the knob up or down. *I'm getting a new car.*

Pulling into Kroger's parking lot was somewhat of a homecoming. The thrill was inexplicable, marking my first public appearance as a multimillionaire, and none would be the wiser. This is exactly what I wanted to preserve. A wholeness with the mundane; aimlessly walking up and down the aisles.

When I arrived back home, after contemplating some of life's biggest decisions in the produce section, it was clear that the reality of my existence would change. My relationships would change, with the possibility of being misunderstood by this sudden affluence; *"He be acting funny now days."* It was a bittersweet revelation. My desire to enhance the lives of those I loved or had grown to love, hadn't changed. But beside that moment of clarity, a pressing matter still lingered. I needed to call my mama.

Later in the evening, I called Mrs. Eugenia Moore, retired secretary of 25 years, with Los Angeles County, and loving grandmother of two, my brother's kids. As I dialed, it dawned on me that I hadn't thought of what to say or for that matter, her reaction. My mother could be a little dramatic. The last thing I needed was her calling half the family, and half the city of Pasadena, California. Tactfully, I decided to do something more clever, and yet, more thoughtful. I'll tell her in person.

Looking for flights to LAX, the prices were incredible. Regardless of my new status, I still cringed at what I saw. *Eight hundred dollars, round trip? Fuck, if I spend that kind of money, I should take the trip to New York*. Having 90 days to collect my winnings was an unnecessary wait in time. And having no clue whether Berber, Morrison & McDouglas would be a right or wrong fit, I bought a ticket intending to see them, solidifying my business. I called my mother, withholding the news.

"Hey, Mama."

"I was just thinking about you," she said. She always said that.

"Yeah, I was just calling, checking on you, everything okay?"

"Yeah, I'm fine…you okay?" she asked, in her usual concerned tone.

"Yeah, I'm fine."

"I actually have some very good news, but it's not final yet, real soon."

"Okay… how was your day?" she asked.

"Fine … nothing much, just another day." *What a fucking declaration*. "Did you walk today?" I asked.

"No, I was tired … on the phone all day dealing with these bills," was her melancholy reply. She lived on a fixed income. My brother and I did what we could to help.

"Mama, things are gone get better real soon," I assured her.

The bittersweet aspect of winning, meant taking care of the people I loved, except for the one who was most influential in my life, my father. Leonard Francis Moore or "Papa Doc," as we called him, was your typical, hard-working, blue-collar man, who worked for the county electric company for 30 years. He was the kind of guy who could make you feel good about yourself, regardless of the truth. He was giving and unselfish to a fault. Mama would often get on him about making "donations," as she would say, especially to those who hadn't paid back previous debts. His death from congestive heart failure, three years ago was untimely. I remember getting the call. It was one of the most painful disappointments of my life.

Sadly, he would never meet the woman I'd eventually marry, or hold my child in his arms. And now with this money, there wouldn't be a trip to Africa, a nice fishing boat speeding on Lake

Conroe, or whatever his heart desired. *Papa Doc, I miss and love you, dearly.*

Then there was my favorite cousin, Andre, who died of cancer the year before I won. We'd always talk of opening some business or participating in some multi-level marketing scheme. We were sick with being stuck in life, and believed for more. This money would've given him the start over he deserved. But for now, my focus was on changing Mama's life, and my brother Devin and his family members' lives. We went through a lot in those lean and in-between years. Welcome to forever.

Gwen, my ex, the woman I was supposed to marry and make a family with, came to mind. Oddly, we'd been cordial in recent months. In fact, we talked a few weeks back. Nonetheless, we ended our four-year relationship earlier in the spring, April to be exact. With all that was transpiring in her life, the death of her sister, the custody battle for her son, and the threat of being laid off, it was just too much between us.

Her son, Morgan, turned me into a surrogate father by happenstance. When we started dating, he was three, full of life and deserving of his absentee father. We'd go and get haircuts together, hit the park, and other father and son shit. Gwen was receptive to my participation, but reserved.

Our separation was really her willingness to relieve me of any further burdensome details of her life. When her sister died, she was functionally depressed. No matter how much I tried to reassure her of my love and support, her pride overruled it all. That was the beginning of the end. One truth remained; I still loved her.

A few days later on Wednesday morning, I called Frankie informing her that I'd decided to go with their firm. Having no reference as to whether the firm was the right choice, I knew the blind trust was a necessary thing. Afterward, I booked kennel service for Buddy Boy, a hotel room, and a flight for me to meet with them on Friday.

Every phone call or personal interaction made with a stranger had a chipper quality to it, like, *"Do you know you're talking to the Mega-Ball, multi-state lottery winner, worth $325 million, roughly $165 million after state and federal taxes… huh?"*

I called in another sick day. The conflict of being absent from Winston weighed on my moral judgment. Beyond having a decent paying job for some sense of security or social standing, I was a teacher for real, a surrogate parent, counselor, role model, and confidant. My biggest prized possession had been my career. With all this money, I still had an obligation to these kids.

A few days later, I was in New York City. I arrived Friday morning excited and terribly nervous. The brisk chill of the morning had an exhilarating affect, a pick me up for what was about to transpire. Not knowing what to expect walking into the office of this Manhattan law firm, I imagined a bunch of white guys in their 40s and 50s, politely smiling at me, grimacing at my fortune. Or maybe I'd receive a genuine reception from a bunch of rich guys accepting me as their own, a member of the one percent fraternity.

The city felt big, and I felt a sense of purpose. The money represented unforeseen opportunities, inspiration, and the changing of lives. Just as quick as I could fathom the good this money could do, my imagination was altered to a nice penthouse suite somewhere near Central Park; going to top tier restaurants and exclusive art gallery showings with some model chick for a girlfriend, spending my money and pissing me off.

As we approached the imposing downtown office building, my nerves were electrified. This wasn't even the actual claiming of the money. The cab driver pulled up to the curb, as New Yorkers hustled up and down the sidewalk, trying to make their way in the world. It was slow motion and yet, everything moved at the speed of life. Stepping out of the car, I took the deepest breath possible, looking up at the building, like a scene from a movie or the opening to a TV show. Afterward, I gathered my belongings and proceeded to walk inside.

Momentarily paranoid, I felt "watched," as I walked quickly through the lobby. Then I remembered to call Frankie upon arriving.

"Hello, Frankie?"

"Mr. Moore, hello, sir. You've arrived?"

"Yes ma'am, I'm standing by the security desk." Some big Italian or Arabian dude was looking dead in my mouth, and then he looked away.

"Okay, Mr. Moore, I'll be right down." Just five days ago, I was a social studies teacher, with a salary of $49,500 a year, living in a shoe box. And now, here I stood, meeting with this New York law firm to handle the biggest business transaction of my life.

Looking around the lobby was weird; my good fortune, this moment, this city, this big ass building, all of it. Unaware of the time, the brightness of the sun washed over the lobby, a precursor to an awesome day. I wanted to live in that moment as long as possible.

"Mr. Moore," I heard someone say. I turned around, and there she stood, this 5'5, 130 - 140 pound specimen of gorgeous womanhood. When I finally saw her, I became a giddy little boy.

"Yes, hello," we both extended our hands for a professional handshake.

"Finally nice to meet you," I said with a bit of enthusiasm in my voice; maybe a bit too much. Her demeanor seemed friendly, while her sexy black framed glasses made her appear to be more of an intellectual type.

"Shall we?" she asked.

"Lead the way."

Frankie looked African-American, but maybe bi-racial. She had a figure like someone conscious of diet and exercise, and her walk ... stunning.

"How was your flight?" she asked walking towards the elevators.

"Oh, it was fine, aside from the guy snoring next to me the entire flight." We shared a laugh, probably at the expense of my uncontrollable corny side. It only happens when they're gorgeous.

"Are you staying a few days?" she asked. I hadn't really intended to. I was a millionaire on paper, but a brother was running on fumes. The flight, hotel, and kennel service put me at around $1,200.

"Not really I'm heading back Saturday morning."

We made our way onto the elevator and all I could think about, besides how beautiful she was, were the people I'd meet. She pressed 39 for the floor and gave a quick little *we're on our way up* grin. We remained silent for the duration of the ride due to the crowded space.

When we finally reached our destination, I was in awe of the reception area, with the law firm's name, *Berber, Morrison & McDouglas* emblazoned on the wall in brass. The decor and lighting suggested modern chic minimalism, and a firm with a lot of money.

Walking through the office, I was greeted with a mixture of trite and welcoming looks. The city view from the floor was breathtaking, something you'd expect from a Manhattan skyscraper. Seemingly all cultures and racial groups were represented, young and mature. They all had a look of sophistication and intelligence. Continuing down the hall behind Frankie, I tried being inconspicuous, but that ass ... I was captivated. *Yeah, she's black or half black.* We eventually arrived at what appeared to be a conference room.

"Mr. Moore, make yourself comfortable. In just a moment Mr. Grantham, Mr. Williamson, and Ms. Strasburg will join us for your consultation."

"No problem," I responded.

Wow, my consultation. My counselors. I have counselors. But sitting alone in the room felt like a job interview. I had to remind myself that I was in charge. Regardless of their degrees and experience, I wouldn't be intimidated. Surely they'd have a line of questions to make sure this wasn't a bullshit waste of time. The lottery ticket was my proof. No matter what, I was the boss that day.

In my peripheral view a small group of folks made their way towards the conference room. It appeared that they were all fairly young, early to mid-40s; the woman was grayish-blonde, the white guy all gray and a black guy who was completely bald. *Cool, a brother's in the room.* As they entered, I stood to greet them.

"Mr. Moore," they all seemed to say in unison. I was impressed.

"Nice to finally meet you all," I replied, as we shook hands.

"Shall we?" the white guy added. We all sat down to the beginnings of a two-hour meeting at 11 in the morning.

"Formally, I'm Cameron Williamson, and these are my colleagues, Gary Grantham, and Paulette Strasburg," he said.

Brother man seemed a bit intense, like the actor who played the captain on "Star Trek, Deep Space 9." He had a really deep James Earl Jones voice, and easily stood about six foot three. Strasburg reminded me of a young Martha Stewart, and Williamson, typical as I imagined; a waspy north easterner.

"So, Mr. Moore, do you think we could see the Holy Grail?" Strasburg asked, in a somewhat coy and cute demeanor. I reached for my messenger bag.

"Not a problem … had a feeling you'd ask me that." From the time I realized I'd won, up until that day, the ticket was with me or very close by. Even the night before the flight, I put it on the nightstand, periodically checking on it. And on the plane ride, it remained in my messenger bag, which stayed in my lap.

When I passed the ticket and printout to the lawyers, they pulled out a document of their own to match the numbers. I looked at Frankie as if to ask, *"What the fuck?"* but she just shrugged.

"Congratulations, Mr. Moore, this is amazing," Williamson spoke.

"Indeed," Grantham added.

"We appreciate your consideration in this endeavor," Strasburg chimed. Their collective front was reserved, and still their elation was evident.

"We're going to go over the benefits of having a blind trust, its legal confines, and formation, but before we do, you have any questions or concerns, Mr. Moore?" Grantham asked.

"Honestly, I wouldn't know what to ask, with my novice understanding of what a blind trust is and how it works ... I'm more concerned with legal fees." Everybody laughed, but I was serious as fuck.

"Generally, our clients are charged in billable hours, so for instance, our firm receives $235 an hour for the services rendered in preparation of a case or presenting documentation of legal representation, which is your circumstance," Grantham replied. That sounded a lot better than a percentage of my winnings.

"Well, as you can see, I haven't cashed in the ticket yet ... wanted to set up the trust first."

"Oh, no problem, we totally agree with that decision. Many lottery winners don't do the homework you've done," Strasburg replied. "When you receive payment, the money will be wired to an account of your choosing, through the name of the trust, which keeps you anonymous."

"That's exactly what I want."

After an hour we finally took a break and with a full bladder for 30 minutes straight, I bee-hived to the bathroom. It was 12:19 p.m. Central Park and Harlem seemed more interesting at this point, but I was handling business. They had me thinking about things I'd never considered; *where was I to put all this money?* I couldn't just have it wired to my savings account, or hire some local H&R Block dude to handle it.

As a protective measure from a shitload of taxes, they advised that I create a charity foundation like the rich and famous do. Difference is, I really wanted to help folks, especially Houston's Third Ward area.

When I returned back to the conference room, Grantham asked, "So what's the first thing you're going to buy with all this money?" I hadn't given it much thought past my dream house, customary new cars, and jewelry.

"I think I'll buy my mother whatever she wants," I replied. Both Frankie and Strasburg applauded.

"Your trust will be an entity unto itself, you should give it a name," Grantham said.

"Decisions, decisions ... can I get back to you all on that?" I asked.

"Well, when do you plan on claiming the money?" Strasburg asked. Her point was evident. The longer I took, the longer I'd wait to claim the jackpot.

"I'd like to claim it as soon as I touch down, probably Monday morning. Will I be accompanied by anyone?" Everybody looked at each other, not sure of an answer.

"I don't see that as a problem, but we'll have to look at our individual schedules and make that determination after today's meeting," Grantham said.

"That's fine, I appreciate that and yeah ... I have an idea for a name; Cypress Financial Holdings."

"Any significance?" Grantham asked.

"Yeah, Cypress is the name of the street I grew up on."

By about 12:50 p.m. we'd begun wrapping up for the day. Just that morning, I was a theoretical rich guy, uneducated in the ways of financial preparedness, without a clue on matters protecting my assets. But by the end of the consultation, not only did I have a blind trust to protect my wealth, I was also more aware of tax havens, philanthropic endeavors, and a variety of accounting firms, ready for my business. My shit was in order.

"Well Mr. Moore, I think we've covered a lot of ground here today. We really appreciate you for choosing our firm to handle this life-changing transaction, and we look forward to nothing but great outcomes from this business relationship," Grantham said. They all smiled and looked at me, awaiting my reply.

"I'm equally grateful for your expertise, thank you very much," I said while looking at Frankie.

"I think we can give you an answer on a travel companion for next Monday, by this evening," Strasburg said. Their support was reassuring; it cemented my status as a bona-fide V.I.P. and soon-to-be millionaire with matters to tend to. We all shook hands and then Frankie escorted me to the reception area.

"It was really nice meeting them. I feel comfortable now."

"Mr. Moore ... "

"Douglas..." I interrupted. She smiled.

"Douglas ... you're in good hands. They handle many high net worth clients, so don't worry. Welcome to your new life," she concluded. It was a defining moment to an unexpected happenstance.

On the elevator ride down, it dawned on me how secretive I'd been with a lot of people. Some of the closest folks in my life had no idea. *Who could I trust with this information?* They'd eventually see me driving something illogical to a teacher's salary. *If I could just keep it zipped 'til Tuesday.*

TAKE THE MONEY AND RUN [3]

When I returned to Houston, it was a balmy Saturday afternoon. Traffic on Highway 59 was congested, but a careless matter. Waking up at 5:30 in the morning to fight it would be a thing of the past. My first stop was at the kennel to get Buddy Boy. We were ecstatic to see each other and get back home. I rushed up the stairs, entered my apartment, walked into my bedroom, and dropped everything.

After taking a shower and a nap, I let Buddy out to do his business, and then went online to check for flights to Austin. Prior to leaving New York, Frankie informed me that an associate, Parker Rose, would meet me at the Mega-Ball office, with all the necessary documentation. We agreed to meet at 10 that morning. I was disappointed it wasn't Frankie, but this was a matter best handled by an attorney.

My cell phone rang, it was Lamont.

"What up nigga?…You been ghost, you all right?" Lamont, my homeboy for maybe a decade now, was the type of dude that shot straight. He works for the city of Houston in the Juvenile corrections department as a probation officer, and his wife Dana, works as a pharmacist at one of the drugstore chains in town. I 'm godfather to their son, Ramsey. For fun, Lamont and I usually went to Carrington's Sports Bar on Main to watch games or Sullivan's Steakhouse on Westheimer to listen to live music.

"Yeah man, I'm good… had to handle some business, but I'm good," I answered. *How would I tell him?*

Lamont and I shot the shit for a good while, with him and his usual tirades about work and Dana pissing him off yet again. We agreed to meet at Carrington's sometime in the near future, before

19

hanging up. Afterward, I scheduled a doctor's appointment for 4:30 p.m., Tuesday afternoon to legitimize my absences for a full week and some days. And I decided to stop by the district headquarters to officially put in my resignation. I figured I'd go in Wednesday and finish out the week and my career.

The redundancy of not telling Mama about the money was beginning to play on my consciousness. Perhaps a random tragedy like a plane or car accident involving my demise would happen and she'd be dealing with the same everyday shit. After accepting the money, she'd be the first to get the news.

Monday morning finally arrived. This was the day that the Lord had made and believe you me, I was truly rejoicing and glad to be in it. It was 6:45 in the morning. I paced the apartment with a cup of coffee, thinking of how long I'd lived there. It was an old friend, much like my good neighbors, Ms. Felicia, a district bus driver; the Robinsons, an older couple from Michigan; and Rocco, my weed connect in the next building over. My existence at 7100 Alameda, apartment number 713, was nice. But times were changing. Telling these folks about the money was like telling a group of people stuck in quick sand, *"Well… I'll see ya when I see ya."*

I received a call from an unknown New York number and suspected it was Parker.

"Mr. Moore, good morning, this is Parker Rose… I'll be representing you on behalf of the firm today."

"Oh, good morning," I replied.

"Mr. Moore, we're scheduled to connect at 10 correct?"

"Yes indeed, I'm about to leave for the airport now, my flight lands at 9."

"Very well sir, I'll be at the lottery office, this is my number, call me when you arrive."

"Will do," I replied.

Her mystique was masked in "professionalism."

Later that morning, arriving at the airport, I went to the ticketing counter without any bags to check. A few ordinary, everyday looking people were working, earning a living. Maybe they'd been up since three, four, or five in the morning.

Secretly embarrassed about the money, a simple dollar changed my existence forever. *Why me?* In that same breath, I proceeded through the security check point, onwards to the terminal, making the resolution to never take economy or coach again; *first class would do.*

After landing in Austin, I immediately called the attorney and went for a taxi. Resorting to covert tactics, I instructed the cab driver to take me to an imaginary building near or next to the lottery office. Riding into the city from the airport, all was well with the world. The sky went on forever, as my thoughts turned to my new situation. The sun was shining, literally and figuratively, on me in the back of that cab.

Getting closer to downtown, I took in the rustic and eclectic vibe of Austin's landscape, reminiscent of California, with its hills and sweeping views.

We made a sharp turn on a busy street, and I assumed we were getting close. Off in the distance, I looked for a sign, anything indicating our location.

"Sir, how close are we?" I asked.

"It's right up the street here, on the right," he replied. My nerves were worked up. I was just minutes and 100 yards away from officially becoming a millionaire. The anticipation put a smile on my face. The driver caught a glimpse of me, and quickly looked away. The traffic was simultaneously painful and thrilling; the space between the closure of one chapter in my life and the beginning of the next.

"Here you go, bud," the cab driver stated.

"Thanks," I said, paying the fare and making my way out the backseat. To my left was the lottery office. I noticed a well-dressed African-American woman holding a briefcase, while talking on her cell phone. I made my way toward her.

"Ms. Rose?" I asked.

"Mr. Moore?" she replied. We both greeted each other with a handshake.

"Hope you haven't been waiting long."

"No, actually my hotel is minutes from here; I took my time until getting your call," she responded. "You ready to do this?"

"Ready as I'll ever be," I replied. We turned towards the entrance of the building and proceeded to walk in.

The feeling reminded me of my days in junior high; that adolescent nervousness of seeing the principal or school counselor. A big sign hung on a wall that read, "Mega-Ball has given over $2 billion to public education across America." Parker walked up to the reception desk, asking where claimants were to go for prizes. After giving our names, we were directed to take the elevator to the third floor, where we'd meet a representative. Finally the chance to take a glimpse at Parker's ass. Upon exiting the elevator, a portly Hispanic woman stood, waiting for us.

"Mr. Moore, Ms. Rose?" she asked.

In unison, we answered yes.

"Welcome to our headquarters," she offered as we shook hands. "Was it difficult getting here?" We both smiled, reassuring her that everything was fine. *Can we get to the damn money?* She escorted us through the glass doors leading to the prize claims department. "Richard Blake, our supervisor of claims will be with you shortly. Have a seat in here would ya?"

"This is exciting, I've never been in a situation quite like this," Parker said.

"You?" I replied. She snickered a bit, revealing a pleasant informal side.

"Hey gang," said some white guy entering the room, presumably Richard Blake.

"Congratulations, who's the lucky person?"

"I am," I proudly announced. Blake walked up to Parker and me, shook our hands and took his seat behind his desk.

"Well let's see here, which prize are we talking?" He uttered with a sly tone. I was a little irritated by it. Motherfuckers don't come up to Austin for $500 scratch-offs. I pulled out my ticket and slid it over for a gander. *Bitch.*

"Mega-Ball, multi-state lottery draw of $325 million," I replied arrogantly. I detected a slight change in his color. *Was he jealous? Certainly not, he works for the damn company, how could he be jealous? Or was it that I won?*

"Oh really?" he said with a weird, sarcastic chortle. Next thing, he took out a big gray binder to match the numbers. Then, he got on the phone and made a quick call.

"Sandy, get Jim in here, we have our winner, bye." I looked at Parker, and she looked at Richard for an answer.

"Jim is our state of Texas lottery commissioner. He has to make the final verification, as well as sign off on the paper work entitling you to the cash option, which you've chosen …congratulations, Mr. Moore, you're a very rich man."

"Thank you, Mr. Blake," I answered. My reserved facade masked the backflips inside … I wanted to scream, but I kept my composure.

About a minute or so later, in walks this big, burly, older white gentleman, maybe in his 50s. He had a limp, with a Texas size gut.

"Hello I'm Jim Brennan," he said as he extended his hand to Parker and me. We shook hands, but I couldn't help noticing something. He was crossed-eyed.

"This is my attorney, Ms. Parker Rose."

"Nice to meet you ma'am," he replied. "Well, can I get y'all some coffee, doughnuts, anything?" he asked.

"Coffee would be fine," Parker responded.

"I'm okay," I countered. After the formalities, the process was underway.

"If you don't mind, let's take this to my office, I have some documents for you to sign."

Walking to Jim's office, my confidence began to build. I was about to collect over $165 million, officially becoming a millionaire. The thought validated my reasons for accepting the money anonymously.

Jim's office was huge and inviting. He had pictures of past winners sprawled across all of the walls. From the look of it, he'd aged with the company.

"Please have a seat." I took a glance at Parker, as she sat with her briefcase. *She's beautiful.* Not forgetting Frankie, Parker's appeal was interesting. Her "reddish" skin tone complimented her hazel eyes and faint freckles. She was tall, maybe 5'8," with shoulder length hair, the color of cinnamon. And when she smiled, her dimples went on forever.

"This is standard procedure regarding the issuance of funds to the claimant," Jim said as he laid documents down in front of us. "You've decided to take the cash option which amounts to $165,876,900 ... man I like the sound of that." We laughed. "Since you're doing so, we need to know how the money is to be wired to your financial institution of choice. Funds in this amount can't be wired outside the United States before 30 days of possession ..."

"My client has a financial institution of choice, with wiring instructions," Parker offered.

"Mr. Moore, are you receiving this money in a public manner, which requires you to make a public appearance for news media and other outlets. Or, are you receiving this money anonymously?" he asked.

"My client will receive the funds through a blind trust," Parker answered. Home girl was on it.

"Wise choice...with this kind of money, I wouldn't want anybody seeing my face either."

Thankfully, the folks back in New York set up an account with Frasier Payne, a private banking institution that handled "high net worth" individuals as myself. A high net worth client had to have assets amounting $30 million or more. The account would be interest bearing, generating dividends every month, more than enough to live on. Once the money was wired, I'd fly back to New York and meet with these guys. I trusted the lawyers on their decision, but I had some apprehension with "Wall Street" after the Bernie Madoff fiasco, and the bank bail outs. Frasier Payne, on the other hand, was a well-known, well respected institution.

"Upon signature of this affidavit, which gives you complete ownership of funds and voids the Texas lottery commission of any responsibility thereafter, your funds should be available within three business days from today. I strongly advise that you maintain all documentation received, in safe keeping," he went on. Parker continued looking over the documents as I looked at her like a sheepish little boy wondering what the hell was going on. Damn, three whole days though. The anticipation was killing me.

At about 11:38 a.m. we wrapped up everything, with me still technically a millionaire on paper, just closer than before. It was surreal, and yet I'd report back to Perkins on Wednesday morning.

"Mr. Moore, Ms. Parker, I think that about does it... congratulations and welcome to the good life," Jim said with sincerity. He made a call to Sandy, asking her to bring the camera in for his traditional picture with the winner; my "celebrity moment," I supposed.

A few minutes later, Sandy walked in.

"Congratulations, Mr. Moore," she said, as she proceeded to give me a bear hug.

"It's safe for me to walk outta' here today?" I asked. Everyone shared in the humor, but I was edgy. Thoughts of them calling up family members and friends saying shit like, "Yeah, I know who won, it's a black guy from Houston ... " crossed my mind.

"Mr. Moore, we're sworn to privacy, based on the option you've chosen. The only people who know about your winnings are Sandy, Richard, and I. If any of this got out, we'd lose our jobs."

"Oh ... just joking." I gave a saving face reply.

After saying our goodbyes, Parker and I went back outside the building in total silence. We looked at each other not sure of what was next; a smile turned into laughter, which led to an unexpected hug.

"I don't even know what to do right now," I said.

"Mr. Moore, it's time to live like you've never lived before," she replied.

After exchanging a few more pleasantries, Parker went her way and I went mine. I didn't know if I'd see her next week at the meeting with the Frasier Payne folks, but lunch or dinner would've been nice. She mentioned changing her flight time since the meeting went so quickly. Maybe she would've made amends. Nevertheless, I caught a cab to some restaurant and later a movie to kill time until my 5 p.m. flight back home.

Tuesday afternoon, I went to the doctor's office in peace. After yesterday's business, it felt good to get settled back in. My doctor of the past six years, Dr. Harrison Miles, was a cool older gentleman, a brother from New Orleans.

"Mr. Moore, you can come back now," the office attendant said. Dr. Miles always had me cracking up, with his dry, dirty old man sense of humor. *Should I come clean and tell him about the money?* He was arbitrary in a sense, removed from my daily life and obligated to doctor/patient privacy. The door opened, and in he walked with that old school dip and grayish flat top.

"Brother Moore, how are you young buck?" he uttered with his nurse assistant by his side.

"Good seeing you Doc. Hi, Ms. Anna," I said. She just smiled and waved.

"It's been a while baby, what's the deal?" he asked. Yeah it had been a while. Hospitals and doctor's appointments weren't my thing.

"I know, just been ripping and running, but I'm catching up," I answered. Doc Miles was the kind of guy that "hooked" up situations, if you know what I mean. This wouldn't be my first time needing a "doctor's note." After explaining that I'd been out for over a week for "mental health" purposes, he obliged.

"Well since you're here, wanna go ahead and have a physical … it wouldn't hurt," he explained.

"I guess so, Doc."

"Anna, prep the patient, I'll be right back." As he walked out the room, Anna gave me the robing to change into, then left. Ten minutes later they both came back in, with an EKG machine, a plastic container with vials, and syringes to take blood samples.

"Mr. Moore can you disrobe and lie down please?" Anna asked. I was a little embarrassed because my midsection was a tad flabby.

Gotta hire a trainer. As Anna applied those cold sensors to my body, the past 11 days of my life were cause for reflection. Nothing in the world could upset me. Even going into work Wednesday would represent the last Wednesday I'd ever have to report to any person or organization again.

After having the EKG, Anna took my blood pressure, four vials of blood, my temperature, and a urine sample.

"Man ... somebody won the lottery here in town, you heard about that?" Doc randomly asked. *Yeah I heard it ... as a matter of fact I know the dude.*

"Yeah I heard, $325 million, right?"

"Man what I could do with that money," Doc joyfully uttered. We laughed, with mine being disingenuous.

"Give us about a week on the lab work. You look okay, just watch the weight."

"Gotcha, Doc," I replied. We shook hands and I proceeded out of the office, proud of myself. Besides the folks in New York, not a soul in Houston knew. All day long I thought *these people driving next to me, these people riding in the elevator, these people in the fast food drive thru line in front of me, none of them know they're just a few feet away from a bona-fide millionaire.*

When I arrived back home, I made a conscious effort to focus on the next day; the bitter sweet ending to an 11-year career and my bi-weekly check of $1,381.56. This week was closure. It was embracing what I'd accomplished as a public school teacher, and equally, "letting go." Some folks would be missed: Coach Jackson, one of the P.E. teachers and Trisha Baylor, a colleague who worked as my co-teacher the year before, helping me with a cluster of special education students expected to fail the state test. With her help we had an 88 percent pass rate.

Also, I would miss Mr. Franklin and Mr. Mackey, two older brothers who always shared their insight on life, and Mrs. Collins, our IT person who always gave me the heads up when she heard things through the grapevine. All these people had an impact on me in one way or another. I realized that they sustained me. Besides my bills, they kept me getting up every morning, coming to work, and doing my job ... all of it would be a memory, a chapter in my life, closed forever. For now, it was "Operation get-through-these-next-three-days."

THE UNCERTAIN FUTURE OF A MILLIONAIRE [4]

Day One – Wednesday: my alarm was set for 5 a.m. Usually I'd hit the snooze button till about 5:45. My routine encompassed a shower, getting dressed, and walking out the door by 6:30 at the latest. If traffic flowed, I'd usually stop by Mickey D's and get that good ass oatmeal, a sausage egg and cheese biscuit, and a large orange juice. I'd make it to school by about 7:10, right before the 7:15 "tardy" mark.

School started at 7:40. During my 3rd period planning, I'd usually walk the campus, catching students skipping, smoking, or fucking in the little nooks and crannies of Perkins M.S. We had freaks running around. Once I saw a line of boys behind what we called the "shack" buildings, getting head from a 7th grade girl … for 50 cents a pop. Another time, I walked into the boys' bathroom and three Hispanic boys were smoking weed. For a second I thought, *pass that shit.*

Our students came from working, lower middle class homes; mainly African-American and Latino, with a few Caucasian and Asian students. The campus was ripe with gang activity. *Bloods, Crips,* Mexican gangs, the whole nine. My heart was heavy for these kids who saw education as a waste. *"I'm selling this weed right now and I'm making money right now. I'm having sex and partying right now. I want to quit school and get a job right now."* In some cases the parents supported their decisions.

Often, I would wonder about some of my former students, what they'd done with their lives. Where was Mario Guzman, a gang member, or Jeannine Spencer, the sassy little something who moved to Houston after Katrina? I wondered what value they'd given their lives. And still the guilt loomed in my heart. *How could I leave a school like this behind?* The fact remained, I cared about these students. Regardless of what was going on in my life, I was teaching and students were learning every day. Whether the lessons of the day or the issues of life, my students knew that I cared for them. My only concern at this point was whether the next teacher would care the same.

When I pulled into the parking lot, I immediately felt drained, as if never winning, like I'd been dreaming the whole time. There were rows and rows of cars that belonged to people who'd been beaten up by life in one way or another. Just then, Ms. Grey pulled up. She was a young first-year teacher from a country town about 50 miles east. I tried to holler at her a few times, remaining cordial of course.

"Hey Moore, ain't seen you in a week … you all right?"

"I was under the weather, thanks for asking," I answered. She had a really nice figure, and always dressed well. I think she was a single parent, too. We had a lot of that up there.

Entering the school building felt depressing. Even though a place of learning, where students were supposed to feel safe, the hallways had the feel of a hospital corridor, or even a mental health institution. Some of my students noticed me, smiled and waved anxiously, while others glanced and looked away. Jamal, a student of mine, ran up to me.

"Mr. Moore, man, where you been? The substitute ain't teach us nothing," he said with pseudo anguish. "People said you got into a car accident or something," he added.

"Nah man, I'm fine." Jamal always kept it 100.

"All right Mr. Moore," he said as he gave me our customary soul brother handshake. Students like Jamal kept work interesting. They kept me current on the latest fads, songs, and dance moves, providing many teachable moments through my lessons.

When I walked into the main office, about ten or so teachers were all scrambling to sign in with the new electronic fingerprint system. A cool "gadget" at first, we later realized it to be nothing more than a way to track us. Greeting folks as I walked in, most seemed happy to see me even if it were a little insincere on my part. My colleagues had the impression I'd been ill, while I was planning to exit stage left.

An unimaginable life awaited me; in a mere two days, I'd receive more money than the entire staff could ever amass in a 20-year teaching career. After signing in, I went to the school secretary to give my doctor's note and head to my room. I caught a glance from Mr. Foster, the school principal–if looks could kill. He always seemed to have a peculiar disdain for me, and for what I didn't know.

Mr. Foster, in his second year at the school, had previously worked at another campus as an assistant principal before being assigned at Perkins. He had a "way" about him, inexplicable even. He was a light-skinned, over-weight, balding gentleman in his early to mid-40s. I ascertained that underneath the arrogance lay low self-esteem by the way he carried himself by wearing frumpy clothes and dusty shoes. Nevertheless, day in and day out, I'd speak to him whenever, wherever, and some days he'd respond. But on this day, he gave me a look that read, *"Mother fucker where the hell you been?"*

When I entered my classroom, a dank funk slapped me in the nose. My seats were out of order, dictionaries were rearranged, and the whiteboard was smeared from different colored markers being improperly cleaned off the board. Yes, I was somewhat of a neat freak, and the cleanliness of my classroom mattered. Even the trash hadn't been removed from the previous day, maybe the previous days. What a fucking return to my old life. In another 25 minutes the bell would ring. I started cleaning and straightening the chairs back, putting the dictionaries where they belonged, and spraying the board, wiping my burdens away.

With a good five minutes left, my room was ready to be filled with students who had no idea I'd be leaving that Friday. Standing in the middle of the room, I looked around, reflecting, similar to the moment in my apartment. Life wasn't all that bad before the money. My career, minus the bullshit, was enjoyable, but surely driving to school in a shiny new Bentley with a straight face was unfathomable. No way could I leave from work and go home to a five million dollar mansion, knowing that some of my students lived in public housing. Separation from that reality was the only way to accept my own.

When the bell rang, I stood at the door, ready to receive students for the first class. My mood had changed with anticipation. The hallway bustled with students, going to classrooms up and down the hall.

Mr. Franklin came to his door. He was an older brother who'd come to the school from another district.

"What's up, Doug ... you back?" he asked with a lisp.

"Yeah, I'm back, had a little bug for a second." *But not for long.* Mr. Franklin, a portly guy, was cool yet the temperamental, sensitive type. If you inadvertently didn't speak, he didn't speak. Or if you hadn't invited him somewhere, without him knowing the nature of the matter, he'd feel slighted.

"Man these kids ... I had some students of yours for a few days. They were pretty good but that damn Sabrina Jones ... I coulda slapped her."

He wasn't lying about Sabrina. If Satan could spawn a child, she'd be it. Her attitude was beyond fucked, her mother unavailable, and our 8th grade principal, too scared to deal with her. She was a pretty girl with a terrible home life. Her mother was a single parent raising four children, with Sabrina being the oldest. She'd been expelled from two previous schools last year.

"What she do?" I asked, as I walked over to him.

"This little nigga gone say, Mr. Franklin, when's the baby due?" I held my composure as best I could, not to laugh in his face.

"I told that little bitch to be quiet and have a seat, but she kept on until I ended up sending her ass down the hall to you know who, but they ain't do shit," he said.

The "you know who" he referred to was Ms. Evelyn Grandberry, a first-year assistant principal who had no clue of what the fuck she did nor how the fuck to do it. As the story goes, she'd been recommended by a friend of Foster's, a typical occurrence in the district. She taught social studies in her previous years, so of course, she stayed on my ass, fucking with me constantly about my teaching approach. At first, the eighth grade staff perceived her to be pretty level headed and knowing that she was a single parent, we shared compassion for her. But as the bullshit revealed itself, we took our compassion and trust back.

"Yeah man, all you can do for that girl is pray," was my *I don't give a fuck at this point* reply. As short a week as it was, no bigger challenge presented itself than simply getting out of bed and going to work for the next two days.

Class after class, my mind stayed on the magic hour, 4 p.m. Yeah, I taught the lessons, squashed the beefs, did cafeteria duty, and at the close of the day, watched as students safely crossed the street, got into cars, or simply walked home. The entire day, my mind and spirit hovered about the halls, giving everyone warm smiles and greetings, even opening the door for a couple of trifling women I didn't particularly like. Then again, I was in the driver's seat. Being a teacher was valuable enough, but in the greater scheme of things, my stock had risen.

Earlier in the day I'd received a text about doing happy hour at Pappadeaux's over on 610. The seafood restaurant was our teacher hang out, a place we could talk shit and flirt with each other. It sounded like a good idea, considering I'd been living in secrecy for the past week.

After a long day, I arrived by five, with the parking lot full as usual. We affectionately called it "Niggadeaux's" for silly reasons. It was home of the "Swamp Thing," comprised of a Hurricane and Margarita, mixed for a lethal combination. One night I remembered getting so drunk, that I actually went out to my car and pissed on the tire. It was one of the best pees of my life.

Our gatherings were therapy sessions. Shit we couldn't freely discuss on campus like bad ass kids, irresponsible parents, incapable administrators, and sexual escapades were the hot topics. The women always outnumbered us and with every chance, "eating coochie" found its way into the conversation. Working at a school where the staff was predominately "black" lent itself to carefree discussions otherwise considered taboo.

Ms. Baker, one of the teachers in the crew spotted me.

"What's up, stranger?" I bent down to give her a hug. Everybody greeted me on this regular Wednesday afternoon, ready to be fueled by a few Swamp Things and seafood fondue.

"Where you been, Moore?" Ms. Ferguson asked. Fergie as I affectionately called her was about my age, single with no kids and a transplant from Dallas.

"Wasn't feeling too good this past week; I had a little stomach virus, but I'm 100 now," I replied. Oddly, she was one of the few I'd actually tell the truth, but I didn't chance it.

Sitting with the crew, that feeling of guilt washed over me again. This was a decent bunch of folks who got up every morning to deal with disrespectful kids and bullshit politics, all for an average salary of $55k a year. Some had aspirations for more with their entry level BMWs and Benzes, and the ladies, with their expensive handbags. Being teachers meant something to us on different levels. It was a noble profession, respected by society, and a sort of middle-class purgatory. When the waitress approached our table, I asked for the usual. Everyone else had been drinking. My only concern was not getting too drunk and spilling the beans.

"Y'all heard somebody won that money right?" Christine Walker asked. Christine was probably the youngest of the group, a new teacher from Atlanta, and a little on the chatty side.

"They say that, but it's probably a lie like everything else on TV," came my anxious reply in a moment of desperation. *Why did I say that?*

"Nah nigga, somebody won that money ... just look for a new Rolls-Royce on 59, come next week," Coach James chimed. Everybody laughed including me. A *new Rolls-Royce sounds good.*

"I know one thing, if I'd a won that money, none of y'all motherfuckers would ever see my black ass again ... nigga I'm going straight to Tahiti or some shit," James continued.

"I think I'd still come to work ... I just wouldn't take no bullshit. First nigga to get outta line with me, I'm heading straight to the car ..." Christine added. Their fantasizing tirades were all humorous, but for me, it was a twisted form of torture, listening to their pipe dreams.

By 8:30, some of us called it quits. It was still a work week. Full with a good enough buzz, I still wanted some Chacho's, a fiesta burrito and large limeade for the road. *Letting myself go* was an understatement, but I hadn't been to Chacho's in so long, I earned that right. On the way home, I decided to call my mother.

"Hey, big head boy," she said when she answered.

"Hi, Mama." It felt good knowing that if no one in the entire world gave a fuck about me, this lady did. "You came across my mind ... just checking on you. I was thinking of flying out there next weekend," I added.

"You have time off like that?"

"It wouldn't be long, Friday night to Sunday morning," I answered. "I haven't seen you since the last time I came for Christmas, and I haven't seen Devin's new son, so no better time, right?"

"Well you know I'm always happy to see you ... that's fine. You called Devin?" she asked.

"No ... I was thinking I'd surprise him, maybe go to dinner Saturday evening, if that's okay with everyone."

"My schedule isn't the busiest these days, just check with Devin when you get here ... he's always on the go," she explained. "I heard someone got that Mega-Ball out there."

"Yeah, Mama, it was me," I calmly replied.

"Boy, if you won that money ... " she said in an imagining tone.

"If I won the money … what?" This was my golden moment, a moment that every man who's ever loved and cherished his mother and remembered the bullshit she went through raising him, longed for.

"I don't know … maybe take a trip somewhere, definitely pay off these bills," she answered. My mother wasn't the type to over indulge, unless it was pork ribs and Coca Cola. She'd never been out the country, nor owned a new car.

"That's it, Mama?" I asked with surprise.

"You know I don't want much, the Lord's been good to me," she countered.

"What about a nice new house in a gated neighborhood, the kind where the security guard stands out front in a booth?" She laughed, considering the idea far-fetched. "And how about a maid to clean that house, so you never have to lift a finger again?" I continued.

"That sounds nice … and a driver too, right?" she replied sarcastically.

"If that's what you want," I responded.

"Boy you crazy … you just make sure you pay your tithes first, that's what you do," she said earnestly. Playing along with her felt good; her imagination was a reality soon to be had. For all that she and Daddy did for us, the financial struggles they endured doing it, nothing was too opulent or too extravagant for her.

After 10 or so minutes of talking, we finally hung up. It was also about the time I reached my apartment. A peaceful moon-lit mist hung in the parking lot. Going up the stairs, I turned around to look at the scenery, one of the last times I'd have here.

Two days later, on Friday morning, I begrudgingly rose from the bed, sat on the side of it and grimaced, *why the fuck am I doing this? I mean okay integrity, finishing what you start, but man, going to work?* I was getting a wire transfer of $165 million. At that realization, my momentum changed. I hopped in the shower, got dressed, stopped for my customary breakfast and rolled into school. At about 7:30, Ms. Grandberry stopped by my room.

"Mr. Moore, good morning sir, I was wondering about you … we didn't see you for about a week," she said in her usual condescending quality. *I know bitch.* Grandberry had this nice-nasty demeanor about her. She wasn't authentic or compelling, but more of a policy manager who couldn't think outside of district mandates and campus rules.

"In the future, can you make sure to give me a call, just as a heads up?" *Yeah, bitch.*

"You're right Ms. Grandberry, I apologize for not communicating with you, but you'll never have to worry about that again, I promise." I meant that shit.

As the day began to unfold, I was a little unsettled momentarily. This school campus had become a major part of my existence and I didn't even realize it. The route to work, the routine of stopping for breakfast, the morning traffic, all of it had become affixed in my life. *What's a millionaire's day like? What, get up at noon? Have my personal chef whip up eggs Florentine with a mimosa?* The insecurity of wealth began to cloud my thoughts. At one point during class I zoned out, so much so that students called my name, while I gazed at the computer screen. In hindsight, it dawned of the significance of walking the hallways, doing cafeteria duty, and talking shit with colleagues throughout the day. I'd miss that.

At about 3:45 that afternoon, after dealing with the daily issues of middle-school students, breaking up more fights, listening to more excuses for being late to class or for not having assignments completed, things were drawing to a close on a day that would culminate an 11-year career. Over the course of that time, I'd taught over a thousand students, some receptive and others indifferent. Some were successes and others failures, but overall I became a man.

Leaving at this juncture was a disheartening decision. Financially I could do more for this community from the outside; more for education as a whole from the outside. Had I continued on, at some point the arrogance of my money would transcend the good deeds done with it. *The school needs new computers, I got it; the girls' gym needs new backboards and hoops, I got it;* all of this and I still report to cafeteria duty?

At a glance, I looked at the clock again. Five more minutes had passed in a blink. It was like the clock was saying, "*you ready motherfucker?*" The time had come to usher in the next era of my life, but after a day like today, I had reservations. *Who would care like me? Would I be replaced by someone incapable of handling the mood swings of my Latino and African-American boys?* Even more daunting was the thought of being replaced by a teacher that couldn't "identify" with the issues of my students, concluding generalities about them.

Walking the hallways felt somber; I didn't make a big deal of my leaving for good measure. Being bombarded with questions about my future was unnecessary. The truth would cut like a knife, and in return, I'd get a bunch of fake smiles and empty well wishes. As I approached the main office, the expeditiousness of a Friday afternoon was evident. Teachers and students alike, scrambled to either sign out or turn stuff in. It was slow motion for me, with no need to rush and do anything, except wrap this shit up.

I sat in the designated area for those wanting to speak with the principal. Ms. Temple looked at me with a smile, unknowing that this was my last working day, and maybe even the last time she'd ever see me. The scenery was familiar, folks laughing, and content with making it through another week. Sadly, Fridays had become a finish line in our lives. All the excitement and joy of whatever the weekend brought would be constrained by the cyclical life of another working week.

A parent was making her way out of Mr. Foster's office and I got butterflies. *Weird.* Ms. Temple looked at me and gave a nod as to say, "Your turn." I smiled back, got up and went in. Foster was on the phone, sitting behind his massive wood grain desk. The walls were decorated with snapshots of his life and accomplishments. What stood out most was his fraternity paddle hanging on the back wall; *us black folks and our letters.* I also noticed a picture of what appeared to be Mr. Foster standing next to a former big shot superintendent of the district. It's all about the people you know.

Foster motioned for me to have a seat as he continued his conversation. By the tone, it seemed he was wrapping up. It's funny how you can see people differently by just observing them talk to others. Foster laughed, and hung up the phone.

"Mr. Moore, thanks for waiting, excuse my delay, how can I help you, sir?" He was awfully chipper.

"I'm doing great, nothing to complain about," I answered.

"Good ... that's good," he replied.

"Well, as you know, I put my resignation in and I wanted to say a formal goodbye and thank you for what has been a great two years thus far ..."

"You're leaving?" he interrupted. *I know the district told this man I was leaving; all that paper work I had to fill out and shit.*

"I'm kidding man ... it's going to be sad to see you go, the kids love you," he added. His statement stung a bit, *"the kids love you."* This process wasn't getting any easier.

"Was there anything that caused this resignation? We didn't get a chance to talk, Doc," he continued. He was pleasantly engaged.

"Well, it was really more of an opportunity that came up," I responded.

"Oh?" Wow, he wanted details.

"I applied for a teaching position overseas quite some time ago, actually during the earlier part of the summer … well they responded three weeks back," I answered. His facial expression displayed genuine interest.

"Where you teaching, Doc?" he asked. Damn, I was expecting this shit to wrap up a little quicker than this, I had to think fast. A friend of mine took a teaching job overseas a few years back, in the Middle East.

"I'll be working in the Middle East, teaching English," I responded.

"The Middle East!" he exclaimed with confused excitement. That oughta do it.

"Where in the Middle East?" he asked. *Goddamn nigga, more questions*? Where did Audrey go, shit, what the fuck was the name of that … ? Oh yeah.

"I'll be going to Abu Dhabi, you heard of it?" I asked with assured cockiness.

"Abu Dhabi … Abu Dhabi, is that anywhere near Dubai?" he asked. *Fuck*.

"I'm not sure, it could be, but I couldn't say for sure," I answered. He mulled over my answer a bit while rubbing his chin and looking up at the ceiling.

For a few moments more, we had small talk about the plight of education, the current political climate, and the state of the Houston Texans. It was actually a welcomed end to a volatile week. When it was all said and done, Foster wished me the best and shook my hand goodbye. I walked out of his office uncertain of the future as a millionaire.

For one last time, I decided to walk the campus as a teacher. I'd eventually come back, but in a different capacity. Maybe as a full-fledged philanthropist, donating funds to whatever school cause at the time, but I'd be back. The distance and time was necessary to acclimate myself to my new life. Actually, I needed to be forgotten.

Walking the main hallway, the familiar smell of the disinfectant being used by the janitors took me back to my first year. I was a new transfer, unfamiliar with the school, and in my fifth year of teaching. I gazed at the encasement holding trophies, awards, and student art. The walls were covered with various encouraging phrases, the kind meant to inspire, but too corny to take serious. The floors were extra shiny this afternoon. The school colors, maroon and gold, were extra vibrant. The school would be fine.

I went back to my classroom to gather my things and a few trinkets collected over the years. It was a cliché moment in need of background music. Hopefully, my absence would create an employment opportunity for someone with aspirations of inspiring kids or paying bills. As I loaded the last item into my cardboard box, Rosa walked in at the usual time.

"Hola señora," I called in my terrible Spanish annunciation. She seemed to always oblige me with her accepting smile.

"Hello, Mr. Moore ... you leaving?" she asked, looking at the bare walls.

"Yeah, I've found another job elsewhere," I answered. I didn't want to lie to her, she wasn't a threat to my discretion, but I had a running theme.

"Oh, Mr. Moore, I will miss you," she said as she walked over and gave me a hug, probably the most genuine send-off I'd receive that day.

By 5:45 in the afternoon I'd finally wrapped up everything and finished conversing with Rosa. The sky had an intriguing orange hue that read *it's done, goodbye parking lot*. I shuffled with my box and messenger bag in preparation to leave that desolate place as I'd done many times before, either staying late to finish grades or on parent teacher night. Wanting to be emotional, I redirected my focus, deciding to catch a motherfucking happy hour, some damn place.

TRANSITIONS [5]

On Monday morning, November 1, I received a call informing me that my wire transfer had been completed. Groggy and incoherent, I tried regaining my composure when I realized who was calling.

"Mr. Moore, my name is Fran Abram, I'm a financial adviser with Frasier Payne. I've been assigned to advise you on your account activities. I'm calling to inform you that the wire transfer amounting to $165,876,900 has been credited to your account and available for your use."

"Oh, wow... okay... uh, thank you for that, I really appreciate it," I rambled. It was a lot to take in at 10 in the morning. It took everything within me not to scream at the top of my lungs, alarming the neighbors and Buddy Boy.

"We'll discuss the structuring of your account when we meet this week. Also, we've taken the liberty of procuring a premium credit account for you with *American Express*, otherwise known as the "Black Card." Because of your financial standing, the card has no limit, so be very wise," she added for humor. The news was overwhelming to say the least.

"Thank you for that ... this is amazing. I don't know what to say."

"I know it's a lot, but don't worry, we'll go over everything in the meeting."

"Okay, well thanks again ... and by the way, will I receive a debit card with this account?" I asked.

The question felt stupid but fair considering this new arrangement.

"Due to the amount, it's more of a money market account, much different from a regular checking or savings. Your account is like its own bank; you're what the financial industry calls a high net worth individual. However, we can wire funds to any bank of your choosing if that's what you prefer," she continued.

"Yes, please do," I replied, anxiously.

"What amount would you like transferred?"

Immediately, I was a ten-year-old rich kid with access to too much.

"I'd like to have $500,000 wired to my bank. Is that possible today?"

"That shouldn't be a problem; give it about two to three hours processing time. You'll receive a call when it's completed."

After I finished giving Fran the particulars for the transfer, I laid there another 10-15 minutes more, contemplating the rest of the day. With absolutely no fucking plans, other than laying my funky ass in bed with my lap top, a box of tissue, and my ambition, I opted to get my ass up and seize the day.

At about 11 or so, after my morning shit, shower, and shave, I booked my flight for the meeting with the law firm and Frasier Payne. At the first consultation, it was suggested I consider starting a philanthropic foundation, primarily for tax purposes. I'd pay fewer taxes based on the charitable donations made.

The process of selecting a beneficiary wouldn't be difficult. It would probably be the United Negro College Fund. Maybe I'd create a scholarship in the name of my mother and father such as "The Leonard and Eugenia Moore Scholarship Fund." It had a nice ring. Also, I would do something for my Alma Mater, Wilberforce University, I couldn't forget my fraternity, specifically my under grad chapter. Finally we'd have a distinguished "frat" house, with all the trappings. My main concern was avoiding beggars and swindlers, plotting and strategizing on my emotions. Having the choice of whom and when I gave, and how I gave was important.

In the meantime, with no plans whatsoever, it was a good day to hunt for a new apartment, somewhere downtown. My taste for the finer things had always overreached the reality of my wallet; living downtown had been a desire of mine. Over the last three to four years, downtown Houston had been revitalized, with the construction of new high-rise buildings and the renovation of old warehouse and office buildings, converted to lofts. After doing a search, two places in particular caught my attention, The Wesley

Tower and Cosmopolitan Square. Both were fairly new, no older than five years. Of course, space would be a priority, but it needed to be pet friendly for Buddy with two or three bedrooms for guests, a nice downtown view, and designated parking.

After making my calls, Cosmopolitan Square would be my first stop. Both places were similar in cost and amenities; about $2,500 a month for a two-bedroom. After arriving, I parked my trusty Ford Explorer in the guest area. I was met with a cautious glance from a woman getting into her C- Class, presumably due to my car or skin tone, or maybe both.

Entering the building had the same feel as the Galleria Mall. The lobby area was massive, like a modern grand ball room. The artistic vision of the architect was evident in the design. High end furniture, lush potted plants, and modern art adorned the entire room. The hanging chandelier was definitely an art piece, with its shimmering, shiny glass pieces, intricately interwoven. The reception desk was flush with a rich mahogany wood, with the name of the building embossed in the center panel on the wall. Standing behind the desk were two young ladies, one Asian and the other Latino.

"Good afternoon sir, welcome to Cosmopolitan Square, how can I assist you?" the Asian lady spoke, in the perkiest voice I'd ever heard.

"I'm here to see Michelle Geist, please. I have an appointment," I replied.

"Sure, sir, let me give her a call right quick. Would you like a bottle of water?"

"Oh, I'm fine, thank you," I replied. She made the call, while I continued looking around the lobby, imagining myself rambling in after having afternoon walks with Buddy, or receiving guests for dinner parties.

"Sir, she'll be down in just a few minutes."

"Okay, thanks," I answered. The windows in the lobby were floor to ceiling, seemingly three-stories tall. Just across the street was a newly constructed strip center with a few shops, convenient for dry-cleaning or ordering Chinese. Even more suitable was my proximity to the Toyota Center for the Rockets games and whatever concerts they'd have.

Turning to walk in another direction, I noticed an older woman was making her way across the lobby towards me. She appeared to be in her 60s, and was a short, grayish-blonde, white lady.

"Douglas?" she called.

"Yes." She greeted me with a welcoming smile and handshake, even if she thought, *"How in the hell could this nigga afford this place?"*

"Welcome to our property...hope you found it okay," she stated.

"Pretty easy... it's right off the freeway," I replied.

"I know huh, makes living here an ideal situation. So are you ready to look around?"

"Sure." Immediately, we went to an apartment on the 10th floor.

"As you requested, Douglas, this is a two-bedroom, two-bath unit, with a gourmet-styled kitchen, breakfast nook, dining area and study. Now, this unit is 1,800 square feet and goes for $2,550 a month, with beautiful western views of Houston," she continued. This was already a red flag for me, considering what I'd pay a month, views of Rice Village and the Galleria area were a letdown. *Gimme a downtown view and a higher motherfucking floor, got-damn it!*

"Ms. Geist, I don't ... "

"Call me Michelle," she interrupted.

"Okay, Michelle, I don't want to come off as difficult, but let me be more specific of what I'm looking for." Her facial expression changed to one of concern. "I really want a downtown view. I should've made that clear during the phone conversation, especially since I'll be paying what amounts to a mortgage." She laughed and regained her composure.

"Okay, Douglas, I've got it. Say no more ... let's walk this way." We walked back into the hallway, towards the elevators, where she pushed the up button, a promising sign.

We got off on the 17th floor. The hallway looked exactly the same, but by Michelle's response, I expected to be impressed. We walked to unit number 1702.

She fumbled with the keys, but when she finally opened the door, my jaw dropped. The first thing I saw was a wall of glass, and off in the distance, the view of a lifetime. "I'll take it," jokingly I responded. She laughed in satisfaction.

"Now this unit faces east obviously, it's about 2000 square feet; it has three-bedrooms, three-bathrooms, a loft area which is your master bedroom, with walk-in closets in every room. It also has the gourmet kitchen and nook, dining area and study," she stated. My focus remained with the view the entire time she rattled off the details.

"So, Michelle, what are we talking per month?" I asked.

She looked at me with a look that said, *Are you ready to hear this?*

"You're looking at $4,000 a month." It was four times my previous rent.

Right then and there, I forgot my millionaire status, or that I probably had in my prestigious financial coffers, what amounted to the cost to build this place. I'd been broke too damn long. My most expensive purchase had been the flat screen TV I bought some months ago. I didn't know how to be rich yet.

"I really like this place."

"You haven't even seen the rest of it, or the amenities on the property and with this unit, you get two designated parking spots."

I was thinking, *for the price, it should come with a maid.*

"Could I get this unit within the week?"

"There's the customary background and credit checks; those could run a few days, but I think we can arrange it," she answered. We went on looking through the apartment, its modern light fixtures, black granite counter-tops and tile flooring. Still with the intent of seeing The Wesley Tower, an equally appealing sophisticated urban hang suite, I was already sold on this place. Coming home would be amazing, especially with that view.

We exchanged information back down in the lobby, before continuing on to my next destination. The drive to The Wesley felt unnecessary, but as everybody's mama would say, *"Don't put all your eggs in one basket."*

After a 15 minute patch of traffic, I finally arrived. The area was as nice as the other with tree-lined streets, mixed in with boutique shops and townhomes. This was *Upper Kirby*, technically the Galleria area, but people like their boundaries.

Approaching the parking structure of the building, I noticed a guard's booth and gate. It was a selling point. The guard was an older African-American man, maybe 50 plus, with a husky build and jet black hair, as if he dyed it every weekend. I pulled closer and let down the window.

"Can I help you, sir?" he asked in an ambiguous tone. It sounded more like, *are you sure you know where you are?*

"Yes, I have an appointment with Vaughn Evans," I replied. He looked away and walked back to his booth, proceeding to make a phone call.

"Okay sir, when you get past the gate, there's guest parking just to your right, park there and proceed to the sliding doors just behind you." I parked my car among a string of expensive European vehicles presumably owned by upwardly mobile individuals. Walking through the automatic doors, I was immediately greeted by a tall, slender brother, maybe in his mid to late thirties, wearing all black.

"Mr. Moore?" he asked, his tone suggested "strangé," with a handshake that confirmed it. "Did you find our place pretty easily?" he inquired.

"I went through a little traffic but it was fine ... I know the area," I replied.

"That's good ... okay then, well let's take a look at the two-bedroom, two bath unit you were interested in," he said. This time I made sure I'd cut to the chase and clarified my request.

"I really want a unit that's high up, with a downtown view."

"Oh, I got you, don't worry."

The walkway led to a more spacious lobby area that invoked a mesh between southern charm and modern minimalism. The smell of orange and cinnamon scents filled the air, while top 40 instrumentals played over the sound system.

"It's hot out there today, isn't it? This weather is so crazy lately," he continued.

It was corny adult banter, but I conceded with an empty laugh. Walking towards the elevator area, momentarily distracted, a fine ass specimen of a woman appeared, probably Ethiopian or maybe a Louisiana girl. She was about 5'6, 135-40 pounds, with a fiery bronze mane of hair, similar to Iman the model. She wore a sweater-like dress with black leather leggings and boots.

"Our property is barely four years old, and we're 75 percent occupied," he stated. "All residents have designated parking, complimentary continental breakfast on the weekends, and the unit I'm going to show you has a downtown view."

He pushed the 21st floor button and off we went. "So, Mr. Moore, are you a Houston native?" he asked. The set up for the real question, *what do you do?*

"Actually, I'm from California. I've been living here for 15 years, so maybe by now ... " We shared more corny banter and empty laughter.

The hallway was completely wood paneled, with soft lighting from the wall fixtures and ceiling lamps, with travertine marble flooring. We approached the unit, number 2112, with its double door entry and brushed chrome handles.

"This unit is over 2,000 square feet, with extra additional square footage from the balcony." *Cool, a balcony,* I thought. As we entered, there was a calmness about the place. It wasn't sexy, or blah, just nice, but more like a single family home within a high-rise. We continued walking about the unit. I was convinced of the other apartment.

"And how much does this go for monthly?" I asked.

"You're looking at $2,850, and additionally, we have a home buyer program where a portion of your monthly lease payment is contributed to a down-payment account," he proclaimed.

"Nice," I offered, but my mind was made up.

Finally after looking at the entire apartment, I walked out ahead of Vaughn. In the hallway, my future baby mama appeared again. The Ethiopian badass from earlier, lived here, or was living with someone here. She bent down to get her bags, and when she raised, our eyes locked for an instant. She went on about her business, entering her apartment, while my future flashed before my eyes. Hopefully the mental picture of her symmetrical beauty, her flowing bronze hair, and curvy ass would last a while; *unit #2109.*

"So Mr. Moore, what did you think of the unit?" Vaughn asked with obvious confidence.

"Oh, it's definitely one to put on my list ... I'm actually going to five other locations, but I definitely liked what I saw." I wasn't lying about liking the place, but after four years of living in a shoe box, I wasn't going to pull teeth over picking a new spot. Cosmopolitan Square would be my home.

I called Michelle with my decision and she asked for a deposit of $6,200 and other documents. My hasty decision wasn't about wanting a new place, but more so a safety concern. Sitting on a ton of money, in a not so bad neighborhood, still felt awkward.

I decided to donate my furniture to Purple Heart, a local goodwill service in town. It was a fresh start with this apartment, from top to bottom. My old bed sheets, towels, curtains, kitchen table, living room furniture, bedroom set, all had to go.

I told my leasing office I intended to move out that week. Janice and Ron, the office managers, were good to me, even when I was late on my rent, more than a few times. Inevitably they'd ask a bunch of questions, but I really didn't want to entertain any of them. Simply put, I wanted to remain anonymous.

My cell phone rang. "Nigga...what the fuck is up?" It was Lamont. We hadn't talked much since returning from the first New

York trip. Another trip back out was scheduled for Wednesday, with my birthday just three days later.

"Man … ain't nothing man, just handling business and shit," I said.

"You know you tripping dog. Carrington's was off the chain last week, too." *How do I tell this man about my money? It's not because I expect him to become jealous and hate on me, but, how does one really process that information? It's equivalent to being told by a friend they have a life threatening disease, and although you say encouraging words, you feel lost.*

"You know my birthday's coming up … you down to get out?" A diversion question, I could care less. My life was swiftly moving in a different direction, with lawyers, accountants, and millions of dollars. This wasn't to dismiss Lamont, but my focus had changed.

"Fuck yeah, nigga," he said with a sort of excited readiness.

"So what's been up lately, you all right?" I asked.

Me and Lamont had our ups and downs and our falling outs, but some kind of way, after all these years, we remained the best of friends. Like I said, that's my nigga, but shit.

BREAKING NEWS [6]

Most folks believe money changes you and your friendships, but that's a half-truth. It's hard for others to genuinely celebrate your good fortune without some hate, when their lives are in shambles. A few years back, Lamont was going through some financial hardships, and me being the friend that I am, offered to help. Dude took offense on some, *"I'm a man, and I stand on my own two feet,"* type shit. But when life is kicking you square in the ass, you gotta let pride go. I never forgot that moment. Now this shit? Paying off his mortgage, car loans, college loans, credit card debt, and putting some money away for Ramsey, seemed a natural expression of my friendship. Nevertheless, the level of his pride would be the deciding factor.

Rather than prolong the news, I figured it was a perfect time to get his reaction, determining the fate of our friendship. Besides my family, he was the only person I considered trustworthy. I decided as we talked, to tell him that evening.

"Say, let's go to Carrington's for happy hour tonight, you down?" I asked.

"Carrington's … I just went Thursday."

After we decided on a time, we went on about our business. I intended to drive to a few furniture stores before going back home, but I got the sudden urge to look at cars. Right off 610, there's a Rolls-Royce and Bentley dealership. As a previous visitor a few times, I would fantasize of one day driving off the lot in one … maybe that day had come. As I exited the freeway and made a U-turn at the underpass, the excitement of my purchasing power actually freaked me out.

I pulled up, not seeing any sales people walking about, which was usual for this place. Other high end cars were parked out front; a couple of Ferraris, Porsches, what have you. I got out and walked around feeling ten feet tall, and if any sales person came at me wrong, they'd regret it.

About five minutes went by, and still no help. A lot of people came up here to sightsee, especially my brothers, aspiring rap artists to be exact. I figured the first person professional enough to engage me would reap the reward of my business. My particular interest was in a new model Rolls-Royce called the Ghost. A smaller version of the Phantom, you barely saw any in Houston. It was unique but a contradiction for me. Remaining anonymous in a 325,000 dollar car? On the flip, denying myself the spoils of wealth seemed unnecessary.

Finally, a guy came out, a young looking George Clooney. His face read unimpressed of course, but obliging. However, in a city like this, with five professional sports teams, world renowned celebrities and business people, you could never size up anyone's money from looks alone.

"Hello sir, welcome to Post Oak Motors." We shook hands as he continued sizing me up, with my polo top and jeans, but he had no idea.

"Anything in particular you're interested in?" he asked.

"Actually, I'm interested in the Ghost, I'd like to get more information on it," I answered.

"Okay," he replied with his dry response and attitude. We walked onto the showroom floor, towards his desk.

"My name is Dino by the way," he interjected.

"And I'm Douglas ... "

"Nice to meet you Douglas, can I offer you any coffee, water, soda?" he asked.

"Water would be fine."

Looking around, I didn't see any people of color working there. Interesting that a product so beloved by "us" wasn't being represented by us. I'm sure a few of the Rockets and Texans had purchased from here, and I'm equally sure they looked like me. Well ,maybe not the same physique, but still.

He returned with the water, and went right in. "The Ghost is a very awesome machine. We have about four or five in our possession. It has a V12 engine, which gives it terrific pick up ... sold one a few weeks ago," he said in a cocky way. "They start out at about 300k, and top out near 350." I'd already done my homework during my pre-lottery winning days.

"Is it possible to see what you have in your inventory," I asked.

"Sure, no problem," he responded. So far so good, I thought.

We went back out to the lot and directly to the car in question. It's design spoke opulence, undeniably prestigious. He continued rambling on about the facts then suddenly, I saw a black one off in the distance that had the signature silver bonnet hood. I interrupted his spiel, "I'd like to see that black one over there." He went inside to get the keys as I walked over for a closer look. This was the one. Something about a nicely designed black car always screamed sexiness.

He came back with the keys in hand, hit the alarm, and I got in. Opening the door was like Christmas day. The interior enveloped my senses, that plush smell of leather. Sitting behind the wheel took me to another place, perhaps the Rockets game, pulling up to V.I.P. valet, or to a concert at Reliant Stadium. "Is it possible to get a test drive?" He seemed a bit hesitant, but asked for my license and insurance to make copies. Afterward, he handed over the keys, explaining the features on it. I was sold. I put the key in, pushed the ignition button, and fell in love.

We approached the feeder road to 610, preparing to make a right and merge with traffic. The magic of the car put a smile on my face, and giddiness inside. Dino continued making more references to the specifications of the car. *Shut up already*, I thought. The drive was so smooth and airy, it was amazing. At the Westheimer light, we made another stop.

"How does it feel?" he asked.

"Like my car," I answered. Looking to my left, I was instantly famous as an older white guy in a pickup truck gave me the "thumbs up."Making a right at the light, we approached the heart of the Galleria area, a perfect location for a car like this.

Driving it put things into perspective for me instantly. *Did I really need a car that drew that much attention?* I rationalized that maybe my "everyday" car could be a little less imposing, but I still wanted the Rolls. We made another right at Post Oak Avenue, up to 610, and then back down the feeder to the dealership. Suspecting the short test drive was due to the value and security of the car, it was still worth it all.

"So Douglas, if you don't mind me asking, what is it that you do?" Over the course of the last few days I'd become introspective about my reaction to people's comments. It was therapy more than anything. Why be mad at this guy? Maybe he's genuinely interested. Equally, he was still sizing me up to conclude whether I was wasting his time. I'm sure the Toyota guys weren't asking the same question.

"I'm into real estate and other business ventures," I answered.

"Oh that's interesting. Maybe you can give me a few tips so I can buy one of these bad boys myself." It was a nice thing to say. I waited for another question to see if he'd continue fishing, but he dropped it. Good for him. We pulled into the lot, and he instructed me to park near the service area. We got out the car. I took a big stretch like a pompous asshole, feeling what a car like this could do for my pussy game.

"So what did you think … is she a keeper?" he asked.

"What's the price tag?" I countered.

"It's 335, ready to go."

"Three-hundred and I'll sign the papers right now," I responded. He looked at me, unsure at first. But with a poker face, I gave him a nod. Presumably he expected me to thank him for the moment of escapism from the piece of shit I rolled up in.

"Let's go to my desk so we can hash this out." Immediately his demeanor changed. His walk was a little bit peppier and his attitude, more accommodating.

"Can I get you more water, anything?" he asked in a pleading nature.

"I'm fine, thank you," I answered.

"I'll get my manager so we can hash the numbers." I gave him a nod as he walked away. *Damn, this is really happening.* A few minutes later, he came back with an older, slender white guy. "Douglas, this is my manager, Trevor Connors." We shook hands.

"Nice to meet you, sir," he responded.

"Likewise," I said.

"So, the Ghost huh?" he exclaimed. "Fantastic car … I think you'll like it."

"I know I will." We all shared a laugh.

"I sold a Phantom a few months back to Derrick Hodges. You know Derrick, plays safety for the Texans," he stated. *Exactly*, I thought.

"Couple years ago, Beyoncé's dad came in and bought a Bentley Azure," he went on. I was thinking, *why all the references to black folks and their purchases? I don't give a fuck, let's wrap this shit up.*

"Nice," I offered.

"So you're into real estate, huh … any project I might know of?" This is the shit I was talking about, the prodding shit. What difference did it make how I made my money or how I'd pay for this car? I was getting agitated.

"Most of the projects I've been involved with were as a private investor," I replied.

"Oh," he countered. Dino's face read, *Please bear with me, he's an asshole.*

"Looks like you've had a good year," he stated.

"Good years," I replied. *Fuck you.*

"So, Douglas, ah, you like the black one with the bonnet, that's a beauty…you offered 300, we're asking 335." I looked at Dino like, *what the fuck?* "This car is awesome and the warranty is impeccable, four years, bumper to bumper … and the value it retains is remarkable as well, so let's entertain a number, how about 330?" he countered. *Okay, so we're off the racist bullshit. That's good, let's get to business.*

"Well, Mr. Connors, I've been looking at this car for quite some time, searching around, comparing pricing. This exact model at a dealership in Miami, is going for 305. I'm willing to make that flight because I really want the car," I responded.

"I see," he replied with a condescending air. "How about 325?" he asked. Actually that was the average price tag, but these motherfucking dealers always mark shit up. I could pay full price, but for what? I've always been a good negotiator. "Douglas, I don't mean to be crass or rude, but this is a fine automobile. Rolls has a reputation for creating a superior driving experience, and such a high end car requires that the value remain in place so that us "little guys" can maintain a living," he lamented. I didn't need the lecture about the economy of selling a car.

"You're totally right, Trevor, I completely understand," I replied. "I want to thank you for clarifying the circumstance you're in. I hope I didn't offend," I added. I extended my hand to both Dino and Trevor, thanking them for their time. Trevor's face turned beet red when I proceeded to get up and walk out the door.

About half way to my truck, Dino came running towards me.

"Hey, Douglas, excuse that guy. He's a dick. He's married to the family, so he throws his weight around. Let me see what I can do on the numbers, and if you don't mind, I'd like to give you a real counter offer," he replied.

I appreciated his hustle, gave him my number and drove on down to the Mercedes-Benz dealership. It wasn't necessary to lose myself in this money. My father taught me that houses and cars were always negotiable.

My other dream car was the Mercedes-Benz G55 AMG SUV. I've always admired the awkwardness of its boxy design. *My everyday car*. Arriving at the lot, I went straight into the dealership and asked for assistance. A young sister came out, kind of fine, too.

"Yes sir, how can I assist you today?" she asked. Pissed from the earlier mishap, I did my best to maintain civility with her.

"I know exactly what I want, and if you have it, I'm ready to go: G55...do you have one in stock?" I asked.

"I'm sure we do," she responded. "By the way my name is Cynthia."

"I'm Douglas," I said as we shook hands.

"Let me go talk to my fleet manager. I'll be right back, but for now, come have a seat in my office." Moments later, she came back with a reassuring smile. "Sir, this is your lucky day, we just received three G55s yesterday, one silver, one white, and a new style that's hot right now, matte black." Matte black sounded intriguing. I asked to see it and she obliged.

About 10 minutes went by, but for some reason, my mind went back to the incident at the other dealership, wondering if the matter could've been handled differently. *Did I swing my dick too hard?*

"Sir, can you come with me?" she asked. We walked out onto the lot, and parked just to the left of the entrance doors was this thing of engineering beauty. I'd never seen a G55 with this matte black color before. The traditional shiny paint job had been replaced with a dull, yet sharper looking appearance. My destiny was to drive this car. "Would you like a test drive?" she asked.

"Indeed," I responded. After the customary copying of my license and insurance, we got in and hopped on 59 South.

The feel of the truck was different from what I'd been accustomed to driving. The wood grain steering wheel and other details were luxuries, in and of themselves. The seats were a mixture of suede and leather, soft and supple, expected of such a vehicle. The feel and drive was intimidating. "So tell me how it feels?"

"I'm trying to get the feel for it. I guess because I drive a smaller SUV that sits a little lower," I explained.

"What do you drive now, if you don't mind?" *Damn!* I felt embarrassed. I didn't know why, but I did.

"Oh, it's a 98 Ford Explorer Sport," I replied.

"Oh ... okay," she replied in a manner suggesting the irrationalness of this test drive. I'm sure she didn't intend to put me on blast. "This particular model, because of the engine type, being that it's a V12, with leather and suede seating, custom paint job and wheels, goes for $125,568," she explained.

"Sounds about right," I replied. What did I know? Deciding I'd live a little and purchase the car, I still hadn't gotten comfortable with its ride, but its vainness was enough. When we got back to her office, I made a cash offer of $115k, and it was accepted. I made plans to pick it up the next day, just before my trip.

Later that evening, back at home, I reflected on the day's events: the new apartment, the new car, the asshole at the dealership. It was chock full of interesting moments. Surely, my lifestyle was changing, hopefully for the better. I felt a little dirty leasing a $4,000 a month apartment, and buying a truck the price of a decent two-story home, but why wouldn't I? *What had I done to deserve winning this money in the first place? And what was to prohibit me from spending it?* My thinking had to change.

While getting dressed to meet Lamont at Carrington's, my thoughts were of the business at hand. I needed to prepare for the meeting with the law firm and the Frasier Payne people in New York to solidify my financial affairs. And ultimately, I had to get back to see my mama, and tell her the news ... again. The days ahead felt promising, granted I needed to keep my wits about me.

When I finally pulled into the Carrington's parking lot, it wasn't packed. It was about seven or so when I got there, and Lamont's pickup truck was off in the distance. At the entrance, a couple of thick sisters walked in, laughing, and ready for a good time. That was the thing about "Caro's" as we called it. It was always about a good time, with down to earth people. I didn't wanna stop coming here, but I knew I'd never come in a Rolls-Royce.

Entering the place felt like home. As soon as you walk in, you could literally order your drink from the door. At the end of the bar, Lamont was flirting with some unbeweavable chick in high heels and a jean dress. As I walked in his direction, he looked back, spotted me and gave the "what's up?" head nod.

"What's up nigga?" we both shouted, unwound, and back to earth. "Oh, this is uh ... what your name is again?" Lamont slurred.

"Loretta, fool," unbeweavable said. She had a fat ass though. Lamont had his usual Long Island in front of him, while I ordered a rum and Coke. In the background, The Whispers' "Rock Steady" played over the sound system.

"This guy right here … this my guy right here," said Lamont, as he motioned for his drink. He could really throw down, and never once did I see him get sloppy drunk. However, his temperament could change in an instant, over the simplest shit. "I ain't seen this dude in like … forever, and this guy was the best man in my wedding, the godfather to my only son, my road dog," he went on. It was true … hadn't seen him in at least two weeks, during the time I'd won, and about a week before that.

"I was just handling business, dog. Ain't nothing man, you know you my dude," I answered. He looked at me and rolled his eyes. "Loretta, can I buy you a drink?" I asked, intentionally ignoring him.

"I already got her, don't be coming in trying to stunt on my girl," Lamont interrupted. She laughed while I smirked at him.

The night went on like any average night, no niggas fighting, no drama, just grown folks doing what grown folks do. About another hour or so, the crowd began to build. The barbecue pork sandwich man set up his station in the back corner, behind the bar area. More women made their way in, and the men were again outnumbered. Good for us and bad for them. By this time, I'd had three or four rum and Cokes, on top of the tequila shots Lamont bought.

"Man, I need some fresh air. I'ma go outside for a minute," I told him.

"Oh nigga, I got something in the truck anyway … " he replied. Lamont and I were functioning weed heads, so whenever he said "something" I immediately knew what it was.

"For real?" I responded, like an addict. We smoked like chimneys, talking about life or whatever else came to mind. But when Ramsey was born, Dana asked him to turn it down a bit, which he did … for a minute.

We sat in the truck and Lamont reached under his seat grabbing his Crown Royal bag, with another plastic bag inside and two blunts already rolled.

"I got some heat, nigga," he said. Lightweight excited, smoking was my extremity; I didn't fish, hunt, or play sports, I smoked. And now with this money I planned to go to Amsterdam, just to smoke. Lamont lit the blunt and the aroma made it apparent that it was indeed "killa." That's the kind of weed that only took two puffs to get right, right fast. He took two deep pulls and passed it over. Holding it felt natural, and no matter how much money I had or the people I'd meet because of the money, I was never going to stop smoking weed.

"Dana's pregnant again," he said.

"Congratulations."

"Yeah, man … thank you," he replied.

"Do y'all know the sex?"

"Nah, not yet, she just found out about a month ago … it'd be cool to have a girl this time."

"You gone spoil the shit out of her." He went silent for a minute while I passed him back the blunt for a couple more pulls.

"It's a blessing man … Ramsey, now this baby. I just wanna do right by 'em. Know what I'm saying?"

"I know man … you will, trust me." The courage to tell him grew, and I figured if I didn't get it over with, we'd be too fucked up to remember the conversation.

"Man I got something to tell you … don't tell no motherfucking body, I'm serious." He slowly turned his head, with a mouth full of smoke, and then he inhaled, with a puzzled look on his face.

"What the fuck, nigga?" He passed the blunt back, and I looked down at it. "You got AIDS?" he laughed.

"If I did, would the shit be fucking funny?"

"Okay, my bad, what's up," he asked, listening intently. I took a deep breath, wondering how to formulate the words, preparing for his disbelief.

"A couple weeks back … first of all, what I'm about to say, I'm not bullshitting."

"Get it out then, okay … what?" he interrupted.

"I won the Mega-Ball, multi-state lottery." The truck went silent as the weed smoke continued to billow about in the cabin. Lamont looked at me with that drunk and high look of suspicion when he thinks he's being fucked with. Then all of a sudden he bust out laughing.

"Fuck you, nigga," he responded as he continued laughing in disbelief.

I played this moment in my mind many times, wondering about the outcome. Our friendship was meaningful enough to consider him trustworthy of my business. His laughing didn't diminish the truth, but stalled its flow.

"I'm dead ass serious," I interjected. His laughter came to a slight end. He took another pull from the blunt.

"Why you fucking with me like this? What's up? You for real?" he asked. You could hear the mixture of sincerity and disbelief in the tone of his voice. It was becoming real.

"The reason I've been under the radar ... I went to New York and got some lawyers to handle my shit, flew to Austin to accept the money, nigga ... my own mother don't believe me. I won that shit." He looked in my eyes with confused excitement, and then all of sudden yelled from the bottom of his gut.

"My nigga!" The ice was broken, and our friendship, sustained for now.

"Why you take so long to tell me, man? What the fuck you gone do now? I bet you quit your job, huh?" His mind and words went 100 miles an hour just like mine did.

"I don't know. It took me a while to tell my mama. I mean I told her ... she don't believe it, but I'm going to surprise her when I get back from New York."

"New York, what you gotta do there?" he asked.

"I just told you I hired this law firm to represent me when I first found out. They advised me to do my finances with Frasier Payne ... they're my accountants now." Lamont's face read like an open book; he was genuinely happy for me. "I'm going out there for a couple days, and then I'll come back Friday night or Saturday morning."

"Damn ... you won," he said, looking out the window with a smile on his face; "My nigga ballin'. Yo bro, I'm really happy ... I don't know what to do or say. Fuck, this shit crazy."

"I know man ... sometimes I don't even believe it."

"So you gone get a whip ... something crazy right?"

"I bought that Benz truck today." His eyes went wider than I'd ever seen, and he leaned over to hug me. Then he started crying.

"Don't lie, Doug ... for real man?"

"I pick it up tomorrow." He let out another big scream. His celebrating my good fortune, meant a lot to me. "You know bro, we friends, we like brothers, and I can't be fly around town and the people I love, struggling. I'm going to help you and Dana." The pivotal moment in our friendship was his response.

"Bro, I don't know what to say. I'm a prideful nigga at times ... with the new baby on the way, I could use all the help possible. God bless you Doug, for real man." We caught ourselves getting emotional, breaking the man code, but it felt good that he accepted my help as I intended.

After we finished the blunt we decided to go back in and finish the night off with one last drink. By then, it was incredibly packed, and the women were all the same. The DJ put on some New Orleans bounce, and the crowd seemed younger all of a sudden. It was time to go. After our last drinks, we went out and said our goodbyes. For the way things ended, I felt confident that Lamont handled the news well. I expected him to tell Dana, but I was sure that they'd keep the shit under wraps.

On the drive home, the buzz from the weed and drinks, mixed with the relief of "coming clean," was a feeling of accomplishment. Facing the responsibility of being blessed with this amount of money would not rest on my shoulders alone. It was important to have an inner circle of trusted individuals who knew my weaknesses.

When I hopped on the freeway, I made an impromptu decision to check into the Hilton Americas Hotel downtown. Staying in my apartment didn't feel safe anymore. Security was becoming an internal issue. The paranoia of the money was setting in and it didn't help that I was high.

GWEN [7]

My flight to New York was on Wednesday morning so I figured I'd stay until then. I didn't pack much, maybe a suit and some underwear to change, but that was about it. I had a shopping spree to commit to.

After going home and picking up Buddy, I drove to the hotel where the valet guys, bellhops, and security guards stood about, shooting the shit. The valet guy motioned over to my truck. "Good evening, sir," he said as I handed the keys over and got out.

"Thank you," I replied, walking towards the automatic doors to the entrance. The lobby's sophistication was overshadowed by the lack of people in it. Buddy and I walked up to the front desk and requested their best room, one of the penthouse suites.

Subsequently, I was escorted to the suite, as a perk. The attention I drew from the front desk was priceless. I quickly discovered that money and "black" weren't synonymous, unless it was a famous "black" with money. Being a non-famous "black" with money seemed to confuse the general population, even those of the same group.

My personal escort was a young, Indian guy named Rasul Rizwan. He'd been working at the hotel ever since it opened about five or so years at the time.

"Mr. Moore, here we are, sir," he said as we stopped in front of the door. I'd been in two high-rise buildings that day, and ended up sleeping in a hotel. He pulled out a golden key card, and proceeded to open the door. The entrance and view were immaculate. The feel was plush with an interesting blend of neutral colors and splashes of a gray, purple and orange, a weird combination that seemed to work. Rasul continued on, discussing the concierge service, the food service, and my complimentary bottle of champagne per day of stay.

After he left, I went straight to the master bath, turned on the water in the Jacuzzi tub, and began to unwind. The king sized bed, off in the distance was my final destination, but first, I wanted to try on the robe hanging on the door. I plopped down on the bed and turned on the flat screen and watched a little cable. Then I took a look at the menu for room service. Eventually I settled on the New York Strip steak, medium well, with the twice baked potato and a bottle of White Zinfandel. After having had my luxurious bubble bath, succulent steak, and few glasses of wine, I was ready to turn in. The curtains were left open to enjoy the view before falling asleep. My circumstance was awesome, looking out over a city I'd grown to love, wishing that my ex, Gwen was right by my side. I wondered about her and Morgan, wondering if life had been treating them fair.

Imagining being with her rekindled a spark for chance sake. I had the means to support them if she didn't mind. Maybe we could start over again, and I could invest in her and her interests. Maybe she could run my charity. She was always knowledgeable and good with numbers. But aside from that, the real question was, *would she consider getting back together*? The urge to call her right then and there, was overruled by the buzz from the wine and the night's previous activities. I'm sure she'd be thrown off by my inebriated rambling.

Later the next morning, I'd awakened to an old episode of *The Cosby Show*. The clock on the wall read 8:43 a.m. With no agenda for the morning, I thought it best to go back to sleep and awake at noon, get room service, and maybe go to the Galleria for some shopping for the trip. I needed new luggage. *Maybe I could call her for lunch*. Her favorite place was Grand Lux Café. She'd always get the buffalo spring rolls, and I, the chicken and waffles. I started dialing her number while lying in bed. The nervousness ensued, but not like the kind that came from meeting someone for the first time and asking them out. This was nervousness like, *we broke up eight months ago and even though we cool, it's still a bit awkward.* And *do I tell her about the money now or do I wait a while?*

I trusted her, but again, what kind of reaction would it get?

"Hey, Doug," she answered.

"Hey, how you doing? You got any plans for lunch?" I asked.

She paused and laughed a good sign.

"Not really, what's up?" she asked.

"I'm thinking we could go to your favorite place for lunch, on me of course."

"Oh, we ballin' today, what's up?" she replied. We started laughing, which was the thing I most admired about us. Even after the break-up we still laughed and talked with each other. Maybe she had moved on already.

"If that's what you wanna call it, that's fine with me," I said.

"I guess so, maybe around 12:30 ... no definitely 12, I have an interview at 2," she added.

"Well 12 it is. How's little Morgan doing by the way?"

"He's good. He was with his dad this past weekend. He's starting to get tall, too."

"Really?" I replied with genuine interest. I missed him.

"Yeah, maybe he can retire his mother in a few years ... get a big NBA contract, something. A sista tired," she continued.

Gwen had been through a lot. To me, the money was a way to correct the ills that came her way, the unplanned mishaps of life, but only if she'd give me the chance. Even though we'd been talking in recent months, the elephant in the room was the break down she had. She was embarrassed, and I, concerned.

"Okay then ... well that's cool. How's your mom?" she asked. We got along with each other's mothers. My mother even admitted to liking her, especially for me.

"She's doing good, thank you. Might fly her out here this weekend," I replied.

"Oh, that'll be nice. Lemme know, I wanna see her," she responded.

"Definitely ... okay, well, I don't wanna hold you too long. Grand Lux."

"Twelve it is ... bye," she said.

When we hung up, a comfort about seeing her for the first time in eight months, settled within. We'd only been talking for a month. I was ready for love again, with her.

After dozing back off, I hopped up, took a good shower, and realized my clothes from last night still carried a dank smoke smell from the weed. It was 10:45. Quickly making my way down to the valet area, I got my truck, and rushed over to the Galleria with the intent of impressing her. Unsure of a look, I wanted something sharp enough to spark her interest. When I entered the mall off

Alabama St., Section 3, I immediately saw Banana Republic. *That'll do.* Lavender, long-sleeved button down shirt, with some gray wool slacks and black loafers completed the look.

The parking lot for Grand Lux was full, and by that time it was 11:56 a.m. I gave the truck to the valet and stood in the reception area waiting for her, after requesting a table for two. All of a sudden, my nerves were worked up. *I thought I was cool. Where's this coming from?* No sooner than I realized how I was beginning to feel, Gwen walked in. She looked so brand new, so refreshed as if she had pushed the restart button to her life.

"Hey there beautiful," I said with unabashed charm. We hugged for what felt like a solid minute, and I didn't care.

"How are you?" she asked with an assured smile. I couldn't stop smiling myself. There was so much to tell her.

"I'm good ... you look really good," I offered.

"You looking good ... loving the shirt, you look good in lavender," she said. *Yes ... she noticed.*

We stood there waiting for the "reservation buzzer," having small talk, and I, at every chance, checking her out. She'd lost some weight, making her ass and hips that much curvier. Gwen had an athletic frame, similar to one of those Olympic level volleyball types, but thicker. Her skin tone was soft and even, just between bronze and brown. Her eyes, a light hazelnut color, similar to mine; we'd often be mistaken for brother and sister. Her hair was what my people called "good," naturally wavy and shiny. Shamelessly I'd play in her hair during better times.

"I must say, you've definitely kept your shape up, if you don't mind my noticing." I was testing the waters. "Have you been working out ... you look like you've lost some weight." She gushed with every compliment.

"Yeah, I've lost a few ... stress will do that, but yeah ... thanks for noticing," she replied in a somewhat sobering quality. Awkwardly, hearing her mention *stress* was something I dared not entertain. Today's get-together was meant to be casual and refreshing, and the day I'd restore her faith in me.

Ten or so minutes went by. The buzzer finally went off, and we were escorted to our table. Off to the side, you could see the chefs and wait staff hustling around in the kitchen area. The atmosphere was inviting as people sprawled about, conversed, and laughed over their meals. When we finally reached our table, there was an older white couple sitting to the right of us and a group of sistas sitting to the left. "Your waiter will be right with you in just a moment," the hostess said.

"Thank you," we replied in unison as she walked away.

"It's been a minute; when's the last time we were here?" My question was an attempt at keeping the ice broken, even though the reference to time referenced the break-up. Before realizing the question, it felt uncomfortable.

"I don't know, maybe last November, December?" she replied. I quickly changed the subject.

"So, I know Morgan just had a birthday ... seven years old now, that's crazy."

"That boy is too much," Gwen said, smiling like a proud mother. "He's so inquisitive, nosey, gets into everything. Sometimes I can't even keep up with him," she went on.

"I'd like to see him sometime in the near future, if that's all right with you," I explained.

"That's cool. He's been seeing his dad lately. I don't wanna confuse him, but maybe you could come over and play with him ... bring Buddy by. How's Buddy?" she asked. It felt like rejection so it stung, but I understood the situation. Morgan was not a baby anymore.

"He's fine ... he misses little man too. Can I ask you something?" She looked at me like, *I know what you're about to ask, and it's none of your business*, but I asked anyway.

"Are you dating?" She dropped her head and started laughing. Either that meant yes or, *wouldn't you like to know?*

"Boy, you crazy right now," she said as she continued laughing. Gwen had a shy side, and I loved messing with it. "No, I'm not dating. I've been focused on getting me together, putting things back in order ... but eventually," she responded.

"Eventually" sounded like an open invitation, possibly reserved for me. *Let's reintroduce ourselves to Morgan, and then work our way up to Mommy.*

"That's cool. Shit, everybody needs love, when the time is right of course," I replied. She gave me a nod of approval. "Well, when you finally decide to go down that road, give me the first dance?"

She looked at me with hesitation. My throat and gut burned for an answer. Her eyes were piercing, as though checking the sincerity of my soul.

"I'll see," she answered. Our "lunch date" progressed quite nicely, talking about our lives, her thoughts of going back to school to become more marketable while I thought about telling her about the money.

"Oh shit, you heard somebody won the lottery here?" *Here we go again ... do I tell her?*

"Yeah I heard ... crazy, right?" In an instant, the idea was no longer interesting for the time being. My focus was on a second chance for us and not the life I could give her. "That's a lot of money ... " I added.

"You ain't lying," she responded. Her enthusiasm was refreshing and helping her was a desirable notion, if she'd let me.

"So tell me, if you won the money, what would you do?" I asked.

"Oh my God ... where do I begin? First I'd pay my tithes ... "

"That's a lot of damn money for tithes," I interrupted.

"You asked me what I'd do, right?" she countered.

"Yeah right, go head ... "

"So like I was saying, pay my tithes ... " she rolled her eyes. "I'd definitely create a college fund for Morgan and all of my nieces and nephews, godchildren ... my friends' kids. I'd pay my mother's bills off, buy her a house, take care of my family's bills, get them new houses ... things like that," she stated. I listened, nodding my head in agreement. "And, I might help you out, give you a little something, something."

"You'd actually help me?" I asked, shocked and surprised, considering our situation.

"I know you got bills. You wouldn't help me?" she countered.

"I would ... " The conversation was pleasant, a perfect time to drop the news, but *not now*.

After having our food, and more good conversation, it was edging towards 1:30. We wrapped up, paid the bill, and walked out. I gave her one big hug, reminiscing of the old days and how we use to be. I wanted to say, *fuck your appointment, let's go get Morgan, and be one big happy family,* but it wasn't in the cards.

"Thanks for lunch. It was good seeing you," she offered.

"Gwen, the pleasure was all mine." We stood there a few seconds more, said our goodbyes and walked our separate ways. *Maybe I should tell her when I get back from New York ... fuck it.*

Unbelievably, our gathering went better than expected, a little uneasiness, maybe tension was anticipated. Talking on the phone was vastly different than facing her. And even though we smiled and behaved as reasonable adults, the past hung over our heads.

The disappointment of not working through our issues was tragic. Even more so disappointing was lacking the balls to tell her about the money.

Sitting in the truck, I thought about life with her and Morgan. Maybe I'd buy a nice house in Pearland instead of River Oaks, or maybe Sugarland. Living in an upper middle-class master planned gated community, with a ready-made family seemed doable. Everyday I'd come home, where she'd be in the kitchen cooking, with the house full of welcoming aromas. Morgan would be in the den area playing, while the TV played some show off Disney or Nickelodeon. Maybe there would be a little sister or brother, sitting in the swing chair in the kitchen with Mommy. I could live that life.

A few years later, Morgan would be in middle school, playing some sport; Gwen and I would be at all the games, cheering and being supportive. Gwen would have her other mother friends, some Caucasian, some African-American, Indian, Asian, and Latino. Of course she'd be active with the PTO and whatever other community based organizations that came with the lifestyle. And I'd have corny male friends, some Caucasian, some African-American, Indian, Asian, and Latino. But for now, the current reality remained. We needed time to heal, and no amount of money could do that.

It was 1:43p.m. The Galleria Mall was right across the street, a perfect time to get a few things for the trip and do away with the raggedy bags I'd had for ages. The Louis Vuitton store came to mind, empowering my motivation to spend. This time the intimidation of the security guard brother dressed in a black suit, shirt and tie, looking at me, wouldn't be a bother.

Like a boss, I instructed the saleswoman to show me the duffel and rolling garment bag in the Ebene Damier print. A few moments later, she returned with both items, for which I gave a quick once over and responded, "I'll take them." I also asked for a toiletry bag, wallet, and messenger bag. Her accommodating, in some ways, encouraged me to buy more. When it was all said and done, everything totaled $10,851.

Walking out the store, through the mall, my focus turned to the next matters at hand ... New York City. This time, I was going to New York as a millionaire. I booked a few days at the famed Waldorf-Astoria Hotel, in the Presidential Suite, that came with a personal butler. I contacted a car service, requesting a Rolls-Royce Phantom for the entire time. On top of that, there was a much needed shopping spree to get in; Bergdorf Goodman, Neiman's,

Gucci, just to name a few. And for the first time in my life, I'd fly first class.

I stopped by the Mercedes dealership and settled my business with Cynthia, arranging for the truck to be delivered to the new apartment. As for my old faithful, a local charity picked it up as a donation. The only thing left to do was clean my old apartment out, the last chapter of my old life.

LOOSE CHANGE [8]

My cell phone rang about 9:58, Wednesday morning. It was the driver informing me that he'd arrived at the hotel. Buddy and I made our way to the elevator, down to the lobby area, and outside to the Lincoln Town Car awaiting us. The driver was an older white guy with "hippie hair" and a handle bar mustache. When we approached the car, he was helpful, taking the luggage off the rack and placing it in the trunk. I tipped the bellhop $50 before getting in.

The morning was fresh and I, excited about New York City. Even though Gwen and I seemed to be getting reacquainted, the anticipation of seeing Frankie grew.

"Going on vacation with your pal?" the driver asked, referring to Buddy.

"Actually it's business, but I'll find a way to enjoy myself," I answered.

"That's nice. Where you headed?"

"The Big Apple."

"Whoa, New York City... I've been thinking of going for my 30th anniversary," he added.

"Congratulations! When's that?" I asked.

"Tomorrow." It was corny, but I still laughed.

"My name's Andy by the way."

"Nice to meet you sir, I'm Douglas."

"Cool," he said. "Are you from Houston?"

"Actually, I'm from California. I've been living here for about 14 years."

"That's cool. I've been here all my life. Just a citified redneck," he replied. We shared a chuckle. Oddly enough, dude was playing a B.B. King CD.

After getting through a little downtown traffic, we finally got on 45 north, towards Intercontinental Airport. Soon the traffic flowed as Andy sped his way towards our destination.

Looking out the window, the fascination of the day continued. I wanted to call my mother, minus the interrogation. The unofficial, official secret was still in play.

"Man I'm sure hungry this morning," Andy chimed. *More small talk*. On the other hand, I was just fine after getting up about 7:40ish, taking a long hot shower, and ordering eggs Benedict, French toast, with a mimosa of course.

"Yeah, there's nothing like having a good breakfast," was my appeasing response.

"I could go for a cold beer and some Boudain," he replied. *Did this guy just say Boudain? What does he know about Boudain?*

"That does sound good. Where do you usually get your Boudain from?" It was my sly attempt at "chin checking" him.

"Well I go to this little meat shop called Smokey's off Jensen Drive," he answered.

Black folks knew Smokey's. Smokey's was smack dab in the hood, on the north east side. It was a shack of a joint, known for having smoked *every thang*. A little shocked with his answer, I had to investigate.

"Now Andy, please forgive me, but how in the hell do you know about Smokey's?" He seemed like a straightforward kind of guy, so I went there and he laughed.

"No problem man. My wife grew up in that area ... she's "black," he answered.

"Oh okay, I gotcha ... the Boudain is really good," I added in a moment of awkwardness. We remained quiet another five minutes. According to the traffic signs, we were about 15 or so miles from the exit to the airport. My heart raced, anxious to fly first class. Looking down at my phone, I noticed a text from Lamont.

"What's up ballin' ass nigga we getting up tonight at Sullivan's?" He must've forgotten about my trip.

"I'm heading to New York, I'll be back in a few days," I wrote.

"That's right, my bad. Bring back a 'I love N.Y.' shirt. Safe travels," he wrote.

"No prob," I replied.

Twenty-five minutes later, we were pulling into the Continental passenger drop off area. In that time, Andy and I continued an interesting conversation. He talked of his three teenaged kids, two girls and a boy, all honor roll students; his love of fishing, and his desire to retire and open up a bed and breakfast near Austin with his wife.

"Here we go," he said while parking the car. The air was a bit dank from the exhaust of the transport buses and other vehicles driving by. Regardless of it all, I was flying first class. With my new duffel and rolling garment bag, looking flyer than a motherfucker, I approached the ticketing counter. A few glances from a group of ladies who worked for the airline made for an excellent start to the morning.

After checking in and going over the particulars for Buddy, I was given my boarding pass, with privileged access to the "Platinum Suite," a lounge area for first class guests. I was even offered a ride on one of those golf carts you see roaming the airport, but I declined. A leisurely stroll felt better. Walking past the different shops, I could only think, *I could totally buy anything I see.*

When I arrived at the lounge, a few folks were already there. The atmosphere was modern chic, with sophisticated lighting, and contemporary jazz playing in the background. A couple at the bar was laughing and clearly enjoying their glasses of wine with a careless air. A swanky leather lounge chair was available by the magazine rack, so I took it immediately as an attendant came my way.

"Welcome, sir. Could I interest you in anything, water, soft drink, cocktail?" she asked.

"Actually, I'd like a rum and Coke if possible," I answered.

"Surely, sir."

My request reeked of alcoholism that early in the morning. Fuck it. I turned my attention to the magazine rack on the wall having almost every magazine and newspaper imaginable. One in particular stood out; *Afrique.* It appeared to be on African culture, but from a worldly, progressive view, with a fashion sensibility. Moments later, the attendant came back with my drink.

"Here you are, sir"

"Thank you ma'am."

I grabbed the magazine, while more people began to trickle in. An Asian guy, an Indian couple, and a brother who looked African, entered the room. Attempting to make eye contact with him, he seemed occupied, unapproachable. By then, the few sips from the drink had me buzzing. Looking through the magazine, I spotted an article on the top restaurants to visit in New York City, making a mental note of the suggested places to take Frankie.

It was 12:38 p.m., and the flight was scheduled to leave at 1:15 p.m. On my second rum and Coke, I felt quite nice. The lounge hadn't received any more guests, which meant the first class cabin would be damn near empty. Seven minutes later, we were called to board the plane. The lounge attendants began assisting us, making sure we had our belongings, and making sure they received their tips.

Walking down the corridor was exhilarating, while on the outside, my composure read *well-traveled*. As we approached the plane entrance, I remembered the promise I made to myself; *stretch out my legs, get a glass of champagne, and enjoy it.*

"Welcome to Continental Airlines, first class... " the flight attendant told each guest. She even said each of our names from a glance at the boarding pass, an extended privilege I supposed. "Welcome to Continental Airlines, first class … Mr. Douglas." The shit was awesome, *I've arrived.*

"Thank you," I replied, with the biggest grin ever. Looking for my window seat, I put my duffel bag overhead and took a good stretch. When I sat down, it was like sinking into a recliner. A 14" inch monitor screen was built into the partition in front of me. Just to the side, was a telephone console, and on the other side, a magazine or book storage compartment. My seating area even had its own sliding door that sectioned off my seat from whoever sat next to me. *Privacy … yes!*

About 10 or so minutes passed. All first class guests were seated, but noticeably, not brother man. Perhaps there was a problem with his ticket, or he had an emergency. No sooner than I thought that, he appeared, looking for his seat. The attendant from the front walked him over to his seat, which happened to be next to me. As he approached, our eyes finally met. I gave him a nod, and he returned it with a lukewarm smile.

He fumbled with his belongings while I focused back on my surroundings, exploring the joys of a first class ticket. My seat had a remote control, allowing it to recline and give a massage. I pushed the button that said, "Deep Tissue," and it did just that. The rolling balls, as I called it, activated, starting from the base of my spine. Slowly it worked up my back, periodically stopping at certain points to emphasize the experience. My toes actually curled, the shit was that good. After it reached the top of my back, it went into a different speed, sort of a chopping motion, which felt even better.

Suddenly, in my peripheral, I saw other guests began to board. My curiosity got the best of me; *are they checking me out?* Surely, every time I looked at the entrance, someone looked in my direction, or around the cabin. I use to be *that guy*.

Another 20 minutes passed, and by then, everyone had boarded. The flight attendants hurried about, fulfilling their duties, whatever they were. Looking around the first-class area, three or four seats were empty at $2,500 a pop.

The atmosphere remained calm; the captain introduced himself and the crew, and the engines were fired up. The plane was pushed back to prepare for take-off, and I, a good nap. But suddenly, I noticed a weird humming noise coming from my first class neighbor. I took a quick peek and saw what appeared to be a man deep in prayer. I didn't know if he were speaking in tongues or his native language, but I leaned back into my chair and business.

The flight attendant began working our area, taking our requests. Not hungry for much, considering the breakfast I'd had, I entertained her anyway.

"Good afternoon, sir ... due to the length of our flight, we will not offer a three course meal, but you are able to select a lunch entrée from our menu," she informed me. *WTF?*

"What do you have?" I asked.

"Here you are sir, take your time." I was slightly embarrassed. The menu selections were foreign to my palate; *Steak tartar, with red wine reduction sauce, Shrimp and Calamari Penne pasta in white wine sauce, Almond encrusted Salmon with lemon butter asparagus...* all of it validating a first class price tag and experience.

I settled back into my seat, enjoying the massage options again. This time I tried the *"circulatory therapy"* button. It seemed to be slightly the same as the previous option, it didn't matter; I'd never flown like this, and regardless of the food or my slightly off neighbor, this was living.

A few minutes later, we were finally in the air and I had to go. I had too many drinks that morning. First class seemed somber as most of the passengers immediately went to sleep. This was normal for them, but for me, lifestyle training. Eventually I chose a romance-comedy and fell asleep. From time to time, the burst of air pockets gave the plane a jolt of turbulence. The inconsistent sleep took its toll on me. I got a mag from the compartment and read, hoping I'd fall back again.

The magazine was a world news type mag, featuring progressive thinkers, businesspeople, and political figures from around the world. Thumbing through it, I stopped on a page with the headline "Africa's Future Now." It highlighted the progress being made in business, environmental development, and politics from different aspects. One article featured a guy who was at the helm of a successful solar panel manufacturing company in Ghana. The picture looked interesting ... just like my first-class neighbor. *Bioko Amana has a very firm grip on the solar panel industry in Ghana* ... a sentence from the article read. I stopped to sneak a peek over into my neighbor's cabin to make the connection. When I peeked over, he was reading a book, but he quickly looked up, above his glasses. Pretending to look past him, I leaned back in my seat.

I felt stupid. *How old am I, afraid to ask another grown man if he's in this magazine? This could be an investment opportunity; maybe I could take a million bucks and turn it into tens of millions of dollars fucking with this dude.* I got the courage to lean back over.

"Excuse me sir, but I'm reading an article ... this picture ... is it you?" He took it for a closer look, and looked back at me with the widest African smile you could ever see.

"This is me, yes, thank you," he said handing the magazine back. I smiled at the humor of him thanking me for recognizing him.

"Nice to meet you," I replied.

"Are you American?" he quickly asked.

"Yes, I live in Houston ... I'm Douglas Moore," I added, extending my hand to shake his.

"Oh that's wonderful, I'm Bioko Amana."

"I know," I countered, pointing at the magazine. We shared a quaint laugh.

"I was here for business," he added in his thick African accent. "What do you do in Houston?" It was a perfect opportunity to embellish the truth.

"I'm actually in private investment banking," I replied. "I have a portfolio meeting tomorrow morning with my business partners."

We began talking business matters, his company, and future endeavors.

"My company has a great opportunity to expand in the next year or so. I've been talking with the current administration of

Kenya about installing solar panels on all government buildings and schools," he chimed. Seeing the opportunity, I wanted to invest.

"If you don't mind, why were you in Houston?" I asked.

"I'm seeking investment money to build the panels for this deal. It's important to have enough equipment and materials to match the order."

Without thinking twice, I blurted out, "I'm interested in possibly investing with you Mr. Amana." He looked at me, sincerely and polite, and replied in a very reserved manner.

"Mr. Moore ... this is a five million dollar project, within a six-month time frame."

Somewhat offended, it sounded like, *dude, if you ain't got no money, take your broke ass home.*

"That's a sizable amount," I countered. What the fuck did I know? I had "new money" smell on me, but the opportunity seemed solid. "Will you be in New York City for long?"

"I will be there for two days to meet with friends and then back to Ghana," he answered.

"If possible, could you take an hour meeting with my staff? I'd like them to hear of your impending project. It's interesting," I offered.

"That's possible, Mr. Moore," he replied. We exchanged information and retreated back to our privacy. A proud moment, seeing a business opportunity and seizing it. Investing in an African enterprise would've made my father proud.

Instantly, I contemplated my decision. A part of me felt like a naïve, thirsty fool. With no research of any kind, or any true knowledge of investing, I'd committed to meeting with this guy when my own affairs weren't completely in order.

You hear about people winning the lottery and losing it over time. Bad business deals, thirsty relatives, and sporadic spending, all equaling to an epic fail of misjudgment. How embarrassing to go through $165 million? *Was this financial suicide?*

After mulling over my verbal commitment to Bioko, I made a pact with myself that I wouldn't invest more than $500,000, 10 percent of the total project cost. A safe gamble, recoupable from the interests off my accounts anyway. Back at ease, it was time for another nap.

About two hours later, I was awake and refreshed, ready for New York. I hadn't been a millionaire a full month, yet, with a business deal in my lap. It was safe to say I was becoming accustomed to living on the other side. The captain announced that we were less than an hour from our destination. Gazing at the clouds outside my window, this feeling of security was something new to me. My life was now like those clouds, unrestrained, free flowing and above all the bullshit. *I'm walking on air now, bitch.*

SOUR DIESEL [9]

Maybe this time, I'd have the balls to ask Frankie out. She was on my list of things to do, so to speak. A few angles could be played; rich obnoxious dude throwing money around, hoping she'd be impressed or naïve and nouveau rich clueless guy, looking for guidance. Either way, she was the target. This wasn't to say that Gwen was no longer "the one." She's who I'd settle down with in the "burbs," eventually. But this weekend was a whole other beast.

Honestly speaking, the idea of being a "sugar daddy" seemed a reasonable feat ... dating some new "hot thing" every month, paying a few bills and having a whirlwind sex life. Conversely, I was never the guy that juggled women in the first place, just the guy who wished he could. And now, with the resources to do it, my heart, mind, and soul, were still tied to Gwen.

Maybe after a solid year of dating, I'd make the right decision. The gamble of course, was biding her time. It's not like I initiated the breakup anyway. I accepted her flaws and qualities, but I refused to be a lovesick, pussy-whipped push over, again.

A burst of sunlight peeked just below the window shade, as we began our gentle decent into LaGuardia airport. The ambition and swagger of this trip gave me an instantaneous feeling of "being on top." The years of just getting by, living check to check, wishing for better days, all came to a head as I realized, *I'm the H.N.I.C. of my life.*

The transition from how things used to be just a month ago, versus now was unbelievable; *we some rich motherfuckers, Mama.* All the toil and heartache of life, the stresses of surviving would be non-existent for her. She deserved a different kind of *life.* However, my heart was prepared for those who'd hate on me."*Money changed*

75

you." As if money doesn't change you. As if the feeling of having no financial worries is the same as eating a good steak.

"Mr. Moore," Mr. Amana called, as he leaned over.

"Yes," I replied.

"Have you ever been to Africa?" A profound question, it stung in a weird way. Here I was, this young African-American male, sitting atop a vast amount of money, with no intended plans to visit my homeland.

"No sir, but I'd definitely like to go in the near future … is this an invitation?"

"Of course sir, you need to see your mother country, it would be good for your soul."

"Indeed it would," I added.

As the flight attendant announced permission to unbuckle seat belts, the movement in first class seemed subdued, opposed to the scurrying of those riding in economy. No one hurried to get their belongings. Actually, some stayed seated, stretched out as if preparing for another flight. I looked around and played the part. *We're getting off the plane first anyway.* My neighbor got up and took a big stretch and yawned.

"That was a nice flight," he said as he smiled. I just nodded, while looking at the ground crew, running about, preparing for our exit.

Finally we were let off, to go our separate ways. I was hoping my very expensive Louie luggage remained intact upon arrival in baggage claim. My mind was also on the suite I booked at the famed Waldorf-Astoria Hotel and the car service awaiting me outside. When I arrived at baggage claim, the first class experience quickly wore off; we were all just motherfuckers trying to get our bags. Mr. Amana and I spoke one last time before making my way to the exit area among the crowd of drivers holding signs of the names of people they'd been assigned to pick up. Noticing my name being held by a light-skinned brother, I acknowledged him with a nod.

"Mr. Moore?" he asked.

"Indeed sir, how are you?" I replied as we shook hands. He offered to take my luggage while we walked outside the airport.

"I'm Raul Contreras by the way."

"Douglas," I responded. *I have a motherfucking driver, how cool is this?*

A shot of cold air hit my body. Regrettably, I didn't pack a jacket. We ended up walking a short distance to the car, parked in all its glory, the most gorgeous vehicle God ever inspired man to make. The color alone was flawless; a sort of arrogant silver paint job, complemented by chrome fixtures about the body. This was a *Rolls-Royce*.

As we approached it, Raul popped the oversized trunk, putting my luggage in.

"Is this your first time in New York?" he asked.

"No, actually I was here a few weeks ago," I answered.

"Oh, okay … please," he said as he opened the back door for me. When I sat down, I was again enveloped in luxury. That familiar smell from the dealership, feel of the leather seats, the wood grain appointments, and the attention from passersby, all made for an extreme ego boost.

"I believe you're heading to the Waldorf," he declared.

"That's correct," I countered with a matter-of-fact tone. *I'm in this bitch*. My meeting with the Frasier Payne folks wasn't until tomorrow morning, so I had a wide open day. The airline made sure that Buddy Boy was delivered to the hotel within an hour of my landing. I'd preferred picking him up from jump, but the delivery service sounded cool.

"If you don't mind my asking … "

"What do I do? I'm in investment banking," I offered presumptively.

"Wow … sounds interesting, how does that work?" he asked. *Damn, a questionnaire?*

"Basically, I look for good business opportunities, invest and wait for a return." This bullshit persona I created was taking shape.

"Oh, okay … so if I had an idea for something, some kind of business, if it made good sense to you, and you thought it was worth investing in, you'd invest in it … right?" he asked.

"Exactly," I answered.

"I know this is unprofessional, but if you have any free time this week, I'd like to run an idea by you." My defenses immediately went up. This was the beginning of what felt like the circling sharks. Making a hasty decision and a condescending promise was unnecessary.

"Well that's a possibility. I'm here on business, but once that's taken care of and my schedule permits it, we can have a chat," I responded.

After 30 minutes or so, with traffic and construction work going on, we finally reached Manhattan. The splendor remained, but maybe even more so from the back seat view of a Rolls-Royce. I hadn't talked with my mother so I gave her a call. Things were still under wraps. On this trip, my plans to create accounts for her and Devin were a surprise. I figured ten million each would do. Also my charity was getting structured, for the following year.

Arriving at the hotel, the ambiance and grandeur justified my $3,500 a night stay. This was the same hotel from *Coming to America* and my black ass had a suite up in that bitch. Raul pulled into the circular drive, and a door attendant came to the car. "Welcome to the Waldorf-Astoria, sir," the gentleman stated with a pleasant, caked on smile.

"Thank you very much. Glad to be here," I replied. A bellhop came with a luggage cart.

"How long is your stay with us sir?" the doorman asked.

"Until Saturday," I replied. Dropping over ten grand on a hotel, from a movie I saw as a kid, the shit was surreal.

Entering the lobby, the feeling was overwhelming. You couldn't help noticing the opulence and décor of the massive marble stairway, sculptures, and chandeliers everywhere. The employees were distinguishable by their impeccably starched uniforms and available smiles.

"Welcome to the Waldorf-Astoria, sir, are you checking in with us today?" the lady asked.

"Why yes," I answered.

"That's great. If I could get your reservation information and I.D. that should do it." When she entered the information my reservation came up, and so did her tone.

"Okay, Mr. Moore, we have you checked in for the Presidential Suite." A colleague working beside her looked up from what he was doing to take a glance at me.

"You'll have personal concierge service the entire time of your stay; take advantage of it, it's a part of the privilege of your suite. He'll be available 24 hours a day until the day you check out. If you need anything, tickets to a Broadway show, dry cleaning, you name it, it's done," she explained. A weird tingling sensation came over me. "Mr. Moore, you'll be accompanied by your personal concierge in just a moment … he's making his way down right now," she added.

"Thank you," was all I could say, as I waited for the mystery guy. I turned to Raul who'd walked in with me, shrugging my shoulders in disbelief, with a slight grin on my face.

"It's good to be you right now," he offered.

"I guess so," I laughed.

"Now my turn," Raul said. "I will also be available 24 hours unless an emergency occurs that hinders my availability, at which time, another driver will be assigned to you. This is my card with my cell and home numbers. Feel free to call at any time. It's what you paid for," he explained.

"Appreciate that," I said as we shook hands. At that time, in my peripheral, I could see someone walking towards us.

"Mr. Moore?" A young, slender white guy, appearing to be in his late 20s or early 30s, approached in a black suit and wire framed glasses. "Hi, I'm Ira Abram, your personal concierge," he said with his hand extended.

"Nice to meet you." I shook his hand.

"Raul, I think I'll take a nap for a few hours but I'll call you later, sir."

"Okay boss, take care ... see you later."

I walked with Ira and the bellhop, towards the elevators, thinking of all the luxury I'd experienced in the last few weeks. "Mr. Moore, can you tell me a bit about yourself ... what you might be interested in during your stay?" A good question. Besides the shopping, and possibly a date with Frankie, I hadn't planned for much, other than a Broadway show.

"You know, Ira, I really don't have any major plans. I'm here on business, but I'd be interested in pleasure – maybe catch a play, see some museums, – stuff like that," I replied. It sounded boring. In the back of my mind I was really thinking, *I need to holla at Raul and see if he has a weed man.*

"That's not a problem Mr. Moore, those matters can be arranged with ease. I'd like to take the liberty of suggesting an option, if you don't mind," he stated.

"By all means," I added.

"There's a private art showing in a few days on the lower east side, by an emerging German artist. It should be an awesome event, and since you're a privileged guest, I can get you on the invitation list."

This wouldn't have been conceivable months ago, fuck, weeks ago. Most of my art came from *Ikea*.

"Sounds interesting. I'd like to attend."

"Any other excursions or personal interests you have in mind?" he continued.

"Well, I did plan on doing a little shopping, maybe a nice suit ..."

"Say no more. I'll arrange a fitting by one of the premiere tailors in Manhattan. Many dignitaries go there. You will be impressed."

This is what "rich" felt like. Complete strangers beckoning to my every whim, for a fee of course. Treatment like this used to be a dream, but now I was living and loving it. Secretly, even if they all hated my guts, with jealousy and contempt in their hearts, that almighty dollar spoke louder than anything I needed to say. The elevator stopped at our intended floor.

"Right this way, Mr. Moore." It was a stately hallway with paintings, and chandeliers hanging from the ceilings. "You'll be staying in the east wing, with great views of the lower east side." Anticipating yet another great hotel room, all I really wanted was a nap. Just ahead I could see double doors, my suite perhaps. "Here we are," Ira replied as he went into his pocket to retrieve the key card. When he opened the room a relaxing aroma immediately hit me. The bellhop proceeded to take my belongings to the master suite while Ira went on about the special features and amenities of the room. But all I wanted was that nap.

Minutes later, Ira finished his spiel and he and the bellhop gave me the privacy I'd been waiting for so patiently. Taking off all my clothes, down to my drawers, T-shirt and socks, I plopped my ass on the bed and off to dreamland. About seven that evening, I'd awaken from a good deep sleep, ready to conquer New York City, with no plans to go anywhere. Hours earlier, Buddy had been brought up to my room, where he ran around frantically like a little kid. I thought of calling Raul to see if he could suggest a restaurant or even a nice club for me to let my hair down, from fear of being cooped up in this expensive-ass room.

When I called Raul, I could tell he'd been napping from the grogginess of his voice.

"Hey, Raul."

"Mr. Moore."

"You can call me Doug, man."

"Okay ... Doug."

"Yeah man, I'm trying to get out, see some sights get into some shit ... where's a good club or restaurant to go chill, meet some women?"

"Oh okay ... get into something huh," he insinuated.

"Yeah, I ain't trying to stay in this room all night ... wish I had something to smoke," I added for a response.

"Word," he responded enthusiastically.

"What … you can get me something?" I verified.

"What you trying to do?"

"A half ounce is good … I'm only here 'till Saturday."

"All right … give me a good 30 minutes, I got you."

Unbelievably, I'd just made a drug deal from the Presidential Suite of the Waldorf-Astoria. Surprisingly so, it felt a little edgy, a little reckless. What's next, a one-night stand with some chick from an escort service? Raul's acceptance was like a flood gate for other shit to get into. As my mind began conjuring up devious ideas, my phone rang. It was Gwen.

"Hey Gwen, what's up? This is unexpected." It really was. After we had lunch the other day, I figured we'd talk again in a week.

"Oh, I didn't want anything … thought about you," she replied. *Was this the beginning of something?* I still hadn't fucked Frankie.

"Oh that's cool. Had a good time at lunch … we gotta do that again," I replied.

"So what's up?" she asked. The timing was off and somewhat confusing. Now she had a sudden interest in rekindling. *Isn't that what I wanted?*

"Actually, I'm in New York City on some family business. I'll be back in a few days."

"Is everything okay? Your uncle, he still lives there, right?" she asked. Yeah my uncle did live here until he moved back to Alabama with his girlfriend a year ago. She didn't know.

"Yeah he's fine, everything's cool … just taking care of some legal stuff."

"When you get back in town, let's go do dinner." *Dinner? Does she know something?*

"That sounds like a plan, looking forward to it."

"Okay, well let me let you go, talk to you later, be safe."

"Okay … don't forget dinner."

"All right, Dougie."

"Bye." The conversation was reminiscent of better times.

Sitting on the edge of the bed thinking about Gwen, I was happy to be reconnecting, and equally upset that she broke our bond. We'd be engaged or married by now. A part of me was suspicious, but for what? I called her for lunch. Subconsciously, I was upset for inviting her back in my life at a time when a man of my means wanted to simply throw caution and commitment to the wind, and live an irreverent existence with an embarrassment of riches.

At 8:13 I got a call from the reception desk.

"Sir, you have a visitor. Raul?"

"Yes, let him up please." For a minute I was spooked, thinking they caught his ass with the shit. When he reached my room he had a, *you won't believe this* look on his face.

"Man ... motherfucking security guard hemmed me up."

"What happened?"

"I was walking to the elevator and dude asked where was I going? I'm like how the hell you know whether I stay here or not, asking me where I'm going and shit." Raul had a reasonable point, but *where's the weed?*

"Anyway, look at this," Raul proceeded to reach into his tattered grayish looking messenger bag and pulled out the prettiest, greenest, puffiest, bag of trees you ever saw. I think a tear welled up in my left eye.

Any and every amazing thing I've ever experienced since winning the money paled in comparison; I was about to get high again.

"You gone roll?" Raul asked.

"You got it." I replied.

"Not a problem." He reached back into his bag and pulled out a small box of mini cigars. Back in Houston we called them "sweets." "So what you wanna do tonight," Raul asked as he proceeded to go through the weed rolling process.

"I'm open man ... I don't know the spots."

"I mean, do you wanna see bitches, go dancing and shit, sit in a classy restaurant with some classy Manhattan bitches, what?" he asked.

"Let's hit a club up ... the hottest club, but let's smoke first." The anticipation of the night was thrilling. Getting high as fuck, riding through the city in a Rolls-Royce, blowing money and possibly pulling a few bad ones back to the spot.

In what seemed like 30 seconds, Raul had finished rolling.

"Shall we?"

"We shall ... you got a lighter?" I asked.

"C'mon, Doug," Raul countered.

"Hold on," I got up really fast, went to the bathroom, took one of those oversized bath towels, soaked it, squeezed it, and it put at the bottom of the front door.

"That's why you get paid the big bucks," Raul added. Then I went to the windows and cracked every one of them.

"I'm ready now, spark that shit." When Raul lit the blunt, instantly an aroma filled the room so funky it gave me second thoughts. Raul read my facial expression.

"You okay with this?"

"Yeah man, I'm chilling."

From the first pull, even the taste of the smoke was unfamiliar.

"Man, what you call this shit?"

"Sour Diesel," he replied. Sour Diesel, huh? I was falling in love on the first date. Ten minutes in, and I was officially flying. With all the uncontrollable coughing, I was a wrap. "We should put this out huh…hit the road?"

"Nah nigga, burn that … " Raul having had more experience seemed more reserved than I. *Did I just call this nigga, nigga?* "I'm ready for these bitches … niggas gone hate tonight." Raul just looked at me like, *shut the fuck up, please.* "Man, you know what… let's go to the mall and get fly…"

"I'm cool, Doug, I'm the driver, I'm still working … "

"Nah, fuck that, we chilling, we smoking … let's go to the fucking mall." Raul just paused, and then laughed.

"You getting high, but that's cool, it's 8:25, we can catch a couple spots before they close."

"That's what I'm saying nigga." *Damn, I just called him a nigga again.*

My state of mind was fuck everything and that's a dangerous mix with money. I had fantasized about this place before. All of P. Diddy's rap videos had influenced me to a degree. When we walked out the room I was on top of the world. Subconsciously, my mother's voice said, *"be careful."*

When we got down to the lobby area, paranoia kicked in. I think everybody could tell I was high as fuck. The self-loathing was incredible. *How could I as an African-American man, be so stupid?* My eyes met with the same corny doorman earlier. I quickly looked away as he proceeded to greet me with another cornball smile. The valet guy came around with the Rolls and I regained a bit of civility. Raul motioned to open the back door but I refused.

"Nah man, I'ma sit in the front, I'm cool."

"All right," he said, walking to the other side of the car. It was unnecessary to spoil the vibe with particulars. When we got in, the radio was playing Biggie, the *one more chance* song. Positioning my seat to lean back, the heat from the air conditioner nursed my buzz. This was a night of high expectations so to speak.

A white family stood at the lobby entrance, with the wife staring at me. She fumbled with her purse as if hurrying to get her phone or camera to take a picture. Flattered, I reached for the knob and turned the music up.

"We can check out Manhattan Mall or one of these boutique joints ... " Raul said in his thick New Yorker accent.

"I'm cool, pick a place," I said. *Man don't fall asleep, please God don't let me fall asleep*, I pleaded. Sitting in that plush leather seat, under that warm air; a Red Bull was necessary.

All the city lights danced with a strange glow through the blur of my vision. Raul on the other hand, looked deep in thought.

"You all right man?" he asked with a docile tone.

"I'm chilling ... just high as fuck." We shared a laugh, but it seemed contrived for Raul. "Life's a trip man ... one moment you looking for an answer, next moment you have the answer and still confused." Prodding him for a conversation, I tried remaining cool. His response was dry.

"Yep ... that's life."

About a few blocks in, the hunt for fresh began when I spotted a store about mid-block. "Let's check this spot, what's that say ...?" I couldn't make out the name except the male mannequin in the window. We pulled up closer, looking for parking, but it was a typical city block situation, so we kept it pushing.

"Oh I know a spot, but it's in Harlem ... you okay with that?"

"I'm cool ... what kind a shit they got?"

"Fly shit, trust me," Raul said with confidence. In the back of my mind I was like, *do we need to be going to Harlem in this car*?

Driving through the city, seeing the transitional scope of neighborhoods, the haves and the have nots, conjured a guilt, mixed with paranoia. The homeless were striving to survive on a cold night in New York's little nooks and crannies. Each street looked to have its own story to tell and I was one of them ... the lucky bastard in the half a million dollar car.

We made a quick left at the light, moving right into an available parking spot. I looked up. "L. Boogie's" was the name on the marquee. Assuming we'd arrived, I motioned to get out when Raul said, "This joint ... you'll like." A few dudes hanging in front of the store provided the typical hood element. Their look was between mean mug and unconcerned, while admiring the car. We gave nods walking in. The vibe of the store was bourgeoisie chic; high end T-shirts and jeans, shoes and accessories, the kind of stuff

I liked. "Bonzi," I heard a thick New Yorker accent say. Looking around, an older husky dude walked towards us. Raul and the guy gripped each other up, embracing like old friends.

"What's good boss, been a minute fam," said the older gentleman.

"Yeah I know, been grinding though." Raul seemed to be genuinely happy, a stark contrast from when he was in the car. "Yeah, I brought my man up here to check you out," he said as he motioned to me.

"What's up brother ... Lamar."

"Doug."

"Looking for something special, exclusive ...?"

"Something fly for the club ... "

"Oh, we got that," Lamar answered with exaggerated confidence.

"All right, well I'll look around."

"Cool." Raul and Lamar continued talking while I browsed. Very few items appealed to my fashion sense. They were almost too hip for my age. The price tag suggested exclusive: $189 for a T-shirt, $335 for some jeans I'd never heard of. With money to blow, I went on walking aimlessly, still high and unfocused.

Nothing moved me, so I settled on some black jeans, T-shirt, and a decent leather jacket. Raul picked up some shit, so we changed in the dressing rooms. I started to collect myself, my high making a gentle descent, with the anticipation of things to come. When I walked out, Raul was already in the clothing area dressed and ready.

"You looking real fresh, Doug, it's a problem tonight ... if you had some jewels to rock with that it would kill."

"Yeah ... I don't have a lot of jewelry though." I wasn't the type to buy gaudy shit. My most expensive piece was a Cartier watch I'd bought back in Houston.

After cashing out, we walked to the car with eyes watching us; some of it good for my ego and equally a reason to be on alert. Immediately, I wanted to smoke again.

"Bro, please tell me you have more of that Sour Diesel." Raul looked at me with a smirk.

"You like that shit huh?"

"What ... that's an understatement." Just as we were getting ready to leave, I saw a young lady and her friend walking up the block, maybe in their early 20s. When she got closer, our eyes locked enough to entice a response. "You see this girl walking up? I gotta holler." I rolled down the window as she got closer. "Hello, what's your name?"

"Huh?" she replied with a face that read, *you talking to me?* I appreciated her attempt at playing hard, but come on, look at the car.

"Yes, you, what's your name?"

"Octavia."

"Pretty … your friend?" Her friend stood to the side.

"Marisa."

"What y'all 'bout to do?" I asked.

"We heading home," she replied in a serious, yet sweet tone.

"Cool … can we give y'all a ride?" Marissa's eyes lit up but Octavia held firm.

"Oh, thanks, but we just up the block."

"We cool babe, we won't bite, just wanna make sure you get home safely, that's all."

"We good, but thanks," she replied.

"All right Hun, be good." I rolled up the window; the reality of the shutdown was refreshing. I got shot down in a Rolls-Royce, good for her.

"Damn." Raul said, and then we bust out laughing.

"Yeah man, let me roll something right quick to get over that bust down."

"I'm cool. She had a fat ass though … saw that shit when she walked up."

"You ain't lying, friend was cute too," he added. The night was just beginning.

By then, it was 9:40ish, way too early for the club, but the right time to get something to eat. "Man I'm hungry as fuck." Raul was puffing on the second blunt as we drove down another Harlem block; gangsta shit. Refusing to tell him the truth, that I was a teacher just weeks ago, my participation in the activities of the evening gave validation enough.

"What you in the taste for, pizza pie, Jamaican beef patties, Cuban sandwich … ?"

"Take me to the spots you go bro, I want that real authentic, New York City cuisine." I was officially at home.

JUST ANOTHER GUY [10]

Driving through another maze of city blocks and neighborhoods, a certain photographic quality was evident in this scenic leisurely drive. It was a unique allure in the hood that never got equal recognition as Manhattan. Other than a Spike Lee movie, I'd never seen such rawness, and I liked it. The obvious difference from Houston was that neighborhoods in Houston's lower social economical stratus still had single family homes as opposed to the throngs of buildings lining each block we passed. Imagining the people who grew up here never having a concept of a front and back yard. The city park was that for them.

In reflection, I was grateful for cutting grass every Saturday morning as a pre-teen and teenager, during those warm spring and hot summer months in Cali. I was thankful for being able to walk down uncongested streets, taking for granted open spaces that didn't restrict views of the sky. A southern California boy accustomed to a much slower pace, whatever sophistication I lacked from that life, made up for my appreciation of the small things nature gave me.

Fifteen minutes and a few pockets of traffic later, we pulled up to another charmingly authentic row of shops and brownstones.

"I'm a go to this pizza joint and leave the car running with the hazards. What you want?"

"Oh, what ever's cool … give me two slices."

"Yo … the slices are mad big."

I was so fucking hungry after the second blunt. "It's cool, I'm hungry."

"All right," he responded as he got out of the car. Leaning

87

back into my seat, the music provided a feeling of carelessness and relaxation. The night was chill enough without the club, but hanging with Raul, probably in his late 20s, early 30s, I had to keep up the façade.

A sudden knocking on my window startled me. It was a woman appearing to be elderly and homeless. Cautiously, I cracked it.

"Yes ma'am?"

"Say young blood, you looking real good in this car right now. Could you help out an old dusty bag like me?" she asked, with a toothless grin.

Reaching for my wallet, I pulled out a hundred dollar bill and handed it to her through the crack. When she saw the amount her facial expression was more than thankful. "Thank you sir, God bless you sir," she kept repeating with trembling in her voice, on the verge of crying. Nodding my head, I realized having the financial ability to give a complete stranger that amount of money was humbling.

Just as she left, Raul came back to the car.

"What's up with that old bitch?"

"Oh, she wanted a little change...hey, what's this neighborhood?"

"This is Brooklyn. I grew up a block down the street ... I live in the Bronx now."

The aroma from the pizza was mouthwatering. He handed over what was the equivalent size of a medium box.

"This me?"

"I told you the slices were big." I opened it to two enormous, greasy, cheesy slices with pepperoni, black olives, Italian sausage, and subtle hints of red pepper. This was New York City pizza.

"Hey you don't mind if I eat? I'm starving, bro," I said.

"Go ahead, I'm eating, too," Raul answered, as he put the car in drive. Taking the first bite was pain and pleasure. I misjudged the temperature, burning the roof of my mouth and getting that dangling piece of flesh moments later. The heavenly mixture of flavors blended for a beautiful marriage of authenticity.

At 10 o'clock sharp, still too early for any club in America, we continued driving through neighborhoods in a car that didn't fit, eating pizza.

"Maybe we should hit up a bar and kill some time ... seems too early for a club."

"Yeah that's cool ... Manhattan or SoHo should work."

"Where's the model bitches at? The sophisticated snobby, too good for nothing ass bitches?" I asked. The atmosphere needed changing.

"I think SoHo is good for that. I take clients over to this spot called the M Lounge, they seem to like it."

The pace of the night was at an even keel, nothing too extraordinary but more drab than anything.

"Hey man, I got a question. When did you realize you weren't broke anymore?" Raul asked. I wondered how long he'd pondered asking me that question. It seemed to come from a place of humility.

"The moment I realized I didn't have to work for anybody else ... that was the moment for me," I answered.

"What was that like, I mean, did you get one big check and say fuck it, or did you eventually save enough money and then one day say fuck it?" Although I heard the sincerity in his voice, it wasn't worth revealing the truth.

"Well ... it was more of a combination of the two. I mean, I worked my butt off, planning, strategizing for the day when I could eventually stop working, and then one day a deal fell in my lap that basically changed everything." Raul sat quietly, nodding his head as if listening to a seminar or lecture.

"That's what's up, that's exactly what I'm striving for. I'm 32, been driving this car for a year now. Before this I worked for another car service for seven years. I'm just waiting on that chance opportunity." The guilt of my bullshit spiel was nerving. The planning and strategizing I spoke of was merely my weekly ritual of playing the lottery, and of course when I won, that was the deal that fell in my lap.

"What's your passion? What most excites you?" I asked. During my lean and in between days, from time to time I'd watch videos and read books from self-help types. They'd always have the same theme ... passion. Mine was living well.

"I don't know ... know what I'm saying? Like I can do a lot of shit, cut hair, fix cars, cook and I like working out ... even thought about being a trainer," he said.

"Sounds like you need to narrow down and find your thing," I replied. The more I spoke to be insightful, the more I felt like a fucking hypocrite.

"I tell you what, you decide on something that best displays your passion and ability, create a business plan and if it makes good sense, I'll take it to my people to consider as an investment project."

"Yo are you fucking serious … man I don't know what to say. Thanks Doug, I appreciate that." Raul's elation was full with possibility.

We reached the M Lounge in a short 20 minutes. Luckily valet service allowed us to head straight to the bar. The atmosphere was eclectic and progressive, befitting this particular area. The walls were covered with abstract paintings, while jazz fusion played over the sound system. The room was brisk as the overhead, exposed air ducts complemented the decor and the beautiful people of New York's night life. As rich as I'd become, I was intimidated. Back in Houston, the black bourgeoisie crowd was made up of people you knew or knew of, some making it and some faking it. But this crowd looked different. Everyone seemed to be in shape, fashionable, and gainfully employed.

Raul and I walked to an open sitting area and tried fitting in.

"This place is chill, cool vibe."

"Yeah it's cool … not really my crowd," he replied. Presumably he felt out of place due to his professional standing or background.

Around the room, the spectrum of attractive women ran the gamut from ethnicity to body type. None of these women would be in my circle back home. The only time I'd seen this caliber of attractiveness was during concerts and other special events. A few interesting ladies caught my eye but my fear of rejection was cemented by the girl back on the block. It's funny. Back home, most of my compliments came from how I dressed or my charming demeanor, but this was New York City, a whole 'nother ball game.

"I think that bitch in the red peeping you out, over at the end of the bar … " Raul saw someone peering my way and occasionally looking in our direction, but not enough to make a move.

"She's nice," was my reply. "Hey man, I'm a get a drink, what you want?"

"Long Island."

"Okay, cool."

Walking to the bar felt like high school, assuming all the cool kids were critiquing my attire. Had I known we were coming to such a swanky, cosmopolitan joint, I might have put more thought into my look. This crowd was smart casual. They had a thoughtful style, versus what I had on which said, "look at me, bitches," rather than "bitch, look at me." Standing there for what felt like eons, waiting for service, I motioned to whoever seemed available, to no avail, until finally being spotted.

"What can I get you?" a young bartender asked.

"Rum and Coke, and a Long Island." She gave a nod and proceeded to make the drinks. I felt accomplished for placing my first bar order in a New York City establishment.

This was a perfect time to be high; my anxiety was far too apparent, that *out of place* feeling. Oddly, this was my type of crowd; young professionals with interesting conversations. Still I was the outsider. A very rich one.

"Here you go, sir."

"How much?"

"Fifty." I handed her $100.

"Do you need change?"

"Keep it." She politely smiled, turned towards the cash register and proceeded to the next customer. Interesting enough, my moment of *flash* was met with indifference.

By 11:27p.m. Raul and I were on our third and fourth drinks, buzzing, my usual cap off. Besides, I had a morning meeting with the Frasier Payne folks, a big day. I was setting up Mom and Devin's financial portfolios, my charity, and asking Frankie out on a date to the art show.

"Hey, man, I'm a shut it down, my meeting's tomorrow morning … no hangover."

"No prob, I'm ready when you are," he responded. "You ain't trying to take one home?" he added. Secretly my being intimidated paralyzed me. Tomorrow was my reason for being here. Tonight and anything after tomorrow was extra.

"Let's do this again tomorrow night and this time, take me to the spot you go."

"Bet."

"Raul … I need one more smoke to get some good rest."

"Me too, bro."

When we got back to the car, Raul sparked yet a third blunt and that familiar aroma filled the car. A beautiful serenade to a decent evening, Raul and I got acquainted within the first day of doing business and I discovered Sour Diesel. Good night.

The next morning, the blare from the TV woke me. The alarm clock read, 8:36. *Fuck, I need to get up and at 'em.* Raul was supposed to pick me up at 9:15. I ran to the bathroom, turned on the shower, came back to the closet, laid out my suit, shirt and tie, called down to room service for a quick bite with coffee, and hopped in the shower.

I gave a quick once over of all the vital parts: armpits, cockpit, ass, and feet, and I was done in five minutes. Hurriedly, I brushed my teeth, walking back in the bedroom to put on drawers and T-shirt, and then back to the bathroom to spit. The clock read 8:45. I called Raul to make sure he was on the way. "I'm down the street Doug ... be there in five minutes." Cool. That put him here at 8:50 and room service at about 9. After we hung up, I got dressed, putting on my first ever Brioni suit. That bad boy cost me five grand flat. It was cashmere and silk blend. I also purchased some Salvatore Ferragamo shoes for roughly two thousand bucks. My attire was the equivalent to seven months of rent at the old apartment.

At 9:05, room service knocked on the door. By then I was somewhat dressed, without my shoes and tie. My breakfast consisted of a small fruit salad with coffee and toast. After tipping the room service guy, I took a quick sip of the coffee and proceeded to put on my shoes. For a moment, I paused to admired the contour of the shoes on my feet. Then I took a couple bites of the fruit salad, and proceeded to put on my tie. All the while, my mind raced a 100 miles an hour. This was a day I'd never forget. From this day forward, life for my family would never be the same.

At exactly 9:15, I was completely dressed, and partially fed. Posing in front of the oversized mirror, I was thoroughly impressed. My suit was an interesting color, sort of a mix between a taupe and gray, with a mauve colored shirt and paisley tie of the same color. My shoes were a rich chocolate brown, monk strap style, with a chrome buckle. Sharp. The time had come to head downstairs and meet Raul at the door. When I reached the lobby, quite a few folks were roaming about, as if a wedding or something were taking place that day. I was focused, dressed to the nines, with my Louie messenger bag by my side. The brightness of the morning bled through the entrance doors, and I was officially 10 feet tall again.

When I reached outside I didn't see Raul. *What the fuck?* My watch read 9:21 a.m. I couldn't be late. The whole purpose of leaving early was to beat traffic. Right at that time I heard a honk. It was Raul. *Six minutes off schedule. Let's go.* He pulled up and immediately got out the car. "Sorry boss, I ran into a bad patch and had to take a detour, but don't worry, I got you," he said, walking around to the other side.

"What's up man? I'm good. I'll ride in the front."

"Sorry Doug, Mr. Moore, sir. Today is a business day and you look too sharp, and paid too much to be riding up front this morning. Your seat awaits in the back." Raul opened the back door. I respected his argument and got in.

As we drove out onto the street, I called Frankie to let her know we'd possibly be late due to the traffic.

"Good morning, Frankie."

"Good morning Doug, how are you this morning?"

"I'm fine … we may be a few minutes late … we're on the way."

"Doug, you realize you're the boss in this whole matter, right?"

"Yeah, I respect that and want you all to respect me. First impressions, right?"

"I really appreciate that," she said. Points perhaps. "But truthfully speaking, we'd still wait on you … we want your business, so relax, you're fine."

"Thanks, Frankie, see you in a few."

Yes it's true, the reason for this meeting was my money, and they'd be as patient as possible for that sake, but a potentially negative back drop could stereotype me as the "Late Black Guy." These people were handling millions of dollars on my behalf and thus my character and timelessness needed to set the tone. It was something my father instilled in me. Just as we were making good time on the road, I received a call.

"Hello, Mr. Moore?"

"Yes, who's this?"

"It's Dino from Post Oak Motors, how are you doing this morning sir?" His tone implied a reasonable counter offer.

"Yes, doing well and you?"

"I'm fine sir, thanks for asking. I wanted to see if we could still earn your business. Again I'd like to apologize for the experience you had, so I took the liberty of talking directly with the owner about your offer on the Black Ghost, and we would like to offer you the price of $315k." I remained quiet a few seconds, even though it was an acceptable offer.

"Is that the absolute best you can do?" I was fucking with him now. He was a snob at first, too. This was pay back.

"Sir, we … I really crunched the numbers on this and … "

"It's fine, I'll take it."

"Oh sir, that's great. I'll draft the paperwork up and have the car washed and prepped for pick up this afternoon."

"I'm in New York now, until Saturday morning. I'll have the money wired, but I'd like the car to be delivered to George Bush Intercontinental Airport for my return flight. Can you arrange that?"

"Quite certainly sir, that won't be a problem at all." I was in a zone, purchasing a Rolls-Royce from the back seat of a Rolls-Royce. Who does that? Afterward we discussed the particulars of the deal and the wiring instructions.

The entire time, Raul occasionally peered through the rear view mirror, during the phone transaction, hopefully motivated for his own dreams.

BIG BALLER, SHOT CALLER [11]

At 9:48 a.m., a comfortable cushion of time between the curb outside to the actual floor of the office eased my nerves. Equally comforting was Raul's knowledge of Manhattan's streets. Traffic was so fucking bad that morning, any possibility of arriving on time was doubtful.

"Appreciate you man," I said getting out the car. Suddenly, jitters hit my stomach with every step closer to the building, a psychological warfare of sorts. *This isn't a job interview, so why am I so nervous?*

Entering the lobby, I set my sights on the elevator and the 39th floor. The usual hustle and bustle was a blur. All I could think about was getting to this meeting, going over the particulars of my financial affairs, a necessary task. With every floor passed, my hands shook, and an uncontrollable heat flushed about my body. *What the fuck man, get it together.* My nerves must've been obvious because an elderly woman to my left couldn't stop staring at me.

When I reached the floor, I gathered myself, and made the conscious effort to enjoy this experience, realizing that it was uniquely mine. In the vastness of the universe, I was chosen to have this good fortune, entrusted with the responsibility of being a good steward over it.

After walking through the double glass doors, I immediately spotted Frankie standing at the reception desk waiting for my arrival.

"Hello, Mr. Moore," she said with her usual warm smile. Wishing I had the balls to lean in and kiss her, better judgment prevailed.

"Hey, Frankie."

"You okay?" she asked sarcastically.

"I'm good, thanks," I responded with a nervous laugh.

"Okay ... right this way." Frankie led me to the back and just like last time, I remembered the sophisticated group of employees, all dressed in their fashionable, professional wear. Some of them even took the time to acknowledge me, as if I'd made a victorious return.

This time however, we didn't go to the same room where I had my initial consultation. Frankie went past that room and kept on towards some massive mahogany double doors. My heartbeat picked up and my mouth went dry. When she opened the door, there was a massive oblong table, exactly like the ones you'd see from a scene of a movie. Grantham and Strasburg sat on one side, but there was no waspy Williamson. The Frasier Payne folks sat on the other side.

I supposed Fran Abram was one of the three new faces sitting opposite the attorneys. Of the other two guys, one appeared older, with a stoic look on his face, as if discovering the meeting was for me. They all stood, greeting me with handshakes.

"I don't believe we've had the pleasure of meeting. I'm Fran, we talked on the phone ... these are my colleagues, Dan Nielsen and Samir Chopra," she offered.

"Good to see you again," Strasburg said. Grantham smiled, offering the same.

"How's your week been?" Fran asked.

"It's been great ... pretty laid back." My comment, met with polite replies, was followed by a dead pan of silence as if waiting for someone to throw in a tad bit more empty banter.

"Well, shall we?" Grantham asked. I sat next to Strasburg, and Frankie, next to me. "As we all know, Mr. Moore has recently come into a sizable amount of money, procuring our services to put his financial matters in proper perspective. Most recently, we decided that for the sake of mitigating his tax burden, the establishment of a charitable foundation should be put in place."

I looked across the table, occasionally reading their facial expressions while Strasburg spoke. Frankie and Grantham were in my peripheral view for the most part, while Fran had a subtle smirk, and Samir, an interested grown up brow. Dan, otherwise, looked lifeless, with his pale skin tone and grayish hair and beard. "As it stands, Mr. Moore has assets amassed at $165,376,900, minus a wire transfer of $500,000 to his home bank, which transpired last week." *I need another $315k for the car.* "Today we are constructing the legalities and financial solvency of the aforementioned charitable trust. Further, Mr. Moore would like to establish financial matters for his mother, Eugenia A. Moore and his brother, Devin H. Moore."

This was a ceremony, the marriage of my family to a new life, becoming instant millionaires.

"Mr. Moore, before we proceed, have you given any thought to the name for the charity?" Strasburg asked.

"I've decided to go with The L.E. Moore Foundation, in honor of my parents Leonard and Eugenia." Everyone applauded, nodding their heads in approval. Frankie even gave me a slight pat on the back.

"Very nice, Mr. Moore."

"Thank you."

"We can now proceed with the legal documentation of the charity, being established as a 501(c)(3) non-profit, tax-exempt organization, having domain rights throughout the entirety of America." The jargon was foreign; I understood "non-profit" and "tax-exempt," but 501 what? Fran interrupted.

"Paulette if I may ..."

"Go ahead," she replied.

"Mr. Moore, the 501(c)(3) is an IRS tax code which allows the foundation to receive monies from the public without any required tax payment.

"I was getting to that Fran ... " Paulette said jokingly. Everyone shared a chortle. I felt at ease. These people seemed to really know their stuff. When Strasburg finished, she asked if anyone had any objections or any additional information for the proceedings. No one replied.

"Now in the matter of the amount to which this foundation will be established, have you given that much thought, Mr. Moore?" Honestly I hadn't. I wasn't sure what the amount needed to be, too hasty to call.

"Well, with all that has happened within such a short period of time, I've not given much thought to an amount. I'd like it to have enough to generate residual income, for donations and an annualized scholarship fund."

"Well that's precisely the question, Mr. Moore. What causes are you interested in making donations towards? In other words, what would you be most passionate about in your giving?" Samir asked.

"Well, that's a good question. I'm most interested in issues affecting education, especially in Houston. In particular, I'd like to invest in inner-city schools, providing better resources, definitely give scholarships through the foundation and financial gifts to historical Black universities and colleges."

"So how much would you put into this foundation? You have a few things to consider," Dan said with smugness. "You have to think about the actual administrative part, who's going to run it, who will you staff, will it be from your home or an office? These are other costs you'll incur." Condescension laced his words. Of course I'd run it, my skill set was considerable, with a Master's in Education Administration. Some friends and former colleagues had credentials to assist me in getting this foundation off the ground.

"I appreciate your concern, and I've already considered those matters," I countered. "I think I'd be able to determine how much goes into this fund, if we could determine how much I'd need in my personal portfolio to sustain a comfortable life for a very long time."

"Okay, so let's start from that side of the table and then we can work our way back this way," Grantham suggested.

"Well, it's simple and plain, no over spending on unnecessary purchases," Dan added. He immediately got on my nerves with the double-speak. Apparently a guy my age with all this money could easily overdose on gold chains and bitches.

"Actually, there are many financial streams available to you; even the foundation itself," Fran added. "By becoming the acting chief executive officer of the charity, you can opt to pay yourself a salary. For example, an interest bearing account on one million dollars would generate roughly $3,000 a month. Times that by 100, now you're looking at $300,000 per month for which you could set aside funds for donations, the organization's expenditures, staff salaries and your own salary."

"What should the salary amount be?" I asked.

"What would you pay yourself?" she countered.

"I don't know, is $100k too much?" I was naïve and they knew it, but coming from a $49,500 annual salary to $100k seemed like a hell of a jump.

"With the scenario I used earlier, if you were to put $100 million into the foundation, it would generate $3.6 million in interest. You could pay yourself a modest 10 percent of that ... $360k the first year." I was numb. That was nearly eight times my salary for probably less than half the effort. I responded with a simple, "Okay."

"We're not advising you to put $100 million into this fund, but if you did ... " Samir replied.

That would leave me with 65 million of which 20 million would go to the family. I think I could live off $45 million.

"But what if I did that, how would you protect that amount of money from say a stock market crash or some Bernie Madoff fiasco?" Without being eloquent, I needed clarity and the confidence that I wouldn't regret the decision.

"Okay, so if we were to allot 100 million into the fund, it would be a trust protected from taxes, any lawsuits or other civil impunities brought on by the general public. Further, the F.D.I.C. insures your money up to $100,000. We can create multi-accounts as a whole insuring each dollar for the life of the charity. The charity will earn interest without the need to invest the money in other risky money-market accounts like stocks and commodities. However, bonds are another safe investment which have the same face value of the dollar amount, and increase in value over a longer period of time," he explained.

I nodded as if on pace with the explanation, but it was all French. Everything still sounded risky; nearly all my winnings in one entity felt like financial suicide. The charity itself was not a bad idea and the salary from the charity was simply extra dough.

"I guess my next question is, if I want access to the funds in the charity for personal reasons, not expecting to run through $45 million, could I still dip into it or what?"

"That's a legal matter ... " said Dan.

"If you construct this charity with this amount in mind, void of any taxation from the government, it's with the explicit purpose that all funds involved be used under the guise of the charity's intention," Grantham explained.

Shit sounded serious. "Further, if the charity accepts public donations, it would contradict its purpose if funds were allocated for your personal use. Your salary is basically an administrative fee based on the initial 100 mill," he continued.

"Well, let's start with my family's financial outcome, then we can work back to the charity afterward, if you don't mind," I offered. Making a hasty decision about that amount of money was unnecessary.

"What were you allocating for your family funds?" Fran asked.

"I'd like to put $10 million in each account. My brother has two children and with that, I'd like a provision that covers college cost and incremental trust payments after they reach 18 years of age." Fran nodded her head, impressed with my call. They didn't realize I'd been imagining and planning for a moment like this for quite some time.

"Man, I wish I was your brother," Dan snidely remarked. The table laughed, but I noticed Grantham remained silent. Maybe he was catching the slick shit, too.

"We could allocate $1 million towards an interest bearing savings account, $500,000 towards a checking account for everyday use, and then we could put $3.5 million into a diversified money market account of stocks, commodities and bonds, all of which could provide additional interest bearing opportunities. The remaining $5 million could be put into a trust for your nephews, covering college tuition at future cost. Additionally, incremental payments of 25 percent of the trust's value could be paid in five-year periods from the age of 18."

I felt at ease with their financial prospectus, hopeful that my brother could appreciate it's intricacy.

"That makes very good sense to me. Let's proceed with that." I felt like a boss, approving the allocation of millions of dollars.

"My mother, she's 58. She's worked for almost 30 of those years, and currently she gets a fixed income. She's not a flashy woman, and she won't need access to millions of dollars, but definitely a comfortable existence with a staff perhaps." Dan frowned, assuming my request seemed over the top, but this is what I wanted. "I'll pay for it, so what amount should I set aside for her in addition to the 10 mill?"

"Who would you like the staff to consist of?" Samir asked.

"Now I wish I was your mother," Strasburg chimed. I actually appreciated her humor.

"She currently lives in California, but I plan to move her to Houston. She doesn't know the city much, other than the few visits she's had, so I guess a driver. I'd also like her to have a live in maid, someone to look after the house, keep it tidy."

"These two individuals would be her employees, so keep in mind that they'd possibly want health insurance and paid vacations," Fran added.

"That sounds fair. So what would that cost, say over the course of five years?"

"It depends on the market in Houston," Grantham responded. "If you're looking at paying these people a salary, the driver could be anywhere from $50,000 to $90,000 a year. And the maid, will she be required to cook?" he asked.

"My mother doesn't trust anyone's cooking." They all laughed.

"Maybe she'd fall in the range of 25 to 30 a year, roughly 75 to 120 in salaries a year, times five years ... "

"Three hundred and seventy-five to six hundred thousand," Fran interrupted. Everyone applauded her speedy calculating.

This process was becoming more real to me. The final documentation for the charity wouldn't be completed for a least another week. The funds for my family had to be documented as a special provision to avoid taxes.

At noon, we all decided to break for lunch. Fran suggested some steak house a few blocks away and we all agreed. I pulled Frankie off to the side. "This is crazy. I didn't know it'd be like this, I'm glad it's almost over."

"You're in good hands, Doug. These are top notch professionals."

"Yeah, but that Dan dude, he's an ass."

"Never mind him, he looks bitter," she said. Her unprofessional opinion gave me the confidence to ask about Friday's art showing.

"Uh, Frankie I was thinking, if you weren't busy this Friday, I have an invitation to a private art showing that evening." She stood there smiling the entire time, but the look in her eyes read *I'm so sorry.*

"Sure, that sounds great, I love art ... where will it be?" She caught me off guard. I was expecting to be rejected for the sake of company policy, fraternizing with clients. "I'll have to get back to you on the particulars, but cool, thank you."

Taking the elevator down, a smile of accomplishment formed on my face. My finances were in check, and possibly my dating life. Once outside, seeing Raul was like seeing an old familiar friend. The stuffy bourgeois business had cracked my face. "Man, this shit here is a trip." Raul had no idea and I had to remind myself to keep it that way.

"How was the meeting?"

"It's cool ... not over yet. We're on lunch break. Do you know Dominic's Steak House? That's where we're going. Lemme get on a blunt first."

"Already rolled." He handed me the lighter, and took a quick detour to smoke.

A few minutes late to lunch, I needed some eye drop solution and space to air out from the smell. When I arrived the group was just getting seated. Apparently Fran was a regular and worked her magic in getting us a private room towards the back. The paranoia kicked in. *I know they smell me.* I looked around for Frankie. I guess the help couldn't attend this affair.

"Is everything all right, man?" Grantham asked. It was our first *brother* connection.

"Yeah I'm cool. I had a call from back home." The back room looked like a gangsta spot from the 20s, on some Al Capone shit.

Samir motioned for me to take the head of the table, "Thanks," I replied. The atmosphere was nostalgic of a forgone era. Pictures from different decades adorned the walls, the 20s, 50s, 80s. Some were of celebs, athletes, and politicians.

"This is a nice joint, Fran," I stated.

"And the food is even better," she offered. Fran was a thick girl, maybe Jewish. She had thick, wavy brunette hair and wore glasses. I was unsure of her sexual orientation because she looked like a box eater. Samir was a petite looking Indian dude with a British accent. He was well dressed, and mild mannered. But Dan, a despicable excuse for professionalism, was the "You Lie" guy today.

The waiter came in and placed our drink orders. No longer feeling like a teacher, I ordered a glass of red wine. The rest of the group followed suit, ordering their elixir of choice.

We continued conversing, sharing glimpses of our personal lives. The humor in adults feeling the necessity to put on airs for maturity sake would soon be thwarted by alcohol.

"So Mr. Moore ... " Samir started.

"You guys can call me, Doug," I answered.

"Okay, Doug," Samir continued. "That moment ... when you realized you'd won?"

"Complete disbelief, even similar to getting a call about the death of a loved one."

"I think I get you, just totally unexpected," Samir added.

"Exactly, unexpected ... but really nice." Everybody burst into laughter while Dan had a shit-faced smirk.

"Everybody, I'd like to call for a toast to Doug, and his new found wealth, and a long lasting business relationship," Strasburg added. Everybody raised their glasses, and I immediately called for another round. Strasburg's face was so damn red, I could tell she got it in regularly. Grantham started to lighten up. But Dan, was the most telling. From time to time he would say and do awkward shit like a typical lush and the type of guy, if drunk enough, capable of using racial slurs. "So Doug, did you buy any fancy cars yet?" he asked. *The bullshit.*

"Actually I did, thanks for asking," I answered.

"Oh what did you get?" Grantham asked.

"A Mercedes-Benz G55 … matte black paint job."

"Sweet," Samir replied.

"Welcome to the G club," Grantham continued. "I have a white one." All of a sudden Dan yelled out, "Homeboys!" The table went slightly silent, and Grantham and I just looked at his ass like *what the fuck did you just say?*

Paulette caught our vibe and instantly tried jumping on the grenade. "That is such an awesome truck, my husband had his eyes on one, but I told him, not until Momma gets her Porsche."

The waiter walked in, took our orders, and most of us with the exception of Samir, a confessed vegetarian, ordered steak. We communed, even with Dan's blunder, eventually getting past it.

After we finished eating, it was quickly approaching two in the afternoon. "Guys, I think we ought to get back to the office," Fran added. When the bill came out, I offered to pay, but Fran ended up taking it.

When we resumed the meeting, the Frasier Payne folks advised that I have my own personal trust. They also advised that instead of buying some big ass house, build one in a choice neighborhood, acquiring instant equity. River Oaks came to mind. They knew their shit, advising me to ease up on expendable purchases, like cars in particular. But unbeknownst to them, I had my heart set on about three or four other dream cars.

We wrapped up about 3:45 that afternoon, supposing the drinks and food had ushered in the itis. However, we covered good ground. I'd eventually make a decision on the amount I wanted in the trust, but I needed time to think. They proceeded with setting up the financial affairs for my family, for which they'd have access in a few days after the tax loophole was addressed. It was perfect timing, since I planned to fly out to California to surprise them with the news.

As for my portfolio, $45 million seemed enough. Personally, there was no need to go out and buy a big ass house, other than the ones I'd buy for Mom and Devin. My budget for Devin was $500k, somewhere out in Sugarland or Missouri City, assuming he'd take the deal. Mom's living conditions were slowly deteriorating. I wanted her home to be regal, palatial, something out of her league. She always dreamed big, but was too humble to believe it. There were times when she'd tell me, "You don't have to do that" or "how much did that cost, was it expensive?" I wanted her to get out of the mentality of believing that nice things weren't for good Christian folk. Ultimately, I decided she'd stay with me while we did some house hunting.

Later that afternoon, after taking Buddy Boy for a walk, I went back to bed. The meeting drained me dry, but I was proud of addressing some very important matters. Even more proud of the fact that I stepped to Frankie and she accepted my invitation. It reminded me that I needed to call Ira to add her to the list.

"Hello?"

"Hey, Ira, it's Doug."

"Yes, Mr. Moore, good afternoon sir. What can I do for you?"

"About the art showing tomorrow night, can I add a guest?"

"Sure, you can add up to three, not a problem … do you have a name?"

"Yes, Frankie Collins."

"Sure, no problem, I'll put Mr. Collins' name on the list immediately." I snickered.

"Frankie's a girl."

"Oh, Mr. Moore, forgive me, my apologies."

"No big deal, Ira, really."

He went on apologizing for another 30 seconds, customary of a concierge I supposed. After that I got the details for the art showing and prepared to plan a magical evening for two. I asked Ira to make dinner reservations at the premiere restaurant in town, whatever that was. Then I called Frankie.

"Hey, Doug," she answered. *She saved my name, awesome.*

"Hey, Frankie, I was calling to give you the details for tomorrow evening, if you have time."

"Oh, go ahead," she replied.

"Yeah, so I had your name added to the list, with no problem. What's your address to come pick you up, say around … ," and then she interrupted.

"Doug, by the way, do you mind if I bring a friend?" *Fuck … a friend? A guy, another girl? How do I play this?* Doing my best to mask the sound of disappointment in my voice, I was accommodating. *Doesn't she realize this was my attempt at having a date?*

"Sure that can be arranged, no problem … what's his name?" I asked, prepared for the inevitable.

"Oh no," she laughed. "It's my good girlfriend, Lacy. She's visiting from Boston." Okay, I guess I could deal with a female third wheel, rather than being the third wheel.

"Okay, cool…I'll set it up," I replied. She gave her address and we agreed on 9 p.m.

YAMI [12]

Later that evening, I'd awaken from a deep sleep, and a weird dream. In the dream, I was back with Gwen, walking down a street on a sunny day, when suddenly, some random chick ran up to me saying, "You gone do me like that … you bitch ass nigga?" Her face was a blur; just her body gestures as she talked with her hands. She pointed in my face the whole time. My only reply was, "Shut the fuck up." That's all I kept saying, over and over again, calmly and reserved. Gwen just looked on and watched the whole thing. Finally she said, "Doug, don't say that please." And then I woke up; *weird*.

The other day I promised Raul that I'd be up to hitting the town again. Now that the important business was done, it was time to celebrate. I called him.

"What's up for this evening man, we getting out?" I questioned him.

"You still down?" he asked, as if expecting otherwise.

"Hell yeah, my business here is done, I'm ready to rock out tonight. Speaking of which, you know any good jewelry joints? I'm looking for a nice watch or bracelet." No sooner than I said that, my mind went back to Fran's advice about expendable purchases—I even heard Dan's voice saying "no unnecessary spending." I wasn't planning on buying anything extravagant … just something to celebrate my situation.

"Yeah man, I know a couple spots … what time you trying to ride out?"

"Can you come in an hour?"

"Bet!" We hung up, and I hopped in the shower.

My birthday was days away. This was something to commemorate the new lifestyle, apartment, cars, and most all, the ton of money I was sitting on. Being my own fraternity so to speak, put things in perspective on how the rich tend to clique up. For me it was an unforeseen challenge, maintaining normalcy with average, everyday people.

With just a few days left in town, I still wanted to meet with Bioko about his solar energy company, so I called Grantham to set up the meeting.

"Mr. Grantham … hey I meant to mention this to you earlier but is it possible for you all to take a meeting regarding an investment opportunity I'm interested in."

"Oh, we're making investment moves already?" Grantham asked.

"Well, it's interesting and I'd like your insight on it,"I responded.

"Okay … can you give me a brief synopsis?"

"Sure. I met this gentleman who has a solar energy company out of Ghana … he's looking for investment money for a project he's doing with the government of Kenya."

There was complete silence. He was either listening intently or simply obliging my spiel.

"Hello … you there?"

"I'm here, I'm listening," he responded. "Well, let me ask you this, how did you meet him … what's his name again?"

"Bioko Amana. I met him on the plane ride here. Funny thing, he was featured in an article of a magazine I was reading, crazy right?" I replied.

"Yeah," Grantham answered flippantly. "Well, what's he asking for?"

"His project is estimated at $5 million. I was thinking of investing $500,000, but of course, to make sure this is a sound investment, I'd prefer meeting with you all. He's leaving soon. Is it possible to take a meeting with him sometime tomorrow morning?" Grantham's reply was leery—unsure to say the least.

"I'll speak with my colleagues and call you back, give me about an hour or so."

"Thanks … appreciate it." We hung up, and I got dressed. Playing the conversation over in my mind again, I hoped Grantham wasn't one of those uppity ass niggas who couldn't do business with Africans. I supposed if it hadn't been for the money, he wouldn't be fucking with me.

Immediately I called Bioko. "I wondered if you forgot me, Mr. Moore,"he replied in that thick and jovial African accent.

"No sir, not at all. Just finished my business and I'm hoping you'll still take a meeting with my consultants regarding our conversation."

"Well, the matter is time. I am preparing to leave tomorrow afternoon. Could it take place in the morning?"

"Indeed. I am actually waiting for a reply for a morning meeting. What time did you plan to leave?"

"I have a 3:45 p.m. flight out of JFK ... I need to be at the airport no later than 2, 2:30. I can do an early meeting, but I must leave by 1," he replied.

"Fair enough, I'll call you later this evening with the details. Thank you, Mr. Amana, I look forward to seeing you tomorrow."

I was on fire. I had a semi-date tomorrow evening with Frankie, a business meeting that morning with Amana, and some New York City night life in my immediate future.

About forty-five minutes later I hopped in the car with Raul, back in the front seat, on the way to some jewelry stores with nothing particular to buy. For sure it was strictly impulsive. At 36, I was conscious of my grown ass man look. Whatever I decided on, it had to be tasteful.

"I'm a take you to Vitalli & Sons. A lot of rappers and athletes go there for custom shit, and then Brewers & Bailey, another joint."

"Okay, cool." Secretly I wanted some ostentatious ghetto bling, knowing damn well I couldn't wear it anywhere in Houston without attracting some kind of attention.

Vitalli & Sons, a moderate sized shop with sectionals of display cases throughout the store and signed autographed pictures of famous rappers, athletes, and others decorating the walls, had an interesting grimy edge. The guys working behind the register seemed almost stereotypical Italian. They were average height, stocky with five o'clock shadows topped off with low-cut gelled up hairdos and gold chains.

"What can I do for you gentlemen?" one of them asked in that classic New York accent. He had thick eyebrows, seconds from connecting with each other.

"I wanna see what you have in the way of diamond watches." I couldn't believe I said, *in the way of*.

"Right this way sir," he motioned to a case just past him. I looked in the other cases on the way—it was your typical gaudy, over the top shit. He opened up the display case and pulled out a tray. Some of the watches were classy. I saw a particular gold Rolex with the diamond bezel; it was subtle enough for everyday wear and tasteful enough for a business meeting.

"How much for the Rolex?"

"You're looking at … $14,875. It's 18k gold, perpetual time and date, pre-owned." *Pre-owned* was the deal breaker; *fuck that … new shit for me.*

"Oh, okay. What about this one?" Another one hundred percent blinged out watch caught my eye.

"This is the Breitling Avenger with thirty carats of diamonds," he went on. Even with the $4,000 a month apartment, the Mercedes Truck and the Rolls awaiting me, I just couldn't see where I'd wear it. After looking around for a few more minutes, I spotted a decent diamond bracelet I liked. It was tasteful and manly, and under five grand. I bought it and we continued on to Brewers and Bailey.

Brewers and Bailey was night and day from Vitalli and Sons. Walking in, we were met with serious glares from the only security guard who had to be about 6'5, 285 pounds solid. A petite saleswoman walked up to us, a refreshing contrast.

"Welcome, how may I assist you?" she asked.

"I'd like to see your watches," I replied. The place spoke class; probably not the iced-out pendant type of store.

"Any particular brand of watchmaker?" she continued.

"None in particular, something nice and classy," I answered.

"This way, sir."

Looking around the store, evidently I'd pay a reasonable amount of money for whatever I chose.

"Yo, this spot is real deal. You want that exquisite shit, right?" Raul added. In my mind I was like, *why didn't we come here first?* The saleswoman asked us to take seats in front of the display case, and showed us a variety of watches, all tasteful and high-end. Then I got a call.

"Mr. Moore, we can have the meeting at 10 in the morning," Grantham said.

"Oh great, I'll let him know, thanks."

Just as I finished with Grantham, I spotted an interesting watch—all black, the band, the bezel, the face and the numbers.

"Can I see that one?" Pointing to it, I couldn't quite pronounce the name. "Hub-lot, is that how you say it?" Raul took a look.

"It's pronounced hue-blo," the saleswoman interjected. "This particular piece has perpetual date and time-adjust until the year 2100; it automatically changes to different time zones once detected and never needs a battery. This is a Swiss made brand."

"How much would this go for?"

"This watch goes for $75,000." I gasped for air; Raul looked at me like, *"yo, who does that?"* I wanted the watch, just not now, especially in front of him. A 5,000 dollar diamond bracelet was one thing, but this? Not now.

After looking at a few more watches, I thanked the lady and we made our way out and back to the car. It was settled, the watch would be mine. I called Bioko to inform him of the meeting for tomorrow morning, and gave him the necessary particulars.

It was getting later in the evening, about 9:30 at the time. We were in the car heading back to the hotel. Wearing my bracelet, I admired the way the street lights danced off the diamonds in cadence to each one we passed.

"Yo, tonight I'm a take you to 'Saba,' a Puerto Rican joint in the Bronx; mad cool, and the girls be up in there... " Raul's expression read, *for sure.*

"Let's go," I replied. Tonight was a night to floss with my new bracelet on.

"Man, I'm telling you, blaze one first and then about 11 we head out."

"Cool, I'm with that," I replied.

When we reached the hotel, the valet greeted us as usual, en route to the suite. Buddy ran up to me, and I plopped on the couch. Raul rolled two more Sour Diesels while I sat and watched a little *Sports Center.*

"Here you go, bro." Cognizant of this grade of weed, it was a battle not to fall asleep. Tonight was a night to see some Puerto Rican women. Secretly, my junior high crush on Rosie Perez still remained. In the opening scene from *Do The Right Thing*, the Spike Lee movie, she's dancing in the red dress so hard it comes up. Right then and there my mother walks in and blasts me for "looking at such filth." I beat off to Rosie that night.

"Yo, my girl might come with us ... she on that shit," Raul said out of the blue.

"That's fine, she gotta friend? I don't wanna be a third wheel."

"Yeah, I can see." Raul picked up his phone and made a call.

"Yo, we leaving in about an hour so be ready ... yeah we coming, just be ready ... yo, see what Teresa doing, my man wanna date too … what the fuck you mean she ain't no hoe, what's that gotta do with anything? Ain't nobody fucking talking to you disrespectful." Raul pulled away from the phone, "This bitch." All I could do was shake my head in pseudo support.

For three minutes I watched the emotional tennis match of Raul's phone conversation while Buddy sat beside me. Eventually we'd pick them up around 11:30, maybe midnight. My attire was the same thing I arrived in days ago. Raul seemed uninterested in changing. He already had on a black suit, white shirt, and black tie—his uniform.

The munchies kicked in and we ordered room service. I got chicken wings, and Raul ordered a burger.

"What's with these bitches today, yo?" Raul asked. A random question, maybe stemming from the other day was the cause for his somber mood. Maybe all this time, he'd been going through some internal shit over his relationship.

"What you mean?" I asked, knowing exactly what he meant.

"I don't know man … between this one and my baby mama … crazy."

"Oh, you have kids?"

"Yeah, my daughter is seven years old, the best thing about my life." Morgan came to mind.

For the next few moments we sat in silence, eating our food. My enthusiasm for going out was replaced by the drab reality of Raul's life.

"Hey man, if it's not a good night …"

"Nah, it's cool. Tonight you get an education on how we do in the Bronx," he answered.

The Bronx had a different edge than Manhattan or Brooklyn. The streets seemed colder than the weather. The night was drizzly and empty, aside from the few homeless folk we'd pass every so often. Feeling a little bourgeoisie, I was uncomfortable in that car, in this neighborhood, but Raul's judgment prevailed; this was his block.

"We on a hundred and forty-first right now, we'll be there in another ten minutes, tell them niggas to put our names on the list, we ain't waiting in no fucking line," he said to somebody on the phone.

"They know we be there, they know us," Raul's girlfriend Claudia chimed. Claudia and Teresa were both attractive Boricuas, with Claudia being the louder of the two. Both of them had straight, jet black hair and tan skin. Claudia even looked like Jennifer Lopez —the loud ass ghetto version. Teresa had a nice thick shape, she enjoyed her food, but she was a little on the shy side. She seemed to be Claudia's sidekick, co-signing everything Claudia said. It was an immediate turn off.

While we continued driving, I glanced at Raul, having that same look from yesterday. Claudia was definitely the cause.

"What kind of music they play here?" I asked, attempting to lighten the mood.

"You like country, right Doug?" Claudia asked, throwing shade. Of course Teresa laughed.

"Yeah, little Charlie Pride and Vince Gill. Reba McIntyre is pretty good, too."

They both replied with, "Oh," and kept quiet afterward. Raul snuck a laugh in. When we arrived at the club, a decent line stretched outside.

"I am not fucking with them, we better go straight the fuck in,"Claudia chimed in. She was getting on my nerves; mad for no reason. We pulled up to the valet, a surprise given the area. We immediately became the center of attention. I assumed that Raul didn't make it a habit of driving this car here.

The average age of the folks waiting in line looked between 21 to 30 with a few old horses sprinkled in. Money couldn't veil the insecurity I felt again, being slightly outside the generation gap. Back home at Carrington's, I was the majority.

Initially, I waited by the car to see how things would play. Claudia was so damn adamant about getting in, surely she'd make a scene. No need in me doing the walk of shame.

Some big ass bouncer came out and gave Raul a pound and Claudia a hug. Raul waved me over. Looking at the faces of the people waiting in line, I could feel the hate like, *"who the fuck is this nigga?"*

We entered the club, met with the blaring sounds of what seemed to be salsa or mambo mixed with a hip-hop beat. Strobe lights and shit were flashing erratically, and people were dancing hard, sweating, and having a good time. It didn't look like the type of place where trouble brewed from mean-mugging thugs holding up the wall. These motherfuckers were light on their feet, cha cha sliding in Tim boots and Air Force Ones. The women were carefree, whipping their hair back and forth, while on-lookers admired their effort.

"Yo, you good?" Raul asked.

"I'm cool…this a cool spot."

"Yeah man…you want something to drink?"

"Long Island."

"Bet," Raul said, walking towards the bar with Claudia. Teresa was off in the distance talking to friends while I observed the scene. Some much older folks, possibly in their 50s, where jigging at the back of the dance floor. This was a Puerto Rican Carrington's. Immediately my age issues were disappearing. About five minutes later, Raul returned with the drinks.

"Here you go."

"That was fast."

"Yeah, they know me in here. I'm here every week when I'm not working. This is my release if you know what I mean," he continued.

Claudia caught up with Teresa across the room. When I first met her, I tried not to check her out in front of Raul, but from my view, she had a sexy fat ass, probably why he put up with her.

"Yo, thanks for being a regular dude, I deal with a lot of rich assholes … dead serious."

"Oh, I appreciate that but I'm just being myself, man," I answered. He looked over at Claudia and leaned in towards me.

"I'm a tell you like this, if it wasn't for the ass, I'd a been gone a long fucking time ago." I started laughing, amused that I was just thinking that.

"What? Claudia?" I pretended.

"Man, c'mon, you ain't seen that ass? Look at that ass," he said.

"Man, I ain't gone look at your girl's ass."

"But you get what I'm saying, right?" he asked.

That seemed to be the theme for many relationships these days. Sexual attraction without love and without the ability to compromise.

"It's like, I wanna marry her, but her attitude is so fucking wack, I can't even see that shit," he continued as I attempted to listen over the boom of the bass and beat.

"How long y'all been together?"

"It'll be a year next January; met her at a New Year's Eve party. She was nothing like she is now. This mother fucker was sweet as pie, cook and clean for a nigga, good sex, all that. Then, she got comfortable." I could see Claudia and Teresa talking, looking our way; maybe saying similar shit about Raul.

Both of them started walking towards us. "Hey man, they coming over here," I warned.

"I don't give a fuck. Fuck them." Nervously I laughed, unsure of where his head was. Apparently I'd become the buffer of the evening.

"Papi, let's dance, this is my song," Claudia said to Raul. He rolled his eyes, and then I looked at him like, *go dance with your girl, I'll talk to Teresa*. Raul reluctantly walked with her, leaving Teresa and I alone.

"Doug, you okay? The music okay?" she asked in a condescending tone.

"Let me get you a drink," I offered.

"Oh, that's so nice. I'll have a lollipop bomb." *A mother fucking what?*

"What was that again?"

"A lollipop bomb. You never heard of that?"

I had to think fast; either go up to the bar, asking for this drink that just felt wrong coming out of my mouth, or take her with me. I took her hand.

"Come with me." Approaching the bar, I saw that all the bartenders were guys, so I made a good call. Noticeably, we never let go of each other's hand, but I wasn't feeling her, nor was I put off by it. The bar area was crowded of course, everyone cool, laughing, and enjoying the music. These were regulars. Looking on both sides of the bar, taking in the scenery, my eyes landed on this exquisite dream of a woman in the flesh standing at the bar in *Saba*. Decidedly, she was my future somebody.

Out of solidarity to this unknown creature of perfection, I let go of Teresa's hand, pretending to lean in for something at the bar, anything I could imagine. Peeking once more at her, I was enamored by her beauty, a sucker for a pretty face. When I got the bartender's attention, I stepped back and let Teresa into the space, avoiding any misconception that we were a couple, especially for this mystery woman at the end of the bar. Looking back at Claudia and Raul, they seemed amicable on the dance floor. I took another look at this woman. If I didn't at least get her name the night was gonna be a heart break.

After Teresa got her drink, we went back to the edge of the dance floor, spectating and being cordial. Yet, this girl's image stayed on my mind. Every time I turned my head, it was to find her and stare for just a moment longer. I even went to the bathroom just to walk in the area where she sat, a discreet attempt at stalking. When Raul and Claudia returned, I had to tell him, hoping he knew her.

"Man, I have to know who this chick is."

"Teresa?"

"Nah man, the chick sitting on the other side of the bar by the restrooms, in a purple dress … she's gorgeous." Raul took a peek, not responding as I'd hoped.

"I don't see her." Turning to look, she was gone. My heart sank, *I know she ain't left, I hope she didn't just leave.*

I was freaking out … this mystery girl intrigued me.

"Right there, standing with the bald head dude by the mirrors." Raul took a look, finally spotting her.

"Oh, Yami? She the home girl … we grew up together." What joy filled my heart for this nigga to say, "Oh Yami," as if to say, *I'll introduce you this evening.* In an instant, my poise for victory was smashed by unwanted additional information.

"She got a man, but he locked up."

The irritation of hearing those words changed my mood.

"Yeah, they got a daughter, too," he added, like I needed to know that. Oddly enough it didn't matter. Being in a relationship with a single parent for four years, I knew how that went.

The deal I made with myself was to fuck around, sow my oats and then settle down with Gwen, if she'd have me. But this chick here was about to fuck up my plans. This girl was, cancel-my date-with-Frankie-tomorrow night fine.

"You wanna meet her?" Raul asked. It seemed unnecessary given the situation.

"Didn't you say she has a dude in jail?" My Long Island mixed with disappointment conjured an attitude in my tone.

"I mean they cool, she ain't rocking with him like that; it's more or less for the girl." Immediately my spirits were lifted, but I couldn't show it, I had to play it cool.

"Yeah, that's cool. I'll meet her," I replied flippantly. Raul walked over, already a foul on the play. Teresa was my "date." He obviously didn't give a fuck. It was easier setting up another time to rendezvous away from the girls. Nevertheless, Yami walked back with Raul in our direction. I looked over at Claudia and Teresa and they were in their usual girl huddle.

"Hey Doug, this is Yami, Yami, Doug." We reached out our hands to shake. I heard the background music to the scene in this movie; she was the love interest, and I, the corny, unlucky, run of the mill dude that everybody rooted for.

"So you're from Houston, that's cool. I've never been there," she said. *It can be arranged.*

Yami had to be about 5'6 or 7, shapely, but in an athletic way. She had bangs which I love for some reason, and shoulder length hair. When she smiled, I noticed her braces, the undetectable kind, if that make sense. Her eyes were hazel with a hint of green, and almond shaped. "So how do you like the Bronx?" she asked, with a cute smirk on her face.

"It's cool, for real. There's a place like this back home ... when you visit I'll take you." *Good one Doug.*

My innocent attempt at breaking the ice was in hopes of getting her number if her situation really wasn't a *situation*. I glanced over at the girls. They looked pissed; maybe I was violating. I supposed I'd feel a way if I were on a "date" with someone I found interesting.

We went on conversing a while, making small talk about the Bronx, Houston, and life in general.

"So what do you do in Houston?"

"I'm in private investment banking."

"Oh?" she replied. "How long have you been doing that?"

"For a while now." Despite the loudness of the music, the conversation was gratifying.

"And you?" I asked.

"I'm a teacher." *What? me too.* The irony of it smacked me in the face—a perfect opportunity to bond lost on a lie.

"Actually my school is just down the street; P.S. 52."

"Yeah, I've always wondered what the P.S. stood for."

"Public School. There's so many here, they couldn't name them all uniquely, I guess." Her humor was dry but welcoming, a contrast to Claudia's brand of crassness. Changing my plans for tomorrow evening was tempting, but selfish.

For the next few minutes, we talked about whatever came to mind, and not once did she mention her dude in prison. For me, it was a promising sign. "If you ever decide to come to Houston, give me a call ... can I get your number?" Claudia continued staring, stabbing me over and over again with her eyes, making faces in disgust.

Yami gave me her number, followed by an innocent hug, and then walked back over to her bald headed friend across the way. Raul looked at me and gave a wink.

An hour had passed, and the dance floor was still packed, but I'd had enough. Yami had left earlier, and there was nothing more to see. Raul looked at me like, *you ready?* I gave him a nod as we started walking towards the door, not noticing the girls had gone.

"Where's the girls?"

"Oh, Teresa got salty when she saw you get it in with Yami ... Puerto Rican girls are some jealous ma'fuckers."

"She feeling me or something?" I asked.

"Don't worry 'bout it."

Regardless, that Bronx morning, I made a move on the chess board of life, and it was a good one.

A REVELATION [13]

Later that morning, lying in that king sized bed, reflecting on the days, I realized I was finally living. Not for the ability to spend money, but the ability to spend my time the way I wanted because of the money. The course of my life charted a new route that left me full of suspense, welcoming the unknown.

Surprised by how early it was, I reached the suite past two in the morning, with Buddy curled up on the couch, and now it was 7:48. The meeting with Bioko was at 10, enough time to order room service and freshen up.

Even still, Yami came to mind. It was embarrassing how easily infatuated I'd get with women, a weakness since my teenaged years. With all this money, *was I destined to become a sugar daddy?* Companionship and deep spiritual love seemed unnecessary, with having the resources to collect bodies and other things along the way. My selfish nature fed by random urges, was an uncontrollable beast, soon to become the prey of life if untamed.

At 9, I called Bioko to confirm our meeting, then hopped in the shower. Minutes later, my usual breakfast of eggs Benedict with mimosas arrived, while Buddy had a plate of steak strips to gnaw on. Some HBO movie played, while we ate. I thought about the leisurely endeavors for the evening.

My flight was booked for Saturday morning, my birthday. A part of me had gotten homesick, longing to celebrate with my people back in the "H." And on top of everything, my family still had no clue about the money. At about 9:40, I made my way downstairs, where Raul was waiting outside. The hotel had gotten used to seeing him.

"Morning, sir."

"Morning, Doug," Raul said with a worn voice. We drove down the boulevard, to yet another meeting. The familiar feel of Manhattan, its bumps, turns, and twists had all become common place. My appreciation for Houston's wide open spaces contrasted this daily routine of fighting congested traffic.

"You sleep all right?" I asked, giving him a good ribbing from last night's antics.

"Hell nah, that bitch jumped all over me yo." I laughed, knowingly.

"Damn, the Yami thing?"

"Like I said … Claudia was supposed to ask Teresa to come out, *not* make a fucking love connection," Raul continued. He had my back, even though I looked like a dog in the end.

"Say bro, what's a decent Manhattan apartment run a month?" I inquired.

"Moving in with Yami already?" Obviously, I was smitten… *why not?*

"Nah, too soon for that, but seriously, for business purposes." Raul went on giving me the breakdown of cost based on area, while I daydreamed about waking up every morning and experiencing the changing seasons, holidays, New Year's Eve in Times Square, with her. Although a pleasant evening awaited me with Frankie and Lacy, with the possibility of a rekindled relationship with Gwen, Yami stole the show.

After reaching the law office, thirty minutes and two cups of coffee had passed and still no Bioko. I called his phone every ten minutes of that thirty minute wait, only to get voicemail. Paulette seemed at ease, while Williamson and Grantham were visibly upset; maybe this was golf day.

On the other hand, the embarrassment of it all gave pause for concern; *was this a sign?* Suddenly, we could see him being escorted down the hall to the room by an office attendant.

"Please forgive my tardiness, I'm usually prompt, but this city, it's so busy," he said while entering the room. I glanced at Grantham, and he was already put off.

"Well, welcome Mr. A-mana…is that correct?" Strasburg asked.

"Yes, very good," Bioko responded with that big ass grin.

"Good, good. Well we understand that you have a great business opportunity that Mr. Moore has asked us to consult with him on. Basically, my colleagues, Mr. Grantham, Mr. Williamson and I, will act as counselors regarding the details of this project, to ensure a clear and concise ..."

"I have a standing agreement with the government of Kenya to install solar panels on all government buildings, new construction, and some existing schools," Bioko interrupted. Strasburg paused, with her standard courteous smile, possibly startled.

"So if I may, what are the details of this standing agreement with the government of Kenya? How will Mr. Moore's interest be protected as an investor on this project?" Grantham asked, with an abrasive tone.

"First of all, let's be clear. Mr. Moore shared interest in investing in this project. I am already doing business in other African countries besides my homeland of Ghana. So let's be clear." Bioko's response caught me off guard ... nigga got buck.

"Mr. Amana, we don't intend to offend you by asking questions; we are simply consulting with Mr. Moore on this matter." My input was necessary or else.

"Mr. Amana, the sole objective of my colleagues is to see the viability of my investment. I've already assured you of my interest; they're only concerned with the details and how I'll be best benefited."

"I understand Mr. Moore, but I am a businessman, too. I would not waste your time or anyone's time with false allegations of my business dealings. I've had many meetings with the minister of energy. This project will cost five million dollars, for which I've already received pledges of three and a half million."

"When will this project be implemented?" Williamson chimed; a good question I'd never thought to ask.

"The current president of Kenya is serving in his last term. The elections for the next presidency will commence in the spring of next year, March to be exact. My contact who works as the minister of energy will remain in office upon the installation of the new president, at which time, his influence will bring light to this project. Kenya has received aid to develop more infrastructures. This project falls under their new policy to develop new energy sources in the country. They have to use the aid for this very purpose or they'll lose it." Bioko's reply was very persuasive.

"There are so many questions to ask in regard to guarantees and actual returns on the initial investment. How sure are you of the project execution, if the current administration hasn't done so? And how sure can you be that the next president and his advisors will support this endeavor?" Grantham asked. He had a valid point, which was to say *what guarantees that the next president whoever that may be, green lights this project, based on aid money, if the current president hadn't thought to do so.*

Bioko chuckled a bit before making his next statement. "Forgive me, but you have to understand my African culture, African people. How you do things in this country is vastly different than how it's done over there. You ask how the minister of energy, who used to be the minister of transportation and before that, the minister of education, can guarantee such a thing. He's what your mafia guys in America call a *made man*. His father was close friends with the founding fathers of Kenya, when they regained control from the British.

"Well that's very impressive Mr. Amana, and we don't doubt the value in that, so the question then is how does Mr. Moore benefit from his investment? Solar panels save money instead of generating it," Grantham stated. That *should've been my first question on the plane, but after seeing Bioko's picture in the magazine, I assumed profitability.*

"As I mentioned earlier, the country has received aid in the hundreds of millions of dollars. This project has a cost of five million. Upon the transition of the new president and implementation of this project, under their energy resources policy, the solar panels will be purchased for triple the value of manufactured cost. The investor will see a 100% return on their money. *Wow … my 500k would turn to a million.*

"Those sound very promising, but let's play another scenario," Williamson countered. "Let's say Mr. Moore invests in this project and this new president decides to take his or her time implementing the new policy regarding these solar panels; what happens to Mr. Moore's investment?"

Bioko cleared his throat and changed the position in which he sat before speaking.

"I understand the questions and concerns, but be aware that I've thought of these things. Remember, I am in business already, not only in my country, but in other African countries as well. Upon completion of the solar panels, the minister and his department will have a 90 day right of refusal agreement. Basically from the day the project is done, they will receive 90 days to take their time, if you will, but on the 91st day, we take the solar panels on to potential new buyers, that simple," he explained.

With slight hesitation, it still made sense. We'd retain the opportunity to sell the panels elsewhere, and still see a return on my investment. Understanding Bioko's breakdown, their approval was considerably important. "Mr. Moore, how much did you intend to invest on this project?" Strasburg asked. I intended to stick to $500,000, but with $1.5 million needed to close the project, my number changed, and maybe my sensibilities.

"Well, I intended to invest $500,000, but if we can close this project and deal, I'm prepared to offer the remaining amount." Grantham made a face like, *what the fuck are you doing?* Strasburg kept a poker face and Williamson jotted notes on his pad.

"That would be a blessing, Mr. Moore," Bioko exclaimed. He seemed genuinely grateful at the sound of my offer, and I, ecstatic at the possibility of turning $1.5 million into $3 million. "Mr. Amana, I think we should continue further discussions with Mr. Moore on this matter," Grantham added.

Our meeting lasted a quaint forty-five minutes, discussing politics and culture. We all thanked Bioko for his time, watched him leave the room and prepared for the real conversation. "Mr. Moore, as one of your counselors, I strongly advise that you give this considerable thought before putting such a sizable amount of funding into a project that could or could not happen," Grantham said. *Did a vain just pop in his forehead?*

His concern was appreciated, but he was talking to a grown ass man.

"I think our real concern is for your financial well-being, coming into such a large amount of money in such a short period of time, we want you to make decisions that will benefit you in the long run," Strasburg added.

"So let's cut to the chase ... should I or shouldn't I do this deal?"

"Don't do it," Williamson said, with a straight face.

"Why not?"

"Look, I gamble on Wall Street. I'm a risk taker, that's how you get ahead, right? This sounds hokey dokey; there's nothing concrete about this other than his word, which doesn't have much weight in today's society."

All reasonable points, but I was looking at this from a different slant. Helping to build an African company was helping to develop an African country. It seemed like a wise and sound business investment based on the trend of the business world, energy development.

"Ultimately this is your decision. All we ask is that you give this considerable thought. Your life has changed drastically. You're in a position to do great things, but at the same token you're in a volatile place, where bad financial moves can stack up and diminish your net worth over time," Grantham said. The table was silent after his statement. My commitment to Bioko was questionable now. Keeping my word was important, but then again, I didn't owe anybody anything.

"I guess I'll give it more thought. In the meantime let's focus on the charity fund." I stood up, shook everyone's hand and made my way to the elevators. My disappointment was primarily with Grantham. How couldn't he see the intrinsic value of this project? Regardless of the enormity of the investment, I could make that back from interest. I thought this out, too.

Raul took me back to the hotel for a quick morning nap. I called Ira to set up a tailor session before heading back to Houston, and then I ordered room service.

My mind went back to the watch at the jewelry store, with the urge to make an impulse buy. I called Ira again for car service for a quick trip to Brewers and Bailey. As soon as I arrived, I spotted the saleswoman who assisted me and told her exactly what I wanted. "The all black Hublot watch please." After the payment arrangement was made, I was assured they'd deliver the watch to my suite by that evening. I didn't need anyone's consultation for that. Later on I called my mother.

"Hey, mom, I have an idea."

"Yes?"

"Why don't y'all come out to Houston for my birthday?"

"What … you got some extra money, Dougie?"

"I'm paying for it Mama. Yes, it's been a minute since seeing y'all, right?"

"But I thought you were coming here?"

"I can't right now, but it would be the best birthday present ever. Please?"

"What brought this on?" My mother's usual suspicion kicked in, for which I'd prepared.

"Just feeling homesick, you know. It'll be nice to have y'all here."

"I understand Dougie, family is important."

"So you'll come?"

"I guess, but I don't want to put you out or …"

"Mama, I got this."

After we finished talking, I called Devin up, knowing I'd get some push back. He was more the reserved and frugal type.

"What's up, Dev, you good?"

"I'm chilling, what's up?"

"I was wondering if you, Grace, and the boys could come out to Houston for my birthday this Sunday?" I waited for some crass, sarcastic reply.

"You serious? Wish we could … money tight nigga."

"If it helps, I can pay for it. Just wanted to see y'all, I'm homesick."

It was a gamble, telling him the truth, without him telling our cousins and other family, but Mama needed to know first. At this point, we could only give her the illusion that she was the first to know.

"Yeah man, I got bills; I can't just take off work."

"Okay, okay…here's the deal, I'm gone tell you something but you can't tell Mama yet, promise me that."

"All right, what, you okay?"

"I'm fine, ain't nothing wrong. Something very good has happened though. I won the lottery." Devin paused to process my words like Frankie and Lamont had done.

"What? Stop lying nigga, don't play… for real Dougie?"

"I ain't lying, for real, I won that shit."

"Which one?"

"The Mega-Ball, multi-state lottery from last month," immediately I heard the dial tone. *Did this nigga just hang up on me?* I called back.

"What happened?"

"I hung up on yo ass." We laughed and tried reasoning with each other. He couldn't believe it, no matter what I said.

"Okay, check this out, are you by a computer?"

"Yes."

"Go to the website, look at the winning numbers for October 16th, and read them to me." I waited while he searched, eventually finding the site.

"Okay, I found it, now what."

"Okay, look at the numbers, read them to me." He went on.

"5, okay … what about it?"

"For Mama's birth month, May … next."

"6 … I guess this is for your birthday?"

"Yes, next."

"10 … for her birthday," his tone turned curious, he was getting the picture.

"Next."

"11, what … for November?"

"Yes nigga, next."

"37 … I don't get this one."

"It's my birth year, 1973 in reverse."

"Oh okay … that was tight."

"Next," I liked saying next, unveiling each piece to the puzzle.

"52 … the year she was born."

"Thank you … do you believe me now?" Immediately he yelled for Grace.

"Grace, Grace…come here!"

"Look man, Grace is okay, but don't tell anybody else." After all the commotion had settled, we worked out the logistics for their arrival. *This was really happening,* something I'd imagined years ago. Afterward, I took another nap in preparation for the evening with Frankie.

Lately, I'd been getting an amazing amount of rest, considering the city that never sleeps. I sat up in bed flipping through channels, thinking about the evening, where it could possibly go. Randomly, I called Lamont to see how he was doing.

"Yo, what's up?"

"Hey, you still in New York getting that big apple pussy?"

"Yeah, whatever, everything cool?" I asked.

"Yeah man, we chilling, you all right Trump?"

"There you go. Hey I wanted to do something for my birthday, but I ain't really plan anything. you got any ideas?"

"Man, rent out one of them reception halls downtown or Belvedere's and have something there," he offered. Belvedere's was perfect, and a good idea for next weekend.

"How 'bout I do the Belvedere thing next Saturday, that way I can give enough notice for niggas to show up."

"Sounds like a plan. When you get back?"

"Tomorrow afternoon. Oh, I went and got another toy, too."

"What?"

"That Ghost … in black."

"You lying. You goddamn lying nigga." Lamont was a car fanatic like me.

"They delivering it to George Bush when I land … I'm driving that bitch down 59."

"Hey, I'm a take a cab up there and ride back with you."

"Fuck it, I land at 3:15."

"Oh shit, the Ghost on these haters ... they gone die when they see that shit." We went on for a few minutes more before hanging up. I got out of bed to stretch and take a shower. It was pretty early, only four in the afternoon.

I hadn't checked my voicemails from home in a while. It was usual shit, even messages from bill collectors, could you believe it? My fault for not closing the accounts as I planned, Lord knows I had the money. But then I heard a message from Dr. Harrison's office, something about making another appointment regarding test results. *That shit didn't sound good.* My mind went to my father and his heart issues, my cousin and his cancer bout. It was hard to believe that at this place in my life, with such good fortune, I'd experience a health issue at the same damn time.

I decided to go down to the bar in the hotel and knock back a few to calm my nerves. Whatever the issue was, I'd face it head on.

For the few days I'd been in New York, I must've eaten two or three steaks, on top of the late nights and the heavy drinking. I put the Long Island down, walked out the bar, back upstairs to get Buddy, back down through the lobby, and out to the circular drive. We continued on down the block, letting the wind and sun wash away my negative thoughts.

In a moment of spontaneity, I hailed a cab and asked to be driven to Central Park—my first time there in two trips. I sat in the back, reflective, doing my best to disregard the voicemail from Dr. Harrison's office. Maybe I was over reacting, but at my age, I'd managed never needing a hospital stay or a major surgery.

We reached the park in a very short time with a good number of people walking around, taking pictures, and doing touristy shit. This would've been a perfect day date with Yami, strolling around, killing time, enjoying each other's company. I'm sure she'd love Buddy. Part of me wanted to call her, but my thirst-o-meter wouldn't let me. It was Friday afternoon, the beginning of every teacher's weekend holiday.

A couple hours, and one ice cream cone later, it was time to head back and get ready for the evening. With today's news, it was the pick me up I needed. Around 7 or so I received a call from Frankie.

"Hey, Doug ... just calling to confirm tonight, with my friend ...is that still cool?"

"Of course, no problem; I'll see you all at 9."

"Cool, can't wait," she responded.

Immediately, the nerves kicked in; *why am I getting nervous, it's just dinner and an art show.* I hadn't been on a serious night outing in a while, let alone with two women. This was nothing like happy hour with "M."

By 8:25 that evening, Raul and I were en route to the girls.

"What's good man, what you get into today," he asked.

"Oh, just chilled. Took Buddy to Central Park … nothing much."

"Man, why you ain't call Yami? That was a perfect opportunity."

"Yeah … I needed to air out a bit, clear my mind, some."

"You got any weed left?" he asked, and I laughed. I was down to two or three blunts worth before flying back tomorrow.

"A little bit, I'm leaving tomorrow afternoon," I replied.

"Call Yami up for a goodbye date, something simple, the movies, go down to Canal Street or some Broadway shit … she'll love that." Although a good idea, I've always had a thing about giving a girl space. Never did I want to seem clingy or pesky.

"Yeah, but it's the weekend, I know how it is …" *Damn I had to catch myself.*

Thirty minutes later, we arrived at Frankie's street, a picturesque, tree-lined view, with a line of cars on both sides of the block.

"Hey, Frankie, I think we're here."

"Oh, okay … you have someone with you?" Delicate moment; I didn't want to say, *yes the driver,* offending Raul, my smoke partner, slash weed connect nor could I say, *my friend,* especially if he wasn't accompanying us on this evening.

"Ah, no it's not like that but … yeah, I think I'm here, 902 right?" I asked, attempting to change the subject.

"Okay, we'll be right down." We hung up.

"What she look like?" Raul asked.

"You'll see. She's bringing a friend, too."

"Okay there big pimping … we forgot Yami already, huh."

FRANKIE AND LACY [14]

Five minutes later, we could see them coming out the front door of the Brownstone. From my view, it appeared that Frankie's friend was white, a red head. Walking closer, Frankie noticed me standing next to the car. "Yo, a Rolls-Royce?" her New Yorker came out and the night immediately began.

"Hey, Doug," she leaned in for a hug, "This is my friend, Lacy, I was telling you about from Boston."

"Hi, Lacy," I said, shaking her hand. She was equally attractive with a pleasant smile, and a firm grip.

"Shall we?" I asked as I directed them into the back of the car.

"Hello ladies, I'll be your driver for the evening. My name is Raul, at your service." He was clearly hamming it up, and the ladies loved it. Frankie pinched my hand, for what I didn't know, but it was cute.

"This is nice, I cannot believe I'm riding in a fricking Rolls-Royce," Lacy exclaimed.

"So... where to first?" Frankie asked.

"We have dinner reservations at Dollop, and then ..." Frankie interrupted me.

"Did you say Dollop? Do you understand that that is the hottest and hardest place to get a reservation?" I smiled, having no idea. *Thanks, Ira.* "My friends are going to fucking flip ... excuse my language," she added. Frankie's *real* side was interesting.

"So, I'm sure Frankie's told you a little about me," I said, looking at Frankie and giving a wink.

I hope she didn't mention the money. "So what do you do in Boston?"

"Actually I'm a trader on the Boston Stock Exchange. I've been there for the past eleven years. I need a new challenge," she replied with a corny chuckle.

"Oh? What would you prefer doing?" I asked curiously.

"I know this is going to sound crazy … well, there's the thing we want to do," Lacy said looking at Frankie. Frankie rolled her eyes.

"It's nothing," Frankie chimed with disdain.

"What? I wanna know."

"Okay, okay … we wanna open a bed & breakfast in Belize," Lacy answered.

"Yeah, with an aromatherapy masseuse on sight," Frankie added.

"Do you have a business plan and target time?" I asked.

"Nah," they said in unison.

The ladies seemed comfortable with me, as I with them. The night was off to a good start, with two beautiful and intelligent women riding along with me in an amazing car, in the number one city in the world, on the way to the hottest restaurant in town. Lucky me.

Periodically I'd look up front to Raul, who'd look at me through the rear-view mirror. Some way, I wanted to include him in the festivities. To imagine just a few weeks back, I'd have the means to do this, that I'd live like this, was unconscionable.

Soon we reached Dollop. The valet line was incredibly long. The valet guys looked like members of a track team running back and forth.

"Wow, it's really going, huh?" Lacy said in her faint Boston accent.

"I'm telling you, this spot here is crazy … the reviews are phenomenal," Frankie added.

Our turn had come to be let out by the valet guy. Frankie was visibly overwhelmed by the experience of eating here; the look in her eyes was appreciation enough.

When we entered the place it was dark and artsy with Asian themed artifacts throughout. The minimal light gave the illusion of intimacy, but the chatter among the patrons made it apparent that it was anything but.

"Reservation, name please?" The maître d' asked.

"Moore, Douglas Moore," I replied. He looked at the list while Lacy jokingly added, "Bond, James Bond."

"Moore, party of three, right this way." We followed, heading to our designated area in this swanky dungeon of a restaurant.

"This place is amazing already," Frankie added, while I responded with "Yeah, it is." I looked around for any celebrities, but it was so damn dark in there, I wondered how anybody could see their plates.

"Right this way," the gentleman said, directing us into a Kabuki styled private room. "Your host will be with you momentarily."

I admired the décor; the walls were a deep dark red, highlighted by the soft amber light flickering from the wall fixtures. This room had ménage written all over, especially with the sliding door and a few drinks.

"Thank you, Doug, for this ... this experience. Not in a million years would I've gotten a table here," Frankie offered. Her gratitude was humbling.

"Stop, you're making me blush," I replied.

"So, Doug, you married? Any kids?"

"Lacy!" Frankie called in embarrassment.

"What, I'm making small talk here," Lacy countered.

"Nope, I'm single and free as a bird."

"So I guess you wine and dine a lot in Houston," Frankie chimed.

"No, not really. Actually I don't get out much."

"So do you date at all?" Frankie asked with concern. *Was she feeling me?*

"I'd like to ... I'm looking." My reply seemed charming enough.

"Yeah, I feel ya, Doug," Lacy said, as our waiter returned.

"Good evening, my name is Serge, I'll be your host," he said, sliding our slightly opened door. "Is this your first time with us?"

"First time," we said in unison. The waiter went on describing the fusion styled cuisine, and their featured items for the evening. Then he handed us the menus made of bamboo, with no visible pricing. "Let's start with drinks. Ladies?" Lacy ordered a dry martini while Frankie asked for a cosmopolitan.

"And you, sir?"

"Is it possible to get a sake bomb?"

"One Kamikaze coming right up."

"Wait, what's that?" Lacy asked.

"It's a mug of beer, with a smaller cup of Sake, Japanese wine, inside it."

"I want that."

"Yeah, make that three."

"Okay, coming right up."

"You're not trying to get us fucked up are you?" Lacy asked.

"Me?" I slyly replied.

Minutes later, the waiter returned with our drinks. I anticipated the ladies not liking them. The first time I tried it, the taste of the Sake threw me off, but the buzz and peer pressure kept me coming back for more. It was an icebreaker drink, and by the look of it, a good call. "Ladies, a toast to the evening … cheers!" We took our drinks straight to the head. The girls had disgusted looks on their faces during and after they finished.

"Good, right?" I asked facetiously.

"Hell nah, no more," Frankie said while they both laughed.

"Fuck it, give me another," Lacy answered. She was the obvious adventurous type.

When the waiter returned, I ordered two more sake bombs for Lacy and I, and Frankie, a cosmopolitan. "Have you all decided?" The waiter asked.

"Did we even look at the menus? Let's start with appetizers, can you suggest something?" The waiter went on about this and that, the available choices like tempura shrimp with ginger Crème Bruleé sauce, or seared Kobe beef strips with melted gouda cheese, sprinkled with wasabi powder; *what the fuck?* "Let's have one of each of those as starters…it'll give us time to order," I explained.

Lacy excused herself from the table, leaving Frankie and I alone.

"Doug, this is so great … excuse my friend though, she's a free spirit…"

"That's totally fine, let's have fun tonight … this is the side of New York I wanted to see, thanks to you," I offered.

For a quick moment we stared in each other's eyes, expressing some unknown language of interest, equally afraid to cross that line.

"So are you dating, do you have a boyfriend?"

"It's complicated," she replied. Right then, Lacy walked back in.

"I think I'm starving now," she said randomly.

After a while, we decided on our main courses. Everything was avant-garde, overreaching, attempting to scream extreme. I settled on a fish dish, taking a break from another steak. Suddenly, something strange happened with Lacy. Periodically, she'd sniffle, as if her nose were running. She hadn't done that until after she returned from the restroom.

"Doug, if you don't mind, the next round is on me," Lacy offered. We were learning about each other, Frankie and her dog, Joey, her love of cop shows, water coloring and sleeping in on Sundays. Lacy was the total opposite; she was the kayaking, crab hunting, bike riding, outdoorsy type.

The main course finally came to the table. It was an opulent presentation, with two women dressed as geisha girls accompanying our waiter. Frankie remained in 7th heaven and I, just hungry. My plate was half square and half round, with dots of sauce, slices of fish, and a small bunch of asparagus as my vegetable. It didn't look like much, but then again, an abundant plate was considered distasteful in a place like this. Lacy wasted no time. She immediately began picking at her food, and then picking at Frankie's.

"Pretty good," she chimed. By then it was 10:40. We had an hour before the art show.

The drinking was beginning to catch up. Two sake bombs and a bottle of Riesling between us, the match was lit. "Ladies, if you can prepare a solid business plan for the bed & breakfast, I'd be willing to take a look at it and consider it for an investment project." Again, here I was offering up shit that no one asked for; a pleading need to feel relevant perhaps. Even though their idea was a far cry in cost from Bioko, it lacked my interest.

"Are you serious?" Frankie asked.

Her eyes dazzled even more from my proposition. I had to commit.

"Yes, I think it's an awesome idea."

"Are you sure, Doug?" Lacy countered. "Give it some time, I think it's the Sake bombs talking," she added.

Slightly stunned at her bluntness, in my peripheral, I could feel the death stare coming from Frankie.

"No I'm serious, it's a no brainer. Belize is a beautiful country,

I've not been, but it's a tourist attraction, correct?" I asked, attempting to deflate the awkwardness.

"Doug, I'm very grateful for your offer; I'll draw up a business plan for you as time permits, now if you would excuse me, I'm going to the ladies room," she stated in a seething yet monotone manner. She was clearly upset, enough so that Lacy also excused herself. *Fuck*; the night couldn't end like this. Lacy was a little direct, but not enough to offend me. I called to the waiter for another bottle of Riesling, hoping they'd drink their differences away.

Momentarily, both ladies returned, appearing more civil. Frankie realized the new bottle on the table, with a smile and wink.

"Doug, I'd like to apologize for my brash behavior; I can get a little crass sometimes after a few drinks," Lacy offered.

"I'm fine, no problem, believe me. Let's have a good time tonight ladies."

"Yeah," Frankie added.

All seemed to be well. The food actually turned out to be pretty good, but the drinks were best. Lacy even ordered one more sake bomb, and got Frankie to finish half of it. We were like a bunch of college kids on spring break in our little Kabuki room. And then I saw it, the sniffles. This time Frankie did it. The only thing that came to mind was cocaine. *Were these bitches snorting coke?*

As our dining experience came to an end, we were offered a dessert menu, but the ladies declined. When the waiter returned with the bill, I took a look and did my best to contain my familiar middle-class reaction. *$639?* I left a hundred dollar tip.

We made our way back through the restaurant, feeling like a million dollars and the celebrities I'd been looking for. Upon our grand exit, Raul was already waiting in the valet queue to pick us up.

"What's your driver's name, he's pretty cute," Lacy said.

"I'll be sure to let him know," I told her.

Raul drove closer and the valet guy opened the back door, letting the ladies in. We were back to normal from a rollercoaster of a dinner.

"How was dinner?" Raul asked.

"Awesome sir; as a matter of fact, a certain someone thinks you're hot," I added with a devilish grin. Lacy instantly gave me an innocent pat on the leg.

"Dinner was great, Doug," Lacy answered attempting to change the subject.

The night had gotten back on course, with us heading towards some area called Tribeca, where the art show was to take place. The city just looked amazing at night, the lights, the skyscrapers, and the mood. I felt bigger than life and wanted nothing to end. The girls were a little more extra than I remembered, the coke perhaps. "What's the name of the artist again?" Frankie asked. I'd already forgotten the day I received the invitation.

"Some motherfucker from Germany ... I forgot," I answered.

"This should be some trippy shit tonight," Lacy added, as we all laughed.

"Yeah, would've been a perfect blunt trip," I continued. The ladies looked surprised.

"You smoke?" Frankie asked.

"Raul, do I smoke," I asked in a matter-of-fact tone.

"Like a chimney, sir," he countered. The ladies erupted in laughter, giving each other high fives, while Raul gave a wink in the rear-view mirror.

"I'm sorry but you can never tell," Frankie went on. It was a perfect invitation for an after party back at the suite.

"I have some left if you guys wanna smoke later."

"Where you staying," Frankie asked.

"The Waldorf."

"Fuck outta here," Lacy fired back.

"Since I landed." Both ladies said "sweet" in unison, and laughed at the humor of it.

"Well, I have something else that might do the trick." Frankie looked at Lacy, to shut her up, but the cat was out the bag. Assuming it was coke, I wasn't interested.

"Ever tried 'x'?" Lacy asked. I did, but it didn't do a goddamn thing for me.

"No. Heard about it. You got some?"

"Yeah, you got some?" Raul chimed. My mother's voice crept into my head. *Be careful.*

"Lacy are you fucking kidding me?" Frankie exclaimed. Maybe she felt it necessary to retain a sense of professional decorum, fearing I'd report her to the guys back at the firm, but I didn't give a fuck.

"Frankie, you're off the clock. Lacy, give me the pill." I popped "x" in front of them, reassuring Frankie I wasn't a narc, and that my sole objective was to have a good time, and maybe get lucky tonight.

"Okay then, fuck it." Lacy handed her one and she popped it.

"Here you go lover boy," Lacy said, handing one to Raul up front. He popped his and kept on like nothing happened. Lacy finally took hers and we were all in, thick as thieves.

"You're gonna feel a warm sensation throughout your body. Just go with it," Lacy explained.

"Yeah, if your hand itches, it'll be the best scratching you ever had," Frankie added.

"Okay."

"And you'll get a super boner," Raul humorously added.

"Well, let the games begin," I told them.

By 11:48, skipping the art show and going back to the suite seemed far more interesting. The "Welcome to New York" song came on the radio and the girls went crazy, with Lacy rolling her window down, screaming the lyrics. Frankie leaned over to me, "I'm having the best time, thanks." She squeezed my leg, causing a moderate hard on, which I tried fighting.

Just three weeks ago, I was a regular dude with bills and aspirations, living in a rut, hopeful that life would miraculously change by no effort of my own. Had I not won, I'd be in bed right now, back in my shoe box apartment, anticipating the weekend before work on Monday morning. Had I not won, I suppose I'd fantasize over "M,"or some other "unattainable" woman. But I won. I was really in the back seat of a Rolls-Royce, in New York City, being driven around with two beautiful women on drugs, on the way to a midnight art show.

WHAT THE FUCK JUST HAPPENED? [15]

"I think we're here," Raul told us. It was hard making out an address. Through a huge glass window, we could see a decent crowd of folks walking about. It appeared to be our intended destination.

"Wow, looks packed in there," Lacy said. It looked alive, filled with beautiful people who lived like vampires in their expensive haute couture, with their sophisticated conversations.

"I'll let you guys out right here," Raul said as he pulled over to the curb. When we got out, the air was chilly, common place for a winter's night on the east coast. The girls instinctively got up under each of my arms attempting to stay warm. We crossed the street back towards the gallery, excited about the show and whatever else could transpire.

Some guy at the door checked for our names and let us right in. The warm breeze of the heating system put us back at ease and ready to explore the evening's fair.

"Doug, we're gonna go to the ladies room right quick, be right back," Lacy said. I knew what it was. I was slightly disgusted in Frankie. It was unconscionable having a relationship with a coke head. I gave them a nod, going in a different direction.

The gallery was typical of my expectations—bleached hardwood floors, exposed brick walls, exposed air ducts, and lights that hung sporadically from the ceiling. Waiters dressed in all black with trays of champagne and wine roamed about, while Johnny Cash played over the sound system. The atmosphere was enchanting by the illusion of highly civilized people interpreting art for more than what it was. *Maybe I'll buy something tonight.*

137

Minutes later, the girls made their way back and curiously, I paid more attention.

"Did we miss anything?" Lacy asked lightheartedly.

"Maybe someone's going to make an announcement." Perhaps, had I attended a few galleries in Houston, I'd know shit like this.

Suddenly all the lights went out, and a voice blared from the sound system, "Greetings you worthless pieces of shit …" The attendees began clapping, whistling, and cheering. "You've come to have your perceptions changed and your hearts broken … welcome to the Claude show." The crowd continued in applause, and then the lights came back on. A guy, presumably the artist, had emerged from the crowd, wearing what appeared to be an old fashioned striped prison uniform.

"Is that him?" Frankie asked. We weren't sure, but we refused to ask whether this strangely dressed man was the artist. We played along, walking through the crowd, amused at the eclectic vibe. And then it happened, but this time it was simultaneous. Frankie and Lacy, while looking at a painting, did the sniffle thing. All I could do was laugh, shaking my head. *She's not the one for me.*

The diversity of the crowd was an interesting mix, an attribute of New York City. Supposedly, living here would make me the small fish in a big pond, blending in with all classes of people. In this city, my money was relatively irrelevant. Conversely, Houston was really home. With every passing day, I looked forward to getting back to the *"H."*

One of the waiters came around with a tray of champagne and I helped myself, intending to nurse the buzz from the drinks at the restaurant. Out of nowhere, Frankie grabbed my hand, and fiddled the middle of my palm with her index finger. *Yes!* My mind went into overdrive. *How do we politely get rid of Lacy?* I looked over at Lacy a few feet away, with a gracious smile, but thinking, *bitch, you gone have to kick rocks tonight.* In that moment of dubious thought, it happened, the warm sensation, the tingling of my finger tips and toes, the euphoria of "x" was kicking in.

Frankie still hadn't let go of my hand and Lacy noticed. She looked back like *oh, okay* and I looked back at her like, *so you know what you gotta do.* It was true. The feeling of her grip was sensual. Every movement of her hand in mine was like a strategic mind fuck for avoiding a visible erection. I'd stare at paintings for a while longer, hoping it'd go down. And when it did, we'd walk to the next piece.

"Are you enjoying this?" Frankie asked. Clearly double talk, and appreciated.

Rethinking my disdain for Frankie's unconfirmed, confirmed drug use, maybe I could influence her that weed was all she needed. Whatever the case, the way she held my hand washed my judgment away.

We continued strolling about, offering bullshit commentary on various paintings as if connoisseurs, convincing ourselves of our interpretations.

"Oh shit, I love this," she said. An awkward painting, one of many, it didn't cut it for me, but she was obviously enamored.

"What do you get from this?" I asked, treading between confusion and sarcasm.

"I can't explain it … it just speaks to me." *Sure it ain't the cocaine and ecstasy pill you popped?*

Just then, Lacy caught back up with us; she was clearly flush in the face.

"You okay?"

"It's the 'x.' Happens all the time," she countered.

"Raul can take you home if you need to go," I offered.

"I'm cool, seriously." *Damn, she missed the hint.* Lacy wasn't the ugly fat cock blocking friend. She was the attractive red-headed third wheel fucking up my flow.

I excused myself to inquire of the painting Frankie liked. It was entitled, *"Not so sure,"* which was exactly how I felt about it. One of the gallery employees gave me information and its price; $14,850. They agreed to ship it to her address. We arranged payment, and I went back to the ladies. At this time, we'd been at the show a good hour and saw most of everything.

"Ladies, how do you feel?"

"I've seen enough … Frankie?"

"Yeah, I'm good." I called Raul as we began to head out the gallery, full on horny and ready to smoke … but Lacy.

"Ladies, I'm so glad you guys came out with me this evening … this is another side of New York that I don't get to see much, but thanks again."

"Thank you, Doug, for allowing me to be a third wheel," Lacy said. We laughed, but she was right.

"Yes, Doug, tonight was much needed, thanks again." Just then, Raul came up with the car and we got in.

"Where to boss?" Raul asked, not sure of what to say.

"Are we still invited to partake of the cannabis?" Frankie chimed.

"No problem … figured you guys were turning in." At that point, my fantasizing was over with; *fuck it, come over and smoke. I'll probably fall asleep anyway.* We'd gotten acquainted with each other over the course of the night. Frankie even leaned over on my side, laying her head on my shoulder. Lacy went to her purse, took her phone out and started playing some game. The previous mood from earlier in the evening had faded, and reality crept back in.

Thoughts of Yami came to mind; *maybe she's free tomorrow for breakfast, I'll call her.* Nothing grand, just some eggs Benedict and mimosas, or maybe a walk around Central Park. I was open.

After a short while, we reached the hotel.

"Here we go ladies and gentleman," Raul said.

"You wanna come up for a minute, bro?"

"Nah, I better hang back on this one. Have fun for me, we'll talk later."

We got out of the car, with the assistance of the doorman. Feeling somewhat ashamed and irreverent, none of these hotel employees had ever seen me bring a woman back to my suite my entire stay. Lacy mumbled something as she stumbled a bit to get out, while Frankie grabbed my hand again.

When we reached the hotel lobby, they were impressed at what they saw.

"This is an awesome place," Lacy said, while looking around. I glanced at one of the receptionists, who looked at me and quickly looked away. She made me feel dirty.

"There's a bar over there if you guys wanna night cap," I offered.

"Wondrous, let's do it," Lacy added. We walked over. A few people were in there, smoking and conversing.

"I'll be happy when weed's legalized," Frankie chimed. Lacy and I looked at her in confusion, wondering what brought on her statement. "I can't stand cigarette smoke," she continued.

"Oh, well, let's have the one drink, and head up afterward," I said. We all agreed.

Within my manly soul, a revelation came to me saying, *you motherfucking idiot, how dare you bring two ladies up to your room, at this time of night just to smoke. You don't think perhaps they'd want more than to smoke your weed? You already know Frankie is feeling you; go for it. If that bitch Lacy wants to be a third wheel, give her a show she'll never forget. Follow through.* My manly soul made perfectly good sense. Never in my life had I'd come so close to having a threesome. Instinctively, I ordered patron shots, disguised as random fun.

"Here's to us."

"I'm ready to puff, puff, pass," Lacy said.

We finished what was left of our drinks. "Let's go." This time around, I was more than buzzed. The drinks from the restaurant, the art show, and bar were adding up. Frankie stumbled, standing from the stool.

"You okay, bud?" I asked as Lacy and I snickered.

"I'm 100 percent ... don't worry about me, just lead me to the trees."

When the ladies entered my suite, Buddy Boy greeted them, barking uncontrollably. "Ahh, is this is your dog, he's cute," Frankie said. More points for me. Frankie went on playing with Buddy while Lacy looked around the suite, obviously impressed with her surroundings. "This is fucking beautiful ... I could live here. Please go fetch the Godiva chocolates," she continued, in a mocking British accent. Frankie went up to the window to see the view while she held Buddy, "I love New York."

While they pranced around, I made myself comfortable, taking my suit jacket and shoes off, and turning on the television. I went to my stash spot, pulled out the baggie with a couple mini cigars, and began going to work. "You know, I could never roll," Frankie continued.

"It's essential for any weed head, darling," I replied. Frankie sat beside me, amazed by the process.

When I finished rolling number one, she took it and asked Lacy for the lighter on the coffee table. I went to the bathroom to soak another oversized body towel for the front door. As soon as it was lit, that familiar aroma did its usual dance, while I continued on blunt number two.

The ladies flipped through the channels, periodically stopping on random shit. They respected the rotation, getting up to pass when it was the other's turn. When the second blunt was finished, I lit it and walked over to the windows to crack them. New York's skyline was an awesome view, along with the moment.

"Where's the mini bar?" Lacy asked.

"Damn, you still going?" I asked.

"Hey man, I'm part Irish, this is what I do." We had a good laugh.

"So when do you leave again?" Frankie asked.

"Tomorrow afternoon ... back to H town."

"We have to visit ... ride some fucking horses and shit."

I got up to sit in the lounge chair, watching whatever they were looking at. Both ladies were on the couch, comfortably sprawled out and relaxed. "I am so fucking high right now, this is some good shit man," Lacy said. I could tell by her blood shot eyes, Frankie seemed more reserved, even somber. By then, Buddy had gone off into his own world.

"You okay, Frankie?" She looked at me with a smile, thumbs up. They were gone.

The weed took us somewhere else, where talking was becoming less and less necessary. By then, Frankie was laying in Lacy's lap, while Lacy gently stroked her head. Lacy asked if Frankie was all right, and then she leaned down and gave her a kiss on the forehead. It teetered between lipstick lesbian sensuality and BFF love. Maybe because of my lesbian fetish, I made more out of it than it really was. Lacy looked over at me and said, "My baby can't hang." I didn't think much of it, and continued on. Soon after, we heard snoring, and looked at each other knowingly.

Afterward, I went to the bathroom to take a piss and change into a T-shirt. When I returned, Lacy was standing at the window, enjoying the view. I sat back in my spot, while Frankie was sound asleep. We were down to just quarters by then. Lacy looked at me."You know how to do a cannon ball?" She was referring to a smoker's trick which entailed one inhaling the smoke from another's mouth.

"Of course," I replied. She walked over and got on her knees in front of me.

"Show me." I took a quick peek at Frankie, took a deep pull from what was left of the blunt, leaned over to Lacy, and blew. She coughed uncontrollably for a few seconds, while Buddy came running to investigate. I tried containing my laughter."Gimme another one." I looked at her like, *c'mon chill*, but she didn't budge.

When I took the second pull, I knew she'd be done. I leaned in, blew, and her lips inadvertently touched mine. I kept blowing and suddenly she leaned in more, at which point our lips fully touched. She started sucking on my bottom lip, and nothing inside of me stopped her. I went with it. Immediately, we were in a full on kiss, tongue and everything. My eyes were closed, consciously aware of the mistake. We went on for a good 20 seconds, and then she got up and went to the bathroom. I sat there like *hell nah; I ain't just kiss this girl*. Frankie was still knocked out on the couch.

A minute passed, and I sat, contemplating my next move. *Fuck it*. I got up, went to the bathroom, where she stood at the sink, and went in for another kiss. This time, it wasn't a mistake, as we grabbed at each other, touching and exploring with no inhibitions. I grabbed at her breast while she grabbed my dick, going harder and harder by the moment. She stopped me, looked in my eyes and asked, "You sure about this?" I wasn't sure, other than being high, drunk, and horny. I leaned back over and kissed her again. Then she pushed me back, took my hand and led me to the bed which was right behind Frankie. We both looked over at her in passing as she lay unaware.

Lacy pushed me onto the bed, climbed on top and continued kissing me. I explored, grabbing her ass and thighs, thinking how crazy things had turned. She started kissing down my neck, onto my chest, stomach, unfastened my belt, opening my pants, and went to work. Thankfully my guy showed up. She paused and said, "So it is true." I smiled and then my smile quickly turned to painful pleasure. She did things no sexual partner had ever done. For a minute I took the liberty of grabbing the back of her head, in a manly moment of sexual dominance.

After she worked me, she pulled her skirt up, her panties down and slid me right in. The warmth of it coupled with the consciousness of not having protection was conflicting. Her rhythm was so natural, I didn't wanna stop. It was another foolish moment of bad adult judgment. At that point, my concern was with my pace. I flipped her over and got on top, thrusting myself harder and harder, looking in her eyes as if at war. It became a battle of who could make who cum first. Our chemistry was undeniable. With every nuance of a move, her body followed. *She'd been with a brother before*. Then I got on my side, my favorite position, and worked her from the back, grabbing at her red hair, as she moaned, assuring me that I was on point.

A million thoughts raced in my head; some of which helped my stamina. We let ourselves go, clearly forgetting about Frankie. Whatever infatuation I'd had, whatever strength of friendship Lacy had, all of it became irrelevant. We were fucking, and violently.

The rhythm flowed, stroking and grinding as she did her best to conceal her moaning. My sexual confidence produced a cocky performance, no pun intended. Grabbing at her thighs and waist, thoughts were lost in this regrettable moment of animalistic lust. And then boom, it happened. I pulled out and let go. It was the hardest nut I'd had in a while, the result of eight months without sex. We laid in silence with only the cadence of our heavy breathing. She immediately got up, and went back to the bathroom.

My mother's voice rang again, *you got yourself a white girl now, huh?* I couldn't believe what happened. It was so fast and unexpected, without a rationale. When Lacy came back out, she came over to the bed, reached for her panties, put them on and kissed me on the forehead. Then she went back to the couch where Frankie remained asleep. I felt used.

In the bigger picture, two consenting adults, living indifferently to the rules of society, chose the joys of free will. I continued lying there, proud and guilty. Proud that I didn't succumb to performance anxiety, yet guilty of sharing this experience with the wrong person. Dazed, exhausted, and careless, I fell asleep.

Hours later, visible sun light peered through the windows after I'd been awakened by a gentle tap on my shoulder. It was Frankie.

"Hey, Doug … Doug."

"Hey," I responded, groggy and a bit startled.

"We're leaving now … it's 6 in the morning."

"Okay, hope you guys had a good time," I said, as Lacy stood off in the distance with a sheepish look.

"Can I give you cab fare?"

"We're fine, go back to sleep. Call me later," she said.

"Okay, you guys be safe."

"Thanks, Doug, for everything," Lacy said. Then they walked out the door.

I over did it. The drinking, the 'x' pill, the weed, was all grown up peer pressure in search of good times.

Sluggish and hung over, desperate for clarity, and removed from reasonable thought, I just wanted to feel better. This conviction of being irresponsible burned inside. *She gave me the pussy, and I took it*. This was a story for Lamont, a fleeting moment of bravado. I turned on my side attempting to fall back asleep, giving reason a break.

Eventually, I pushed myself to get up, take a shower and retreat to the couch, with nothing but my drawers on. Buddy jumped up and laid beside me. My nigga. I ordered breakfast and sat there, watching movie after endless cable movie. Raul called, probably to get a play by play of the goings on of the hours before, but I ignored the call. The hangover needed to end. Looking forward to Houston, I was mostly excited about the plans for my mother. They were scheduled to land on Sunday morning. Their arrival would ground me, especially after the week I had.

The desire to see Yami before leaving felt wrong, dirty, and unworthy of her time. What happened in those early morning hours wasn't me, but rather the realization of a hyped-up fantasy, common amongst heterosexual, "black guys."

Even though the Lacy thing was the spice of life, it was equally a mishap. More so, lessons in civility, self-control with sexual opportunities, awaited me. If I didn't fasten my head on straight, I'd be somebody's baby daddy, or worse.

Around noon or so, I sat on the edge of the bed, eager to get home and enjoy myself. Raul assured me he'd be downstairs in half an hour, for my two o'clock flight. In the background, the TV played while I stared out the window.

Right on cue, Raul called. He was downstairs waiting. I called for a bell hop for my bags and checked the room once more before leaving. The excitement of returning home was beginning to overshadow the guilt.

Walking through the lobby, I greeted the familiar faces I'd come to know in that short span of time. Even Ira came to walk me to the car. The suit I had custom made would ship to my new address in a few days.

Raul came out to help with my bags, while I wrapped up business and small talk with Ira. "Well, Mr. Moore, it was a pleasure having you stay with us. We look forward to your speedy return," he said. I thanked him for all he did and got in the car, airport bound.

"Hey, man, I brought some doughnuts on the way in, want some?"

"Hell, yeah," Raul handed the box over, full of glazed doughnuts.

"Back to the crib, huh?"

"Yeah man, it's time … had fun, handled business."

"Most importantly," he added. "So what now? What's your plan back home?" he asked. I guess he thought I forgot my offer from a few days ago.

"I guess get back to looking for things to invest in… did you create that proposal for me?" No sooner than I said those words, he handed me a spiral bound book that looked to be 20 pages long.

"Here you go boss; thought it could be a good read for the plane ride. Take your time and give me your honest feedback. I wrote my email and cell number on the back page." His ambition was respectable. If I'd met someone like myself, I'd do the same thing.

"So you know I wanna know ..." Raul continued. I started laughing. There was no way of getting around the questions. Raul had been my New York City road dog. I owed him some intel.

"We chilled, smoked a little, talked shit, but nothing really popped. They ended up leaving an hour after you dropped us off," I told him. Concealing the truth was my way of showing a genuine interest in Yami.

"I wanted to come up there, but Claudia, know what I'm saying? With the late nights and all, she been giving me shit lately."

"Honestly, I figured that," I responded.

"Yo, I'm giving it 'til New Year's ... if she don't fucking show me something different, it's a wrap, for real." His ultimatum made no sense. Did he really think she'd change in less than two months? Curiously I wondered why he never pursued Yami. Maybe she was bipolar, or had too many vagina miles.

"Why you ain't never go for Yami?"

"Yami? Your girl? Nah, she's like my sister ... we grew up together. We know each other's families, all that."

"Yeah ... but they say the best relationships come out of friendship first." My mind went immediately to Gwen. "Well, I wish you the best on whatever you decide man." I continued.

"I'm a be all right, find me a new situation, something drama free. Matter of fact, what's up with that redhead chick?" A weird guilt hit me, like I betrayed him, for not telling about the sexcapade with Lacy, a chick he found interesting.

"Yeah, she was a little cutie, but she talked too fucking much."

"Word?"

"Word, my nigga."

That afternoon drive to the airport seemed to flow with ease. Everything was a blur, while Raul sped on the expressway. The sooner I could be seated in first class, the better. The first thing on my list of things to do, after getting my car, was to stop by The Breakfast Klub and get an order of fish and grits.

My mood was mellow. Life was back in order. New York City no longer felt necessary to feel alive. My resolve was accepting the mistakes made in my life as lessons to be learned. After checking in at the airport, going through security, a good forty minutes passed before boarding the plane. My mind was set on another nap for the duration of the flight. With a quick call to Lamont about my arrival time, my heart was set on home.

Later on, during the plane ride, I contemplated my love life. *If I were supposed to be in a period of free love, how serious could I be about a relationship with Yami; and if I were seriously thinking about her, where did Gwen fit in all of it?* The plan was to get all the fuck shit out my system, and then settle down with Gwen in the end. But something changed. That weakness of mine stuck for one face, one body … one woman.

BREAKING BREAD [16]

I re-imagined my previous plan of pre-monogamy. That plan involved coming back to Houston, fucking around with the most beautiful and coveted women in town until sexually well fed and ready for marriage to Gwen. Yet, my heart had spoken, saying otherwise.

First and foremost, this new found infatuation meant nothing without developing a real relationship with strong mutual feelings for each other. Never mind the long distance thing—would she even consider moving to Houston? The more I thought of it, the more I began to give doubt about it; *maybe it's easier to fuck around and have random, meaningless flings.*

Hours later, Buddy and I were back on the home turf. Eager to see some familiar faces, I immediately called Lamont.

"Hey man, I just landed, where you?"

"Hey, I'm out front. I think I saw your car, too."

"Oh shit, let me call them niggas, I'll call you back." I quickly made a call to Dino.

"Dino, my man where are you guys, I just landed."

"Mr. Moore, glad to have you back. I am waiting in the arrivals area. When you get here, we'll drive to the car. We weren't allowed to unload it on site."

"No problem man, gimme a minute to collect my things."

After collecting my bags and picking up Buddy, I made my way through the exit doors where I saw Dino cheesing hard as hell.

"Mr. Moore!"

"Dino, how's it going?" We shook hands as we continued walking.

"Hey, my friend is here waiting for me, let me call him." I dialed Lamont.

" We walking outside."

"I thought your car was black, I see a white Phantom," he countered.

"It is. That's for us to ride to the car. Hold tight, I'll see you in a minute." I felt like a first-round draft pick arriving in town for the home team.

When we got outside, Lamont was standing by the car, looking fly on his cell phone.

"How was your flight, sir?" Dino asked.

"Okay, had a good time in New York, but I'm glad to be home ... Lamont!" I called out. He turned and noticed me, raising his hands like I'd just finished a bid.

"What's up, man?"

"What's up," we gripped and hugged each other.

"Yo son, you good, yo?" Lamont said, mocking my temporary choice in words.

"Yeah, whatever." We started laughing and shooting more shit.

"Oh, by the way, this is Dino from the dealership." Lamont and Dino shook hands, and then Dino popped the trunk and started putting my luggage in.

"Man, I love this car ... how much you letting it go for Dino?" Lamont asked jokingly. Lamont grounded me, and with my new found wealth, he'd "shine" too. He wasn't my sidekick or flunky, and neither would he allow himself to be.

Driving out from the airport, I sat relaxed and excited to see my car, on such a bright and warm Saturday afternoon.

"We took the liberty of detailing the Ghost with a double coat of wax and tire dressing for the wheels, you'll love it," Dino said.

"I hope so for what I paid."

Minutes later we pulled into a parking lot about half a mile from the airport. We could see the truck that hauled the car, and just a few feet away, the Ghost, shining like a pretty black diamond. "That's you, man?" Lamont asked. We both started laughing uncontrollably. Even Dino joined our contagious illustration of pure car joy. Smiling from ear to ear, my cheeks started hurting. Dino drove right next to it, and we all got out in awe.

"Here's your car, as requested," Dino said. We gazed at it like stunned fools. My very own, first Rolls-Royce. Lamont was so focused on the car he didn't pay me any attention. "She's all gassed up and ready to go. At some point, either today or later this week, stop by the dealership so we can discuss warranty and maintenance stuff."

"Yeah, that's fine. I'll come by this week for sure."

"Well, that about does it for me, if you don't have any more questions."

"I really appreciate this, thanks for everything." We shook hands and went our separate ways. Lamont and I got in the car and sat there for at least ten minutes exploring the buttons, the sound system, everything.

"Hold up, I got something," Lamont said. He reached in his jacket pocket and pulled out an old *UGK* CD and put it in. We started jamming to "Pocket Full of Stones."

"I think it's time to hit these motherfucking streets, nigga," he added. Buddy paced from door to door, "You ready Buddy Boy?" I put the car in drive, and got on the William Clayton Expressway, ready to stunt.

With the air condition blowing, and the music bumping, I was on cloud nine. My best dude was with me, my mama and Devin were coming tomorrow, and I had no financial worries. Just as I basked in the euphoria of it all, the voicemail from Dr. Harrison's office, popped into my mind.

"I'm hungry as hell. I'm a drop Buddy off at the crib. Let's go to The Breakfast Klub."

"Yeah, that's cool," Lamont replied. Pushing the acceleration, speeding pass others, we didn't give a fuck about the police.

Finally reaching downtown, we made a quick stop at the apartment. "This where you at now... I fucks with this," Lamont commented. This was Buddy's first time in all 2,000 square feet of his new home. Afterward, we hopped back in the Ghost and continued on.

Driving down Elgin was adrenaline-charged but laborious, as we dodged potholes. People were turning their heads, left and right, trying to get a peek in. Lamont was enjoying it the most.

"Nigga we should go to T.S.U. and shut that shit down." At every stop sign and stop light we could feel the eyes peering at us, wondering who the hell these dudes were. "Man, motherfuckers going nuts, man."

An older black gentleman pulled up alongside us at the next light and motioned for me to roll down the window.

"Say, young blood ... what kind a car that is?"

"It's a Rolls-Royce Ghost," I said, while Lamont smacked his lips.

"How this nigga don't know what kind a car this is?"

"Beautiful car."

"Thank you, sir," I replied before the light changed and we pulled off.

Due to the small size of the parking lot at The Breakfast Klub, it stayed full, with a line of folks hanging out the door, but I felt like stunting anyway. We pulled in, waiting for somebody to leave.

"You know you not gone find a parking spot, right?"

"Just checking, is that all right?"

"Shut that shit up ... everybody see you," Lamont replied in a mocking tone. Of course I wanted some attention.

"Man, come to think of it, don't park here ... too risky." He made a reasonable point.

"All right, I'll go to one of these parking garages, grab us a spot in line." Lamont got out and I went down the street to park. As I walked back, appreciating Houston's downtown scenery, a homeless man sitting on the sidewalk was just up ahead with a sign that read, *"Homeless Veteran, just trying to survive, anything would help, God Bless"* I reached in my wallet and gave him some money and continued on.

My mind went back to the homeless lady in Brooklyn, wondering if she spent the money wisely or on her usual vice. In reality, the act of giving meant accepting not having control on how the money was spent. All that mattered was the deed, and the positivity in doing it.

The Breakfast Klub was packed as usual with Lamont second in line to be seated. A beautiful crowd of "black" faces were laughing, talking, and enjoying themselves over good food; *home again.*

"They in here, man," Lamont said, referring to the *fine* women.

"Fish and Grits here I come," was my only reply, I was hungry.

"So did you smash something up there?" Lamont asked. Lamont and I usually shared our fuck stories, even though I hadn't had any after Gwen and before Lacy. The Lacy thing was still a regrettable moment.

"Yeah, a little unexpected rendezvous ... wasn't nothing, just some late night freak shit." I was breaking my own promise to keep it hushed. The awkwardness of the conversation in line was uncomfortable.

"Was she bad?"

"She all right ... white chick."

"You knocked off a white chick?" Lamont's over reaction was amusing. "You fucked a white bitch?"

"Damn nigga ... you loud enough," I answered, laughing nervously. An older sister was standing right behind us. Just then, a hostess led us to our seats. I looked around the room to see any familiar faces, and sure enough I saw an old co-worker.

"Hey, Fergie," I called out. She was with some other girlfriends.

"Hey there, Moore," she responded. I went over and gave a friendly hug. "So when you coming back?" We laughed, but she knew that'd never happened.

"I'm good."

"So did you go to another school? Where are you now?" she asked. Here we go again. The charade was never-ending.

"I'm actually going back to school."

"Oh really, that's good. What are you working on?"

"I'm going for my masters ... looking at education administration."

"That's good ... you know everybody going to PV, is that where you are?"

"No, I'm doing mine online..."

It was like a tennis match, going back and forth with her questions.

"Well, it's good seeing you...come by happy hour Wednesday."

"Yeah ... it's good seeing you, too," I told her, proceeding on.

When I took my seat, Lamont looked at me with that puzzled face he gets when he smells bullshit.

"Have you told any of your co-workers about the money?"

"You, my mama and brother, the lawyers in New York, that's it."

"I feel you dog, but be realistic ... you driving around in a $300,000 car, and a month ago you was clocking into work. C'mon dude, think about that." Lamont was a voice of reason, for a conversation I wasn't ready to have.

"I'm a figure it out some kind a way. Maybe I don't drive the Ghost around town much." It was a silly notion, believing I'd maintain some sense of privacy.

Later on after finishing our breakfast, I offered to show Lamont the new apartment and my other new toy. His earlier statement stayed with me a bit. *Did I need to get rid of the cars?* Eventually someone was going to see me whether it was at a supermarket parking lot or valet service in front of some club. There wasn't a way to formally tell someone, "By the way, I'm the mystery winner of last month's lottery jackpot." The delicacy of it hinged on my ability to stay under the radar, balancing my anonymity, with my taste for the finer things in life.

"Man, I forgot to ask. Did you tell Gwen?" he questioned.

"I thought about it, even thought about getting back with her, but I met this girl, man. I'm feeling her."

"The white girl," Lamont interrupted.

"Nah, man … Puerto Rican chick. Met her at a club in the Bronx, she's a teacher."

"What she look like, she got a fat ass?" Lamont chimed.

"She got that, but more than that, she got good conversation. As far as Gwen … I still got love for her. We had lunch a few days ago. She called when I was in New York. You know I'm a look out for her."

"I ain't gone lie, Gwen was good for you, bro."

"She was, until she decided we couldn't work. You forgot that shit?"

"Nah, I know she fucked up, but before she fucked up, she was a good woman." The oddity of talking about Gwen in the past tense was surreal. Even though seeing her was cool, Yami was that new business.

"So this new chick, how you gone do that? You gone move her out here, fly back and forth every other week?"

"I don't know hater, let me think about it."

Lamont was hitting me with questions worth considering. But ultimately, it was Yami's decision to make. "You need to run through these hoes first, see how you like single life, you might wanna stay single, take it from me."

Most of my married guy friends discouraged holy matrimony. With Gwen, it was as if we'd already taken vows; we never lived together, but did everything else. Maybe for her, the concept of marriage was fleeting. You just never know what's going on in someone's heart, why two people grow in different directions. Gwen got tired of me … tired of life.

"If she wanna move out here, it'll be after we do the long distance thing first. I'm a still date though," I replied.

"You talking all that mess, you ain't gone do shit you one woman man you. You ever cheat on Gwen?"

"No."

"See, that's what I'm talking about. You need to date, you too rich to be falling in love right away. Mother fuckers ready to trap that ass with some pregnancy shit and that child support shit." Lamont was being hilarious as usual, and in some ways, truthful.

"Nigga, my pull out game is impeccable."

We decided to go to the Galleria to kill some time. Driving through Houston felt different in this car. It's weird, but in a way, I wasn't "black" anymore. Rich was another race. Having money meant people listening to me, catering to my every whim.

Every time I went to the Galleria, I'd stop at three stores: Footlocker, Gucci (to look around, while being watched), and Macy's. Today, I was buying something in every one of them, just because I could. In Footlocker, I saw some Jordan's and bought them while Lamont looked around. Then we went to Gucci. Immediately the program began, but I was clowning today.

As soon as we walked in, those familiar glares from the sales people, all dressed in black, with their strictly professional and stoic faces, welcomed us. In my broke days, I never asked how much shit cost, or tried shit on, to not raise their hopes. I'd look at something, admire it, and move around.

Today, it was all about shoes, being a shoe head, especially for loafers and tennis shoes. "Ma'am," I motioned for the attention of one of the salespeople. "I'd like to get this in a size 11, please." The saleswoman proceeded to inventory.

"$695 for these nigga," Lamont said.

"C'mon man, quality is always worth it. Just try 'em on" When the saleslady returned with the shoes, I asked her to get Lamont the shoes he liked in his size. I put on the pair I requested, getting a feel for them. I briefly turned my head and saw one of the sales guys hovering at attention; *no big deal*. When the saleslady came back with Lamont's shoes, he tried them on.

"How you like 'em?"

"They cool, they fit," he said.

"Ma'am, we'll take both pair." Lamont did a double take.

"You sure, nigga?"

"Man, you tripping dog," I told him. After selecting a few more items, we purchased and left out with two *Gucci* bags in each hand. Shit was fun.

"You know Dana gone be mad as hell."

"Why?"

"I was in mother fucking Gucci and didn't bring her back shit." We laughed about it. I offered to go back, but he declined. I appreciated that he wasn't trying to "come up." More was in store for my brother.

We went a few other places, but didn't see anything interesting, so we bounced. "Hey, I have to go to the Benz dealership a quick minute. You got something to do?" I asked.

"No, I'm straight … getting hungry again though." We got to the garage, packed all the goods up and got back onto Westheimer.

"Man, I appreciate the shoes, but you know I ain't no Gucci nigga."

"It ain't nothing … you're welcome." An awkward silence followed.

"Don't go changing on me, Doug, that's all I ask."

"What made you say that?"

"Nah man, I'm just saying, you in a good space right now. Just don't act funny with me, that's all I'm saying."

"You ain't got nothing to worry about."

We pulled into the dealership and parked right up front. Amazingly, a sales guy came dashing out to assist us.

"Good afternoon gents, how may I help you?"

"Well actually, there's a young lady working here, I forget her name, but she worked with me on the purchase of my G55. Is she here?" The sales guy's face cracked a little.

"Oh, that would be Ms. Cynthia Rodgers, I'll go get her. Come have a seat." We followed him in and about five or so minutes later she came walking from the back. "You bought the truck from her? She bad," Lamont whispered.

"Mr. Moore, good to see you again. How's the S.U.V. running?" she asked.

"It's great, hadn't had a problem, yet."

"Well that's good, we aim to please. So what brings you by today?"

"Well, this is my good buddy, Lamont."

"Nice to meet you, Mr. Lamont," she said while shaking his hand.

"He's also in the market for a new vehicle, so …" Lamont immediately looked at me like *what the fuck?*

"Doug, what you doing?"

"Hold on a minute, Lamont … so I brought him here to take a look around and for you to give him the good deal you gave me."

"You know that's not a problem …" she said before Lamont interrupted again.

"Ma'am, can you excuse us for just a moment, please?" Lamont asked.

"No problem," she said as she walked back to the reception area.

"Man, what you doing?"

"What you mean, what I'm doing? I'm buying my best friend a car."

"Man you ain't got to do ..."

"I know I ain't got to do it, but I'm able to. God blessed me, now I'm blessing my friend ... you see a problem in that?" Lamont went quiet.

"I appreciate it ... don't get it in your head that you gotta buy me stuff."

"You been knowing me 10 years. I saw Ramsey when he was born. When you met Dana ... we niggas, stop tripping. Enjoy this shit with me." We dapped each other and called Cynthia back over.

"Like I was saying, my friend is in the market for a new car, so I'm going to let him tell you what he wants, 'cause I don't know."

"Well, Mr. Lamont, what did you have in mind?" she asked. Lamont was so bewildered. You could almost read his thoughts. His facial expression was like a kid on Christmas day. "Well, think of it this way, how would this car benefit your lifestyle?" she asked. Lamont looked at me with a devilish grin, knowing exactly what it meant. "Do you have a family?" Immediately, his demeanor changed.

"Yeah, I'm married with a son. I guess a family car would be nice." Lamont grimaced at telling the truth.

Cynthia took us on a test drive of several cars, one in particular being the S-class. I knew it was a bit much for Lamont, Dana, and Ramsey, but again, this was my friend and his family, and money was no object.

We also checked out the CLS and the E. The CLS was cool, with its coupe like design, even though it was a 4-door. The E was okay, but it looked boring.

"So what you think, man?" Lamont asked. It was about 6 by then.

"I mean, it's up to you really ... if I had to pick, it'd be between the S and CLS."

"Yeah, those two, but damn ... it's a hard choice."

"It's a nice hard choice," we all laughed.

"I think I'm a go with the S, it's a nice big body, spacious car ... Dana gone trip when I bring this home, man," Lamont exclaimed.

"Okay, so we're going with the S, all in agreement?" Cynthia asked.

Lamont and I responded in unison with "yes." We dapped and hugged each other and walked back in the dealership. That familiar euphoric feeling happened, my secret drug ... doing nice things for people felt good spiritually and physically. Somewhere was a balance to find, but for now, it felt right.

After we finished with the particulars of the business, Lamont asked if I'd follow him to show Dana, but I declined. I didn't need to be the star of the show a second time. Lamont's genuine appreciation was enough. Afterward, back at the crib, I made plans for the next day, booking limousine service for my family's arrival. Then I decided to take a leisurely drive in the Rolls down Westheimer.

Driving down that pot hole-riddled stretch of road, pushing the sunroof back and putting on my Robert Glasper CD, the sky was beautiful at dusk, with hues of burnt orange, lavender and gray. Block by block, basking in the attention I received, the scenery was awesome with a new set of eyes. Every iconic landmark looked different from the driver's seat. When I reached River Oaks, just past Lamar High School, a River Oaks cop pulled up behind me, seemingly to be inconspicuous. I hadn't any plates yet. Then, he pulled off, and I laughed out loud.

Another five minutes down the road was the bourgeoisie Highland Village area, with all its high end restaurants, stores, and shops. Usually you'd see the yuppie crowd roaming about. Just down the way was Sullivan's, where Lamont and I would go for live music and Tavern steak. Continuing on, driving under the 610 overpass, I was in the Galleria area, another high end spot for Houston's well to do, and aspiring. Because of the attention, I realized I was in a small fraternity—the Rolls-Royce fraternity. So many people of all ages and races just stared at the car and me. Presumably, I was one of the Houston Rockets or Texans, the not so famous one.

I finally reached the Fountain View intersection, my old stomping ground, my former apartment was just around the corner, down the street from Chacho's. No damn way would I travel such a distance to pass up a large limeade, chicken fajita nachos with refried beans and queso cheese on the side. Pulling into the drive thru line in my $300,000 car, I placed my order. My previous promise of never eating in the car was overruled. This was Chacho's. Pappas barbeque would've been a different matter, with the sauce and shit. But on this day, after receiving my order, I pulled over to the side of the parking lot, engine running, and prepped my box of chicken fajita nachos, carefully pouring the hot queso cheese evenly over the nachos, ensuring that every chip was blessed with hot, gooey, goodness. Afterward, I popped a few chips for satisfaction, following a few swigs of cold and tasty limeade. I put the car in drive, and continued down Westheimer, to Highway 6.

These were the simple things worth maintaining and perhaps had I done the media thing, the unnecessary attention would eventually diminish its value. The car wasn't necessarily under the radar, but the driver was. If I wanted to, I could go to the movies, the mall, or grocery store in ambiguity. I took I-10 east back downtown, reflective of my discussion with Lamont. The idea of being a recluse and victim of my new found wealth didn't sit well with me.

MAMA 'NEM [17]

The following morning, the time had come. Today's agenda was pretty simple: get Mom, Devin and his family from the airport, drop their shit off at the apartment, go somewhere for breakfast, ride around town for a 99 cents store for Mom, go get some pork ribs for Mom, take her home for a nap, then look up movie showings, and then dinner.

However mundane the day would be, it'd be with my family whom I loved and hadn't seen in over two years. The driver called and said that he was downstairs and waiting. I got my things and made my way down. The limo was a white Cadillac, a definite dramatic presentation. Her facial expression would be priceless when she realized she'd be riding in this and not my 98 Ford Explorer Sport.

I greeted the driver and got in. It was your standard plushness with TV screens, wet bar and partition. I felt like a boss riding in the back of the 'Lac, while traveling down 45 south, towards Hobby Airport. Suddenly, for some reason, the urge to call Gwen hit me.

"Hey, Doug," she answered.

"Hey Gwen, what's up with you?"

"I'm good … you back in town?"

"Yeah, I'm back, just wanted to see how you were."

"I'm good … I got the job from that interview I had last time we met."

"Oh, great … good for you."

"Yeah thanks, I start tomorrow … today's my last free chill day, thank God."

"I heard that. Well congratulations again."

"Thank you. So how was New York?" When she asked that simple question, one that should've been met with enthusiasm, it burned my gut like a guilty little boy about to lie. "It was cool. Didn't do much, just handled some biz for the family. But I called to tell you, I'm on the way to pick my mama up from the airport, in case you wanna see her while she's here."

"Yeah, I'd love to see her."

We continued talking about getting together, and bringing Morgan around, but it felt weird. Since returning to Houston, I hadn't called Yami. All this daydreaming shit, playing myself for a woman who probably didn't think twice about a nigga.

We reached the arrivals area and I called Devin for their location. Based on the flight time, they were to land by11:15. His phone rang, but no answer. We tried staying in the area but HPD made us move, but not before I asked for the cop's attention.

"Officer, I'm waiting for my mother, it's her birthday... I'm trying to surprise her. Is there any way we can stay a bit longer?"

"I'll give you five minutes, then you're gonna have to circle around." I thanked him and informed the driver of the extra time.

Devin pissed me off. I called another four times. I tried my mother's phone and got her on the first try.

"Hello? Yeah we just getting off the plane, we in baggage claim right now."

"Is Devin with you?"

"Yeah, he's right here, you want him?"

"No, but tell him I've called 50 times trying to reach him." I could hear my mother actually pull away from the phone to tell him verbatim what I said.

"He said he turned his phone off."

"Okay, well, let me talk to him for just a minute."

"Hello."

"Man, turn your phone on."

"Yeah, I turned it off and forgot. My bad."

"Okay, well look, I got a limousine. It's white, so when y'all come out call me right quick, cause we may have to move since it's not a parking area."

"All right."

Ten minutes later, there still was no call from anybody. I was getting frustrated. We had to circle around twice before getting a response. Devin called me, "I had to take Jabari to the restroom to change his diaper. We heading out the door now." We circled for a third time when I spotted them up ahead. Devin noticed the limo and waved at us. When my mother saw the limo, her facial expression read pure shock, then laughter. Devin, his wife, and kids, all looked good. I hadn't seen the oldest nephew since he was two. I hugged them all.

"Now, now birthday boy. Is this how we do it?" my mother asked. She thought this was a big deal but the news I had would surely blow her mind.

"Y'all had a good flight?"

"Yeah, pretty good. Jabari was restless though." The driver started putting their bags in the trunk, as they got in. I looked at Devin like, *don't say anything.* I decided rather than waiting till dinner, I would tell her early. Too many other people knew already.

"Let's drop y'all stuff off first, then we can get some breakfast."

"Yeah cause I'm hungry," my mother's usual reply. She and I were "foodies."

"Doug, this is so nice, what made you get this?"

"Just something different," I answered. Devin and Grace looked at me knowingly.

"Where y'all wanna go, I.H.O.P., Denny's …?"

"I don't care, y'all decide," Mama said.

"Let's just figure it out after we put everything away.

Denny's…I.H.O.P…really? I don't wanna tell her in any of those places; maybe wait 'till dinner. Then again, when she sees my apartment, she'll get suspicious and ask questions, I don't know.

The ride back made up for the occasional talks on the phone, the difference in being with them, being able to touch them and look them in the eyes. "So, you got a girlfriend, huh?" Mom asked. Devin and Grace looked at me, waiting for an answer, but I smiled, slightly embarrassed. Mentioning Yami was premature.

"Nope, free man right here. Y'all got somebody for me?" We all laughed, but I knew the elephant in the room, or should I say limousine. *Think ahead and diffuse the bomb.* "Gwen and I talked on the way to pick y'all up, she said 'hello'… she wants to see you Mama."

"Oh that's nice. How's her son, Morgan?" The relief of addressing the issue early on eliminated any tension.

"Morgan is doing well, he just turned seven," I replied.

"Oh, that's wonderful. Glad to know they're doing okay."

By the time we made it back downtown, we had chosen Denny's. I decided to tell her at the apartment. There was no need in her fainting or speaking in tongues in public. When we reached my building, Grace and my mother were awestruck, "Wow Doug, you live here?" Grace said. "Nice." My mother just looked at me, shaking her head.

"What's going on?"

"What you mean?" I replied, concealing my laughter. The driver pulled up to the lobby entrance and Devin and I proceeded to get the bags out the trunk.

"You better tell me what's going on," she kept saying.

"Mama, what you mean?" I replied facetiously. When we entered the lobby area, they all looked around, taking in the elaborate layout.

"Man, how much you pay to live here?" Devin asked. He saw the look on my face and got the picture. One of the ladies at the reception desk recognized me and spoke. I introduced my family and proceeded to my apartment.

In the elevator, my mother kept looking at me, suspiciously of course. Devin, Grace, and I, did our best to maintain the charade. As we walked down the hall, they began oohing and aahing over the details, making me proud of my choice.

Opening the door, a cool breeze from the air conditioner hit us, along with the immediate view of Downtown Houston and the sound of Buddy Boy's barking. "Doug, this is nice ... how long you been here?" my mother asked, with her usual investigative tone. With a shred of discernment, she could tell this wasn't from district money.

"Not that long. You like it?"

"Do I like it?" she asked rhetorically. "I love it." Her approval was important, but the best was yet to come.

Just before the last New York trip, I put furniture from a local chain in the guest rooms. It wasn't over the top, just something to make it comfortable. Down the line, I'd eventually upgrade to some higher end stuff.

I pulled Devin to the side. "I'm gonna tell her now before she acts up in public, crying and shit. Let's just get it over with." Another five minutes of her and Grace walking from room to room went by, while the boys played with Buddy. I called them all into the living room.

"I'm really glad y'all made it."

"You know we love you, Doug," my mother replied.

"I know, and I love y'all too, which is why I wanted y'all here in the first place." My heartbeat raced, with that familiar flash of heat rushing through. I was coming clean. "Well, mom, I actually told you this already, you just didn't believe me."

"What? What you tell me?"

"Remember when we were talking, maybe three weeks ago, and you brought up the lottery winner?"

"Yeah, I said somebody won in Houston," she replied. I smiled, waiting for her to process it. When it clicked, her eyes grew large and she became speechless. She even pretended to faint.

Devin, Grace, and I, even the kids began laughing. What took weeks to get out was officially said and done.

"Doug don't play with me. Are you for real?"

"Wait right here," I said, going to my bedroom to get the ticket which I framed and the printed page from the lottery website. When I returned, she was gasping for air, still in shock."Here's the ticket I purchased, and here are the numbers from the lottery website." She looked at the numbers meticulously, then looked at me and started crying.

Overwhelmed by her emotion, I cried along with her. The realization of finally making it, with no more bills to play catch up with, or living check to check, came true. All the whimsical imaginations of "one day" were now, instead of looking at life through the likes of *Oprah* and *them*, she was now one of *them*.

"Words cannot express ... words cannot express," she kept repeating, as she occasionally spoke in tongues. Grace even teared up a little, while Devin looked on, indifferent.

"Mama, you know this means you'll never have to worry about a bill for the rest of your life." The tears flowed down her face as she listened to me. Her immediate happiness was worth more than anything I could give her.

"I've already set up accounts for y'all; and the boys have a trust fund."

"Thank you, Doug," Devin offered, pretending to cry, mocking Mama, who in turn gave him a stern look.

"If you don't mind, I'd like for y'all to consider moving down here permanently. I'll buy houses for y'all, so we can be together. I'm not saying you have to live here, it can be wherever, but the cost of living is cheaper." Devin and Grace remained quiet, while my mother raised hands and rejoiced.

"You know I love Houston, that's fine with me, thank you son." She got up to give me a hug, while I looked over at Devin.

"Listen, it's not a deal breaker, I just thought it'd be nice to live in the same city, plus you can get a lot more house for your money than Cali … y'all know that."

"I know, it's just all of sudden. We need to talk about it. It's not a bad idea, we just need to plan for the move and all, get junior set up in a new preschool, stuff like that."

"Well you know I'll help with all the transition stuff. We can go looking at neighborhoods, all that."

The hesitation on his part seemed weird for something most people wouldn't have thought twice about. My intentions were simple and transparent. Maybe the issue was Grace's side of the family. I wasn't sure.

"Let's just enjoy the rest of the day. You guys will stay with me so go put your bags in the room. Any room is fine, except my room, the big spacious one on the left." Devin smirked, while Grace and mom snickered.

After we put the bags away, we decided to go for breakfast, but of course I had to show my new cars. "Doug, a Rolls-Royce? This is so beautiful, ooh I love it," my mother exclaimed. Devin on the other hand was smitten with the truck. "Man, you gotta let me drive this," he responded. *Fuck it, I'll buy him one.*

I reserved the limousine service for the entire day, so after we took a look at the cars, it was time to eat. My mother looked at me, shaking her head, crying again. I gave her a quick hug to console her. "So what now? What are you gonna do, still work?" Devin asked.

"Hell nah … I quit the same week, but none of my co-workers know."

"Who knows?"

"You guys, the lawyers I hired in New York, Lamont, that's about it," I replied.

I supposed that Devin was being concerned for my well-being. He was the strong, silent type. The questions were inevitable but accepted. There was a time when we weren't as close, but I appreciated the men that we'd become and proud of his ability to carve out a life for himself with just a high school education.

My mother sat back, visibly reflective of all that went on that morning. I wished I could read her thoughts. I'm sure she thought of Dad, imagining how much more the moment could be with him here. We stopped at a Denny's on the corner of Southmore and 288. The limo guy tried finding available parking while we walked in. It was semi packed for a Sunday morning and we were led to a booth, enjoying the normalcy of the environment. Exactly what I loved.

We all placed our orders, and Mother being who she is, remarked about the cost of the items on the menu, temporarily forgetting she was a millionaire. From time to time I'd look at her like, *c'mon*. Afterward, we got back in the limo.

"Where to now, Mama?" I asked. In the back of my mind, knowing, pleading even, I hoped she wouldn't mention the 99 cents store.

"I don't know, Devin, Grace, did y'all have some place y'all wanted to go?"

"You mind if we go to the Galleria?" Devin asked.

"Of course not."

"Yeah that's perfect. They should have a 99 cents store in there," she said. We all gasped for air, even Grace.

"What? I can't go to the 99 cents store no more?"

"Mama, you can do whatever you want," I replied.

When we reached the mall, we made a plan to meet back up in about an hour. Devin and Mom had visited before and were somewhat familiar with the layout. Devin and I went in our own direction, while Mom, Grace, and the boys went theirs. It was a perfect time to discuss what I'd done for Devin financially.

"So man, what does it feel like?" Devin asked.

"What? The money?"

"Yeah, when you won, what did you do?"

"I just froze up. At first, I wanted to call y'all, but for some reason I just froze up."

"I would a went crazy if I won," he said.

"But you won, too … we family," I replied.

"I mean, I know we family and everything, but it's still your money."

"Devin, I created an account in your name with lawyers and accountants and shit. I put $10 million in it. Half of that is a trust fund for the boys. On top of that, I'm buying you a house … we won." Devin stopped walking and just looked at me.

"Are you fucking serious? $10 million?" In sheer amazement, he gave me the tightest hug I'd ever experienced from him, aside from the day of Dad's funeral. "We balling now bro, it ain't a game," I told him. Devin got teary eyed, stopping by the railing to take a break.

"You all right?" I asked, humored by his reaction.

"$10 million, that's a lot of money."

It was a perfect moment for explaining my reasons for living in the same city. "This is why I was saying y'all move down here. Maybe we start up a business or something; the cost of living is way cheaper. I'll take y'all around town, looking at neighborhoods." After I made my appeal, I waited for his response.

"I like it out here though. Y'all got sports and shit, nice restaurants. Let me just see what Grace says," he answered.

We went on walking, while I tried rationalizing his response. *It's a married thing*, supposedly. A few feet away, we saw a jewelry store. "Hey, let's go in here right quick, and see if we can find something for Mama." We walked in, greeted with smiles as if they knew we had money.

"Yes, how may I assist you today," the older saleswoman asked.

"Can we see some diamond tennis bracelets and earrings?"

"Surely, right this way," she replied, directing us to follow her. This was my fourth jewelry store visit in two weeks, the most I'd ever done in my whole adult life.

"So is your place a condo?" Devin asked.

"It's an apartment. I'm a look for some land and build something later."

"Oh, okay," he replied. We weren't savvy business people, but I was learning a lot from the lawyers and accountants. Maybe we'd start a McDonald's franchise or car wash, shit like that. I'd always wanted to get more into real estate, own an apartment building or build some houses, but never really anything more technical than that.

We spent a good 30 minutes looking at bracelets and earrings before deciding on something. Total cost, $7,695. Couldn't tell Mama that, she'd freak out and probably insist on returning the items after slapping us silly. We purchased them anyway and called up Mama and Grace to see where they were.

"She said they looking for the 99 cents store," Devin responded. I grimaced in bourgeoisie disdain.

"Tell her, we can look for one outside of the mall when we leave."

My mother's thriftiness was one of her good qualities. Using her approach, I'd never go broke.

Later on, we all met back up in the food court area, probably not the wisest decision. My mother and I had issues with food; we didn't know how to say no. Just the smells were enough to entice unnecessary eating. "Y'all ready?" I asked. I looked at my mother who had a suspicious look on her face. She had a funny way of playing dumb when she wanted something.

"Ah, what's that place there ... Taco Ca-ba-na?"

"Yes, Taco Cabana, Mama. You hungry again? We just ate." A little stern, her complaints about weight and high blood pressure didn't warrant an afternoon snack.

"Just wondering, that's all, we don't have to stop," she answered. After another 30 minutes of walking and stopping periodically, we finally decided to leave. The limo guy was parked at the front entrance. Finally situated in the back seat, I handed her the bag from the jewelry store. "Mom, this is for you." She immediately went into dismissal mode.

"You know you guys didn't have to do this." Getting her used to this lifestyle required patience. "What is it?" she asked, opening the bracelet box. Her amazed reaction with all five carats of diamonds said it all. Mama didn't really have a lot of fancy jewelry other than when she dressed really nice for work and church. She started crying again, and we endured.

"Dang, Mama, you ain't even get to the next box," Devin said.

"There's another one? Oh my God," she replied. When she reached in the bag she noticed the smaller box, the earrings, with the exact reaction of pure disbelief. The earrings were three carats.

We were proud of finally being able to do shit like that. We weren't athletes, entertainers, or prominent businessmen, just randomly blessed, a non-sacrilegious way of saying lucky. And the shit wasn't over. Tomorrow was house hunting day, while Devin and Grace had a decision to make.

After finding a 99 cents store, she made her little purchases and afterward, we went back to the apartment. It was nap time for me. Reservations were made for a really nice Latin restaurant on Gray Street near River Oaks, for my birthday dinner. "Hey y'all, I made dinner reservations for 8, we can go to the movies afterward." Everyone agreed, and I retreated to my suite to lie down, and map out the next day. Then it hit me: *Dr. Miles—you need to go handle that.* Without realizing, it was good that my family had come. I called the doctor's office. Luckily for me I had a doctor who liked working on weekends for his golfing Mondays.

"Hello, this is Dr. Miles' office, Anna speaking, how may I help you."

"Hey Anna, it's Douglas Moore, how are you?"

"Mr. Moore, yes good to hear from you. We got your lab results and we thought it was necessary for you to see a specialist regarding traces of blood in your urine." *Was this a minor or a serious issue?*

"Does that mean something?" I asked.

"It depends, which is why we recommend you see the specialist for an in-depth analysis." Those were probably the most words I'd ever heard her say, and the least desired. She gave a name and number of a specialist, and later, I made an appointment that week.

Blood in my urine, what the fuck could that mean? I immediately went to the internet, searching the topic, panicky with a million negative thoughts. A term, *hematuria* popped up. The description gave origins for a cause, from something as simple as kidney and bladder stones which caused bleeding, to having some type of urinary tract infection, or ultimately cancer along the urinary tract. Cancer was the last thing I wanted to see, given Andre's death a year ago.

Blocking negativity out of my mind was all I could do. *I'm too young to die.* Was this supposed to be a sick joke God was playing on me? Neither Devin nor my mother could know; she'd instantly go ham. Lamont was the other option, but I wasn't even sure of the issue. Confused and tired, I decided to calm down, take a few breaths, go to my trusty porn site and whack one off before taking a nap.

An hour later, refreshed and determined to enjoy my birthday, I went out into the living room where the family sat, watching TV. "You get your nap out?" Mama asked.

"Yeah, I'm hungry now, what about y'all?"

"I think you know the answer to that," Devin replied, giving Mama a side-eye.

"What you saying, Devin?" Mama responded.

"The limo guy is still outside, y'all."

"Can we go somewhere without the limo, I wanna ride in that Rolls-Royce," Mama answered. Devin just shrugged his shoulders.

"Okay, but we can't all fit, so Mama you can ride with me ... Devin you drive the truck."

"So, where to?" I asked.

"What's that place you took me for the ribs ... Pappis, Pappas?"

"Pappas, Mama," I said sternly. She knew exactly why. With high blood pressure, pork was the last thing she needed to eat.

"You know you ain't supposed to eat pork, right?"

"I can't live a little?" she responded.

"You keep eating like that, and that's exactly what'll happen."

"Good one, Doug," she responded sarcastically.

"All right ... suit yourself, only trying to help. But I'm a cancel dinner plans."

"Why, son?"

"After Pappas, you ain't going to want anything else." She looked at me, rolled her eyes and smacked her lips. I held firm.

I decided to relieve the limo driver for the rest of the evening, and we hit the streets in the cars. Mama took pleasure in riding shotgun in the Rolls; she kept oohing and aahing over every little detail.

"So, how much for this?" she asked. I was tired of dodging the issue of money.

"$315,000. This watch I'm wearing, it's called a Hublot, pronounced hue-blow ... yeah, it cost me $75,000. That bracelet and set of earrings we just got you ... eight grand." She needed to know and get used to it.

"Okay big timer, just wondering."

"It's okay, Mama ... just telling."

SAME SHIT, DIFFERENT DAY [18]

As we drove, the guilt of conceding over the pork ribs, lingered.
"Mama, I'm glad y'all came out here ..."
"Glad you brought us out, Doug."
"Yeah, you know I care about you, right?"
"I know."
"Mama ... pork ribs with high blood pressure?"
"You acting like the food police, Dougie. I'm on vacation, can I have some ribs?" She responded in her typical sing-song defensive way. It was a regrettable break down in our attempts at adult communication.

"Fine, but just think about the reason for the conversation." She went silent. "I'm sorry if I upset you, just caring ... one day I hope to have kids. Don't you wanna see that?" She seemed at ease, aside from her usual dramatic breathing.

"You're right. I need to be careful, but I just really like the barbeque here. You know we ain't got too many barbecue places like this back home."

About 10 minutes later we reached the rib joint. The welcoming aromas reminded me of how much of a guilty pleasure this place was. A real down home atmosphere, with an oversized menu board on the wall.

One of my favorite things to get was the stuffed potato. I never saw a potato the length of boys' size 3 shoes until I moved to Houston. And forget about the fixings; scoops of butter, sour cream with gobs of cheese and whatever choice of barbecued meat with barbecue sauce splattered on top. It was a ridiculous collage of decadent demise and the ribs ... fall-off-the-bone-deliciousness.

173

"How the drive feel?" I asked Devin. Obviously pleased, he was cheesing from ear to ear.

"Man, I like it … I'm buying one of those."

"Huh, excuse me?" Grace interrupted.

"What? I like the truck, I want one," Devin replied. To hear him flippantly declare that he was buying a $100,000 S.U.V. and being financially able to do it made me proud.

"Well, you make sure I get something, too," Grace demanded.

After an enjoyable lunch, Mama looked like a big o' pacified baby. I can't lie. I was ready for another *itis* nap myself. When we left out I told Devin to follow me for a leisurely drive through River Oaks to kill a little time.

"Mama, tomorrow we can go looking around for houses…" Her eyes lit up.

"For real, Doug?"

"Mama you can't live in that place anymore, especially all alone. That neighborhood ain't what it used to be."

"So what you saying?" she replied, sounding offended.

"I'm saying you can stay with me, until we find a nice new place out here."

"You really want me to stay with you? That's not gone cramp your style?" She had a point. Hopefully we could find something within a good month of shopping around.

"It's fine. We'll look until you find something you like."

About ten minutes or so, we were in River Oaks. Immediately my mother reveled at the obvious contrast and stateliness of the neighborhood. "This looks like Beverly Hills." From time to time, I'd take leisurely drives, street by street, imagining what coming home would be like. Back when I dated Gwen, we talked about the "what if" of moving to a place like this. Her reply was simple: "They don't want us here." It was disappointing the way she thought in the 21st century. My belief was that all possibilities were mine. My mother never told me what I could or couldn't do based on my skin tone, and I was grateful for that.

"This is a real nice neighborhood … what do the homes go for?"

"It depends, but nothing's less than $2 million, easy." We kept driving until we noticed a for sale sign; the house was decent, stately, and older.

"Do you like that, Mama?"

"It's okay, not my cup of tea." We kept on, from street to street, where every new turn revealed something better than the last.

"Ooh, I like that," she responded. A French Chateau styled, newly constructed home, had a for sale sign. We pulled over looking for any flyers attached to the sign. When I got back in the car, I gave her the flyer to read.

"How much is the house going for?" I asked. She reached in her purse to get her glasses.

She looked down at the paper, and then back at me, "$3.8 million."

"Is that too much?"

"Ah, a little rich for my blood," she replied sarcastically.

"But I'm the one paying for it, the price shouldn't concern you."

"I don't need that much house, too much."

"Is it the price you don't like or what?"

"Doug, you know I have a simple taste and I like nice things, but nah…too expensive." I didn't wanna push, so I dropped it.

"Okay, Mama, we'll keep looking."

"Doug, you know I'm blessed to have a son who can buy me whatever, but the super fancy things ain't me and I don't need them to be happy." As whole-hearted her words were, she confused me. When we were growing up, she was always considered one of the best dressed women in church. Back in those Reagan 80s, we had aspirations for more. Dad would drive through the nice parts of town, while marveling at the palatial homes. That desire and knowledge came from them, and now this?

"Mama, I appreciate what you're saying. I don't wanna push you into anything. Spending good quality time with family, having good conversations with friends, things like that mean more. But I'm in a position to change what life was. The struggling, barely getting by, I don't think that's the life God intended, and surely I don't think this money is a sin. All I'm saying is for once live like you've never lived, experience the things you've only read of other people experiencing. It's not a sin for you to have a big old house worth millions of dollars. If anything, you deserve it."

She remained quiet, looking straight ahead. "Well, let's just keep looking, but I don't need that house." We continued driving for another 30 minutes, going through almost every block until reaching the other side of River Oaks Boulevard. "You got a sweet tooth, I have a sweet tooth. Ever had a beignet?" I asked.

"No, what's that?"

"It's like a doughnut without the hole, with powdered sugar sprinkled all over it. Wanna try one?" It was my attempt to lighten the mood that carried over from the previous conversation. We pulled into Crescent City Beignets, a small shop right on Westheimer, across from Lamar High School. I went in and ordered two dozen. "Here try one." Mama reached into the bag, and picked one up.

"I don't wanna get this sugar all over the car ..."

"Mama, don't worry, I've already eaten in it." She took a bite, and seemingly enjoyed it. "These are big in Louisiana ... I first tried this in New Orleans at this place called Café du Monde."

"Oh, it's French, huh?"

"Yeah, you like it?"

"It's pretty good, but all this sugar, going everywhere."

Devin called."What's this place we just left?"

"It's kind of a pastry shop, they make beignets. I got enough for everybody."

"What the hell is that?"

"You'll see when we get back to the house."

"Okay cool, by the way I think you need to get some more gas."

"For real? I ain't been driving that thing that much, but okay, I'll pull up to the first gas station I see." We drove a few blocks heading back towards downtown until I spotted a Texaco on the corner at the Montrose intersection. Montrose, an interesting, eclectic part of town is mostly known for its gay community.

Devin drove up to a pump while I pulled to the side. I jumped out to start the pump, while Mama waited in the car. Out of nowhere, two youngsters pulled up in an old school Chevy Caprice, which was somewhat odd for this urban, yet yuppie neighborhood. I played it cool, not wanting to think the worst of anything. They went to a pump, and I continued minding my business.

I took pause, looking at my two beautiful cars, feeling like the motherfucking man. *Who does this?* Then I pulled it back in. *Calm down.* For a minute, lost in my reality, this new baller status was what many "black" men my age, craved.

The urge to be pissed at the escalating price of pumping gas, irked me. The shit was just going and going, until at the end my total was $89. Eighty-nine fucking dollars to fill up. Crazy. At least with the Ford, most times it was between 49 and 55 bucks, a major difference.

Just as I finished, the two youngsters pulled off and circled back around to exit by the Rolls. When they got closer to the car, they slowed down, creeping by it, while I took notice, ready to rush to my mother's aid. They sped off, jocking I guessed. My assumption was embarrassing. During my broke days, had I seen a similar car at the gas station, I'd use more discretion than they did, but all they wanted was a good look.

Maybe Lamont had a point. If I was gone do this thing, do it all the way, or not at all. And since I desired this life, and actually got it, accepting all that came with it, was equally important.

After I finished pumping and paying, I hopped back in the car with Mama, exiting back to Westheimer with Devin right behind. Our hot little caravan held the attention of onlookers, getting the best show of the day. We were two black men, who'd never been to jail, who'd never sold any drugs of any kind, driving some expensive cars, in anonymity.

"You okay, Mama?"

"I'm fine. Didn't know what they wanted," she replied.

"They wanted to know who the pretty lady was in the pretty car." She chuckled a bit, and all was right with the world again.

The afternoon had turned out to be a pretty good family excursion of good food and some sight-seeing. Everybody looked to be visibly tired, or at least under the spell of the *itis*. When we reached back to the apartment, I decided to break away for a bit and head back to my room for a quick nap. Lying in bed, Yami came to mind and the sudden urge to call followed. It was around 4:45, 5:45 her time. *Fuck it,* I thought. I'll give her a call and leave a quick message. The phone rang and the nerves jumped.

"Hello?" *Oh shit she picked up the phone.*

"Hey, Yami, it's Doug … the guy from Houston, I met you at the club with Raul and …"

"Hey, Doug, yeah, how are you? I was looking at this number like, what's this area code?" We shared a laugh, while I rejoiced that the conversation had legs.

"Yeah, so how are you?" I asked.

"I'm good. You're actually catching me right at a good time."

"Good for me," was my corny reply.

"So you're back in Houston, right?"

"Yeah, I should've called before leaving. I wanted to take you to dinner and a play on Broadway, but I didn't know if you were into that sort of thing."

"I love Broadway, even though I've never been. Are you kidding me?" Her laughter put me at ease, and shot my confidence up. "So why didn't you call me?" she asked. *Good question.*

"I got a little busy at the end, my schedule, but I kept thinking about you. I hope that doesn't sound creepy." I could feel my body melting, crucifying any shred of self-dignity left in me.

"That's funny 'cause I asked Raul about you a few days later …you took my number, but never gave me yours." *Damn baby, you asked about me?* For a quick second, I pulled away from the phone, rejoicing—her fine ass asked about me.

"Raul should've given you my number … any way, I just wanted to call, see how you're doing. Are you on Facebook?" *What an adolescent question.* My voice might as well cracked.

"Yeah, friend me or I'll friend you, either way," she answered. "When are you coming back to the Bronx?" she asked with a slight tone of humor.

"I was thinking of coming back for a weekend. My family is visiting from California, so I'm playing host right now."

"Okay, when you decide to make that trip again, give me a call this time."

"It'll be sooner than later," I replied. "All right, Yami, it was good talking to you and I'm glad you remembered me."

"I can't forget Douglas. Call me, talk to you later." We hung up, and I beamed like a teenager.

Immediately I began fantasizing about our lives together. Yami was now in Houston with her daughter, our happy 21st century, blended family. We'd live in a nice townhouse somewhere, I'd teach her how to drive if she didn't know already, and I'd pull some strings at the district.

We'd take nice family vacations, and of course fly to New York every six months so she could catch up with family. Her daughter would attend the best private schools in town. We'd pick her up from soccer practice or ballet. As a family, we'd go to the movies on Saturdays and church on Sundays. It was a quick playbook I'd drawn up in my head of how things could be. My desire to have a family, to be responsible to and for someone else like I was with Gwen and Morgan. I wanted that feeling again.

The thought of being used or taken advantage of hadn't crossed my mind. Whether Raul described me as a wealthy businessman or some nice guy with paper, for some reason, in my spirit, the bigger fear was falling head over heels, jumping out the window, too soon.

I decided to call the limo driver back because Mama still wanted to go to the movies. Everyone, even the boys seemed poised for a night out. So many thoughts about all that transpired in just a few weeks bombarded me. When I got like that, I usually ran to the aid of a blunt, but with the family around, it made it difficult to steal away.

A HOUSE IS NOT A HOME [19]

The next morning we all got a fresh start eating a homemade breakfast of cheese grits, scrambled eggs with cheese, bacon, sausage patties, and biscuits with grape jelly. My two-week old apartment was officially lived in with the traditional aromas of a morning feast, reminiscent of home. We were all together again, laughing, enjoying each other, void of any thoughts of wealth or status, like the good old days on Cypress Street. My mother was standing by the stove in her element, happy and humming while she cooked.

"So what's the plan?" Devin asked.

"Today is house hunting day, so more neighborhoods. I was thinking we could drive to Sugarland." Sugarland is a suburban city just outside of downtown Houston. Appealing, it interested family-oriented folks, represented by different cultures and racial backgrounds. A decent two story home could start in the $170s and run into the millions with areas like, Avalon, Riverstone, Sienna Plantation and of course Sweetwater.

"Sugarland, interesting name, why they call it that?" Mama asked.

"Sugarland was a major producer of sugar back in the day. There's actually a factory out there, but it's closed down now." The Sugarland area had a lot of interesting tidbits, including the numerous hidden prisons you wouldn't know existed out there.

By about 11:30, we were heading out the door. It was the same arrangement. I drove Mom, while Devin and family followed. The other night on the way home from dinner we stopped at Target to get car seats for the boys, realizing we'd been breaking the law.

The blessing of another beautiful brisk fall day, met with the sun shining brightly, was perfect for a convertible. *Hmmm, a convertible, that sounds nice.* Looking over at Mama who was looking down at her crossword booklet caused a moment of gratitude. "Can you believe this?" I asked her.

"What's that?" she replied.

"Just everything." My reflection, usually reserved for friends in weed cyphers, was a realization of the transition our lives had made, with no true effort of our own.

Then my mother hit me with, "You just make sure you pay your tithe." That was a hard pill to swallow, due to the guilt of my Pentecostal upbringing. Tithe for me meant $16.5 million. Surely, I wasn't giving one church that amount of money. With the recent scandals going on at these mega churches around the country, my confidence was shaky.

"Do you know how much money I got after I paid all my state and federal taxes?" She looked at me in anticipation. "$165 million and my tithe, based on the 10 percent rule would be $16.5 million. Mama, I ain't giving one church that much money. I'll donate to churches and causes, something like that, but nah."

She looked at me, shrugged her shoulders and said, "What you want me to say?"

"So you think I should give a church that kind of money ... like who? T.D. Jakes, Creflo Dollar, TBN?" She could sense the sarcasm. My issue was with the misappropriation of hard-working people's money for personal gain in the "business" of religion. Not that the men and women of God shouldn't be blessed and receive financial gifts, but to have a million churches in the hood with no true affect?

"I'm starting a charity. As a matter of fact I created it in your name and Daddy's name." She looked at me in astonishment.

"Really, Doug? That's a blessing, God is gonna bless you for that."

"Yeah. You think a church would've done that?" I snidely remarked. She looked at me and the smile quickly went away.

"I'm not looking to fight with you over this money. Do what you feel God has led you to do, just remember you're blessed."

My upbringing was extremely religious. As kids, going to church at least three to four times a week was normal. Mama was the church organist, and Dad was on the deacon board.

My mother's comments bothered me. Donating to a few churches wouldn't hurt. Public donations through my lawyers would keep things transparent. "Tell you what, I'll donate $1 million to your church, or whatever church you want."

"You'll be blessed, Doug. Don't forget how we raised you."

The traffic on 59 south ran pretty smoothly on the way to Sugarland. My regular speed of fast, weaving in and out of lanes, caused her to glance at me with contempt. She hated my driving, but the blame was the V12 engine. The pickup was ridiculous and I loved it. "You looking for a ticket?" she asked rhetorically. I smirked, looking in the rear-view mirror for Devin.

Exiting at Highway 6, amidst a plethora of shopping centers, any and every major franchise store and restaurant was in that dense populated area. It was middle class paradise. "Dang, sure are a lot of shops around here," she commented with that familiar tone.

"After we drive around, we can stop somewhere for lunch," I replied.

The blandness of Sugarland provided a contrived sense of security. Neither close nor far from downtown Houston, in just about every subdivision was a rolling neighborhood security guard, covertly racially profiling.

We rolled into one area, a secluded neighborhood, with a faux manned gate, immediately stocked with Spanish and French influenced mansions and lavishly adorned wrought iron fences and gates. "What do you call this area?" she asked.

"This is Sweetwater." She seemed impressed.

"What do the houses go for out here?"

"Some of these homes cost the same as River Oaks." She continued looking.

"How far is this from your apartment?"

The question really meant, *how far is too far in case of an emergency?* As much as I love my mother, I needed the space and ability to be alone. Even with my willingness to house hunt every day, I secretly held a time-frame in which to complete this task— six months tops.

"Are there black people out here?"

"I'm sure there are … maybe a few of the Houston Texans."

"Oh yeah, you know some of them?" she asked with childlike interest.

"I don't know them. It's rumored that some of them live in the area."

The type of house I envisioned for her, could easily cost over a million dollars. Besides the occasional family visits, it needed secure grounds and space, but not the look of ignorant gaudiness. With her being a southern girl, having a big lush back yard, and possibly a lake view was key. We could hire a landscaping service to take care of the grounds once a week, while she sat, sipping lemonade and looking on. Furthermore, she would have a live in maid, someone young but not too young, who'd clean the house and cook if Mama wanted it. She wouldn't have to lift a finger for anything.

"Ooh that's a nice house over there," she said, looking up to the left. It was more like a vain monstrosity, the exterior was off-white stucco with natural wood shutters and window seals. It had a Spanish tiled roof and an elaborate wrought iron fence in front of the property.

"You like it, huh?" I asked, hoping it wasn't for sale.

"It's nice, I really like it." The properties she seemed to gravitate to were reminiscent of the homes in California. Maybe subconsciously she didn't want to move and was only appeasing me.

"Mama, you sure you wanna move here? I ain't trying to force your hand. If you wanna stay in California, it's fine with me." She looked over with a mixture of anger and confusion. The question posed a tone, a delicate line between genuine concern and proximity, at least in her mind.

"Are you sure you want me living here?" *Here we go … irrational.*

"I'm just making sure … these houses look like the ones in Arcadia and South Pasadena."

"I don't see it that way," she laughed.

After a few turns of a few blocks, the entrance to another gated neighborhood was just ahead. "That looks interesting, what's that?" she asked. We drove closer, turning right into the community. A sheriff's car was parked on the corner, and it immediately triggered my middle-class nervousness.

In my temporary lapse of reality, I forgot that I had enough money to buy 10 to 15 houses in this neighborhood if I wanted. My composure and confidence re-aligned, and we drove right past.

These were the grandest, most extravagant homes. They were on par with River Oaks and probably any other affluent community in all of Texas. "Wow, these houses are huge … I couldn't live here by myself," she said.

"You wanna leave?" I asked.

"No, I'm still looking."

After driving around in two big circles, we realized there were only ten houses in that entire neighborhood, a plus for privacy. It was just day one of house hunting, so it was important for me to be patient. Even if it meant her living with me for a year, there was no way she was going back to the bullshit. I called Devin to check on him.

"Y'all all right back there?"

"Yeah we fine ... this is a nice neighborhood. Does she like it?" he asked.

"I guess so. Mama, Devin asked do you like this area?" She looked at me, smiling.

"I like what I see so far, but y'all not gone pressure me into nothing," she replied.

"She likes it," I told him.

We drove through a few more neighborhoods in the area before calling it a day. I had some personal things to do, Particularly, I needed to find a Houston-based attorney for my charity stuff. The local chapter of the N.A.A.C.P., my fraternity grad chapter, lodge house, T.S.U. and Prairie View A & M University were local organizations I wanted to get involved with.

Choosing a Houston lawyer to handle local matters made sense, now that I had my other affairs in order. The boys and girl in New York were my big dogs; they handled the bigger issues. My Houston attorney would be my mouth piece. His or her main objective was to act on my behalf, while I maintained my anonymity as much as possible. Whomever I hired would need to possess a working knowledge of Houston's elite culture, and the savvy to keep me unscathed by the hounds that would do me in.

The morning soon became the afternoon, by which time we had gone through several neighborhoods. Sienna Plantation turned out to be promising, despite the fact that I hated the name. Both Devin and Mama saw houses they liked. Afterward, we stopped for lunch at a restaurant in Sugarland Town Square. Town Square was a manufactured collection of shops and restaurants, attempting to replicate a modern version of a small town shopping center, adjacent to First Colony Mall, where it was typical to see Caucasian, Asian, Indian, Latino, and African American families milling about in middle-class purgatory.

"I liked that last house ... I could really live there," Mama said convincingly. A decent sized, one-story brick on an oversized lot, it was something manageable. Devin on the other hand, found interest in a two-story house that went for a million. It had five bedrooms, a four-car garage and pool with Jacuzzi out back. It was a drastic upgrade from his two-bedroom apartment.

Besides the excitement that goes with looking for a new home, it was important to be level-headed. Though I promised to buy whatever they wanted, I doubted if Devin and his family were ready for a five bedroom, million dollar house. The transition seemed too fast. In Mama's case, I wanted the best for her, no matter the audacity. Ultimately, I wanted her to be comfortable and not fearful of living alone.

After lunch, we drove back home. I dropped her off and continued driving through the city without plans. I thought about calling my old weed-connect for an ounce. A good buzz always put things in perspective.

"Yo, Doug, what's good, bro?" It was cool hearing Rocco's voice. Rocco was a New Orleans nigga who moved to Houston after Hurricane Katrina. We clicked because of my two favorite things: weed and the French Quarter.

"Hey, man, what's good with you?" Maybe a month had passed since my last pick up. As a matter a fact, the last time I bought from him was two weeks before winning.

"Man, I ain't seen you in a month, nigga, what's good?"

"I'm good. I moved out the complex two weeks ago."

"Oh, okay, that's what's up."

"Yeah man, lemme holla at a zip right quick."

"Yeah, I got that. You on the way right now?"

"Yeah, 'bout 15 minutes."

It hadn't dawned that I was driving to my old neighborhood in a $300,000 car, to get a $40 bag of weed. The etiquette of being rich hadn't settled in.

When I reached the complex, I opted to park at the reception office, the safest place, presumably. Getting out the car was bizarre. I lived here, and not too long ago. The old mailbox center, the community pool, all of it was just the way I left it. For a slight moment, I experienced homesickness. The routine of coming home from work, walking up a flight of stairs, going to Rocco's every week, for years, was second-nature. As hard as those days were, they shaped me as a man who could deal with everyday struggles and keep my sanity.

In a sense, my lottery win was like skipping the line. The guilt of it popped up from time to time, but reality prevailed. *If not me, then who? And why not me?* When I got to Rocco's, it was that old familiar smell of weed and more weed. A mix tape by D.J. Screw played while a young broad sat in the corner of the couch. Rocco was a slender built dude with a high-top bald fade. He wore gold fronts and had a tear drop tat by his left eye.

"My nigga, wassup?" Rocco and I gripped and hugged each other.

"Man, what's the deal? Been a minute, I was starting to get worried," he laughed.

"Nothing like that, just moving and shaking," I replied.

Rocco went to the table and picked up the baggie. It was just like old times, a little small talk, the hand off, and out the door. But today was different. The thought of not seeing him anymore had sentimental value. This type of trip would be risky from now on.

Rocco introduced his friend and then turned his attention to my watch. I'd forgotten I had on the Cartier with the brown alligator strap and the diamond bezel. "Man that watch fire! Where you get that shit?" I looked down at my watch like a proud father would his son.

"This shit, ah man I got this on Harwin, right behind one of them Chinese luggage stores." The Harwin area of Houston was known for selling knock-offs of everything, but his enthusiasm remained.

"Man I don't give a fuck that shit cleaner than a bitch." He had a good eye for quality. Nevertheless, I continued to play it down.

As we wrapped up, I begin walking out, but he followed. I believed it was to see me to the door. "All right my nigga," I said, as I walked off.

"Hold up, I'm going to the mailbox." *Fuck!*

What are the odds? This was one conversation I didn't want to have. "Yeah man I been fucking with that bitch a good month now she cool," he continued.

"Oh yeah, that's cool, where she from?"

"Shreveport."

"Oh, so she can cook up some shit," we laughed.

"Yeah, man, but shit you know me ... stay on the hunt."

The mailbox was just a few feet ahead of us and my mind went into overdrive. *How am I gone shake this nigga?* "Say bro, I'm a go to the office and hit the restroom. I'll holla at you later," I said, walking off yet again.

"All right my nigga stay up," he replied. I walked into the office, went to the restroom, and stood for five minutes, like a dumbass, updating my status. When I finally walked back out, there stood Rocco on the phone, still by the mailbox.

I walked by him and waved, heading towards the car. I hit the alarm, planning to jump right in and start it up, when all of a sudden I heard, "What the fuck nigga?" I held my head down, trying to ignore him, and again he yelled, but specifically, "Doug …say, Doug, man." I looked up and he had both his hands in the air, shaking his head like, *what the fuck?* He had the biggest country grin, with all his gold fronts shining like laser beams. Finally acknowledging him, I looked and shrugged my shoulders. He started walking towards me, his hand over his mouth, admiring the car even more, and literally salivating. "Is this you, nigga? This you?" I had a decision to make, either continue lying to everyone who knew me before the money, or come clean, one by one. I looked him square in the eyes.

"Yeah, man." He went on oohing and aahing, while I sat there watching.

"What'chu doing bro? How you living?" It was a naked moment of truth.

"Got a settlement from a lawsuit I was involved in. Finally over."

He reached in and gave me a dap, congratulating my good fortune. I obliged, thinking, *at least I owned the money.*

"Man, that's good bro. You beat the rat race man."

"Yeah, I guess so." We went on talking, with him imagining what he'd do if he had money.

"What this bad boy run ya?"

"Oh, it was about 300."

"Oooh nigga, three-hundred thee." He looked and just shook his head.

"Man if I had your hands, I'd cut mine off." The conversation went on a few more minutes about the car and my settlement, and then we parted ways. I drove along, thinking about what just happened. It was a mixture of emotions, all expected. *Should've parked the car and took the truck*, like that was any better. *Was I becoming a prisoner already?*

I went to a corner store, picked up a pack of cigarillos, hot Cheetos, and a bottle of cranberry juice, then I went to Hermann Park, found a secluded spot, and rolled. The serenity of being alone gave me the space I needed to think some things through.

My perceptions about being rich, the transition from middle-school teacher on a budget, to multi-millionaire with time on his hands wasn't hard, just awkward.

For a good hour, I sat in that parking lot, burning and blowing, grateful about life. In the back of my mind, the doctor's appointment for tomorrow lingered on. Whatever news they had for me, I'd deal with it.

Mama called, asking my whereabouts and requesting I pick up some double A batteries and Coke but not before stopping at Frenchy's, a local creole chicken franchise. Afterward, I'd gotten another call. It was Bioko.

"Hello, Mr. Bioko."

"Mr. Douglas, how are you, sir?" *We just talked a few days ago.*

"I'm fine, how are things with you, my friend?"

His phone call was no surprise. He was checking if I'd made a decision. The opportunity was still interesting, but I thought about Grantham's point of view. And yet, part of me doubted Grantham's honesty, wondering if his advice was bourgeoisie, *us against them*, bullshit.

"All is well, Mr. Douglas. I'm in Accra and I figured I'd give you a call."

"Yeah, I'm still interested in the project, just got home a few days ago. Do you have a contract for me to go over?" My tone was firm, exact.

"Mr. Douglas, are you confident about your decision? It seems your attorneys had common concerns. This has been my business for over a decade."

"Mr. Amana, I'm sure you know your business. They only did what I pay them to do." Bioko went quiet and I held firm. My investment would remain $500,000. Grantham rather I not invest at all, but the value in this transaction was a no-brainer, or so I thought.

"Are you still a part of this project?" he asked.

"Indeed, Mr. Amana, all I'll need is a formal contract and we are good to go."

"You don't trust me, Mr. Douglas?" He asked with a tone of cynicism.

"That's not it ... only business."

"All my investors are given contracts, Mr. Douglas. You needn't worry."

"Understandable. This is a major transaction. All t's must be crossed and i's dotted."

"It appears we want the same thing," he replied.

Bioko promised to have a contract e-mailed by that evening. It was satisfactory enough, and yet I'd have another attorney look over it. As interesting the deal was, I had to trust my judgment.

Later I called Lamont to see what he was up to.

"What's the damn deal, homie?"

"Chilling, wanted to see if you were down to get out ... get a drink?" I needed to be around a friend and talk shit. We decided on Niggadeaux's. Not wanting any extra attention, I dropped the Rolls off.

THE DOCTOR'S NOTE [20]

The place was packed as usual, with beautiful black people laughing, drinking, and dining, like any normal night. Lamont called me. "Hey man, you there yet?"

"I just walked in. I'm looking for a seat at the bar now."

"Okay cool. Had to get permission to get out. You know how that goes."

"Nah, nigga, I don't," I replied.

"Give it time buddy. Anyway, I'm driving that cocaine thang, be there in a minute." *I think I created a monster.*

A few minutes of waiting for a seat at the bar and the bartender's attention, my usual swamp thing was ordered. The crowd was a mixture of 30 to 50 somethings, having an average middle-class night out to push the week along. I remembered those days, not too long ago.

Looking around the room, I didn't see any recognizable faces—a plus for the evening. At the right side of me sat a group of sisters, having a good time over some drinks. They looked like some of my former co-workers, usually married with pre-teen and teenaged kids. In front of me sat a younger couple. She was light-skinned with an average build and short brown hair. Her dude was tatted, with a gold cap and wire framed glasses, kind of like Pimp C.

To my left were a group of older brothers, the ones usually seen at Red Rooster, a bluesy night club off MLK. Farther down the bar, I saw another couple preparing to leave, so I made a mad dash towards the seats. I called Lamont.

"Hey man, I got us some seats. You close?"

"I'm parking right now." Five minutes later he came in with

that, *I drive a Mercedes* swag. I laughed at the sight. I knew that look. "Man, I was already here in the parking lot trying to find a decent spot. Motherfuckers park bad out here."

"Yeah, you good though?" I asked.

"Yeah I'm cool. Some chick was tryna' holla ... I ain't wanna make you wait.

"All good, homie, don't blame me," I replied jokingly. Although I didn't condone it, Lamont was a huge flirt and from time to time, he'd slip up. I remember when he and Dana weren't on the best terms. He started seeing a girl from work, the worst possible move. She even claimed to be pregnant. In the end, the girl lied, but Dana and Lamont ended up separating. In the back of my mind, the fear of him stepping out again with his new toy caused me to feel responsible.

"So whose car is it?" I asked.

"You know it's hers, although technically, it belongs to the family."

"All right, don't be getting caught up."

"What you trying to say, Doug?" He knew exactly what I was saying. He hada smirk on his face.

"Don't let these chickens blow ya mind. You know you be out there."

"I'm a changed man, Doug. I've learned my lesson."

"All right, we'll see."

His bullshit put our friendship on the line at times.

"Man, Dana will not shut up about the car. She done took it to her mama's house, aunties, cousins, co-workers ..."

"I'm glad man, y'all deserve it."

"Bro, I can't thank you, enough."

"It's all good. Y'all family."

Lamont ordered a Long Island and I, a plate of seafood fondue, which quickly reminded me of my bad eating habits. No wonder I was pudgy, and facing some shit with Dr. Harrison.

"You know it's gone be popping at Belvedere's. You ready?" he asked.

"Yeah man, you bringing Dana?"

"Nigga, what? Do I have a choice?"

"See what I'm talking about."

"Man, Dana knows what's up."

"You like playing with fire, man?"

"Depends on how I feel. Anyway, you talked to Gwen, yet?"

"Why you keep pushing the Gwen thing? I'm a tell her when the time is right." I couldn't tell him how much I'd fallen for Yami, without him giving me shit. Giving up my pursuit of Gwen for someone he knew nothing about would draw unnecessary chit-chat.

"Besides, I don't want her acting strange around me."

"I got you. I'll fall back, nigga."

Lamont's attempt at being a good friend was met with anxiety, my fear of telling him the truth about this newest infatuation. Maybe even the world knew how much of a sucker for love I could be. Lamont could say the one thing to snap me out of this daze, even if I wasn't ready.

"Hey man, I'm a be honest right quick, and don't use the shit against me."

"C'mon, man," he said.

"The girl in New York ... I'm really feeling her. I think about her a lot." Lamont looked at me with a smirk.

"Are you serious? I mean, that's cool. She bad as fuck, huh?" I had the proudest smile, the first time in a long time I beamed about love.

"Just don't get no niggas pregnant man."

"Shit, we ain't even been on a date," I replied.

"I mean, if you really feel like it's something there, you should go for it."

I was startled at his encouragement. Normally, Lamont would shut down the conversation if I hadn't "hit" yet. Maybe my expression showed the genuineness of my attraction.

"You think she'd move here? Houston's slow. Hope she don't get bored." We laughed.

"I don't know. It's a little too soon. Like I said, we ain't even been on a date, never mind the long distance thing." What did I know? I was hopeful of everything about a relationship and equally unprepared. Just because I had previous experience with a single parent didn't mean we'd jive. First and foremost, she was a New Yorker, and I, a native Californian living in Houston for over a decade. I understood Houston culture, steeped in religiosity and "heritage." But would she? Would going to the annual Rodeo Festival be boring? Would she miss her subways and cold weather? We didn't need to be casualties of monogamy.

The following morning, my thoughts were occupied by the doctor's appointment for 9:30. Dr. Katelyn Dobbs, a urologist at MD Anderson Hospital in the medical center, was to give me my official prognosis. The thought alone caused spastic allusions of my impending doom. We use to visit Andre at the very same hospital, and although it's a world renowned facility, he still died.

All the positivity in the world could not shake the fear of going to MD Anderson, the cancer hospital. Why did I have to see her there?

As I prepared to leave, Mama was already in the kitchen, cooking and humming as she always did.

"Hey, Mama. Got an appointment for 9:30. I'll be back by noon."

"Everything okay?" she asked.

I hated lying to her, but I got accustomed to it in the last few weeks. This wouldn't hurt.

"Yeah, it's for business. It shouldn't take long. When I'm done, I'll call y'all and we can go get lunch." I gave her a reassuring hug and walked out the door. The hallway seemed much more narrow and desolate. I wasn't rich anymore, just desperate. When I reached the garage, I looked at both cars, surmising which to drive to receive this news. *Should it be the Rolls or would that be too pompous of me? I should be more humble today.* I jumped in the truck and off I went.

The drive was solemn. I and Dr. Dobbs were the only people in the world that day, waiting to have an exchange. For a brief instant, I tried to reinforce a sense of carelessness. *Maybe it's more gibberish about my weight or what I eat ... I can change, no problem. I'm serious this time.* This space felt disappointing. How confusing was it to win all this goddamn money. I wanted to see what 60 felt like, even 80. I wanted to be the old fucker with the pretty young thang by my side at Essence Fest.

The luxuries of my life were meaningless. The sunshine alone should've been enough for inspiration, and yet I felt duped by God. *What lesson is this supposed to teach me?* As the traffic light changed to a blaring red, I took pause from my thoughts, realizing that the spiraling effect of the assumptive state I was in had not prepared me for the actuality of the prognosis. *Maybe it won't be all that bad, but if it is, do whatever it takes to get back. Just get back.*

By the time I reached the hospital's parking structure, I mustered up a pseudo sense of calm. For no other purpose than not having Dr. Dobbs see me "scared," I wanted to portray something else. Not a flippant arrogance, but more of an acceptance of the matter at hand. The information was to enlighten me and cause some fervent action on my part. After a five minute stint, I finally found an open spot and parked. I made my way through the confusion, otherwise known as a hospital parking structure; "Level 3, row c, level 3, row c, level 3, row c," I kept repeating. My ritual for times like these.

Walking through the hospital lobby, my mind went back to those days when we'd visit Andre. Our optimism was blind to the fact that he'd been in stage four of his cancer bout for quite some time. Praying teetered belief and the act of. Some days were unbearable, seeing his helpless state, a contrast to his former athletic prowess. I remember the days we'd play basketball and he'd dunk on motherfuckers, or when we'd go to the club and he'd shoot game and pull some of the baddest bitches. He was that dude. To see him reduced to a shell of his former self was heartbreaking. And now I was in the same fucking hospital? *Fuck.*

I reached the 24th floor and went straight to the receptionist desk.

"I'm here to see Dr. Katelyn Dobbs for a 9:30 appointment."

"Name, sir?"

"Douglas Moore." As the nurse looked my appointment up, I glanced around, seeing nothing but signs of death. I hated hospitals. Seeing people in wheel chairs or walking with those transportable IV's was depressing.

"Yes sir, please have a seat and we'll call for you."

I obliged and went to the waiting area. I hated waiting areas too. Maybe as much as I hated appointment times to doctor's visits. Why would the appointment be set for 10 if it meant being seen at 11:30?

Fifteen minutes later, others remained sitting, waiting to be seen. The waiting area consisted of an older white guy looking like a college professor or pedophile; an older black couple, maybe in their 60s, and a Hispanic woman with her child. The child appeared to be the patient with his thinning hair implying chemotherapy. For some reason, I'd periodically glance at the couple, imagining their lives together. I wondered about the length of their marriage and the obstacles they'd overcome—their lessons learned. The somber feel of the reception area charged my motivation to make a conscious go at Yami.

"Mr. Moore?" the nurse called.

I got up and met her at the door with a gracious smile that masked the jitters inside.

Today's meeting contrasted the time I met Jim Brennan back in Austin or the lawyers in New York. This was my health. A few feet ahead I could see another receptionist desk followed by a scale and more chairs.

"This way please," the nurse instructed, walking towards the examination room. "Dr. Dobbs will be with you in just a moment." I thanked her as she walked out, closing the door behind. The silence was deafening. Alone with my rampant thoughts, I chose to distract myself by pulling my phone out and checking my timeline. The temptation of "checking-in" for some sort of sympathetic attention was quickly subdued by rational thinking: *motherfuckers don't need to know my business, and I'm not that weak.* Instead, as a status update I wrote, *"Always remember the power of prayer… as I pray for you."* It was the same difference, but in a vague, generality sort of way.

Moments later the doctor walked in with spryness reserved for good news.

"Mr. Moore? Hi, I'm Dr. Dobbs," she said as she extended her hand. After exchanging pleasantries, there was no further desire for small talk or empty banter. *Tell me what's wrong.*

"So, we want to discuss your lab work from Dr. Miles' office, specifically the matter that came to his attention."

"Yes. I'm freaking out right now. I've been thinking about this appointment ever since." My statement was an admission of fear and I didn't care.

"Well, we don't want to make any premature assumptions about the lab work. As you know, blood was discovered in your urine. Now that can mean a number of things. Primarily, my role as an urologist is to diagnose the cause. Once we find the attributes, we fix it, that simple." I was beginning to feel some comfort in her assurance. Still I wanted a clue as to the possible causes, today, not in a week.

"So, Dr. Dobbs, uh, what could be the cause of the blood?"

"Well first off the medical terminology is hematuria, and the causes could stem from a kidney or bladder infection, to an enlarged prostate or even prostate cancer."

Cancer? Every word she uttered from that point on was lost in the abyss of my anxiety. I refused to believe that a year after Andre's death, I'd face the same fate. The devastation it would cause my family was too much to imagine.

"What's the probability of it being cancer?" I wanted straight talk.

"Well, we need to do some examinations. One in particular would be your prostate. Prostate cancer is highest among African-

American males between the ages of 40 to 55. How old are you, Mr. Moore?"

"I'm 37."

"You fall within proximity to the range. For your benefit, we should check your prostate today and also take some more blood and urine samples," she offered. My willingness to do whatever she asked seemed a dreadful process, but a necessary evil. She could see the look of concern on my face, so she offered some encouragement.

"Mr. Moore, don't let your imagination get the best of you. If it's an infection, I'll prescribe some medication and within a week or so it should subside. But first, excuse me. When I return, I'll check your prostate. By the way, are you familiar with the location of your prostate?" she asked in a forewarning manner.

"Honestly, Doc, to be a teacher, I'm embarrassed to say no." She raised her brow.

"Okay, no problem."

When she walked out, the anticipation overwhelmed me. My education and money were insignificant. In an effort to spare my family and friends the burdensome obligation of being hopeful, the conviction to keep the shit secret brought resolve. For a brief moment, the examination room became an interrogation room, as questions began to loom through my mind. The anguish of assuming that somehow I'd brought this upon myself was thanks to my Pentecostal upbringing. I'd been living in sin. Hell, the lottery was a sin by church standards.

"Mr. Moore, I'm going to exam your prostate which is just behind your scrotum area, but before I do, I must inform you that this will be invasive, yet quick." *Big deal, check under my balls, no problem*, I thought.

"Okay, Doc, do what you do," I replied unknowingly.

"Well, I'm gonna need you to stand and drop your pants for me, sir."

"Okay."

"Now turn around for me and bend over. You can lean on the examination table." *What the shiggady?* I thought she was gonna fiddle underneath my sack, have me do the cough thing. This motherfucker proceeded to spread my left butt check and insert her right index finger in my ass. My feelings were hurt. No way in hell could I ever tell Lamont that shit if I didn't wanna hear about it for the rest my life. Her awkward prodding lasted 10 to 15 seconds, and I stood there compliant, patiently awaiting my dignity. My focus was laser sharp on the wall, as she took liberties no other soul had ever taken. The hardest thing about the ordeal was having the ability to look her in the eyes as if none of it ever happened.

"That's it, Mr. Moore, we're done," she said, as she pulled the latex gloves off. The thought of what could be on the glove was embarrassing enough. "I'll have my nurse to come take some blood and urine samples. Your prostate felt fine so I suspect we'll need the samples to gather more data. Well, it was good meeting you. Give me about a week to ascertain a diagnosis."

"Thank you, Doc." I sat there, somewhat dejected but understanding. My prejudice concerning all things medical was overcome by the reality of the circumstance. Moments later, a nurse came in to take blood and later, collect my urine sample. Giving urine was always a crazy mind-fuck act of humility. Standing over a toilet to collect a fraction of a stream while having the ability to avoid "wetting" myself, was always a humorous self-deprecating slice of life.

The drive home was a reflective appreciation for the oddity of it all. As much as I wanted to feel sorry for myself, if only for assuming, the emblem on my steering wheel put things in perspective. I was still rich as fuck and capable of getting the best medical attention money could buy. *Time to get serious about my weight, cut out the bad eating, drinking, and maybe even smoking. Well maybe not entirely. One blunt a week couldn't hurt.*

When I got home, everyone in the living room was watching TV. It appeared that they'd just finished eating breakfast.

"What's up?" Devin asked.

"Chilling. What y'all just finished eating? Hope you saved me some."

"It's still some food in there," my mother said. I went to fix a plate, easing my mind from the morning fair. The distinction of my high-end kitchen with all its bells and whistles, were met with my mother's Alabama, down-home cooking. Home-made biscuits, scrambled eggs with cheese, cheese grits, pan sausage and bacon, all culminated for an ensemble of love. I sat down at the kitchen table looking out over the city, blessed for such a time as this. With every bite, my spirit was restored and a new resolve was forged. *This is the day that the Lord has made …*

PARTY OVER HERE [21]

Finally the weekend. The reservations were set at Belvedere's for my extended birthday celebration that Friday evening. My intent was to get fucked up, ignoring the realities and pampering the possibilities. Self-indulged and alienated far too long, tonight was the unofficial debut of "Doug." Tonight I'd ball out, hiring a local celebrity DJ and buying the bar, allowing the drinks to flow and the ladies to lose their inhibitions—my gift to the fellas.

Unbeknown to my invited guests, this private soiree was costing a whopping $30,000. In essence, it was my "coming out" party. Tonight I'd wear the Hublot, the Louie, the ice, and when it was all said and done, I'd leave in the Rolls.

Mom decided to stay home with the boys, giving Devin and Grace a break for the evening. Unfortunately, they didn't smoke, so I had no partners in crime. I settled on knocking back a few Crown and Cokes. At 10:20 p.m. it was still early for the club. Guests were told to arrive at 9, so leaving fashionably late at 10:45, we'd get there right around 11. I pulled Devin to the side to give him the plan.

"Hey man, y'all can drive the truck, I might go somewhere else afterward." It was a lie. As much as I would've liked the idea of having my own after party, I had no plans other than smoking in the car on the way there.

As for my attire, it was a time to kill. My custom suit from New York was the weapon of choice; a silk and cashmere blend, two-button charcoal gray master piece, paired with some patent leather Louis Vuitton loafers, cashmere sweater and Damier scarf.

As the time drew near, we kissed Mother goodnight and made our way toward the garage. I got in the Rolls in rock star mode, lit the blunt, and turned the defrost all the way up. Any car connoisseur would've cringed at my deplorable act, my real life music video. Devin, sitting behind the wheel of the truck, looked over at me and shook his head, while I politely offered him a middle finger.

When we reached Belvedere's parking lot, we conveniently pulled up to valet service and popped right in. To my surprise, the crowd was fairly decent, maybe 50 or so people, mainly frat and co-workers. Ms. Ferguson, Coach Jackson, Mr. Franklin, and Ms. Baylor, even "M" showed up. Off in the distance, Lamont and Dana sat at the bar as I strolled their way.

"There's my birthday boy," Dana said in elation. We talked on the phone the day Lamont bought the car, but this was the first time we'd seen each other. She was genuinely grateful, hugging and thanking me over and over again. Oddly, I hadn't thought much about it. They'd do the same for me. I greeted Lamont, thanking him for showing, with a look that read *glad you brought Dana*.

"Damn nigga, you loud as fuck," Lamont said referring to the scent of weed. I thought the cracked windows washed the scent away. *Fuck it; I ain't a teacher no more.*

"Damn, you can smell it?" I asked.

"Hell yeah. You brought some?"

"I smoked that shit down to about a half, it's in the car."

"What you drive tonight, the Rolls?"

"But of course," I replied as we shared a pound and a laugh. "Devin followed me in the truck. You remember my brother, Devin, right?" I motioned for Devin to come over to re-introduce him and Grace. Lamont and Dana gave each of them a hug and carried on small talk as I immediately noticed "M," who appeared to be staring at me. We held a slight flirtatious gaze.

The DJ put on Frankie Beverly and Maze, "Before I let Go," and it was over. Every damn body went into rhythmic pandemonium, mouthing the words, dancing with their libations in hand. For a minute, I was Diddy. I relished in everybody's enjoyment of *my* party.

"Man this shit off the hook," Lamont said, double talk for, "*they in here tonight.*" He wasn't lying. From the look of things, some attractive unrecognizable faces, maybe friends of friends, friends of co-workers, had come to my party.

"Hey bro, what's the silver bottle with the ace of spades on it?" I asked as I turned my attention to the bartender.

"Armand de Brignac champagne, would you like some?" he asked.

"Sure, man." I was unaware of the brand or that the shit was $500 a bottle. I bought the bar. After getting my drink, I walked into the crowd to work the room, greeting and thanking people for showing up. Just then, Mr. Franklin came towards me.

"I see ya, brother. This how you do, huh?"

"Glad you made it. You know it's an open bar right? Get whatever you want."

"Man this is nice, what's going on, you quit, now this?" he pried.

"Ah, I just wanted to do something special for myself. I hadn't had a good party in a while. And of course I miss y'all," I countered. The whole time he was giving me a *don't shit me* face. I held firm, ascertaining that other folks would eventually ask the same question. The vulnerability of spewing at the mouth after a few drinks was a clear and present danger. Keeping folks in the dark was fine with me. Soon enough, the hate and the fake would reveal itself, allowing me to maneuver and remove them from the guest list of my life.

Thirty minutes in and I was already on drink number two. Gradually the crowd began to swell, and what appeared to be initially 50 or so folks, was now easily 100. *I didn't invite this many damn people.* The DJ had the room going with song after song and the bar looked like a government cheese line. My ego was fed by it all.

The time had come to turn on the charm and make my rounds, with discretion of course. The dim lighting fared well for this egocentric plan. My interest had turned to the ladies—three in particular. First there was the obvious, "M." Our happy hour rendezvous had only been weeks ago. Effortlessly, she wore a form-fitting, teal colored mini-skirt, black jacket, and stilettos. Her shoulder length hair was brushed to the side. She wore very little make-up, just enough to complement her gorgeous caramel skin tone. From time to time I'd check for her, seeing which nigga was up in her face at any given moment.

Then there was Grey, the country girl of the two ladies. Grey was that everyday chick, that take home to meet Mama and friends type chick. She was beautifully low-maintenance, and still bad as fuck with that soul-food fed body. Even with the failed attempts in the past, we were now on different playing fields. Reconsideration came to mind. And last but definitely not least was mystery girl number three. This fine and tasty looking individual was accompanied by another colleague, Ms. Proctor, a gym teacher. She was possibly her cousin, sister, friend, or even lover. *Damn, I hope not.*

I'd accepted the probability of being watched all evening. The young, fly, rich, buzzed, high, horny, single and ready to mingle dude. The tact I'd employ was constant flow. This meant engaging in short, witty banter, no more than five minutes, making sure the drinks were topped off, transitioning to the next lady. It was my "triangular prose" for the night. The only issue was deciding the order of the conquest. Definitely not mystery girl. I'd have to get an introduction from Proctor and that could mean a good five to ten minutes of talk time. Let me start with Grey.

Grey was sitting in the lounge area with other teachers, mainly women. Other guys had tried their hand, but she seemed to elude them all.

"Hey, ladies y'all doing all right?" I asked. Six of them sat together, making it damn near impossible to holla. Everybody seemed to be enjoying themselves, as I periodically made eye contact with her.

"This is real nice, Moore," Ms. Ferguson said.

"Thanks," I replied. Assessing from the look of it I had to retreat. I looked for "M" who was across the room with another teacher colleague, Mrs. Riley the music instructor. I encouraged the girls to continue having a good time, giving Grey a flirtatious wink, before heading to the other conquest.

Walking towards "M," she noticed me and perked up. Riley noticed me as well but kept talking.

"Hey ladies, hope y'all having a good time," I said.

"Yeah, Moore, this is nice. What, you won the lottery or something?" Riley facetiously countered.

"Damn, can't get nothing past you, huh?" I replied. Riley was shaped like a hot mess and a bag of dirty laundry. Being a bitch was her thing, but she didn't intimidate me. "Y'all want anything to drink?" I asked, looking at "M" the entire time.

"What, you buying?" Riley asked.

"It's an open bar, Ms. Riley, you can get whatever you want." Her demeanor immediately changed.

"Well, girl, if you could excuse me for just a second, I'll be right back," she said as she walked her dumpy and frumpy ass to the bar.

"She's a trip, huh? So what's up? Glad you could make it tonight."

"Me, too," she answered.

Somebody was watching and discussing our conversation, and it didn't matter. Judging from her disposition, "M" didn't mind either, considering the gossiping repercussions to come Monday morning.

"I really had a good time on our little happy hour date," she offered.

"Any time and you're rather stunning this evening, might I say."

"You're not looking so bad yourself, Moore. Loving the suit, and I see ya with the Louie loafers."

"I try."

For a brief moment I looked around the room and sure enough folks here and there, peered at us anticipating our collective body language. A part of it was flattering, considering the situation. Lamont was definitely on the scope, even flashing a supportive "thumbs up." Tactfully, I made it a point to keep a professional distance from her, refraining from any body contact or touching, even though her body was killing me softly. "So where are you now?" she asked. Everyone suspected I'd be at another school. Ferguson was the only one I told about the college thing. I could run with that, or come clean with someone as bad as this. Tonight was about introducing the new and improved Douglas Moore, not Mr. Moore, the teacher, Bro. Moore, the fraternity member, or Doug, the all-around, respectable tax paying good guy. Tonight was an announcement that I, last month's lottery winner, was also Houston's most eligible bachelor, until Yami gave further notice.

"Can you keep a secret?" I asked.

"Yeah, what's up?"

"Well, I'm pretty much done with teaching. Last month I received an inheritance from my uncle. He left me some property and paper. I'm looking to start a business, maybe a cleaners or something like that."

"Oh, okay, that's what's up. Congratulations," she replied as Riley headed back our way.

"But please don't tell anybody. Too many nosey people here tonight, feel me?"

"I got you, Moore. Mums the word." Riley arrived.

"So we can get anything we want, all night long?" Riley asked.

"That's right."

"Oh it's on tonight, my husband bet not wait up for me."

The temptation to say something vile was met with constraint, as I offered an appeasing chuckle.

"Ladies, y'all enjoy. I'll be right back."

Riley was killing my vibe as it was, a perfect time to check out mystery girl. Searching around the room, I saw Proctor, mystery girl, and a frat brother of mine standing near the DJ booth. I casually strolled towards them, with the intent of getting her name.

"What's up, frat?" I spoke to my brother and good friend of 11 years, Dion Conners. Dion was one of the first "bruhs" I met when I moved to Houston.

"You, brother. This is real nice, man," he replied.

"Hey, Ms. Proctor, thank you for coming," I said.

"Yeah, Mr. Moore, no problem," she replied in all her studly glory.

We all had our suspicions about Proctor, wanting her to fess up. But for now, my focus was on her guest.

"This is my cousin, Cambria," she continued. *Yes!*

"Nice to meet you, Ms. Cambria," I offered. I did my best to subdue the thirst.

"Nice to meet you. Cam is fine," she said as we shook hands.

"Y'all having a good time? You know the bar is open right?"

"Straight?" Dion responded.

Obviously everyone wasn't aware of the open bar. Management was instructed to have the bartenders inform my guests, allowing for generous tips.

"Can I interest you ladies in anything," I asked.

"Man, I really don't drink," Proctor replied. A healthy stud, perhaps.

"What about you, Ms. Cam?"

"Oh, I don't know, maybe a White Zinfandel if they have it?"

"Sure thing. Frat, let's go to the bar."

It was an opportunity to clear the air with Dion. Did he intend to holler at Cambria? If so, the gentlemanly thing to do was to politely fall back.

"Say bruh, the Cam chick ..."

"That's you, birthday boy."

"You sure? I ain't trying to block ..."

"Nah, cause I see some ladies tonight who should be having my baby..."

"Baby!" I countered, in tribute to Biggie.

"Matter fact, who's the chick in the green dress and black jacket, standing by the fat old chick?" *Damn, he talking 'bout my "M."*

"Oh, that's my co-worker, you wanna meet her?"

"Yeah nigga, set that up."

My generosity was unbelievable; but Dion had just did the same for me.

When we reached the bar, the confliction of my carefree pronouncement of "M" stung. My jealous Scorpio side reared its head. She was fine as fuck, a trophy for niggas to claim. Her being nice to me, talking with me, even sharing an evening with me, did more for my ego than my spirit, and I needed to be cognizant of the difference.

After getting our drinks and getting back to the ladies, we continued having small talk, while I soul-searched the origins of my curiously addictive behavior. *How could I have a serious, monogamous relationship with one woman if I'm wagging my tongue and tail at every chick I find halfway attractive? Could I really be married with all this money? Be resolute about something and someone.* If Yami was going to be the *one*, then it was time to make that commitment before making a commitment.

"Here you go, Ms. Cam."

"Thanks. What's your name again?" she asked. Proctor rolled her eyes.

"Douglas Moore. You gonna friend me?" She laughed a bit.

"Yeah."

"Cool."

Dion and I began talking about our fraternity stuff, road trips, and the national conference coming up in New Orleans the following summer. It felt good being the ambiguous center of attention, roaming the room as if a king among his royal subjects. By the look of things, my guest list had been dwarfed by another 100 or so people; motherfuckers must've called niggas up like, "Come drank, it's on the house."

I excused myself to the restroom as the crowd was in full party mode. The DJ brought it back down south with DJ DMD's "25 Lighters," a local favorite. Even for me, it was reminiscent of my arrival to Houston in '99. On the way, I was tugged at, unaware of whom it was, due to the thickness of the crowd. Taking a second look, it was "M." She motioned for me to dance with her and I willingly obeyed. Finally able to maneuver closer, our bodies immediately clashed in the façade of the dense makeshift dance floor. This was the closest I'd ever been to her and it was problematic. *He* was aroused at the feel of her hips, thighs, and back, and firmly supported by a full bladder. Instantly, I'd become the representative for all heterosexual men in Belvedere's. The enchantment served well to distract my urgent need to pee. As the crowd moved in unison, it didn't matter who was watching or discussing our apparent lust. We were lost together. With every enticing rhythmic move she made, my confidence and comfort level harmonized. She knowingly pressed up against "it," allowing me the liberty of exploring her waist line. Then the DJ continued his ghetto symphonic spell by mixing in Mystical's "Here I Go," which blended perfectly. She turned around with that blessing of an ass pressed up against me, giving me permission to do away with social etiquette. Ambition called.

Before completely letting go, the urge to look around for spectators nudged at my consciousness. My hypocritical teacher side preyed on my sense of decorum. Teetering passionate dance and dry humping, the most popular girl on campus was letting me have my way, and didn't give a fuck. For an instant, in my attempt to portray "a regular guy doing a regular thing as he looks around the room," my eyes locked with Cambria, who looked disappointed. She was instantly out of play. And then I looked for Grey, but the crowd was too sporadic to spot her.

For a good four to five songs, at least 12 to 15 minutes straight, I danced, generously grinding and marking my domain. Looking to my right, Dion observed us, putting both hands up as to say *what the fuck?* I just shrugged my shoulders and looked down at her. The scrutinizing over our carelessness was null and void. This was the night of my life and I was riding it till the wheels came off.

"M" finally granted me pardon from her erotic confinement and a quick dash to the restroom allowed for another one of those lovely inebriated pees. When I was done, I stood in front of the mirror in admiration of an insignificant vainglorious accomplishment. Relishing "my" moment, I took care in washing my hands, avoiding the splash of water on my $2,000 suit. Just then, an unfamiliar gentleman walked in. With a slight glance from the mirror he replied, "I saw ya doing ya thang, brother." Perhaps in reference to "M," that was how Monday would be.

RATED "M" [22]

Walking back out to the blaring force of the sound system, I took a detour and went outside for some fresh air. It was 1 in the morning, about an hour before the night concluded. The moon provided a romantic mist meant to be enjoyed by two. Silently, I thanked God for the oddity of my life; the ups and the downs and the all arounds. None of it made sense, but it was all appropriate for this space and time in my journey.

The idea of having my car pulled up to finish the doobie, seemed a good one, but instead I chilled. This was another one of those over indulgent moments that needed reeling in. Peaceful and resolute, I entered the club ready for what remained of an already awesome and memorable evening.

At this point, almost everyone was lit. Usually at this time, it was commonplace to see folks taper off, but an open bar seemed the antidote.

Just to my right, Proctor and Cam were talking with some ladies from work. To the left, was Devin and Grace, still under the watchful eye of Lamont and Dana.

"Man, dog, y'all fucking?" Lamont asked, referring to "M." I looked at Devin who looked happy just to be in the place. Grace and Dana were people watching, laughing spontaneously.

"Was I out there bad?" I asked with slight apprehension.

"Shit, it's your birthday nigga. You was doing it. She bad, too," he replied.

"I wasn't doing anything more than the rest of these ma'fuckas," was my inebriated defense.

"Like I said, tonight's about you."

I felt responsible for whatever shit talking gossip came her way. *We* love keeping up mess, especially at someone else's expense. Making more rounds, I noticed a few co-workers being consoled by their entourages from the excessive drinking. I was even approached by a waitress informing me that a female guest was lying on the ladies restroom floor, passed out. The embarrassment killed my vibe. I went directly to Proctor for her studly assistance.

"Ms. Proctor, do you mind going into the ladies bathroom? Apparently one of my guest has passed out on the floor."

"What you want me to do?" she countered snidely.

"Well, I can't go in there. Can you just see who it is, if it's one of us?"

Reluctantly she obliged and a few minutes later she came back.

"It's Riley ass laid out. I can't get Riley, you gone have to do that."

I grimaced at the thought. Riley was easily 260 pounds. Looking around for other available options, I went to "M" who was still in party mode and pulled her to the side.

"Hey, this is awkward but I need help with your girl. She's laid out in the restroom."

"What's wrong with her?"

"She's probably drunk. Can you get somebody to help get her out? I feel uncomfortable going in there," I replied.

"I guess, but who?"

We were instantly linked to another circumstance, light years away from the dance floor. In an effort to avoid stirring interest away from the party, I went looking for the messiest, most gossiping instigator I could find to help "M" get this girl off the floor. And then it came to me, Thibodeaux.

Behind Riley, Ms. Thibodeaux, a reading teacher on campus, who'd been known to be a snake in the grass a million times over, was the perfect one for this task. The fact that I even invited her and Riley was the grace of God. She was standing with some unrecognizable folks, laughing, and probably talking shit.

"Ms. Thibodeaux, can I speak with you for a moment?" I asked. She looked at me with one of those snobbish "sista-friend" looks.

"Yeah, wassup?"

"This is crazy, but I got a problem. Ms. Riley is laid out on the restroom floor and I need some ladies to help me get her up. You mind?"

"Ooh, Ms. Riley? She kind of big-boned."

"Nah, I'll find someone to help. I didn't wanna go in there for obvious reasons." She looked up for a moment with a sigh.

"All right let's go, but you owe me, Moore." *Yeah some dick in that gossiping big-ass mouth of yours, bring yo ass on!*

"Thanks so much, I really appreciate it," I replied.

When we reached the restroom, a small crowd of about three ladies were standing at the door. "M" and Thibodeaux excused themselves through to help out. By this time, Riley was literally snoring, for which Thibodeaux got a good laugh.

"Okay, now what?" Thibodeaux countered snidely. Every second made for good juicy gossip, diminishing the hate against "M." Hopefully the strategizing worked.

"C'mon, girl, you gone have to help me with this heifer," Thibodeaux shouted.

"M" and Thibodeaux tried every possible maneuver to get Riley up off the floor. First, they had to turn her over from lying flat on her face, attempting to sit her straight up. The whole time, Riley was completely removed from the commotion, slightly murmuring and in and out of consciousness.

"Moore, you have to get in here," Thibodeaux stated as they continued struggling. I was stuck on the unwritten law of entering the girls' bathroom. All I had to do was drag her out to the hall. *Fuck it.* It was pitiful seeing those two, both in heels, reeling back and forth with this mammoth of a woman. The crowd of three grew to seven with Grey, who eluded me most of the night, spectating along with the others. We both looked at each other, shaking our damn heads.

"All right ladies, I'm just gone drag her out to the hallway and give her some air, y'all take her shoes off." As I bent down to get a firm hold, the murmuring became louder, with her attempting to mouth the words to the hell she was in.

"Ooh Jesus … Lord Jesus, help me," she repeated, while her eyes rolled.

"It's gonna be all right Ms. Riley," I said comforting her. The pungent smell of alcohol permeated her body. She was lit. Just as I got a firm grip under her arms, with her slightly up in a 45 degree angle, she burped with a girth reserved for a manly man. It was an indicator. *This bitch 'bout to throw up, let's move, let's go!* No sooner than I thought the worst, the worst happened. Riley, of her own strength and will, leaned upward and to her left side, releasing a most vile and repugnant mixture of gut juice all over my left Louie loafer and pant leg. A consensus of sympathy rang out, while she completed her business. Afterward, I continued to drag her and her sludge out the door.

When I reached the outside area, I gently laid her down, while going on a mental tirade. *My fucking shoe and suit, are you fucking serious?* Grey's sympathetic look was gratitude enough. "M" and I were becoming less and less of a topic. Once word got out about this, it could last for months, even years. Poor Riley.

I went straight to the men's restroom to mend my wounds. It was an unbelievable twist to the evening—my ego was slightly bruised more than anything. The shoe, the left pant leg, and the misery of cleaning vomit from a woman whose character was equally grotesque, caught me off guard. Casually, I re-entered the scene with members of the restroom crowd graciously empathizing with what took place. Lucky for me, most guests were unaware of the previous event dubbed restroom gate. I went straight to the bar and ordered a double shot of Crown and Coke. Devin and Grace appeared out of nowhere.

"What's up man? Been looking for you. Everything okay?" Devin asked.

"Yeah, I'm cool. Y'all all right?"

"Yeah, Grace fucked up though."

"No, I'm not, shut the hell up," Grace replied.

The little bit of comedy between them brought civility and calm back. I no longer had the desire to strangle the shit out of Riley. It was 1:15 in the morning and the DJ was still rocking while motherfuckers kept drinking. The open bar alone made my party a thing of legend. By then, some of the guests began going home, while a good number of folks held on. I was actually in the mood to leave, with or without someone. Off in the distance, Lamont and Dana danced a jig in their own little world. It was a welcomed sight.

From the looks of it, Proctor and Cambria had left, along with Mr. Franklin and a few others from the job. Some of my frat still hung around, occasionally hopping to whatever song they felt. Mrs. Riley was escorted by two of the P.E. coaches to another co-worker's car who offered to take her home. Grey was huddled with the girls and unavailable again. I felt a tap on my back, it was "M."

"Man, you okay?" she asked, sympathetically.

"I'm good. Glad someone could take her ass home. You okay?"

"I'm fine, tripping on that bathroom business. Happy Birthday?"

"Yeah, since you came. It made the night." She giggled and I immediately calibrated back to my happy place. "Is somebody doing any after hour spot, Waffle House, something?"

"Oh, I don't know, you ain't tired?" she replied. I was, but willing to extend the night with the pleasure of her company.

"Well, I'm down to get some breakfast if you want, or you could just cook it." I was feeling myself, smelly left pant leg and all. She looked at me with a "c'mon" smirk, but I held firm. All inhibitions were gone, thanks to our little dance.

"I don't know, I'm going to check with the girls over there and see."

"You scared to go to breakfast wit'cha boy?" She started laughing again. I was breaking down the barrier that our professional lives had built. Honestly, I was looking for a one night stand. There was nothing to lose. I had money now which meant options and with options came patience. Don't get me wrong, Yami was still the candelabra, the centerpiece of my desire so to speak, but "M" was right in front of me.

"What you trying to do then?"

"I can follow you to a Waffle House if you wanna take it that route, or we can kick it up a notch." She raised her brow in slight protest, but my liquid courage was on a thousand, trillion.

"So what's the notch?" she countered.

"It's whatever, but if you're asking me, it involves getting room service at the Hilton downtown by the Toyota Center. You know where that is, right?" She looked at me stunned, impressed even. She'd never seen me come this hard, but tonight was the night.

"You so crazy. You gone be all right to drive?" she asked humorously.

"Ah babe, my car can drive itself, either way, we riding together," I countered. She gotta kick out of that and laughed longer and louder. "Leave your car here and ride with me. We can come pick it up in the morning, you tripping." She remained quiet for a minute, staring me down, reading every nuance of my face for clues to where this was going. My poker face remained.

"I need to go to the bathroom," she replied. Consciously, I reverted back to the old Mr. Douglas Moore. *I think I've offended her. I'm such an irresponsible, brash, and untactful goof.* I sat there regretful of my approach, feeling embarrassed and dejected. Devin walked my way while I looked at my half empty glass.

"Hey man, we going home. You gone be all right?"

"Yeah. You remember how to get back to the apartment?"

"Yeah, it's easy. Be careful." We gave each other a hug and I waved to Grace who was already standing at the door. Lamont and Dana walked my way as well.

"Nigga, can you drive home or do you need a ride?"

"I'm cool, thanks. I had fun tonight." Dana reached in for a hug and Lamont, a pound, and off they went. It was 1:37 by now, and the DJ had just announced last call. People were still drinking, the greedy bastards. I received pats on the back and well wishes for the evening. At least they were grateful. The club manager came by and went over all expenditures, resolving any outstanding financial matters. It was time to shut the shit down. Suddenly I felt a vibration from my cell phone. It was a text from "M."

"I'm parked by the cupcake shop on the other side. Meet me there in your car."

Those words did wonders for my libido and self-esteem. I hopped up off the bar stool, gave farewell salutations to everyone, and made my way to the valet where others were waiting. They also thanked me for the lovely evening they had at my expense. I texted her back informing that I was on the way.

"I'm waiting for my car, look for a black Rolls-Royce."

"Okay, I'm parked right in front of the window area...white Lamborghini ;-)"

"Lol," I replied.

Moments later, more guests started to file out, creating a larger crowd. A part of me loved the idea of having my whip pulled up front, but on the flip, my anonymity would be compromised. Five minutes later, in my peripheral I could see that black thing making its grand entrance. Bonita El Negro, I called it. As the valet guy slowly approached, the reactions to the car fed my ego even more. Someone yelled out, "Everybody ain't able." Embarrassed and equally flattered, I looked at the ground with a slight grin on my face. I waited until the car pulled completely up to the front, in all its glory, and in an impromptu moment of bravado I addressed the audience. "I just wanna take this time to thank y'all for coming out tonight, some faces more familiar than others but loved just the same. Y'all truly made this a birthday to remember, thanks again."

Everyone clapped and cheered while I made my way to the driver side of the car. When they realized the owner, the cheering grew louder and my head, bigger. When I got in, I strapped on the seatbelt, adjusted the rear-view mirror and waved back at the crowd again. Asshole heaven. The rendezvous of a lifetime waited. Heading in her direction, I slowed down to spot her car, parked right where she said, with faint smoke billowing from the exhaust. Pulling up behind her, I honked, and rolled my window down. She opened her door with a look of disbelief, got completely out of the car and starting walking towards me.

"You ain't lying, huh? I'm riding with you."

"Get in then," I replied.

When she got in, she looked around, admired her surroundings and then looked at me with the sexiest, most conniving look I'd ever seen. "Where we going?" Even the tone of her voice changed. It was sultry, domineering even. It took everything within me to prevent my voice from cracking.

I simply cleared my throat and said "Just ride, I got you." For the duration, we remained silent, possibly strategizing our next moves. What would occur in the coming hours was a mystery and hopefully consenting. This was my graduation night. Finally a realm of manhood I'd only lived vicariously through the pages of *Black Men* or *King* magazines.

I-10 east seemed a logical means of travel for the ensuing mood. In an effort to mask my thirst, I turned up the CD playing in the background. It was a new album from Big Boi of Outkast. From my peripheral I could see that she was slightly nodding her head, giving ease to the sexual tension that built from the moment she got in.

"What you know about this?" I asked.

"Shutterbug ... please, what you know about this?"

It broke the ice, maintaining my level of confidence for the intended foreplay. I continued speeding towards the Hilton, in awe that this woman was riding with me. My focus overreached the desired destination. No sooner than I could fathom an outcome, Houston's skyline appeared. The closer we got, the city lights rang of a potentially promising affair.

"Oh, okay. We really going to the Hilton?"

"You really don't wanna go?" I replied matter of fact.

She remained silent, looking at me, with me dividing my attention between her and the road. Then she put a smirk on her face and looked ahead. For a minute my flippant façade battled with the nerves raging within. I had to make her decision worth it all.

We made the exit off the freeway headed for the hotel and it became a leisurely drive. I purposely slowed down to soak it all in. Downtown city lights illuminated the path to our impending sexual activity. Occasionally I'd look over at her, stealing glimpses, imagining her thoughts.

"I'm hungry for real now," she said.

"Me too. What you got a taste for?"

"Anything. Is room service still open?"

When she said that, it solidified everything, and I got hard.

"Trust me, you can have whatever you like." She laughed and all bets were off.

We reached the circular drive, with the same guys that met me under a different circumstance weeks ago. This time I was driving something a bit more sophisticated and accompanied by a most lovely companion. The door attendant reached for the passenger side letting her out as I gave the keys to valet. We walked into bustling lobby activity, appropriate for an early morning weekend. It could've been the ending of an exhibition from across the street at the George R. Brown Convention Center or maybe the hotel restaurants.

We approached the reception desk where I asked for the penthouse suite. Luckily it was available. I was asked how long the stay would be, ensuring an afternoon check out. I had to be cognizant of my guests in town, specifically my mother. Surely she'd freak out if she hadn't seen my 37-year-old face by a certain time. We got the key and this time around we were escorted by a white girl who looked as if she were still in college, maybe at U of H or Rice. She assured us of the privileges we'd have with the room and her availability for the length of our stay. She rode in the elevator with us to the suite and gave the same spiel I'd gotten from the last guy.

After she finished, we were left to our own volition. The tension was immediate. Someone needed to take the reins before the situation became lame. I could see it now—us sitting on the couch talking about our families, our lives, our hopes and dreams …fuck that, what that pussy do?

We'd already been through the formalities. *But now what? Take it slow and order this girl some food.*

"What you want from room service?"

"They got grilled chicken or fish?" she asked.

"And that's it? You want something to drink?"

"Some type of fruit juice, mango, lemonade …"

"All right cool."

I called down to room service, ordered her grilled chicken and myself, a Caesar salad with grilled chicken and a slice of strawberry cheesecake. When I hung up, I stood to stretch and take a leak. She was already on the couch watching TV. My mind went back to the episode I had in New York with Frankie and Lacy, unsure of how this scenario would play. There wasn't a need to force anything or ruin the opportunity with some unnecessary fly shit. *Take it easy.*

When I came from the bathroom, I sat beside her, watching what she watched, gauging this mental game of double-dutch.

"So this is what you do? Bring girls up here and knock 'em down?"

"What?" I replied in shock with a nervous laugh; I wasn't expecting that.

"No, I'm just saying, is this how you get down on the regular?"

"Honestly, I don't do this. Just trying to have a good time that's all, maybe impress you a bit," I replied.

"Waffle House would've impressed me," she said in a matter of fact tone, and we shared a laugh.

"I'll make note of that."

"So do you find me interesting? What do you like about me?" she asked.

Her tone was serious and straightforward, somewhat removed from the giddy valley girl act she'd put on before. Assuming the intimacy of the situation, she was on guard. I had to drop the bullshit.

"You're very attractive, educated, and I can be myself when I'm around you. I mean, it ain't like we hang out all the time but the few times we have, it's been cool."

"So like buddies?" she asked. Now the shit was turning into an interrogation. Her chess moves were precise and calculated while I was on checkers. It was easy to assume she'd been here before, with eligible bachelors vying for her hand, promising the world with it resulting in unrequited love. She was a pro at discerning "game," and mine was greener than ever.

"So, what are we doing?" she asked.

"About what, tonight?"

"I mean, you got this penthouse suite. What's next?"

"You tell me, I'm going to follow your lead."

"Nah nigga, you got this room, what you trying to do?" she asked. She was pressuring me towards the truth and the vulnerability was painfully naked.

"I'm tryna eat that pussy and fuck," I said. Those unredeemable words floated from my lips in anguish, but it struck a chord. She leaned in and gently kissed me.

"That's all you had to say."

She gracefully stood and walked towards the bathroom while I sat there stunned at the last 10 seconds of our conversation. Lamont would've been proud. I picked up the remote and flipped through channels to distract the onslaught of performance anxiety wrestling with my libido. My only wish was that I'd been prepared for a night like this. I wished for a little blue pill. This was the beginnings of a rejuvenated sex life.

In the background, the sound of the shower played. Curiously, I wondered about her sex drive, if she were insatiable, or conversely the demure type. Either way, I'd hit the bad bitch jackpot and a benchmark to a new standard in my dating pool.

It was about 3:30 in the morning. The food was just delivered, and by the sound of things, she was out of the shower. I continued sitting on the couch, prodding my erection, while I waited for her to join me. The anticipation of seeing her "after shower" glow was amplified. Whatever the imagination, the unveiling would supersede it. The door opened and I immediately looked back; she had her hair tied in a ponytail and was wearing a bathrobe.

"Hey pretty lady, the food is here." She stood there with her hands on her hips, almost in a pose and replied, "You'd rather eat that or this," while she proceeded to undo the robe to unveil a most wondrous interpretation of the female body. I gazed at her like a dumbass pimple-faced teenaged boy. Words couldn't formulate a justifiable narrative of her body. My eyes were fixed upon her luscious breast, athletically flat stomach, child-bearing hips, cornbread fed thighs and most of all, the piece de resistance, that giver of life.

I stood up, unaware of what to say or do, and simply replied, "shit." She stood there matter of factly with an arrogant smirk that read, *"I know."* I began walking towards her thinking, *you better put it down.* The pressure and the excitement began to rage within, for a tumultuous mix of arrogance and nervous energy. The closer I got, the stronger the façade as I rubbed my hands together in mischief for what was about to happen.

We stood face to face, staring in each other's eyes, her naked and I, fully dressed. This was a face off and someone had to give. Courageously, I made the first move, leaning in for a kiss, while she slightly tilted her head in submission. This awkward dance symbolized the transition from cordial colleagues, to flirty friends and now sexual partners. My actual moment of fantasy, strong, wild and free had been realized. She began undoing my belt buckle as I took my sweater off. I tossed it like a piece of trash even though it was a $600 garment. She had nothing on but that beautiful caramel skin that went on forever. Mannishly I grabbed her ass cheeks as my pants fell to the floor.

In unison, we took the commotion to bed, a much suitable means to going nowhere fast. We laid on our sides, continuing the vigorous act of French kissing. Then I made the brave and brash decision to explore elsewhere, breaking our stride, but resuming on her breast. By the look of her nipples, I'd made a wise decision. She began to slightly moan, a much needed sign that things were going in the right direction. My inner man was prodding me to take it a step further, and go for the gusto. I gently kissed her on the stomach, just under her breast, in a teasing manner. Knowingly, she repositioned her body for what was next. I continued kissing her torso area, dragging out the process as she squirmed in pleasurable agony. Then I made it to her lower stomach area, looking back up at her.

I went all the way live, putting my head square between her thighs as the aroma of her excitement gave cause for motivation. Lips upon lips, the tart sweetness of her blossom signified new ground in this burgeoning liaison. My tongue took liberties that the arch of her back seemed to condone. The moaning became much more pronounced and meaningful, and I, a free spirit in a confined space, the opening act of what was to cum. Masterfully, I engaged the orifices of her lower extremities, acting under the auspice of the zodiac sign for which I was born—Scorpio.

Ten minutes in, it was clear she had a newfound respect for me. Her body shivered and convulsed more than once, thanks to a steady tongue and index finger. Time for round two. Arising from what I considered a "good showing," she continued laying there in blissful glee. Momentarily, the self-loathing for my body disturbed my thoughts in fear of her judgment. Hurriedly, I went to the light switch just outside the bathroom, turning off the modernized chandelier to the bedroom. Walking back towards the bed with the faintness of the moonlight peering through the curtains, my T-shirt and briefs were removed. Poised and erect, I kneeled before her temple prepared to give her an offering. The touch of our bodies signified the crossing of a vulnerable threshold. I was thankful for the dark, shielded in expressive anonymity, managing to conjoin ourselves as one. The slickness provided the very support necessary to begin anew. The calculated motion of my body was that of a ritualistic tribal mating ceremony, or in other words, a daddy long stroke. Pump after pump, grind after grind, the luxury of our "fucking" was only matched by the bed itself. We were gone. At some point the octane of my confidence had me in overdrive, causing her to forewarn, "Not so hard."

Fearful of finishing, I slowed even more, regrouping for stamina's sake. When I'd pick back up, occasionally I'd hear "yes" or "fuck," for which I'd reply "shit" or "damn." Our grown up teeter-totter ride was enjoyable in every way. Feeling adventurous, I suggested a new position with her being on top this time—another favorite of mine. She took to the transition, adding her own, "dutty wine" like a Jamaican dancehall queen. The seduction of her control was a euphoric culmination to that early morning hour.

We went on and on till the break of dawn, literally, enthralled in the act of vigorous unprotected sex. We spooned and she came, we doggied and she came, we even did reverse cowgirl, a move I learned from a flick, and that time, I came. After a wondrous sexathon of self-exploration, we mutually agreed to retire, feeding our sexual desires rather than ourselves.

Later at about 9 that morning, I'd awakened from a deep sleep thanks to the kitty. She was settled on my chest like a familiar lover, comfortably secure. I looked at the crown of her head, still in amazement of what went down. *If the guys at Winston Perkins could see me now.* I reached for the remote on the nightstand, struggling not to wake her. Stroking her head gently, I was thankful for my performance. Somewhat disturbed, she came to, gradually turning towards me with a slight smile.

"Good morning," I said. She replied the same while putting her head back down on my chest, and then she added, "I'm hungry."

EBB & FLOW [23]

Nearly a week had gone by with no communication from "M." Maybe she was *'bout that life,* and not at the mercy of my phone call. *Should I call her, get it over with?* I didn't wanna be *the guy that doesn't call.* This attempt at being a playboy wasn't as gratifying as I'd imagined. A spiritual emptiness coupled with the guilt of having an intentional one-night stand convicted me in a way I hadn't expected. *First Lacy, now this?* On the contrary, calling her too soon seemed needless and love-struck.

Earlier in the week, I received a call from Dr. Dobbs' office about a possible Friday appointment. Hopefully it would be a conclusive follow-up with a positive outcome to ease my mind once and for all. In times like these, I'd take solace from the fellowship of the saints, but it'd been so long. Instead, I'd watch T.D. Jakes on YouTube. That was my new "thing." My prayers had become frequent, too. Nevertheless, it was all hypocritical. I was a reactionary Christian rather than a consistent believer.

In spite of the slight bumps in the road, the journey was still good. Mom and I were back on the house hunting thing, making appointments to see a few properties. One in particular grabbed her attention. It was a two-story, Spanish-style stucco house in a subdivision called *Riverstone,* right off Highway 6. Somewhat of a gated community, residents had an entry code.

The neighborhood was typical of a master planned suburban area complete with a retention pond masked as a lake. The area was perfect with easy access to the 59 or 288 highways and plenty of malls, supermarkets, Target, anything her heart desired, just 20 minutes from my place.

Buddy was our third wheel for the day. Devin, Grace, and the boys went to the Galleria. Slowly but surely, they were getting acclimated to life in Houston. The dream was becoming more and more of a reality—my family and I living well, finally enjoying life the way it was intended.

"Mama, you should get a pet for the new house to keep you company," I suggested.

"Like what? A dog … a cat … so I can clean up boo boo and hair all day long?"

"You can hire someone to house train 'em," I offered. She'd taken a liking to Buddy since her arrival and with the size of house I'd eventually buy, this pet, whether cat, dog, or fish, would act as a physical surrogate for my time.

"Let me pick the house first …"

"Got it, Mama." It was funny, looking back on how I'd even had a dog considering the size of my old place. When Gwen and I were in better times, she'd often talk about a pet for Morgan—a small dog, something manageable. One day we were watching TV and a pet food commercial came on. In the commercial was a pug. Gwen and Morgan instantly reacted.

Hunting for pugs all over Houston, my first stop was a major pet store at $550 a pop. My check was barely $1,100 every two weeks back then. Andre suggested Traders Village, kind of a Saturday swap meet. There would usually be a variety of folks selling their wares, and in particular different breeds of puppies, but I could never find a pug. Then Coach Jackson recommended the Houston Humane Society, a pet rescue outfit that allowed the general public to adopt abandoned pets at a fraction of the cost. Every week for close to two and a half months I'd call, checking for new arrivals. Obsessed, I wanted to show Gwen my family man swag. Finally, on a Tuesday afternoon two years ago, Buddy came into our lives.

He was a frail and nervous little pup who'd been neglected by his previous owner, an elderly woman who was diagnosed with Alzheimer's. He was purchased for companionship but the onslaught of the disease made it impossible for her to maintain the responsibility it entailed. The woman's daughter brought Buddy to the shelter when it was discovered her mother hadn't properly fed nor cared for the dog. Needless to say, it was just my luck. Prior to adopting Buddy, my patience had run thin with waiting on the shelter and I was about to settle on purchasing a pug from a Craigslist post, when I'd finally received the call. Nothing was more fulfilling than being able to give that little boy a dog. Full of pride, the ideas began formulating in my head for a surprise presentation. I was absorbed by ambition, deciding to keep Buddy a secret from the both of them. We decided to meet at Hermann Park that following Wednesday afternoon, a contrast to my usual couch potato self. After beating around the bush, doing my best to veil the truth, she finally complied. Purposely, I arrived late after receiving two calls from her asking, "Where the hell you at?" The intended visual was supposed to be of me walking up with the pup in my arms and handing it to Morgan, immediately bonding the two of them for play time in the park.

Off in the distance I could see her sitting on the park bench while Morgan played on one of those bendy doohickeys most of us rode as kids. When she noticed me she gave a *what the fuck* expression, but then it changed to delighted disbelief when she saw the bundle of fur nestled under my right arm. She instantly jumped up and ran towards me.

"Oh my God … you found one?" she replied enthusiastically. It was an opportunity to gloat, especially after the time and effort it took, but I simply replied in a reserved yet triumphant tone, "I told you I would." She gently held him in her arms and the expression of care she showed assured me that we'd found our family pet.

"Morgan," she called out. "Where did you find it?" she continued.

"I did a little hunting here and there; got some tips. You like him?"

"He's cute," she responded, continuing to fawn over him.

Morgan ran over and as he got closer, he discovered what his mother held. He had the biggest smile ever on his face. *I done good.*

"Mommy is this doggy mine?" he asked, anticipating a hopeful truth.

"Yes, baby, and guess who got it for you?" He immediately looked up at me and now I had the biggest smile ever.

"Thank you," he replied.

"You're welcome, lil' homie. Give him a name," I added.

Morgan looked up at his mother, unsure of such a hasty decision, while I remained silent waiting for his reply. "How about Buddy Boy?" she asked.

"Why Buddy Boy?" I asked. The name was so bland it hurt. For the time it took to find him, it lacked in originality.

"Well, this is Morgan's new buddy, so Buddy Boy," she replied.

You'd be better off naming him, Dog, I thought. I suppose I was becoming attached, however, Morgan instantly took to the name, repeating it over and over, and eventually it stuck.

Gwen and I had no idea the level of responsibility being a pet owner demanded. With veterinary visits, pet food, supplies, and cleaning up piss and shit, it was an unbelievable undertaking. But eventually, as Buddy grew and matured, the ease of taking care of him developed into a reasonable routine.

Initially he stayed at Gwen's. She had a small patio that served as Buddy's backyard. However one faithful day, after about three months of this arrangement, she discovered that having a pet was against property policy. The landlord had heard him barking. It was a difficult decision to make, but I offered to take him in. Imagine my one-bedroom, one-bathroom apartment, with no balcony or patio, and the only other rooms being the kitchen and living room/ make believe dining area. My love for Gwen translated to an act of generosity that infringed on my space.

What was once a decent smelling, pleasantly appearing bachelor pad, gave way to chew toys, a cage, a water-feed bowl combo and a damp, dank, funk that mysteriously came from an animal no bigger than a sofa throw pillow. Of course I adjusted over time, and eventually made Buddy a part of my life. Gwen and Morgan would come over or I'd bring him over there, basically co-parenting, In hindsight, it worked out for the best that he was in my "custody" at the time of our break-up, or I suppose I'd never see him again.

Another part of the adjusting process had to do with the looks I'd endure walking this little ass dog around. Being a *"black guy,"* nine times out of ten, the expected dog of choice was either a pit bull or a Rottweiler. This pug went totally against that stereotype. Regardless, I grew to love Buddy, proudly walking him around the apartment complex or at the park or any other place that allowed domesticated animals. In some cases, Buddy's appearance helped to break the ice and spark conversations with some very attractive women.

"After we see this place can we go get something to eat? I'm getting hungry again," my mother said. We'd eaten breakfast a few hours ago, but to avoid an unnecessary debate about her health, I responded with a simple "Okay, where you wanna go?" My doctor's appointment was the next day and I needed all the positive energy I could muster.

"I'm in the mood for Mexican," she answered.

"I know a great Mexican restaurant with a drive through. I'm sure you'll like it." Just as we finished discussing our next "feeding," we reached the street where the house was located. Attractive, fairly new, and not quite occupied, every other house seemed a shell ready to be filled by some family in search of the expensive American dream.

"What's the address again?" She looked through her purse for the piece of paper she wrote it on: "3909 Shasta Court."

I slowed down, checking each address until finding the right one. There was a fire engine red Mazda Miata, presumably the realtor's car, parked in the drive. We pulled up alongside it and got out.

"Looks better in person," I offered, perhaps my superficial attempt at encouraging her to make a decision. This was house number six.

"Yeah, it does. can't wait to see the inside," she countered. We rang the doorbell and within seconds, an older woman, maybe mid to late 50s, came to the door.

"Welcome, welcome, come right in," she offered. She appeared to be Latina or even Arabic with super caked on Elvira make-up. Her hair was jet black with gray roots and she wore a multi-colored sweater in honor of the kaleidoscope. "Can I offer you a bottled water or soda?" she asked. Mom and I thanked her but declined. "Okay … well my name is Bianca," she said.

"I'm Douglas and this is my mother, Eugenia."

"Great, nice to me you all," she replied. "Is it chilly enough for ya?" she added.

"Yeah it's getting a little cold out there," I replied.

"So are y'all Houston natives?" she went on.

"Actually we're Californians, but I've lived here 11 years. We're house hunting for her," I replied with a proud smile.

"Oh great; well this is definitely enough house for you," she countered. The interior, although typical of the houses we'd seen, had some character but no "wow factor," at least not to me. Yet, I'd imagine family gatherings—Yami and I coming over for Christmas—a beautiful notion. "Let's take a tour if you don't mind," she suggested. Besides the stainless steel appliances and black granite counter tops in the kitchen, or the open floor plan that seemed to be the trend of most new homes, the look on my mother's face was most telling. *Was this the one?*

My willingness to buy whatever house she desired became questionable. *Did she need this much house?* On the other hand, after the night with "M," the possibility of future rendezvous seemed conceivable in my new bachelor digs, minus the roommate. *It's gated, better than where she is now, but it's a lot of house.*

"So what do you do?" Bianca asked abruptly, catching me off guard.

"I do private investment banking." My mother had a slight smirk on her face, unaware of the running theme.

"Oh, that sounds interesting. My daughter works in the lending industry, primarily construction loans. You guys should talk," she offered.

"That does sound interesting. Let's exchange information later," I replied. Suddenly my phone rang. It was Devin so I excused myself.

"Yeah, what's up?"

"Y'all still looking at houses?" he asked.

"Yeah, why? Everything okay?"

"Yeah … I wanted to go to the Mercedes dealership and look at the truck. How long y'all gone be?"

"Maybe 10, 15 minutes, but she wants to stop to get something to eat. I'll call you when we done. Y'all still at the Galleria?"

"Yeah, we 'bout to get something to eat though … just call us."

"Okay, 'cause the dealership is right around from there."

"All right, later."

While Mama and Bianca talked house stuff, the random urge to text Yami came out the blue.

"Hey Yami it's Doug. I was thinking about you … hope all is well. TTYL."

The thirst-o-meter within said, *Don't write or call anymore until she replies.* This fantasy of a Yami Christmas or at least a Yami New Year's, wouldn't happen unless I kicked up the game.

"Doug," my mother called out. Walking back up the stairs to what appeared to be an open game room or family room area, my mother's doe-eyed expression, presumed satisfaction. "What do you think?" she asked.

The idea of this much house was becoming a concern, solely for her safety and security. She was getting up in age, so the thought of her climbing stairs every day was an issue.

"It's a nice place, Mama … you like it?" I asked. A deal was a deal.

"It's pretty nice ... spacious, all the better for my future grandkids," she added. They laughed as I stood there put on blast.

"Well, do you want it?" She continued looking around.

"No need for a rushed decision, but this is definitely number one on my list."

"What's the asking price?" I asked.

"This property is going for one million, two hundred and sixty-seven thousand dollars. Of course the price is negotiable." My mother's poker face made me proud, refraining from any outward disapproval. She was coming around.

"Well, I guess we'll discuss this a little more and get back to you," I replied.

"Thank you both for coming out and oh yeah ... let me give you my daughter's information," she added. We exchanged numbers, saying our final goodbyes before walking out.

"Investment banker, huh?" my mother said with an amused tone.

"What, you want me to tell the truth?" I asked rhetorically.

"I get it," she answered.

After our little excursion we were en route to Chacho's. It was a beautiful late morning, brisk and full of potential. The meeting with Dr. Dobbs was tomorrow, but today was a day meant to be sporadic and blissful. Mama had apparently found her house, Devin, his car, and I, the nerve to text Yami.

"Mama, I want to tell you something."

"Okay."

"I met someone in New York a few weeks ago ... "

"Is she pregnant?"

"Mama," I said in a tone that warranted common sense. "She's not pregnant. She's interesting to me and I'd like for you to meet her." I paused for her response, hopeful she'd say something encouraging for the sake of my love life.

"I don't mind meeting her. Is she coming here for Christmas?"

"Well, that's the thing. We haven't really talked on that level of commitment. Honestly, she doesn't even know how much I'm attracted to her. I mean, I think she knows that I'm interested, but I hadn't made it a full on pursuit, yet."

"So, what you saying?"

"I haven't officially started courting her," was my sarcastic reply.

"So what's your plan?" A good question. *What was my plan?*

"Well, I wanted to know how you felt about going to New York for Christmas. We could stay in a really nice hotel, do some shopping, maybe go sight seeing, stuff like that." She listened as I made my case. Her opinion was important, especially now.

"What about Devin and Grace, and the boys?"

"They can come too, Mama, but I'm asking you. Would you mind spending Christmas there?" Her approval, necessary for different reasons, meant a pivotal effort of commitment on my part, while avoiding any feelings of guilt from leaving them behind for someone I barely knew.

"If Devin and his family can go, then I'll go. This girl must be something special."

"I don't know, but I really like her. I can't stop thinking about her."

"Well, go for it." Those four words were all the ammunition necessary to grow a pair and pursue this woman with the vigor of a man hunting his prey. *Yami Conchita Orozco you will be mine.*

Receiving my mother's blessing was empowering. Her opinion mattered. She was my example of finer womanhood and the only one capable of telling me what to expect in a future mate. But after four years with Gwen, the thought of loving again was so far removed from my sensibilities that the hurt and anguish of what I'd been through made it seem impossible. Maybe the excitement of Yami was the representation of love resurrected—not the kind of fanatical, sexual pondering of a random chick on the street, but a deep-seeded, spiritual connection indistinguishable to the naked heart.

"Thank you," I said.

"You're welcome. Just be sure to pray about this. There's no reason to jump the gun." She was right, and I hated it. Throwing caution to the wind, as if in a neatly tied plastic bag, down the trash chute of my fancy new apartment building, was a better, more selfish choice. The cons outweighed the pros in this picture, which I valiantly ignored. For once, being in love with a woman who enticed my senses, enthralled me with her beauty and intelligence, invigorated the possibilities about the rest of my life.

"She has a daughter, too," I added for a response.

"Oh? How old is she?"

"Ten."

"And the daddy?" she asked in that familiar rhetorical tone.

"He's in prison."

"Hmmm," her vocalization of thought said it all. "What does she do?"

"She's a teacher."

"Oh, okay." In a way her reply blessed my imaginable courtship, despite the baby daddy reference. "Like I said, pray about it ..." As embarrassingly painful to express my motive for a Christmas in New York, my mother's reserved charm and grace pardoned me. An exciting and volatile holiday vacation worth having awaited us—I hoped.

Later, in the earlier part of the afternoon, we caught up with Devin and family after lunch and proceeded to the dealership, but Cynthia wasn't in. In the back of my mind, I questioned my spending. This was Benz number three in less than a month—rich nigga shit. I hadn't really blown through money, except for the cars, and now this house if she wanted it, but the Bioko deal and charity stuff was still on the table. The tendencies to be extravagant were easily accessible. Suddenly I felt the vibration of my cell phone.

"Hey Doug, sorry for the late reply, hope all is well with you," Yami wrote.

I was relieved she replied.

"I'm doing well, thinking about coming there for a white Christmas with my family," I nervously responded.

"For real, ahh that's so cute," she instantly replied.

"Can I see you while I'm there?"

"That's cool. Who's all coming with you?"

"My mother, brother, sis-n-law and nephews."

"Great. Have they ever been to New York? We can take them to Rockefeller Plaza to see the Christmas tree and the ice rink. They'll love it."

My heart was elated at her usage of the word "we." It was a sign of approval in my pursuit of another shot at love.

"Well I'm definitely looking forward to it and looking forward to seeing you. :)"

"Ahh...thanks and you to:)"

All I could think about was Stevie Wonder's'"Overjoyed," the background music to the sappy lovesick disposition I was in. To avoid suspicious inquiry to my presumable obvious glow, I excused myself to celebrate alone. Looking up at the sky in wonderment, I simply said, "'Thank You." No sooner than that moment of grateful reflection, another text message alert came. Thinking it was Yami, I expected more sugary sweet comments about the impending holiday plans or simply another corny smiley face icon. But instead, it was a text from "M" that read, *"What's up playboy?"* I couldn't believe a woman once considered most desirable was now second fiddle to someone else. Grappling with my approach, the moment was debatable: *Should I respond right away, or play it nonchalantly?* She did give me the night of my life. The least I could do was be respectful and reply back in a decent time-frame.

"Hey, wassup witchu?"

A dickish reply. She didn't deserve cold and callas treatment when she'd done nothing wrong. My pride shouldn't have been a factor for simply checking up on her. My actions probably represented an ongoing theme of the uncommitted "black" men that ebbed and flowed in and out of her life. Shamefully, my posturing was partly steeped in the belief that I was *protecting myself*, while the underlying truth lingered ... *I had options.*

"Nothing much, you good?" she responded. Obviously, the tone of her text implied more than the question asked. *Even though a night of consensual adult sex, Mr. Douglas Moore, the lucky social studies teacher, got to fuck.* Her text obviously referred to the audacious length of non-communication time, after giving me such good pussy. The guilt of obligation prompted a response that lacked the ability and charm of delivering a sophisticated, yet gentle let-down.

"Chillin', just out with the family right now."

"Alright, didn't want much, TTYL," she replied.

Damn. Say something else, offer something more. If not, it would've solidified my status as a "dog," regardless of how our encounter really happened.

"What you doing tomorrow? Wanna go see a movie, get out?" I asked.

"What? Like a date? lol"

She was being cute at my expense to regain her sense of self-respect, masked as simple humor.

"What's wrong with that?"

"I'm just kidding. What time I need a babysitter."

"Let's do 9ish."

"Okay"

"See you tomorrow."

This goodwill act was an end all, be all, forever, amen date. Even if I got the pussy again, I'd still stick to my guns, my noble yet strange commitment.

My prior intention for reconciliation with Gwen ended up being this unscripted longing for a total New York stranger. Maybe aesthetically enamored lust at first, it was surely an undeniable spiritual connection. "M" was fine, with a body just as banging as Yami's, but Yami had that "something" I consciously decided to call love.

An hour or so later, Devin was the proud owner of his first Mercedes G55 AMG S.U.V. You could see the wonderment in his eyes, reminiscent of our Christmas mornings back on Cypress. Mom smiled with contentment as Grace played with the boys, during the final details to the purchase. My wealth wasn't from a best-seller, a multi-million dollar company or some life changing invention. A simple lottery ticket created moments like these with more to come.

"Where to now?" Devin asked. He was clearly on Cloud 9.

"Oh, I don't know, maybe to get my BMW?" Grace said sarcastically.

"Devin?" Mama and I asked in unison.

He just smiled, at a loss for words. We broke out in laughter. We hopped back in the "whips" and gave Houston yet another car show. Mama randomly looked over at me.

"Seek God about all your decisions, Doug."

"I will, Mama."

As soon as we got back to the apartment, parked the cars, and rode the elevator, I went straight for my suite and laid it down. My follow up appointment with Dr. Dobbs was in the morning. On the surface I displayed a calm that my eyes masterfully disguised. The intensity of my throbbing temples was a direct result of my nervous anticipation. But through it all, the support of my family, and specifically my mother's prayers, gave me the confidence to face the good and the bad of tomorrow.

FAREWELL "M" [24]

Weeks before Thanksgiving, life seemed promising. Besides the doctor's appointment that morning, my religious upbringing suggested a victorious outlook in times like these. The drive to the doctor's office was paced, and my attitude resilient; *He wouldn't bring me this far to leave me, for this is the day that the Lord had made.*

Sitting patiently in the reception area with magazine in hand and lacking the desire to update my status, maturity was faced with uncertainty. I was called to the back to be seen after an unusually short wait in time.

But with a leisurely stroll, my confidence instantly waged a war on what was otherwise intuition. *Science and religion don't mix; faith and diagnosis are at the opposite ends of the spectrum.*

I scoffed at reason, opting for the security blanket of faith. I was directed to the "isolation room," remaining positive in the midst of ambiguity. And yet again my wait time was considerably shortened as Dr. Dobbs casually walked in within minutes of my entrance.

"Mr. Moore," she stated with her hand extended in greeting.

"Hello, Dr. Dobbs," I replied with a forced smile.

Something was immediately different that morning. Aside from the reduced wait times, Dr. Dobbs didn't display the spryness I'd expected. She exuded a sensible somberness as if preparing to deliver troublesome news. Her flush appearance implied possible stress, heightening my curiosity and diminishing my faith.

"It's been one of those days you know ... but otherwise, how are you?" she asked.

"I feel fine ... my family's in town visiting ... everything's great," I replied.

She took a seat on the stool before speaking another word and immediately my stomach churned in anticipation. Everything was in slow motion now.

"So I got your results back, it looks like your hemoglobin is low. Are you anemic?" She could see the confusion. "To clarify, your red blood cell count is pretty low, attributable to a variety of factors. Possibly you're anemic or some iron deficiency is going on." I was slightly fucked up. *What's this medical mumbo jumbo shit mean?* Besides my weight, there was nothing else to pinpoint as a problem. If being a lazy ass couch potato was a symptom of something, then maybe, but otherwise, today's diagnosis was an anomaly.

"I don't think I'm anemic, never had a doctor tell me that before."

"Really? The other possibility could be internal bleeding. We should schedule an x-ray of your urinary tract and kidneys." *Great, more medical shit.* As irritated as I was by the news, I was equally relieved it wasn't dire. I could go home and genuinely smile in my mother's face. Before leaving, she suggested talking with a family member or friend about this process. Afterward, Dr. Dobbs scheduled the exam for a week later, with the hopes of finding conclusive evidence. I walked out, lost and drained from the anxiety of yet another appointment. In my 37 years, not once did I require medical care beyond the chicken pox and measles.

Later that afternoon, after driving aimlessly through Rice Village in search of peace of mind, the sudden urge to smoke came about. The nervousness of this random medical happenstance bombarded my thoughts similar to when Gwen and I thought we were pregnant the first year we dated. Today's briefing wasn't the end all be all, but the beginning of confusion in my world. Winning the lottery was supposed to be my happily ever after, not this. For simply going to church every now and then, paying my tithe every so often, being kind to random people, helping my mother financially when I could, for these things, this matter seemed untimely. And then my phone rang. It was "M."

"Hey what's up?"

"All good. What's good with you?" she asked.

"Ah, nothing just handling business. You good?" I asked.

"Yeah, I was on break and thought I'd give you a call. We said nine tonight, right?"

"Yeah, nine is cool."

"Okay, just making sure. Gotta get my babysitter straight."

"All good."

"All right, see you later, Mr. Moore."

"All right, Ms. Lady."

"M" was thirsty now? *Interesting how the tables had turned.* But then again, she did witness *that life*; nice car, penthouse suite, and good dick. Albeit a moment to gloat, it was merely a distraction by a woman I once fucked. The hunger for answers remained. *Why me? Why now?*

Rocko came to mind as a quick fix. I could whip over to the spot, pick up a zip, and chillax for a couple of hours before seeing Mama. But for some reason the idea seemed dismal. Before I knew it, I'd be back over there every week like old times. Nothing against Rocko, though.

The thought of going to some local bar and knocking back a few felt reckless and addictive at this time of day. Calling Gwen was pathetic option number three.

Man up bitch, nothing's wrong. This was perpetuity all over again. Part of me wanted to sulk and the other part wanted to go buy some random expensive thing, as if this shiny new expendable item could somehow provide clarity.

Apparently, the x-ray was the beginning stages of exploration. Calling Gwen for this matter seemed reasonable.

"Hey, Doug, what's up?"

"Oh, nothing, just wanted to holla at you right quick."

"Oh, okay, I'm actually about to go into a meeting … you all right?" *No I'm not.*

"Yeah, I'm cool, just catching up. Call me when you can."

"Okay, call you back in a little bit."

Back at square one, with a butt load of money and time on my hands, I was clueless of a next move. The day was bright and delusional. The only reasonable thing to do was go to Chacho's for a second day in a row before heading home.

When I reached home, everyone looked pleasant. Even Jabari ran up to me.

"Uncle Doug!" His smile and wonderment from being lifted above my head was the temporary cure to my frustration.

"How was your meeting?" my mother asked. Another unfair lie formed at my lips, offering positive reassurance of something that never took place.

"It was good, nothing much. Did y'all eat already?" Deflecting the question gave ease to the guilt of another lie. Getting through the day was more important.

After a few more minutes, they'd decided on going out to Memorial Mall off I-10 west, while Buddy and I stayed in. Surfing the channels, and periodically nodding off on the couch, the evening with "M" seemed a perfect opportunity to take my mind off things. With that resolve, I turned off the TV, went to my master suite to watch porn and masturbate for a proper power nap until my next episode.

Knock, knock, knock. "Doug." Knock, knock, knock. "Doug." Incoherently, I could hear Devin speaking through the door. Well rested and lifting from a damp spot on my pillow, I groggily replied, "Yeah."

"We back." *Okay mu'fucka, damn.* My much needed power nap was disturbed by an insignificant announcement, but when I looked at the clock it was 7:08. I'd been out six hours. With about an hour and a half of prep time, I got up, took a shower, and picked out an outfit for the evening. The effort and suspense of seeing "M" again put me in a weird but welcomed happy place. When I walked out the room, Mama looked at me with that wipty-doo look.

"My, my, someone's looking sharp tonight. Where you going?"

"Meeting up with a friend for dinner."

"Oh, okay, well, be careful."

"As always."

I went to the kitchen, pulled the Crown from the pantry and a can of Coke from the fridge, fixed up a quick drink, took a minute for a few swigs, and walked out the door. Tonight I'd take the Benz truck to switch things up.

Driving towards Highway 59, I realized Gwen never called me back as promised. Maybe she'd forgotten. We use to joke about her good memory. She usually never forgot anything—one of the main reasons I'd lose most of our arguments. Whatever the case, she was still the one I wanted by my side next week.

The anticipation with seeing "M" after the night we had gave me jitters all over again. *Could we repeat that … tonight?* As selfish the thought, another luxurious sexual escapade, with the result being another, unattached "nut," was all right with me.

Twenty minutes later I arrived at her apartment complex, right off Richmond Avenue. The sign out front read "The Gables." "M" struck me as someone accustomed to the finer things, but more affording of the appearance of having them. She was always well-dressed at school, yet low-key. She wasn't one for gossip, but knew everything. And for the most part, she seemed liked by all—even those jealous of her. *She bad.*

Truthfully, even while Gwen and I seemed to have a loving and functioning relationship, my private bedroom fantasies in apartment 713 were imagined with "M." She was the unattainable trophy girl; my *freak bitch.* With every stroke, I vigorously fucked her, disrespecting her in ways that went against our trite little hallway greetings. And to think, this was our *conscious* date, where this time, we *knew* each other. No conscionable space for shyness, I knew the curves of her ass and back, the stretch marks on her stomach and the tattoo on her inner thigh. I was there.

Next in line at the security gate, I called to inform her of my arrival.

"Hey Doug, when you come through the gate, make a right at the first building, go all the way to the end then make a left. I'm building G 119."

"Cool, am I coming in or are you coming out?"

"I can come out, gimme 'bout five minutes."

"All right."

Driving slowly, I took my time knowing five minutes really meant ten. Among the rows of middle class vehicles and manicured grounds, sat these seemingly newly constructed apartment buildings light years ahead of my former place. I wondered if she had a *sponsor* to be living here. She had to be paying at least $1,500 a month.

Just as I made the left to her area, I saw what looked to be Gwen's car parked at the first corner parking space—a 2008 Honda Civic, dark gray with her sorority license frame. Coincidence? After my momentary gasp, I proceeded to look for G119, and for a quick exit. Oddly, the building "M" lived in was next to the building where Gwen's car was parked. *Fuck.* I almost honked the horn in haste, but decidedly remained cool, backing into a parking space, sending her a text, *"I'm here."*

True to form, "M" came out minutes later, not ten, but not quite five. In those moments before, my focus remained on the area of Gwen's car. She didn't tell me she moved. Maybe she was visiting a friend. My curiosity piqued. *Was she at a dude's place? Are they in there fucking? What kind of mother is she to be fucking some dude? Where's Morgan?* Jealousy, the strongest trait of us Scorpios, nearly made me black out, until I focused back on "M." She stood at the curb, looking left to right, so I flashed my headlights. She unsurely looked in my direction, and cautiously walked my way. The closer she got, her facial expression gradually changed until a big thirsty smile totally manifested itself. She walked to the passenger side door and slid in.

"I see how you do. Switch it up, huh?" she responded, referring to the truck.

"Sometimes you gotta switch it up."

"My, my, somebody's fly."

"It ain't like that," I responded with a smile on my face, a little embarrassed.

"I mean, first the Rolls, now the Benz. What's really going on?"

"I told you about the inheritance, remember?"

"Yeah, but you doing it real big."

Unsure of her point, I fired up the engine and drove out in the opposite direction.

I hadn't made any reservations anywhere. This wasn't that type of date. As a matter of fact, this was the *gentle let down, but you still cool with me, end all, ba'bye, but if possible, could I hit one more time? Date.*

"So what you been up to today? Buying cars and shit? Mansions?" she asked bluntly.

My genuine laughter was in gratitude for her ability to distract me. Oddly, to imagine where our conversation would go by dinner seemed scary. As beautiful, shapely, sexy she'd been to me, I was afraid I'd be visibly bored. However, the more she talked, the more layers were removed from this delicate flower I once revered as my dream "chick." She was more *fine* than interesting, but a plausible good time.

"No house yet. Working on it," I answered.

"Oh, well make sure you get a house, Moore," she responded.

"You right. I'm a start looking soon."

She seemed genuine in her concern, or plotting at the least, but thoughtful.

We continued on to Edwards Cinema off Greenway Plaza, a decent venue with a lot of options for someone who forgot to check on movie times, much less a particular movie. The old me would've made up some bullshit like, "Damn, I forgot the movie I picked."

The new me didn't give a fuck. We'll park, we'll walk in, we'll look at the gazillion movies and times, she'll pick what she wants to watch, I'll oblige, and that's pretty much about it. "So you got everything straight with your daughter ... the babysitter?" I asked.

It was an attempt at pushing the conversation forward and off my personal business.

"Yeah ... had to bribe my cousin into doing it. My regular babysitter was sick."

"Oh okay. So how old is your daughter?"

"Thirteen, she's autistic."

Immediately a pitiful, guilt-riddled feeling washed over me, punishment for my ill intentions. This woman had bigger issues than my libido. She didn't look like a mother of a 13-year-old, autistic daughter. Instead, she looked like someone ready to have a family for the sake of her daughter, rather than the countless meaningless encounters with men drawn to her beauty and not much else. Humbled by the information she shared, I vowed to be on my best behavior for the rest of the evening.

"Damn, I wouldn't have imagined it," I replied.

"What?" she responded defensively.

"That you have so much on your plate."

"Had her when I was seventeen. I was a lil hot mama back in the day."

As uncomfortable the conversation was becoming, her transparency was refreshing. Maybe the night we had, wasn't her usual seductive swan song but simply a moment of escapism. The plight of raising a child with autism was something unfathomable from the perch of my selfish, bachelor existence.

"Yeah, I love my baby. She's a handful, but she's my heart."

"That's beautiful. I need to be honest and tell you something," I interrupted.

"You don't date chicks with autistic kids?" she responded facetiously

"Funny. No I didn't pick a movie I was running behind and ..."

"Don't worry about it. We'll figure it out," she replied.

For some reason, I billed "M" as this sexy boughetto, high maintenance, one dimensional female, good enough for the "look" I wanted, but not an intellectual equal.

"And I didn't make reservations for dinner."

"Damn. Where we going?"

"You have a preference? I'm open." I replied. I was embarrassed, especially after opening up like she did. The least I could do was have dinner reservations. *Guess I'll have to splurge tonight.*

In a short time, we reached the theater. My focus for the evening had changed. Tonight seemed a conceivable therapy session for us with our realities. Of course, she was still the attractive sex kitten I'd quickly grown to admire.

We settled on "For Colored Girls," an interesting break from Tyler Perry's usual comic shtick. Next, we made a pit stop at the concession stand, where I convinced myself that a large popcorn, a box of Raisinets and a large Coke was fair game. And then my phone rang. It was Gwen. *Damn why is she calling this late.* I ignored the call. We collected our calories and continued on towards the hall to the theater.

Cheesy abstract carpet and sticky cement floors provided a welcomed setting for this curious date of sorts. After our dialogue in the car, a good laugh was necessary, but our choice was an obvious contrast. Tonight was not the night to be depressed. "M" who walked just ahead of me under the dim lights, periodically looked back for approval until we settled on the middle of the incline of steps, and the middle seats of the row.

With a decent gathering of "black folks" waiting to be entertained, we sat in quietness, stuffing our faces with comfort food. "M" reached in her purse for her cell phone, turned off the ringer, while she looked at me and suggested I do the same. I obliged with a simple smile, but not before hitting Gwen with a text that read, *"sorry I missed your call, I'm in a meeting. Can I call you later tonight?"* Then I put it away.

As the previews came on, the ancillary anticipation of watching a movie was overshadowed with the realization of being on a full fledged, albeit trifling date with "M." In the darkness, with my head ever so slightly turned in her direction, I was in awe again, and for a moment, I imagined this date happening regardless of the money.

Her eyes danced from left to right, illuminated by the brightness of the screen. Her laser sharp focus was amusing, a different look perhaps. All the while she chomped on popcorn, leisurely taking sips of her drink. Her innocence was a refreshing difference to the sexual romp we had a week ago. Maybe tonight, we could just be friends, enjoying each other's company with no intentions or reservations, no pun intended.

As the night went along, the pleasant surprise was the film; enjoyable and introspective. *We could have a good conversation over dinner after all ... at least 30 minutes worth.* During the film, "M" became emotional, possibly reflective of the demons in her past. Those deep dark places never seem to leave us. Even I was touched by the story line, the grit of life in the big city, which made me think of Yami and her daughter. *What was she doing right now?*

When the movie was over, the mood in the theater seemed somber. Despite the circumstance I faced, I was grateful, thankful for the possibility of hope. "M" appeared drained but cordial. Her eyes were visibly red from crying throughout the film, a matter I chose to ignore. *Let her be.* Instead I tried lightening her mood.

"I'm so damn hungry right now."

She responded with a simple smirk, a promising sign for the rest of the evening, despite the fact that this was probably my first and last dating encounter with her.

"Hey, let's go to Houston's. That's cool with you?" I asked.

"Yeah, that's cool," she replied.

Walking out towards the parking lot, the brisk winter air of that November night sky jolted my senses, striking my emotional chord. *Yami's the one.* Not to be insensitive, but I didn't owe "M" anything, I didn't owe Gwen anything. These women were concurrently of my present and past. But of my future, maybe Gwen, for reasons other than love.

Our short drive down Kirby was welcomed with a five minute wait for a table. We ordered drinks, her Cosmopolitan, and my trusted Long Island. Thankful for this elixir, my nerves were settled in such close proximity to this woman I once adored. If possible, I would steer clear of relationship questions and sexual innuendos.

"M" had regained her composure after the first round. With a brief rehash of the film, we talked school politics and travel. She spoke of her desire to one day visit London and how she always wanted to see a fashion show in Paris, all things I could make possible, unfortunately. I shared with her my desire to see Africa and to be able to reconnect with my ancestral roots. Overall, the flow of the conversation was comfortable and safe over a basket of bruschetta and olive spread, but then she hit me with it.

"Are you dating anyone?" she asked. In the pit of my gut that strange uncomfortable churning of pain, met with a moment of truth, stung fiercely. My charming schoolboy demeanor was second nature. I hadn't developed my inner asshole quite yet. Being a straight shooter wasn't easy for me. Feelings mattered, more so those of others over mine.

I wanted to say, "No, but I'm interested in this chick I met in New York last month." Not imagining how that would sound, I opted for a different response, "No, not really."

Surely her question was an invitation that made perfectly good sense. We already did the sex thing, we had some familiarity as colleagues, a factor, and financially, I could support "us." Again, I understood it and if it hadn't been for a chance encounter with another woman, perhaps the stars would've aligned. But for once in my life the conviction of heart and a determined will had to prevail.

"Actually, I was in a relationship for four years. We broke up this past April. I'm sure I'll date again but for now, I'm chilling. I don't wanna bring the baggage of my last relationship to another one." Brilliant bullshit. Hopefully it was enough to quell any further interest from her. I sat quietly for her response.

"So basically, you just fucking for now." Another upper-cut from across the table that landed. It was true. If we could fuck again I wouldn't hesitate, even with the knowledge of her daughter and my infatuation for Yami. But again, I didn't owe her or anyone else an explanation.

"Is that a bad thing?" I asked.

"I mean, don't you want to settle down, get married, and have a family?"

"I did, and I thought I would with my ex, but she had other plans." My tone turned serious. "M" backed me into a corner momentarily, but I came back swinging. Her condescending attempt at thrusting a life decision on me was enough. *Eat your bread.*

Saturday morning, I lay in bed disconnected and frustrated with millions of dollars in the bank. Something wasn't right. As beautiful the sun rays that beamed through the curtains, with the billowing smells of my mother's cooking, the morning was uninspired. The pleasantries of last night's date had worn off. After dinner, I drove her home and kept my hands to myself, although secretly wishing for a blow job along the way. She asked if I'd come in, but I declined. Meeting her daughter seemed weird for me, almost a nefarious prodding to the inklings of a serious relationship.

At that moment, I knew I needed to call Gwen. She deserved having the choice of attending my next doctor's appointment. Desperately, I hoped she would. She was the only one worthy of entrusting the ambiguity of what was ahead. It was 10:15 in the morning, *maybe she's still sleep or dealing with Morgan.*

Suddenly, my mother came to the door, "Knucklehead, you up?" Technically I was but my mind, body, and heart weren't aligned. *What's Yami doing right now?* Immediately, I reached for my phone and before calling Gwen, I chose to text Yami.

"Good morning beautiful just thought about you." And then I called Gwen.

"Morning, Doug."

"Hey, hope I didn't wake y'all."

"Nah, we been up since nine, Morgan has a game today."

"A game? What he play?"

"I signed him up for soccer a few weeks ago … kept bugging me."

"You're a soccer mom now?" We laughed.

The beginnings of the conversation proved a welcome difference from my morning mood. More so, the lightheartedness of it made it difficult to transition to the real matter at hand. *How would she react*? The oddity of revealing this information, but withholding the news about the money, was plain stupid.

"So, what you been up to?" she asked.

"Nothing … chilling. Went to see that Tyler Perry movie."

"Oh how was it? I wanna see that, too."

"Yeah it was good. Didn't think it'd be that serious."

"Don't tell me nothing. I'm going to see it, maybe tomorrow after church."

"Yeah, but it was good. I wanted to ask you a huge favor though," I replied.

"Okay. What's up?"

Before uttering another word, my mouth quivered in hesitation. Basically, the pride of my inhibition gave way. The pause was deafening but reflective of my fear of asking my "ex" to a doctor's appointment.

"Well, ah, long story short, I had to see a specialist, and ah … they wanna run some test to see why I've had blood in my urine. It's not anything serious yet; they just wanna get a better diagnosis. My doctor suggested sharing with close family and friends about this process … I guess for support. I thought about you. I haven't told my mother yet … she freaks out over everything. It's nothing serious, just needed to let someone know." I went silent, waiting for her response.

"I mean, you know I'll do whatever I can to help. When's your appointment?"

"Yeah, it's next Friday…"

"I'll put in a leave request Monday morning for Friday. I'll come with you."

I wanted to cry right then and there. Her willingness to appease me, even after the drama of our break up, after the months of being separated from each other, made her amazing all over again.

The only thing left to say was, "Thank you ... thank you so much, I really appreciate it." And I did. Option two was Lamont. Explaining the situation to him felt tedious for his over dramatic ass.

After a few minutes more of going over the particulars for next Friday, we ended our conversation on a high note. We were definitely still friends. The ease of knowing she'd have my back made the days ahead bearable. Consciously, I could ride around town with my mother looking for houses, participating fully in the process. I'd actively be engaged with whatever topic of discussion, however mundane. The effort to keep this from my mother was a necessary evil. With all that had transpired in our recent family history, this happenstance would only deepen the cut, and I surely didn't want to hear, "God has a reason for everything."

A DIAGNOSIS FOR FEAR [25]

A few days had passed since sharing the intimate details of my life with Gwen. Within that time, a lot had transpired. Devin and Grace secretly found an apartment of their own, a move that Mom and I hadn't expected. They even quit their jobs, a definite sign that they'd transitioned to Houston completely.

Mom had actually shown interest in a single-story brick house in a newly planned community called Rivercrest. We went as far as negotiating the price, asking for changes in the fixtures, among other things. *Was this the one?*

Lamont and I caught up, shooting the regular bullshit. I was fighting the urge to tell a new secret. Albeit deceiving, we laughed and talked like any other time.

"Nigga, what's up with that girl you was dancing with at the party, in the green with the long hair ... the teacher?" he asked.

"She cool." I responded.

Immediately, that famous grin of his was followed by, "Did you hit?" All I could do was laugh. His usual interrogation and my classic ambiguous laughter neither confirmed nor denied the truth.

"Man, I told you who I'm after."

"So what's up with that?" he asked.

Yeah, what was up with that? Yami and I texted back and forth the other day, the simple shit, *"hey how you doing? hope all is well, thinking 'bout you,"*

"Hey Doug, doing well, how are you?"

"Good, just chillin'."

Continuing this adolescent approach to a possible real love connection was doubtful and depressing for my age. I really wanted to say, *"When I come for Christmas, you'll stay with me in my fabulous penthouse suite at the Waldorf-Astoria ... we'll shop till you drop by day, and by night ... leave that to me."*

"I'm a see her when I go back for Christmas. My mother and 'nem coming too."

"Dang, you for real, huh?"

"I really like this chick man, for real."

Of all the bullshit lies I'd told over the money, this moment of clarity was refreshing. Never lying about her, or hiding her, now both my mother and best friend knew that I was really in *like* with Yami.

"Damn, nigga, I can't wait to meet her. Your nose wide as hell."

He wasn't lying. The next time I'd see her, I promised myself at least a nice respectable hug, a peck on the cheek and then I'd say, "You were the Christmas gift I've been waiting for." *Too much?*

Earlier in the week, I'd made some strides with my business affairs. A frat brother referred me to an attorney for my charity stuff, Bioko sent a contract for our deal and finally, I decided to put half my winnings into my foundation. Seventy-two million dollars was more than enough to live on.

Tomorrow was the follow up appointment with Dr. Dobbs. I tirelessly assured Gwen she didn't have to come. She fervently insisted, and I conceded. Her persistence and willingness meant more than the act of accompanying me, and yet the guilt of my feelings for Yami felt selfish. *Was I indebted to Gwen?*

The Day

This is the day that the Lord has made and I'm scared. No positive affirmations. I hated hospitals and all things diagnostic. At 4:17 that morning I lay staring at the ceiling with a million possible outcomes. Imagining the worst, being melancholy was easy. In just the other room laid a woman who'd lost her husband and nephew to illnesses.

I pushed myself to get up a few hours later, retreating to the living room with a bowl of cereal. Everyone was still asleep, while I watched the local news. Sitting there thinking of the day, I decided to book taxi service for the appointment. Gwen would meet me there.

By 9:27, I'd taken a shower, got dressed, and was heading out the door, when my mother, half-awake called for me.

"Doug, is that you?"

"Yeah, Mama, be back in an hour," I answered.

"Wait a minute," she replied.

Concerned for the taxi downstairs, I impatiently obliged. She walked over and gave me a hug, something she hadn't done any other morning. Then she offered a prayer. Standing there on the verge of ruin, I held her hands with my eyes closed, blessed to have a mother with spot on intuition.

"Love you, son. Have a good day," she added.

"Love you, too, Mama."

The elevator ride was long and nerving. As soon as I exited, my usual smile and nod to the girls at the reception desk was replaced with a stern focus to the taxi waiting outside.

"The medical center please. MD Anderson."

The driver took off as I sunk into the seat, looking forward to Gwen's face. Her look could ease my mind, this tension, this over thinking.

In 20 minutes time, I'd arrive at the hospital to some wanted or unwanted news, but at least I'd have the support of an old friend, my ex love. *Awkward.*

When I arrived, Gwen was already sitting in the lobby area on her cell phone. I walked up beside her to get her attention.

"Hey, girl let me call you back. Okay bye," she said. "Hey Doug." I bent down and gave her a hug. Her eyes had that morning look and she smelled wonderful.

"You been here long?"

"Nah, just a few minutes," she replied.

We sat there, not sure what else to say. The appointment was at 10:30, but it was barely 10.

"Thanks for coming."

"Ain't nothing. How's your mom?"

"She good, getting on my nerves a little, you know how that goes."

"When I'm going see her? Set that up," she replied flippantly.

Our conversation was a cute distraction from the moments ahead. We went on a few minutes more before deciding to go up. When we reached the reception area, only one other person was there. Depressing.

"Dang, you should be able to go right in," she said.

Problem was I didn't wanna go right in. I didn't wanna go at all. Whoever this other person was who was waiting, I'd oblige them graciously. I went to check-in. The nurse made note and asked that I take a seat. This shit was getting old fast.

"I prayed for you, Doug. Everything's gonna be all right, you believe that?"

"Yeah, but you know how much I hate hospitals and shit."

"Well, get over it. You are here now."

It sounded simple enough, but it was hard to do. My imagination always got the best of me. Once, Gwen and I didn't talk for a week after a disagreement during our relationship. I immediately assumed another dude. Maybe that's my current situation—paranoia.

"Mr. Moore," the nurse called as she stood by the door. Gwen and I got up and walked to the back area. A familiar scene, we were led to the room where I received the previous prognosis. "Dr. Dobbs will be right with you." I offered a polite smile as she walked out, closing the door behind her.

"It's a little nippy in here," Gwen stated.

Somewhat perhaps, I wasn't giving a fuck about the air conditioning. *One more random observation.* We continued our empty banter, choosing to ignore the obvious reason for being there. The lifelessness of the room juxtaposed the anxiousness of seeing Dr. Dobbs. Two minutes had gone by noticeably, then five, and then ten. Gwen continued playing some game on her phone, while I checked my timeline.

"Hello, Mr. Moore, sorry for the delay," Dr. Dobbs said as she walked in. *Damn, where the fuck you been?*

"Good to see you, Doc," I replied as we shook hands. "This is my friend Gwen, she's accompanying me for support," I added.

"Nice to meet you, Gwen."

"Likewise."

"Mr. Moore, we're doing the x-ray today."

"Correct,"

"Yeah, we're checking your kidneys and urinary tract. Let's take a look at that first and then proceed."

"Well, okay. Do you think it's serious?"

"I wouldn't say that just yet. Again, these are only preliminary measures."

"Okay," I responded. There wasn't much else, but to wait on her next call.

"I've scheduled the examination a few floors down. They'll take the x-ray, send it back up, and then we can proceed. Should take 30 minutes tops. As a matter of fact, Gwen, you could wait here or the waiting area while Doug gets the x-ray done."

"Oh, well I prefer to go with him, if that's okay." *Ride or die.*

"Sure, no problem. Give me a minute. I'll go fetch the lab room number," she said as she stood up to walk out the room.

"You don't have to go if it's just downstairs," I said.

"I know I don't, mind your business," she playfully replied.

Moments later Dr. Dobbs returned with the floor and room number. We thanked her and walked out towards the elevators.

A re-occurring theme, no one sat in the waiting area. Aside from the lab technicians and receptionist, we were it. I gave the lady my name and again was asked to take a seat. Gwen and I looked at each other. *Here we go again.*

Moments later, I was called to the back, asked to disrobe, put on a radiation vest, and laid on the cold examination table. A chubby Asian guy toiled with the x-ray lamp as I laid there watching and waiting for this to be over. The process took a quaint 10 minutes. Afterward while I was getting dressed, he informed me that the x-rays would be sent up to Dr. Dobbs.

We were back waiting again for Dr. Dobbs to hear the results. "Okay, let's see what we have here," she said, entering the room with a vanilla folder. She sat on her stool, put on her reading glasses and began to hold the x-rays up against the light for a better view. Gwen and I looked on, waiting. Judging from her facial expression, something was wrong. Her concerned look was intensified by the wrinkles of her face. The longer she grimaced, the more I wanted an answer.

"Doc, you see something?"

"Well, something is interesting. I'm looking at your bladder. I see an odd blur worth investigating," she went on. *An odd fucking blur…what the fuck is that?* She continued looking and then got up and walked out the room, "Excuse me." Gwen looked over, offering a comforting smile. This unexpected *blur* went against the usual moments of my life, where things kind of just worked out in my favor. Gwen put her hand on my back, rubbing it to console me I suppose.

Moments later, she walked back in the room and went right in. "Doug, what's your schedule like today?"

Off put by the question, I shrugged and replied, "I'm free." I turned to Gwen, "What about you?"

She looked hesitant. "I have to pick Morgan up by two."

It was already twelve. "Doc, whatever it is, will we be done before two?"

"Well, let me tell you what I'd like to do before we proceed. When I left the room I consulted with a colleague about the blur I saw on the chart, and we agreed that it would be advantageous to further investigate it for true analysis. I'd rather not send you home without gathering more data, so with that said, I'd like to perform a cystoscopy exam of the bladder to see just what this blur is. Shouldn't take more than 25 minutes from prep to finish. We'll be done before 12:30 max."

"Okay, Doc. I have no objection to that. So what does this procedure entail?"

Funny I would ask. It was a more amusing choice of words, *entail*. She went on to explain the need to "invade" my privacy, with the aid of a 10 inch scope and freezing jelly, used to numb the feel of the telescope going through my dick, into my bladder. This was the first and only woman to literally be in my ass and dick within a month. I looked at Gwen who did her best to conceal a slight smirk.

"Do I have any other choice?"

"It's not painful, it won't take long, and to be honest, this is the only way."

Not in the mood to debate, I simply conceded. This whole ordeal was getting much more serious than anticipated.

"I'll do the cystoscopy exam in another room. You'll need to disrobe. We'll provide you with dressing."

We followed a nurse to the examination room where the procedure would be performed. Twenty minutes later, after putting on those drab, powder blue hospital robes that barely closed and Gwen leaving for the reception area, I sat alone at the edge of the examination table, distraught and eager to get home. *I want my Mommy.*

"Okay, Mr. Moore, we're back," Dr. Dobbs said as she entered the room with a nurse who rolled in what looked to be the device and monitor.

"Is that the machine you're using on me?" I asked hesitantly.

"Yes sir," she replied as she prepped herself with rubber gloves. "At first it'll feel a little odd of course. The movement through the urethra to the bladder ... a cool sensation, that's the jelly and then your bladder will feel full like you have to pee." My focus was on the *blur*.

Moments later I was asked to lay back, while being injected with a localized anesthesia. Avoiding eye contact with any of them, I looked at the ceiling, but in my peripheral I could see the scope, a thin black plastic flexible shaft with a light at the end of it attached to some hand held remote, with knobs. The nurse applied jelly to the body of it, while Dr. Dobbs looked at the monitor, ensuring it worked properly. Then the nurse handed the scope over.

"Ready, Mr. Moore. Just relax."

"Okay, I'm not ready, but okay."

Suddenly she began to insert this thing into my dick ... *damn it.* I focused back on the ceiling as a collage of thoughts rushed through my mind. *This shit here.* My natural reflex was to clinch, but I couldn't feel anything.

"Mr. Moore just relax ... take a few breaths, okay?"

"All right, Doc."

I guess she figured talking in the tone of a kindergarten teacher would make things easier. I grabbed at the side of the bed as the scope was inserted, slowly, and without my control. As she continued pushing upward, it felt like I was pissing backwards. Her focus was zeroed in on the monitor, while the nurse stood to the side watching. "You're doing good, Mr. Moore." *Thanks, but what am I doing good at? I'm doing good by having this plastic wizard wand gently pushed through my dick? I get a gold star and lollipop afterward?*

I continued looking at the ceiling when suddenly I heard her make an interesting noise as if realizing something. She stopped pushing the scope and asked the nurse to go get the x-ray sheet.

"You see something, Doc?"

"No, just want to make a comparison between the x-ray and the area of the scope," she replied.

If I didn't know any better, it sounded a tad misleading, considering the need to *compare.* Occasionally glancing at my obstructed view of the monitor, the hope of seeing what she saw was hopeless. Soon after, the nurse came back with the x-ray, handing it to Dr. Dobbs. She paused from the exam to juxtapose the monitor and x-ray. I lay there, concerned with a scope protruding from my dick. She continued her meticulous note taking and probing while more thoughts came to mind. *My next blunt, five piece wing combo from Frenchy's, Yami.* I was bored now.

"Okay, Mr. Moore ... we're done. Told you it wouldn't take long," she offered.

"Cool," I responded.

Moments later after getting dressed, Gwen and I were called backed to Dr. Dobbs' office to discuss the exam. We sat there, waiting her diagnosis, while a lingering pain of nervousness sat in the pit of my gut. It was *the principal's office all over again.* Just behind her was a window view of a sunny bright afternoon undeserving of depression. Her degrees, family pictures and cheap art hanging on the walls were slight distractions, but the question still remained: *what the fuck is up?*

"So, Mr. Moore, after looking at the x-ray, and then doing the exam, I saw what appeared to be a golf ball sized growth on the inner lining of your bladder. Have you been experiencing any pain lately?" I was still stuck on *golf ball sized growth.*

"Not that I can remember. Maybe a sharp pain every now then. I thought it was from holding it too long."

"Well, I don't want to alarm you, but the growth appears to be a tumor."

At that moment in time, everything about my sugary sweet existence was stripped away with those words. This wasn't the day I was expecting from the Lord. "Now, what we need to do is discern whether it's malignant or benign. If it's malignant, it's cancerous. We would immediately need to begin chemotherapy treatment to contain the tumor, shrink it, and remove it. If it's benign, we can remove it surgically."

"I don't know what to say right now, Doc. Whatever you think is the best option, let's just do it. How soon can we figure it out?" Gwen grabbed my hand in support. My words raced, panicked, and unsure. I tried expressing myself as articulately as possible in the face of fear. My mouth moved but this was a conscious out of body experience. *I have cancer?*

After discussing the matter a few moments more, with more random questions on my part, Dr. Dobbs did her best to assure me of what she didn't know, and I knew it. I needed to hear *everything would be okay ... I get cases like this all the time ... you'll be back to normal in no time.* A new reality superseded $165 million; possible death. Gwen put her arm around me the entire time, from the walk to the elevator, to her car. She occasionally wiped tears from her face, as I looked on, confused about this outcome. Lost for words, I questioned everything. *What was the meaning of this?* We hugged goodbye as she got into her car. Mustering the strength to wave, the sadness of seeing her leave weighed more than the news I'd received. What a difference from six weeks before. *I need to smoke.*

THE CHRISTMAS ANTIDOTE [26]

October 16 and November 19 had become two of the most significant dates for 2010. In a month's time my emotions and resiliency were stretched to the opposite ends of the spectrum; following the last appointment and diagnosis, we scheduled a biopsy two weeks later.

After the December 3 surgery, it was discovered that the tumor was in fact malignant. Heartbroken and scared, nothing mattered anymore. Gwen was the only one who knew. We cried together, had long conversations on the phone and seemed to be strengthening a resolve as friends. As much as I wanted to tell my mother and other close folks in my circle, I refused. My façade seemed easier to maintain than the outpouring of sympathy I'd receive.

Dr. Dobbs suggested chemo treatments before Christmas. A definite downer, it didn't fit well with my plans. On the contrary, my family was excited about New York City. With reservations at the Waldorf again, limousine service to accommodate us, this was a worthy diversion with Yami in play. And still, at the crux of it all, the fear of dying lingered, clouding the ability to control my random acts of stupidity.

My usual bi-weekly zip lock baggie was increased. I started buying an ounce every Sunday from Rocco. Every night, I found a reason to hit some club or bar, attempting to inebriate my somber life, against the doctor's orders. Even with Yami in the horizon, random chicks were fair game. My self-pity was rationalized with the belief that my time was limited, that every moment was to be lived as my last, even though it was a tumor detected early enough to be treated.

In keeping with the randomness of my life, one Saturday morning I woke up and decided to go to a luxury car dealership and bought a $400,000 Lamborghini, bright yellow with black suede and leather interior, and yellow stitching. I even drove it to Carrington's one night, not giving a fuck. *At least if I died, they'd remember the nigga in the yellow Lambo.*

The days were indifferent; between December 3, the day of the biopsy, and December 23, the intended date we'd all fly to New York, everything was a blur, no pun intended. The chemo treatments were draining, painful, and uneventful consisting of needles, IVs and long hours. All the while my mother had no clue of her son's private hell.

In the mornings we'd have breakfast together, sitting at the table or in the living room, and occasionally, I'd see her staring at me, wondering, discerning if something was wrong.

"You know you can talk to me about anything, Dougie," she said.

"Why you say that, Mama?" *She knew something.*

"I feel something ain't right,but you gone lie anyway. You been secretive all your life, even as a kid."

She was right. I could keep a secret, any secret, until I'd eventually forget it. She deserved knowing, but it was too early to say. By then, I'd only had two chemo treatments. My hair wasn't thinning and I hadn't lost any weight.

"Mama everything's all right, you worry too much." Keeping it together was important regardless of how much her sympathy could heal my soul.

Three weeks and five chemo treatments later, the day arrived for our White Christmas/ New Year's Eve adventure. Just as before, I'd made reservations at the Waldorf-Astoria, for three penthouse suites and reserved limousine service for the family. I called Raul and Yami about my return visit. I decided not to call Frankie for obvious reasons.

As we were boarding the plane, seeing my mother experience first-class for the first time made me proud. Prior to my winning, she barely traveled, much less like this. My mother grew up in the deep south, the youngest of two. Her father, my grandfather, was a factory worker, and her mother, my grandmother, a domestic. Her stern Baptist upbringing permeated everything she did, from washing clothes, to cooking, to whipping our asses ... the Lord was in it. Funny enough, on the plane ride she requested a couple of glasses of White Zinfandel for the sake of turbulence. The will of the Lord I supposed.

When we finally landed, collected our luggage, and made it back to the pick-up area, our shiny black Cadillac limousine awaited with an older brother appearing to be in his 60s, holding a sign with my name.

"Hello sir, that would be us," I offered. Slightly surprised, he replied with a welcoming smile and firm handshake.

"Welcome, sir. My name's Rayford."

Devin and I began loading the luggage in the trunk with the driver's assistance while the ladies and children sat inside. This time we came prepared for the harshness of a New York winter. We took mom to one of the premiere fur boutiques in the Galleria area for her first full length chinchilla coat worth $50,000. She cried like a baby.

"So, Mr. Moore, where are you from?"

"We're all Californians residing in Houston," I replied while smirking at Devin.

"Okay, I've got a few family members down there, small world."

"Oh great," I replied tritely.

Being used to the question, *what do you do*, my expectation was pleasantly disrupted when he continued on to the driver's side of the car. We begin driving towards our intended destination, excited about a family vacation well overdue. That moment in the back of that limousine was something straight out of a Hollywood screenplay. If someone had told me I'd win the Mega Ball, jet set to Manhattan with my mother and brother, stay at one of the most prestigious hotels in the country, all while having a cancerous tumor, I'd cussed them out.

"You stayed at this hotel before, Dougie?" Mama asked.

"Yeah, my last trip here. You're gonna love it."

The excitement in her voice was pleasing. To imagine the thoughts in her head, the wonderment of going from living check to check to a $50,000 jacket had to be mind boggling. Being a two month old millionaire was still surreal for me.

"What's that place where they do the ice skating, with that big Christmas tree?" Grace asked, obviously excited, too.

"That's Rockefeller Center," I said. Grace immediately began clapping while Jabari followed suit.

"Look, whatever y'all wanna do let's do it. We here for about two weeks. We gone have fun. You only live once."

Approaching the entrance area to the hotel provided that same familiar tingly feeling. I looked at Mama and Devin who seemed preoccupied with the people walking about, while Grace looked down at her phone. Jabari just kept jumping up and down while their youngest son, Julian, was sound asleep.

"We here y'all," I said. No sooner than saying that, the passenger door was approached by a doorman.

"Welcome to the Waldorf. Mr. Moore?" he asked in puzzlement. It was the same cornball white guy who'd seen me high as a kite, who'd seen me ramble in with Frankie and Lacy after one late night of heavy drinking and an "x" pill, and now with my family.

"Yes, forgive me, I'm not good with names," was my bullshit reply.

"Bradley, no problem, sir," he answered with that caked on smile.

"Yes, Bradley, okay great. Yeah, back again. I love this place obviously, huh?"

We shared another one of those disgusting empty laughs. Bradley reminded me of the doorman on *The Jeffersons*, the kind of dude you'd slip a couple of dollars to keep things quiet. "I brought my family this time for Christmas."

"Very good, sir. Enjoy your stay and Happy Holidays."

"Same to you, Bradley."

The family continued to the lobby and reception desk. My mother was awestruck as I'd been with the ambiance. She roamed around, wide-eyed, while Grace started taking pictures with her phone. She was slightly embarrassing. Checking in to more fanfare, we were all waiting for our own personal concierge. A little ghetto fabulous, but it's what I paid for. With a 10-day stay, including the first-class tickets, this trip was already at $100,000. *Ballin'.*

Before arriving, I requested Ira again, so I was interested to see who Devin and Mom would get. Five minutes later, Ira, with two other well-dressed employees walked in our direction.

"Mr. Moore, so good to see you again, sir. Who do we have here?"

"Good to see you, too, Ira. This is my mother, Eugenia, my brother, Devin, his wife, Grace, and their sons, Jabari and Julian."

"Oh. that is so wonderful, and I must say you all make a beautiful family."

We thanked him for his excessive ass-kissing before being led to our suites. "So before we go up, I'd like to introduce you to your staff. First Ms. Eugenia, you will be accompanied by Mr. Carter Bailey, a 15-year member of the Waldorf-Astoria family, and Mr. Devin and family, you will be assisted by Ms. Stephanie Garner, the newest member to our family. And of course, Mr. Moore, it will be my pleasure to serve as your host once again."

"Really appreciate it and by the way, this is my family's first time in New York City, so we want this to be a very memorable Christmas and New Year's stay," I added.

"Mr. Moore, we will do our very best to make this an awesome stay that you and your family will never forget." Grace and Mom continued googling over everything while Devin dealt with his sons. Then we all followed suit to the elevators and up to our suites.

After getting settled in, I called them asking if everything was okay. Of course my mother went on and on about everything, especially the bidet. "How am I supposed to use this? I just squat over it?" She was on some Jed Clampett shit and I loved it.

After everyone had gotten settled in, we agreed to have lunch at one of the restaurants in the hotel. I made a call to Ira to arrange it. Then I made another call to Raul.

"Papi what's popping?" he asked.

"Nothing man, you. Just landed in town today."

"Ah shit, that's what's up. You called Yami, right?"

"Nah, not yet, I'm a call after … just wanted to say what's up. Brought my family, too. Want you to meet 'em. And I read your proposal. We should talk about it."

"Ah man, for real? That's cool, and I'm looking forward to meeting them. Now call Yami, my nigga. Peace."

"All right," I answered with a laugh.

Raul had become a quick friend. His encouragement towards my campaign for this amazing chick felt good. *Yeah I should call her but I'm nervous again. Dumb shit.*

For a minute I paced back and forth, thinking of what to say, how to say it, and her possible reaction. This was the time to be more assertive than before. All the nice guy shit wasn't getting me anywhere. I called.

"Hey, Doug, you made it?" she answered.

"Yeah, we landed about an hour ago … just wanted to say hello." *Doug, you're being a bitch … step it up.* "Ah yeah, but I was wondering if we could get together for dinner after Christmas. I'd like to see you again." *Good shit nigga.* I jumped off a cliff hoping she'd catch me. Understandably she could refuse due to visiting family members or other pending obligations, so I readied myself for polite rejection.

"Sure, that sounds great. Will I meet your family then?"

"No, no. Just us, we'll be here 'til New Year's Day. I wanna get to know you a little better if that's okay." She snickered some, a good sign. My courageousness in throwing caution to the wind paid off. Whatever happened from this point forward had to be purely natural.

We agreed on dinner reservations for Monday at 8, without a restaurant in mind. I asked her to leave it to me. Immediately after saying our goodbyes, I called Ira.

"Ira, my friend, I need your help again."

"Sure, Mr. Moore, what can I do for you?"

"I have a date Monday with no clue where to go. You did such a great job making reservations at Dollop last time, but for this, I want something memorable and romantic … what do you suggest?"

"Well, Mr. Moore, it depends. If I may be direct, is this for your significant other or someone you're getting to know?"

Fair question, albeit nosey. I replied, "Someone I really like."

"The reason I ask, we could put together a real elaborate showing depending on your, let's say … budget?" His question really meant, *how much you willing to spend motherfucker?*

"I gotcha now. Well, I'm all ears." It was like letting loose a kid in a candy store. Ira with his fantabulous imaginations about my first date: a horse-drawn carriage ride through Central Park, or a helicopter ride overlooking the city. Budget didn't matter but common sense did. As much as I wanted to impress her and make the date something she'd never forget, most of all, I wanted her to get to know me, my character, and my interest in her. If it back-fired, I'd never forgive myself or Ira. Thirty minutes later, after careful deliberation, we devised what I considered a master plan. Hopefully she'd agree.

On Christmas Eve, everyone gathered in Mama's suite to watch movie after endless Christmas movie. We ordered hot chocolate and blueberry scones, laughing and sharing memories about Dad. The pleasantry of it all besides the obvious comfort was our togetherness. Being able to spend Thanksgiving and Christmas together wasn't always easy. When I was dating Gwen, we'd alternate which family we would spend holiday breaks with. Our schedule could fluctuate with Thanksgiving in Houston and Christmas in Pasadena, and then the following year, vice versa. But now that we lived in the same city, Devin and I could share in the responsibility of looking after Mama.

"Y'all 'member that time Daddy caught the Christmas tree on fire?" Devin recalled.

How ironic, my father, an electrician with years of experience, didn't think the 1,000 strings of light he draped it with would eventually overheat that old plastic tree we'd had for ages. Mama ran straight to the closest thing she could find, a punch bowl filled with egg nog, and dumped it on the tree. Her quick thinking saved our gifts and our house. Moments like that made her a hero in our eyes, and for that unwavering dedication, I arranged for one special gift, something worth more than money could buy.

The clock read 12:05 a.m. Our traditional midnight unwrapping was kept alive with the boys. Eagerly, Jabari went first. Devin and Grace bought some crazy looking, oversized Lego set that he went nuts over, while Julian looked on. Mama began helping Jabari unbox the set while Devin and Grace shared their next gift with Julian, one of those dancing Elmo dolls. He laughed hysterically with every gyration Elmo made. The pureness of their joy did more for me than they'd realize. It gave me hope.

A couple of hours in, Grace and Julian crashed while Mama watched "It's a Wonderful Life." Me, Devin, and Jabari fooled with the Lego set when I finally got the call I'd been waiting for.

"Yes, okay, we're in Mrs. Moore's suite," I answered.

"You ordered something?" Mama asked.

"You'll see." I replied.

"I don't need anything else now, what y'all up to?"

Devin and I just smiled at each other. We were both in on the planning of this surprise gift she had no clue about. In just moments her reaction would be priceless.

The doorbell rang, and as I jumped up to answer it, I asked, "You ready, Mama?" She looked at me with contempt, afraid to answer. "It's okay, I promise."

I opened the door and there stood her big brother, whom she hadn't seen in over five years. Although they spoke on the phone at least once or twice a month, it didn't compare to this moment.

"Uncle Junior. Good to see you man," I said as we hugged. I hadn't seen him in just as long a time.

He was the spitting image of our late grandfather, thus the nickname "Junior." He'd gotten a little grayer and pudgier than recent memory.

"Good to see you, too, young buck," he responded. Mom stood up with her hands over her mouth, her eyes welling with tears, flushed with emotion.

"Ooh, I'm a get y'all," she kept repeating. Uncle came in and they shared a big hug while he tried consoling her.

"Genie, stop all that crying now."

This was truly the best Christmas of my adult life, despite the money, despite the tumor. I was beginning to realize the value of "catching up" among ourselves. Mama finally gathered herself and walked over to Devin and me for another hug.

"I really appreciate this boys. Y'all are the best sons a mother could ever have."

A DATE WITH DESTINY [27]

Christmas day was perfect. The ruggedness of the city with blankets of snow made for a picturesque holiday view outside my penthouse window. We all managed to get some sleep before reconvening around 11 that morning, refreshed, and ready for breakfast. Mom and Grace listened to Devin and I speak of our masterful undertakings for Uncle Junior's surprise visit from Alabama.

"At first, I didn't see how it was gone work," Uncle Junior said. We had to accommodate his night-shift schedule in order to catch the last available flight to New York. He would've arrived by the afternoon, but it would lack the same effect.

But now that her special surprise had been executed to satisfaction, my attention had turned to Monday's date. With Ira's keen sense of taste, we decided on an interactive dating experience, allowing Yami to choose the course of the night. Option one was dinner at Tavern on the Green, a swanky upscale restaurant located in Central Park, followed by a horse-drawn carriage ride and to top it off, tickets to the Broadway play, "The Color Purple." The second option was dinner at Bistec, a top tier Argentinian steak house, a helicopter ride around New York City, and finally tickets to "The Lion King," on Broadway.

I arranged for Raul to pick her up, but before driving off, she'd receive two envelopes with the options. After making her decision, I'd receive a call and have the driver take me to her chosen destination, where I'd wait with a dozen white Tulips. Yeah, it was a bit much for a first date. I was spending an insane amount to do it. Simply, it was an opportunity to have an amazing night with someone I'd become deeply infatuated with. All day, I received Christmas well wishes by text from friends, family, old co-workers and especially one from Gwen which read, *"Merry Christmas, hope you're enjoying one of many to come :)"* Her positivity was sustaining at a volatile time in my life. And for all her support, I wondered how she'd react to my interest and possible relationship with another woman. Loyalty was important to me, but so was true love.

Just as I sat thinking these things over, my uncle asked a random question.

"Doug, what's up man? When you gone get some kids?" His lighthearted inquiry had been a secret burden of mine. I wanted kids. It was hard enough, my little brother already had two, not to mention my other cousins, friends, and frat brothers I'd known before becoming fathers.

Easily by now, Gwen and I would've been married with at least a son or daughter. Even though Morgan was my surrogate son, it wasn't the same.

"I guess when the time is right, Unc'. Gotta find the right girl first."

"Yeah, buddy, don't wait too long."

Coming from a man twice married with three baby mamas, completing the act of fathering a child was good enough, but I wanted more. Having a family like the one I grew up in, with a mommy and daddy, who didn't agree all the time, but never lacked the ability to love each other, was what my future deserved.

At 2:36, Monday afternoon, I scrambled unnecessarily through the city looking for white Tulips. A simple phone call to Ira would've handled it, but I needed space from Eugenia and Junior. Mama and Uncle Junior's constant reminiscing, caused my patience to quickly run thin. And to add, I hadn't packed a suit, so I needed something classy and understated, for tonight's date. Rayford, God bless him, drove block through city block, waging a war with congested mid-day traffic, for some damn flowers. Our first stop was a quaint shop Rayford spotted half a mile from the hotel. I hopped out while he put on the hazard lights, thinking it'd be a quick turnaround.

"Hi, excuse me ... do you all have white Tulips?" A woman appearing to be Middle Eastern sat behind a counter, while a miniature color television played.

"White Tulips," she countered, as if an anomaly. Then she called to the back, asking the others who worked there the same.

They all responded "no." Slightly irritated, I thanked them as I proceeded back to the limo.

"No dice, my man?" Rayford asked.

"No sir. One down and I don't know how many more to go."

The whole idea behind the white Tulips came from some blog I read about 21st century women being unimpressed with red roses. The point of the color and flower choice was about being dramatic … different. That's exactly what I wanted for this date.

Looking at the time, I suggested checking one other place before making the call to Ira. The eagerness of getting the flowers showed some effort on my part, rather than leaving everything to him.

"Hey boss, there's a place I think might have what you're looking for," Rayford said.

"Oh, okay, cool, I'm game."

He continued driving and before I knew it, it appeared that we were in another area similar to where Raul had taken me during my last visit.

"Is this Brooklyn?"

"No, this is still Manhattan. Washington Heights."

Looking around, every so often I'd see a Dominican flag—either a sticker or actual flag hanging from or on something. "I live in this neighborhood."

"Oh, cool," I replied.

The richness of culture throughout the city was appealing and one of the reasons I'd contemplated buying a place here. Mama would kill me. *"You got me to move to Houston, now you moving somewhere else? That's not right."*

We approached another floral shop, in a much seedier area, barely noticeable from my back seat view. "We're here, boss," Rayford said. We followed the same routine before, as I motioned to get out. "Tell Hector I sent you, buddy." The confidence in his voice was promising. When I entered to the sounds of a clanging door bell and Spanish music, it felt right.

"May I help you?" The barely 5 ft. tall, older man with an even smaller voice and distinct accent, had a reassuring and welcomed warmth, capable of influencing me to buy anything. He stood over a bouquet of flowers spraying water, while looking my way.

"Yes sir …do you have white Tulips?"

Optimistic, I stood there ready to buy and move on to the next task at hand.

"Ah, papi no, sorry my friend."

"Okay, no problem." Disappointed and ready to leave, I asked, "Are you Hector by the way?"

"Yes," he replied with a bright smile, "How do you know my name?"

"Rayford sent me." I answered.

"Oh, my friend … yes, I know him, he is my friend," he replied. I smiled, nodding my head in recognition of his awareness, while backing towards the door. *I had shit to do.*

"Tell him I said hello … but why white Tulips, papi?" Knowing he was only trying to help, I held a polite posture. *It's what I want pops.*

"I have a special evening planned," I replied. Figuring that was enough, he continued on.

"Your wife? Girlfriend?" *Nosey much?*

"No, actually it's a first date. I wanted to get something different from roses. Everybody buys roses you know?" He put his hand to his mouth as if devising a master plan. I was set to call Ira when he offered an alternative.

"How about a beautiful bouquet of Thespesia Grandifloras."

The way he said it rolled graciously from his lips, to my ears, intriguing my interest enough for me to say, "Never heard of those, can I see them?" He walked to the back while I scoped the joint, barely 800 square feet, small for a floral shop. The bright fluorescent lighting, along with the ferns and shit hanging from the ceiling made the place appear even more congested. Five minutes later he emerged with a white bucket full of these exotic looking flowers.

"These are very beautiful for your friend. She will love these, trust me."

The flowers were larger than normal, a vibrant red with a golden stem in the middle. They were beautiful, huge, and different like I wanted.

"They're beautiful. How do you say the name again?"

"Thes-pes-eya, gran-di-flo-ras," he pronounced using hand gestures. "These are very special. They don't grow all year-round. I keep them hidden for special occasions like yours," he continued. Although the white Tulips seemed a dramatic choice, these were definitely romantic. I was swayed and said, "I'll take them."

He took great care in prepping the sheets of paper that would make the bouquet, laying each stem one by one, creating an arrangement fit to make any woman with half a heart, feel loved. Afterward, I paid and thanked him for the suggestion, hit the limo and asked Rayford to go to Macy's for a suit and shoes. Then it was back to the hotel. My watch read 5:10. Still with a cushion of time, I called all parties involved, ensuring tonight would go off without a hitch.

"Yo, what's up, you ready for tonight?" Raul asked.

"Yeah, I better be. You good though?" My nervousness got the best of me. Raul couldn't be late, Rayford couldn't be late, and everything had to align as I imagined. "You got the envelopes right?"

"Yeah. Picked those up from the Ira dude hours ago. Don't worry man."

"All right just making sure."

After hanging up with Raul, talking with the family, and playing with Buddy, who joined us on the trip, I took a quick power nap in preparation of the night's festivities. *Please don't over sleep, Doug.*

Two hours later, I was back scrambling. After a quick shave, hot shower, and spritz, I quickly got dressed to meet Rayford downstairs, but before that, I went to see the family. Everyone had gathered in Mama's suite as usual for the last few days. I knocked at the door and Devin answered. "Ah, that boy fly than a mug."

"Whatever. Where's Mama?"

"She in there."

I walked passed Devin as Buddy ran up to me, jumping on my legs. Thankfully I wasn't wearing another one of those two thousand dollar masterpieces. "Buddy Boy, calm down, you're messing up Daddy's suit."

"Oh, that's your son," Uncle Junior offered mockingly.

"I gotcha, Uncle," I snidely replied.

Mama was sitting, watching television with everyone when she turned and noticed me. "Well, well, hope we can meet this Yami one day soon, buying pretty flowers like that."

"Yeah, Mama, on New Year's Day at the parade, remember?"

"All right, be careful out there. When you getting back?"

As grown as I thought I was, I struggled to give her an answer that would satisfy her nosiness and still be close to the truth.

"I don't know Mama, maybe midnight. Just pray for me," I answered sarcastically.

Suddenly, I received a call from Rayford, "Mr. Moore, I'm downstairs."

"Yes sir…I'll be down in just a minute." I hung up and prepared myself for a hopeful evening. "All right y'all, I'm 'bout to go …

love y'all, peace." The nervousness of the night hit my gut again. It was 7:56. Raul was supposed to call me between 8 and 8:10 with Yami's choice. When I hit the elevator I prayed that I not miss his call. The look could throw Yami off.

Finally exiting, I made a dash for the limo, got in, spoke to Rayford and sat patiently. Seven minutes later Raul called. "Hey boss, she chose Bistec, see you there."

"All right man, see you there." My nerves again, this was some covert ops shit. "Mr. Rayford, Bistec restaurant please."

"You got it," he replied.

I sat alone with my thoughts, wondering how she'd look, the first thing I'd say. It placed me in a weird yet euphoric state of being. This excitement was healing for the tumor attached to my bladder wall, this oddity, this glitch in an otherwise storybook tale of how a lucky bastard met the love of his life.

The city lights with its warm illumination from behind my tinted view assured me that everything would be fine. I just needed to get through the night, the formalities of a first date.

Some jazz played softly through the speakers, causing my nerves to subtly subside. I could feel my swagger rebooting. My game plan hadn't totally materialized, but as promised, my first move was a sensuous hug, the kind of embrace that could say all the words my sensible barriers wouldn't allow. I could only imagine her reaction ... *accepting*.

Thirty minutes later, after bad traffic and stop lights, we arrived to the valet of Bistec. Rayford graciously hopped from his driver side seat to open my passenger door.

"Thank you, sir, and thanks again for Hector," I responded.

"My pleasure, Mr. Moore."

I got out with this rather large display of flowers, feeling eager and equally stupid, but most of all anxious. Confident about the night, the beginnings of phase one had begun. Raul called me a few minutes later, "We're heading around the corner, buddy." *Damn, I can't believe this. I feel like a teenager. Shit, I forgot breath mints.* And to add, the weather was brisk. Doing my best to conceal how cold I was, I moved from side to side, looking up and down the block. One of the valet guys glanced at me.

"I'm waiting on someone," I said.

Sure enough, in my peripheral view, the Rolls was gingerly making its way up the street, with my heart rate increasing the closer they got. Finally, Raul pulled up to the valet, went to Yami's door, and out she came, a sensational presentation that immediately hypnotized me. From the way she got out the car, to the style of her hair, the glimmer of her eyes when they met mine, the contour of her overcoat to her body, all of it was to the glory of God. I looked at Raul, proud of what I saw, while he shook his head smiling. Yami began walking towards me, until she completely stopped, noticing the flowers. Her eyes grew larger as she put her hand over her mouth. "How did you know?" she asked. *How did I know what?*

"These are like my favorite flowers in the world," she went on. *Thank you motherfucking, Hector!*

"Really? I just wanted to do something different," was my modest response. This was a perfect start to the evening. We continued on to the entrance of the restaurant, met by the maître d.

"Good evening, do you have reservations?"

"Yes, under Douglas Moore." He checked his list, noticing my name.

"Right this way. Madame would you like for us to check your coat?"

"Ah, sure," Yami replied. When she took her overcoat off, it revealed an even more pleasing sight, familiar as the night we first met. She wore a form-fitting charcoal gray, V-neck cashmere sweater and hound's-tooth skirt, black sheer stockings and black patent leather high heels. Doing my best to avoid an awkward moment of gawking, I simply stated, "You look very nice."

"Thank you, sir. You, too."

We were led to our table, where I helped with her chair as she sat and the date began. Sitting across from her obligated me to be charming, funny, spontaneous, thoughtful, and most of all worthy of a second date.

"How was your day?" I asked. She had a cute way about her. Before she spoke, she clasped her hands together, swayed her head to the side and looked up, doing her best to make the mundane seem interesting.

"A lot of my family members are in town from Puerto Rico. My grandmother who's 93 years old, my sister, my mother, uncles, aunts, cousins, and my daughter … it's a lot right now," she replied as we shared a laugh. "It's Christmas time, you know how it is … isn't your family here?"

"Yeah. my mother, brother, sister-in-law, my two nephews, and my uncle who we flew in secretly to surprise her."

"Ahh, that was sweet of you guys," she replied.

"Hopefully you'll meet them at the New Year's parade if I don't kill them first."

We shared another laugh, understanding the semantics of dealing with family. Our conversation launched smoothly. We continued on with her speaking of her 10 year-old daughter, Jocelyn, her life as a middle school teacher, and being single.

"When it's cold like this, sometimes a girl just wants a warm body to cuddle up next to," she stated. Clearing my throat made her laugh at the implication. I joined in, glad that she got the joke, but then again, *I'm just saying.*

"So when's the last time you went on a date or had a serious relationship," I asked. Going for the gusto, what was the point of waiting on the aid of alcohol to ask what I really wanted to know? She looked at me like, *wow.*

"Honestly, to be exact, this is my first date in over a year," she replied. *Damn. Cob webs on that thang, okay.* This was an opportunity to restore her faith in men, relationships, and love … with me. "Being a single parent … my hours at work … it's kinda hard to find time for the extra stuff."

"I know, huh." *Shit, be careful, Doug.*

How awesome the opportunity to swap teacher stories, I had to remind myself to steer clear of school house talk. Just then our waitress came to the table, introduced herself and took our drink request. "May we try your best bottle of wine?" I looked over at Yami and she obliged. The waitress went on explaining the chef's specials for the evening, another eclectic barrage of culinary bullshit meant to validate the cost for our dining experience. We settled on an escargot dish to begin.

"So Doug, enough about me, what's going on with you? Any kids, wife, rap sheet, drug addictions?"

Cute and direct, her inquiry was investigative, masked as small talk. Even still, I could appreciate it in today's society.

"No wife, no kids, never been to jail or plan to go, and occasionally, I enjoy a good tree." My willingness to be forthright about smoking came from the lessons learned during my relationship with Gwen. Upfront honesty was important, especially if this was the beginning of something, otherwise I was wasting her time.

"Oh ,you smoke, huh?" she asked with a raised eye brow; "You got some?" *Yes!*

"What you saying?" I countered with a sinister smirk.

This was going too good.

"Well you know, every now and then, but it's been a while."

"Just say the word. I got you." We shared yet another laugh and by then all nerves were gone, a perfect moment for a nice glass of wine. When the waitress finally returned with the bottle, she continued on, pouring glasses for us. I called for a toast, "Here's to a wonderful first date, with the possibility of a second." My confidence had grown quickly, and would continue to grow glass by glass, and laugh by laugh.

"Are you ready to order?" The waitress asked, but we'd been talking much of the time, paying less attention to the menu. In a short period, I learned that Yami was the youngest of two at 32 years of age, a Capricorn, and the biggest Mary J. Blige fan in the world. She also spoke of her mother, a retired nurse, and a father who passed some years ago. She was reluctant to go into details, even as I shared of my own father's passing. She continued to speak about her daughter, Jocelyn, and very vaguely, Jocelyn's father, who she only referenced as "being away," but I'd known the truth. Surprisingly, she'd never been to a Broadway play, maybe off Broadway. Luckily, "The Lion King" was one of her favorite films and thus the reason for her choice.

"I can't wait for the rest of this evening, so many firsts for me. First time I ever ate here, first time I ever rode in a helicopter, first time to ever see a musical on Broadway."

"Yeah, this is a first for me, too," I offered.

"Which part?"

"You." She blushed with a suspicious gaze.

"Good game, Doug," she countered.

"What? I'm for real." I laughed, as if cornered by guilt.

We looked back down at our menus, pretending to focus on anything other than the obvious connection taking place. Maybe it scared us. The ease of the conversation had grown natural, welcoming any mundane pleasantries just for the sake of being together.

"Found something?" I asked.

"This parmesan scampi and clam dish sounds interesting. Do I have a limit?" she asked facetiously.

I returned her remark with a smirk, "Get what you want, silly." I, on the other hand had to be cognizant of diet. With the weight gain and the tumor shit, the act of making the conscious effort to be healthy was good for my conscience, especially since I hadn't had any chemo treatments the previous week. I decided on a salmon dish. When the waitress returned, we placed our orders while enjoying more glasses of wine. The mellow atmosphere provided a romantic backdrop for this wondrous first date. The lighting was comfortably dim with Argentinian artifacts and art placed throughout. The wait staff was dressed in traditional Argentinian garb, with a pianist and guitarist playing Spanish-themed songs. Our occasional eye contact went well with the ambiance, making for a real-life romantic cliché.

"Why aren't you married, Doug? You seem so romantic and thoughtful. I can't understand how you're still on the market." Easier said than done. In that instant I realized how insensitive the question was for women, as if the underlying mystery somehow had to do with the person being asked.

"Love is crazy that way. I was going to ask you the same thing."

"Well, I think any woman would be lucky to have you," she offered.

"Maybe it's your lucky day." She smiled when our eyes locked again.

A while later the food arrived. By then both of us had gone through our fair share of wine, presumably buzzed. The presentation was inviting, her scampi and clam dish, my salmon with capers and asparagus with white cream sauce. Before we began, she looked over at me, assuming that I'd offer grace. Afterward, we continued on talking with her discussing recent cuts in the New York public school system. Friends of hers were recently let go due to budget issues, and so the fear remained. But in my mind the matter was resolved; she could move in with me.

"How long do you see yourself in education?" I wanted to know of her other interests, something I could possibly invest in.

"This is my eighth year teaching. I love what I do, but of course you have some days when you don't wanna get out of bed, or the kids are out of control. It's a love hate relationship."

"So what would you be doing if you weren't a teacher?"

She took some time before giving an answer, assuming she'd never been asked.

"I don't know, maybe a writer of children's books," she added.

"Go for it. You're young, smart, educated, you only live once," I replied. Thinking of my statement, at some point, revealing the truth would be a necessary evil if this supposed "romance" went past a month.

"What about you? What would you do if you weren't this successful, investment banking guy?" she asked.

"Probably be a teacher."

An hour later, after more wine, good conversation, and a delightful piece of almond encrusted cheesecake with mango sauce, I called Rayford for our next adventure. Part one had gone so well, skipping to the musical seemed a more mellow finish, but I had to commit. During the limo ride, we shared more small talk about sports, politics, and the fate of rap music, then all of sudden she asked, "Does this have a mini bar? I need some water." I looked in the small fridge built into the side of the back and sure enough there was a bottle.

"You okay?"

"Feeling a little nauseous. I'm cool."

"We can skip the helicopter ride. No problem."

"No, no, I wanna go for real."

My intuition said no, but for a first date I didn't wanna seem domineering even if it benefited her. *Fuck it, we on the way.*

Rayford pulled into the parking lot of this helicopter hanger with a sign that read "City Choppers," off the Hudson River. The setting was perfect, a cinematic moment disguised as real life with the lead actress by my side. She looked over at me and said, "I can't believe this." I smiled, knowing I'd done good. We got out the limo, went to the office announcing our arrival, and sat in the reception area until being called to the back.

Moments later an Asian guy walked into the reception area, "Douglas Moore?"

"Yes," I replied, standing to shake his hand.

"I'm Scott. I'll be your pilot this evening. Are you all ready to fly?"

"Sure man. Let's do this." Instinctively, as we began walking to the helipad, Yami grabbed my hand, possibly out of nervous fear or hopefully from feeling completely comfortable with a guy she barely knew. Her innocent act made me nervous, fearing my hand would tremble in hers, but I held firm.

The helicopter awaiting us was a black and gray Bell 206 Jet Ranger with red stripes. The cold night air and bright cityscape backdrop instantly ingrained a memory never to be forgotten. This was the night that the prettiest girl in the world allowed me to forget about the reality of my Houston life. When we climbed in, we were instructed to put on seat belts and headphones with microphones attached for communicating against the cabin noise. Again, Yami grabbed my hand as Scott fired up the engine and propellers to begin this adult roller-coaster ride.

"You ready?" I asked. Looking at her, she held a smile full with anticipation. We began lifting from the ground, and noticed a visible gust of wind. Quiet as it was kept, I was scared as fuck, pretending to be a thrill seeker. The higher we went, the more my heart raced. Soon after, Scott had us over a thousand feet in the air, gliding through the sky with a view lost for words. Off in the distance, the first recognizable landmark was the Statue of Liberty. The closer he got, the more we fell in love.

Our tour had become an even more elaborate showing with Scott's descriptions and historical references to the views we had. "To your right is the construction site for the new World Trade Center building." We were awestruck, sitting atop a world of lights, with the people below, living their lives, at work, walking the block, driving their cars, having dinner, and us, removed, exclusively in the sky.

Imagining that we were already in a relationship, the ups and downs of love, the fights, the break-ups and make-ups, and of course an established sexual compatibility, the setting was perfect for a marriage proposal. "Oh my God, is that Madison Square Garden?" she asked with child-like excitement. Things couldn't get any better with the views, the company, and Scott's skillful aviation teetering daredevil mastery. All of a sudden she said, "Shit." Not thinking it more than another reference to an amazing view, she clutched her hand to my arm. I continued looking on when I noticed her grip getting stronger. When I looked her way, her previous disposition was replaced with a more dismal look. "I think I'm gonna throw up." *Shit, not here babe.*

For a second we both went quiet. The view didn't matter any longer as we waited on a verdict. Looking for a bag or something to catch it, we were shit out of luck and time. Yami leaned forward, letting loose on the cabin floor, portions of the bottom of her overcoat and shoes. I immediately tapped Scott on the shoulder, "We gotta go back, she's not feeling well." She stayed bent over, preparing to go again while I continued doing my best to console her. When she sat back up, her eyes were watered. "I'm so fucking sorry, Doug."

"Don't worry about it, we're heading back now." Maybe she was embarrassed and understandably so. We were stuck in the air with the smell of vomit. She looked in her purse for a napkin to wipe her mouth and face, while I continued to look after her.

"I can't believe it."

"What?" she said.

"Even the way you throw up is beautiful." She laughed a little, breaking the tension from the previous moment. *I should've insisted on not going, we could've rescheduled.* I felt embarrassed for her, and sure that the next time I felt convicted enough to make a judgment call, that I'd act on it.

Minutes later we were back on the ground. Yami had taken her overcoat off and folded it. "Doug, I'm so sorry. I think I had a bit too much to drink. I don't know, maybe the seafood didn't agree with the wine or the helicopter ride."

"It's cool for real, don't worry about it. "The Lion King" starts in an hour, we can go back to my suite, get you cleaned up."

"I don't know, I don't wanna throw up again, in public, on Broadway."

"Trust me, you'll be fine. We'll go rest up. No hanky panky, and then off to Broadway." She stood looking at me, mulling the idea over as Rayford stood by the back passenger door waiting for us to get in.

"All right."

We were off to the hotel, poised to recoup for the third act of the evening. On the drive home, she felt comfortable sitting next to me, laying her head on my shoulder. At this point, the date remained interesting simply because of her. When we eventually reached my suite, after all her gushing over the luxury of the place, we retreated to the couch and put on a movie. Less than 30 minutes later, she'd fallen asleep. After six weeks of texting and phone calls, the date ended perfectly.

POMP & CIRCUMSTANCE 28

By midnight, she woke up a little dazed but obviously feeling better than before.

"Doug, I'm so sorry," she said exhaustively. Her apologetic manner was appreciated but unnecessary.

"It's okay. Do you feel better?"

"Yes, thank you. Wasn't expecting that."

She continued sitting on the couch a few moments more then said, "I better go. Don't wanna hold you up, plus my mother and grandmother get antsy when I'm late."

"You sure?" I asked in the thirstiest tone ever.

"Yeah. I'm 32 years of age, go figure."

"Okay. I'll have Rayford take you home."

"I really appreciate that."

After calling Rayford, she began gathering her things, preparing to walk out. "I just wanna say thank you so much for an amazing evening, tonight was the best time I've had in a long while." Her gratefulness was attractive.

"Seeing you made it worth it all, and you're welcome," I replied. We held a gaze appropriate for a good night kiss, but instead, we walked out towards the elevators.

When we got to the limo, we stopped and hugged each other. I could feel all the secret places of my heart once occupied by Gwen, being gradually replaced by Yami. A painfully pleasurable revelation, saying goodbye was like ending the music, this awkward song that she and I created, a love song perhaps.

"Text me when you get home if you don't mind. We still on for Saturday?"

"Yes, definitely," she replied.

I gave her a kiss on the cheek, Rayford opened the door, and I watched them drive off. Romantically cynical, I feared that my usual love sap daydream would eventually break my heart. Nothing was concrete about "us" other than her willingness to spend time with me and my ability to pay for it. Thankfully, she didn't seem to be a gold digger, especially after falling asleep on $300 Broadway tickets. The only thing left to do was introduce her to my mother, the "Queen Bee" and masterful bullshit reader.

Throughout the week, the family and I did the New York "thing," shopping, dining, and enjoying the Big Apple altogether. During this time, we pulled Uncle Junior in on our fabulous big secret. Of course he went ballistic, and being that he was Mama's big brother and only sibling, I offered to retire him, pay all his existing bills, and buy him a place off some master planned community lake down in Birmingham. Of course, he graciously accepted.

During that time, I also checked with Bioko about the solar panel deal. The time was soon approaching to make the transfer of funds to Ghana to complete the Kenya project. Despite the main negative in my life, everything else about it seemed to be batting a thousand.

I even called Raul to share the news of my plans to invest in his fitness gym proposal. It made sense, especially the low maintenance of the business. The major cost for now was rent, electricity, and a few employees.

On New Year's Eve, Friday night, Unc', Devin, and I decided to hit the town. Curious and courageous, we were ready to brave the city streets to catch the action in Time Square. This was something I'd always dreamed of doing, and now here we were, flooded by the marquee lights, sights, and sounds of 42nd Street. Mama and Grace decided to stay behind with the boys and watch Dick Clark do his usual countdown on TV. On the limo ride in, we helped ourselves to the mini bar in preparation of the cool night breeze ahead.

"Any Courvoisier in that motherfucker," Unc' asked. "Uncle Junior," a.k.a. Eugene Taylor, being our favorite and only uncle on my mother's side was too cool for school. Mama would tell us stories about Unc' and his rebellious younger days, cuttin' up in the streets, his womanizing, and his eventual full scholarship ride to Fisk University. He was a "smart thug" Mama would say. After college, he joined the Air Force for one term before moving to Florida on a dare from a girlfriend.

"You miss living here Unc'?" I asked.

Before he answered, in dramatic fashion he swirled his cup of rum, a substitute for the Cognac, thoughtful of his next words and replied, "Hell, nah." We all laughed in response, expecting his usual exaggerated rant. "I take that back," he continued. "You know what I miss? Spanish pussy." We all laughed again.

In the time that Unc' lived here, he'd had relationships with two women: Tia' Teresa, or *titi*, Spanish for *'auntie,'* and Tia' Irma. Teresa was Dominican. She had a son from a previous relationship, Alex, much older than us and barely around. And then there was Irma who was Puerto Rican and the mother of his last child, our *prima*, Cecilia. Cecilia was younger than us, probably a teenager by now. Besides Cecilia, Unc' had two other daughters, one in Florida, Lisette his oldest, someone we'd never met, and Tatiana, who was my age. Tatiana and I talked from time to time, even visiting each other back in Cali where she lived.

Tactfully, I chose not to reveal Yami's ethnic background for fear of Unc's dirty old man seal of approval, high-fiving me for the fact that somehow I'd carry on his preferential tradition. He'd find out soon enough. Honestly, I'd never had a preference in woman other than thick, educated, and STD free. She could be light, bright, and damn near white, chocolate, or honey brown. My prejudices hinged on hips, thighs, ass, breasts, and a lovely face. Hair, good or bad, didn't matter. I'd just prefer it not be on the coochie.

"Hey guys, I'm gonna let you out at the corner. I can't get any closer, but it's only a two block walk," Rayford said.

"Yeah, Doc, we cool. I use to live here," Unc' replied.

Rayford pulled over a few feet up and we all got out, immediately met with the brisk night air. Thankfully I came prepared this time. When we bought Mama's fur coat, I saw a rust colored, quarter length leather jacket with a fur collar that had my name written all over it. A bit pretentious, it was luxury none-the-less. I was also wearing thermal pants under my jeans and a pair of Red Wing boots I picked up earlier in the day at Unc's suggestion.

"Look alive, look alive. We in these streets now, baby," Unc' said. Presumably he was attempting to forewarn us of the "block" with its gats and knives, thieves, and schemers looking to do us in. He hadn't known that this was trip number three in as many months, or that I'd been to a club in the Bronx. And judging from the multi-racial mix of the crowd, this was the United Nations, assembled together at this tourist attraction, all for the purpose of gazing at a glass ball with lights, to commemorate a new day, year, and for some, a second chance. *Thank God I made it.*

The next morning was filled with the enchantment of 2011. I was geeked to show off Yami to my mother, ever since the day I first talked about her. This steady journey towards New Year's Day, for this parade, was in effect, judgment day. Assuming she wasn't her usual self, I was looking for her approval.

"Y'all hurry up, we gone be late," I hollered. We were all in Mama's suite, the guys sitting watching TV, the boys playing with Buddy, and the ladies, doing whatever to look their best for a damn parade in 30 degree weather. Since we were seven deep, I arranged for a second limo to pick Yami's family up and follow us. Some of it reeked of desperation, maybe to impress them, assuring that I was nothing like her baby daddy or that I could provide her a fairytale existence, opposed to the harsh realities of a single parent life in the city.

"Who you yelling at boy?" Mama spoke playfully, walking in the room with her fur coat on. Grace followed behind, modeling just as well. They looked like the members of a well-to-do family, and by American standards, they were.

"Look at Genie," Unc' said, admiring her grand entrance.

"Y'all divas ready?" I asked.

Rayford again, was waiting downstairs, while the other limo was en route to Yami and family. The nervous jitters of the moment we'd all meet played over and over in my mind. *If we're late it'll look inconsiderate. Are two limos too showy?* And to top it off I wasn't feeling well. Assuming it was something to do with the tumor and a second week without chemo treatments, there wasn't anyone in my immediate grasp to share my concerns with.

When we finally made it down to the limo, I did my best to mask my discomfort. Today was important on many levels and I didn't want my attitude fucking it up. I made a call to Yami informing her we were on the way and that the other limo would be there within a few minutes.

"Hey, Doug, Happy New Year!" Yami answered cheerfully.

"Same to you beautiful. Just to let you know, we should be there in a little bit."

"That's fine. It's just me, Jocelyn, my mom, and grandmother."

"Oh okay, can't wait to meet them. My mom, uncle, brother, sister-in-law, nephews, will be with me. I thought about bringing my dog, but this weather might turn him into a little bitch." We shared a laugh. I liked making her laugh, making Gwen laugh, making women laugh. It was the one thing that made me feel most relevant.

Fifteen minutes later, we were smack dab in "Alphabet City" where Yami lived. The throngs of buildings, block by block, made for an interesting look at Manhattan's contrasting neighborhoods. Riding down 4th Avenue on the lower east side must've been a sight at 8:43 in the morning. Suddenly my phone rang, it was Yami.

"Hey the limo guy is here, how far are you all?"

"We're on 4th Avenue. Are we close?"

"Yeah, okay, remember left on East 10th … right on Avenue B."

The anticipation was more overwhelming until Unc' said, "Why didn't you just have the limo bring them back up town …much easier."

"True, but I figured if we traveled together, we wouldn't be lost in the crowd, and I wanted y'all to meet them before all the parade hoopla."

"Fair enough. I see we're in Alphabet City. What's your girl's name?" I could see the wheels of my uncle's mind turning, his detective work in full effect. Playfully I responded, "Lawanda Jenkins." He looked at me, assured that I was bullshitting him.

"You don't look like a Lawanda, my brother," he replied. Everyone laughed, me included, but sadly I'd come to realize he was color struck. Just then, Rayford made the right on Avenue B and just about a half block up we could see the other limo parked in the street with its hazard lights on.

"Is that them?" Mama asked.

"I think so," I answered.

The brightness of the morning sun provided a beautiful orange glare off the side of the other limo, as smoke from the exhaust billowed. The closer we got, we didn't see anyone. Assuming they were sitting inside, I called her back.

"Hey is that you guys coming up behind us? We're inside, it's cold," she said.

"Yeah. We're gonna park right quick so everyone can meet. That okay?"

"Sure. I wanna meet your family."

Rayford parked just a few feet up from them and proceeded to get out, and opened our door. Mama who was sitting on the driver side was let out first.

"Watch your step pretty lady," Rayford said, innocently flirting

I supposed. While we were all being let out, Yami and family were getting out just the same. When we saw each other, I couldn't conceal my big ass, thirst bucket grin. We walked towards each other and hugged, forgetting everyone else.

"Happy New Year!" we said. It felt like an engagement party of some sort, the immediate blending of our families, even though it was for a simple parade. She waved her mother over and began introducing everyone.

"This is my beautiful mother, Sonia." We shook hands providing each other cordial smiles. She was much shorter and darker than Yami.

"Nice to meet you," we offered each other.

"This is my lovely, lovely, grandmother, the best nana in the whole wide world," Yami gushed. We shook hands and offered pleasantries. Yami's grandmother only gave a polite smile, providing her English wasn't that good. Finally she introduced her daughter, Jocelyn, who I'd heard so much about. She seemed a bit shy but shook my hand anyway.

Then, as I prepared to introduce everyone, I caught a glimpse of Unc' with his sinister smile and wink. I ignored it and proceeded on. When I introduced my mother, Yami, her mother, and grandmother, everyone provided her with hugs and kisses. It was a promising sight. They did the same for Grace and the boys. When I introduced Unc', of course he had to be extra.

"Buenos dias...como estas." Yami, her mother, and grandmother, applauded and praised his greeting. Even Jocelyn giggled. I rolled my eyes. Afterward, I introduced Devin and we prepared to take off for the parade. When the family and I got back into the limo, the commotion immediately began.

"Dougie, she's beautiful," Mama said.

"Boy, now that's how you do it," Unc' offered. His expression of approval was humorous but fleeting.

"Dude, that's the one right there, bro," Devin said. Grace looked over at him with a bit of contempt.

"Oh, really?" she asked.

"What babe? I'm just saying they make a nice couple."

We all looked at Devin and bust out laughing. *Approval of Yami ...check.* Throughout the time of the parade, our families seemed to mesh quite well. My mother and Yami's mom enjoyed themselves side by side, while Yami and I let everything flow naturally. It felt a little too fast, too familiar, too soon, but undeniable. From time to time, I'd put my hand on her back, or she'd put her arm around mine. We we're touchy feely that day. And oddly, none of it felt strange, just accelerated.

Soon after the parade, Ira arranged lunch for us at one of the hotel restaurants, for an informal gathering, perfect for getting to know each other. Yami's mother sat at one end of the table, and my uncle at the other. The oddity of the moment was striking.

By the time Gwen's family had dinner with mine for the first time, we'd been dating for almost two years, and here we were, after six weeks of long distance communication and one date.

"Ms. Eugenia, how did you like the parade?" Yami's mother asked.

"It was very nice, especially for my first visit to New York City," she replied.

"Oh this is your first time? I hope you like it with this cold weather of ours."

They shared a grown up, complimentary laugh, as the table watched this formality of pleasantries. My biggest fear was an interruption from Unc', with more of his superficial attempts at speaking Spanish.

"You know I use to live here a few years ago. Washington Heights area," he offered.

"Oh, really? I have friends over there," Yami's mother responded.

Immediately I was nervous with the thought that one of his old flames might've been friends with her. I could easily see him saying something about Teresa or Irma, and Sonia saying something like, *Oh … that was you?* I had to think fast.

"So, Ms. Sonia, do you all attend the parade every year?" I interrupted. I couldn't care less about her answer. I was doing preemptive damage control. Reason being, any dumb shit he could spew about his past with Latinas, could very well create a negative perception of my intentions with this woman's daughter.

"Off and on, but not every year. I can easily watch it on TV," she responded. Again, the adults at the table offered a polite round of laughter as our lunch gathering gracefully dragged along. *God help us.*

An hour and a half later, after a pleasing meal, a few glasses of red wine, and Yami playfully pinching and nudging me under the table, it was time to call it a wrap. The *itis* was coming. We all walked out together, a bit more knowledgeable of each other but presumably precautionary, Sonia with me and my mother with Yami. Despite it all, the mission was accomplished. My mother finally met the woman who I'd perceived to be something special, and now, all I needed was her "take," good or bad. After saying our goodbyes, we watched them load into the limo, back en route to Alphabet City. *If I could be a fly on the wall.* Hopeful that I left a good impression of my character, I looked forward to talking to Yami again, about the day, about everything.

"I don't know about y'all, but a nigga sleepy," Unc' said. We all agreed. Me and my napping ass had no problem retreating to the suite for one more daydream in the city. A lot had been accomplished in a quaint five hours.

"Y'all wanna do something tonight before we check out in the morning?" Mama asked.

"How about you and Grace go see "The Lion King" tonight … my treat."

For the past two weeks, my family and I lived a glamorous lifestyle in New York City; big fancy hotel, chauffeur-driven limousine everywhere, exquisite dining and fabulous shopping to boot. None of it would've mattered had I not shared a moment with Ms. Yami Conchita Orozco. *I think I'm in love.* My fear factor was life after the plane ride home. Could we maintain this thing? The thirst inside seemed to battle with sound rationality. Gwen was the longest relationship in my adult life. I'd forgotten the complexities of dating, but I was sure of my feelings.

As we all sat in first class, the myriad of thoughts about my Houston agenda began to bombard me. Resuming my chemo treatments was number one on the list. My will to fight, to be resilient, was recharged with this trip. But If possible, the whole process needed to remain under wraps. At some point it was only fair that I'd come clean about the money with Gwen, simply for her having information more dire. Also, my business affairs with the charity needed organizing. I wanted to kick 2011 off with some significant donations.

Mama, who sat in the cubicle next to me, looked relaxed and ready to get home. It seemed a perfect time to pick her brain about a lot of things, such as, whether she'd decided on a house from the many we'd seen, and most importantly, what she thought about Yami.

"You all right over there?" I asked. She fumbled with her seat, reached in her purse, and pulled out her reading glasses.

"I'm fine," she replied.

"You enjoyed the trip?" I continued.

"Yes indeed. Had a good time my son, thank you again."

"So, what did you think about Yami?" I asked.

"She seems to be a nice young lady, respectable, pretty."

"I mean, do you think she's right for me?"

"I just met the girl, it's a little too early to make that call. Is she right for you?" I hated when she got rhetorical. Even as kids, right before an ass whooping, or some other form of punishment, she'd always ask whether or not we deserved it. In hindsight, it was her way of teaching us critical thinking, but now, I just wanted a straight up answer.

"I mean, Mama, you always operating in the spirit and all. Do you see something wrong about this?" She turned to address me, looking over the top part of her glasses.

"I think you want me to give you my blessing, approval, whatever, so you can go gong ho, but don't let looks and a feeling get you caught up. You have time. Get to know her."

Optimistically, I had time, but the status of my health was ambiguous. Dying was the furthest thing from my mind, and although I believed I'd be okay, Yami was figuratively my last meal. More so than the money, the feeling of love, of giving and receiving it, could do wonders for my spiritual and physical well-being.

"Nah, I mean I am very attracted to her, looks matter somewhat, but she's really nice to me and she makes me feel like, like I wanna be in a relationship again."

"Does she know about the money?" she asked sternly.

"Well, she knows that I'm a business man, an investment banker."

"You need to keep an eye on your heart and your money, in that order."

Eugenia wasn't budging, thankfully. Had it been left up to me, with my usual act first, think later approach to women, I'd already be working on a wedding proposal within the coming weeks. *It's time to chill.*

WHAT HAD HAPPENED WAS ... [29]

Four weeks after Manhattan felt like yesterday. There was no daily grind to resume, no appointments to keep other than the chemo treatments, and thankfully no house hunting to do. Mama finally chose a one-story home in a newly developed subdivision in Sugarland, close to all the shopping she'd like, and enough distance from me for civility's sake. The 2,500 square feet house with three bedrooms, three bathrooms, and a nice backyard faced a man-made lake, and had a two-car garage with a brand new 5 series in it. She was set.

Devin and Grace followed suit. They liked Mom's house and neighborhood so much, they broke their lease and bought a two-story, similar in style, just a couple of blocks from where she stayed. It seemed a perfect arrangement for the grandkids.

With all the beautiful transitioning of their lives, the tumor remained in mine. Gradually, there was a slight change in my appearance, particularly my hair. It looked translucent, thin ... sickly. Soon after, I started rocking a baldy to keep suspicion at bay. Even my weight dropped some as a side-effect to the chemo and my subdued appetite. One day my mother asked, "You losing weight, Doug?" It nearly broke me.

Another biopsy was scheduled to check the size and fervor of the tumor. If it turned benign, we could proceed with full removal. Otherwise I'd maintain the twice a week chemotherapy. My frustration came from the fact that this was the most extreme situation ever in my life. I'd never had a broken limb or any serious illness, just the average everyday cold and occasional flu. On a positive note, Yami and I continued communicating by text,

Facebook, phone calls and emails. It was promising to say the least, and all without ever having sex. I longed to see her, to smell her hair, feel her touch and be whole again. My mother was right about guarding my heart. I'd been there before, but this was different, or so I believed.

Lamont and I planned to meet up. He wanted to run some business ideas by me, something I hadn't expected. Being in my financial position made it only right to invest in my friend. At least that's what I thought.

Since my mother moved out, I was truly living in a bachelor pad. There were clothes everywhere that needed washing, dishes piled high that needed cleaning, and the dank funk of stale weed smoke from the freedom of walking around my apartment half naked, smoking whenever I wanted. Hurriedly, I picked up around the place before Lamont arrived. Twenty minutes later, I heard the doorbell.

"What up nigga?" I answered as I opened the door. Lamont, holding a bag presumably with alcohol, already had red eyes.

"Oh, Thurston Howell the third ass nigga," he replied, walking in. "Damn! You need a maid in this bitch?"

"Man, it was worse than this. What you got in that bag hoe?"

"Fuck you trick," he responded, then with a devilish grin, he slowly pulled out a 1.75 liter bottle of Paul Masson. *Fuck.* On doctor's orders I was to cease all alcoholic drinking. Back in New York I'd occasionally have red wine with dinner. *I don't feel like explaining myself tonight. Stick to your weed.*

While I prepped my tray for a couple blunts, an old episode of *A Different World* played in the background.

"Man, I would a fucked the shit out a Jaleesa thick ass ..." Lamont said as he poured himself a cup.

"I know, huh," I replied, meticulously separating the stems and seeds from the small bushels I'd broken down. Of all my accomplishments and skills, I was proud of my ability to "roll." After cutting and dumping the *cigarillos,* I carefully stuffed, packed, and tucked the contents into the paper, tightly rolling and licking the seam for closure. Reaching for my lighter, I called Lamont in to begin this pow wow session.

"So, nigga I was thinking, where do we always go and spend money just to get out the house and shit?" he asked. I could see where he was going but entertained him anyway.

"Carrington's ... Sullivan's."

"Right, don't you think we should open up our own spot? Think about it—upscale sports bar—kind a like a *Hooter's* but black." Oddly, I was interested.

"Okay, so like a spot niggas could watch the games, eat and shit," I replied, maintaining the exhale of smoke through my words.

"Exactly, and for the menu, all soul food shit—ribs, fried chicken, macaroni and cheese, greens—all that." The more he spoke of it, the more the concept became believable. A bona-fide upscale soul food joint/sports bar in Houston could work. But he didn't stop there.

"So that's my first idea. Second, think about this, a top notch strip joint where niggas have to have special membership cards to get in. It'll be like a compound with a guard gate at the entrance. We could charge annual fees for members and $100 entry fee for non-members. Only bad bitches from around the world, like Brazil or Atlanta, would dance there." Immediately, I could already see the outcome of that scenario: Lamont, with all his swaggering, accidentally slipping in some employee pussy, and there I'd be sitting with the blame for their divorce.

"Yeah, could work," I responded hesitantly. "On the cool, I like that first idea better." Pleasantly surprised that he'd been thinking business, I was willing to explore it a little more. "Maybe with the sports bar, all the waitresses could wear sexy ass referee uniforms, what would you call that shit though?" Lamont looked over at me after taking a pull from the blunt. He exhaled and smiled knowingly.

"Fullbacks."

"Fullbacks? I like that shit." We immediately laughed in agreement. The name flowed like it was meant to be. I started fantasizing, imagining a place like Fullbacks being the new hotspot, the new hangout in town. Motherfuckers would be like, "We going to Fullbacks to watch the fight," or, "They showing the Super Bowl at Fullbacks." The idea stuck, but for now, with my obligations to the Bioko deal and Raul's gym, it was time to be wise about the heavy spending.

"A spot like this gotta be in the Galleria, maybe Memorial," Lamont added. Of the other pending business ventures I'd already committed to, this felt special. Driving up to Fullbacks to watch the game and get some ribs after a day at the office or just on a whim could be a nice routine. "How much you think it'll cost to get going?" he continued.

"That's a good question. We got some homework to do."

On Wednesday, February the 3, my second biopsy was set to take place. Gwen agreed to take off yet again, and accompany me. For some reason, it felt like the perfect time to come clean about the money, primarily out of guilt. Keeping it a secret any longer was unnecessary. Possibly she'd feel offended after asking her to be a confidant in one area of my life and not the other, as if untrustworthy of it. Not sure of her reaction, I decided to tell her that day, right before meeting with the doctor.

"Hey there," I said as she walked closer to where I sat. Arriving first gave me the time necessary to formulate my thoughts, taking care in how I delivered the news.

"You been here long?" she asked.

"Five or so minutes now. Not long." My mouth was going dry, my gut burning with anticipation. *What should I say first?*

"I see you rocking the baldy. The treatments?"

"Kind a sort a … yeah."

We shared a good-natured laugh, a likely moment to introduce the other news. Right as I began to speak she spoke as well.

"When I'm a see your … oh, go 'head," she started.

"No … go 'head, what were you gonna to say?"

"Oh, I was just gonna ask about your mother. How is she doing? I want to see her."

"She's still here." I answered. She looked at me slightly confused. Gwen didn't know about the move from the "shoebox," our nickname for my old apartment. Imaging the 800 square feet, one-bedroom space for non-couple living was unreasonable.

"She's been at your apartment this whole time? I know that's cramping your style, right?" This conversation was turning into double-dutch. I needed to jump in. I held my head down, working up the nerves to say the next few words.

"Hey, ah I need to tell you something. I should have told you this a while back but the timing wasn't right, I punked out. I just hope you're not mad at me after … can you promise me you won't get mad?" She continued looking confused, her head slightly tilted to the side, with a smirk, anticipating my words.

"It depends," she said. We held a gaze, the kind that used to be enough, that said everything necessary, but this time the connection was vague.

"A few months back in October, remember when the Mega-ball jackpot was like $325 million?"

"Yeah," she responded nodding her head. I took a pause, a deep breath and a sigh.

"I played it and I won." She remained with a confused look, silent yet intently waiting for an explanation. Hoping my quaint summary would suffice, she continued looking at me. "What?" I asked, followed by a nervous laugh.

"Doug, are you okay, I mean, I'm sorry, this is confusing. Are you serious?"

She had every right to process the information any way she wanted. Actually she deserved to cuss me out, but like everyone else, the news didn't register as quickly as it was told. "So what are you saying ... I don't understand ... you won $325 million and then found out you had a tumor, a cancerous tumor at that?" *Yes motherfucker just like that.* Her tone turned sarcastic. "Boy stop ... let's go to this appointment, I ain't got time to play with you," she continued. As she motioned to get up, I remained seated, wrestling with the opportunity she provided for escape. What would it be worth in the end, losing a friendship? "Why are you still sitting down?"

"I wasn't finished," I replied. My tone was serious. This was once and for all.

"Doug, please, what's wrong? You're really confusing me now," she answered.

"I need you to believe what I just told you. I'm not lying."

"Okay, so if this is true, why you just now telling me?"

"It was awkward for me to even ask you to lunch that day. The breakup was still fresh, only five months. I'm a tell you I won the lottery after we'd just broke up?"

"Oh 'cause you thought that I was gone try to get back with you?" she replied. Her statement cut deep. Her assumption was fair but not in the way she phrased it. The thought of her being a gold digger never crossed my mind, but only a fear that money could superficially heal *our* wounds. I wanted "us" for us. "So what was I expecting for coming to these appointments with you, taking off work, taking a cut in my own damn paycheck, you thought about that?"

I sat there feeling stupid as hell, ever so slowly sinking into the lobby sofa, dying to disappear in that instant. This thing that I worked out in my mind, this master fucking plan, backfired. She remained standing in silence, waiting for my reply. Feeling like I'd just been reprimanded by my mother, I continued looking down at the ground, the noise from the lobby of elevators bells, people walking and talking, the world turning, continued.

"I think that you need to man up … tell your family what's going on in your life, accept how your mother will react. I can't do this."

"Gwen, I'm sorry. I over thought the whole thing. I wanted us to get back together regardless of this money. I never thought of you as a gold digger. All those years together, I ain't have shit then. I didn't want you to act funny, be weird around me because of this money. I wanted you to want me back for me."

"So when I came to lunch that day, what was that? When I called you a few days later or sent you a text on Christmas day, or these few times that I've gone with you to your appointments …what was that?" If this were a game of chess, her last few points were all checkmates.

"You're right, I am so sorry, I truly apologize. I read the situation wrong."

"No, you read me wrong," she countered.

I sat there continuing to look dumb, but at least into her eyes, hoping that she could see through me, into my insecurity … *I fucked up.*

"I still can't believe you, but if it's true, congratulations. It's a blessing. But I think we should go ahead upstairs now," she said in a reserved and somber tone.

I rose from my seat, humbled by her maturity to remain with me. Intending to reconcile with a hug, I walked in her direction, but instead, she walked away and ahead of me, never looking me in the face the entire time.

When we reached the reception area of Dr. Dobbs' office, we sat cordially in silence. Soon I was called to the back, but she stayed behind. I changed into the hospital robing, while my thoughts were with her, and the foolishness of my rationality. When I laid on the bed for the cystoscopy exam, my thoughts juxtaposed Gwen's reaction and Dr. Dobbs' findings. *Had the chemo treatments worked at all?*

"Well, good news, Mr. Moore. Looks like the tumor shrunk some, that's always a good sign."

"That's the news I need to hear, Doc, thank you so much …"

"Well, we're not out of the woods, yet. We still need a sample to check if it's in remission. If so, of course we remove the whole thing."

A half hour later I was prepped for my second surgery, hopeful for a positive outcome. I lay there under the flush of bright lights, submitting to the sedative rushing through my blood stream for another knock out. I was a pro now. Quietly I said a prayer, as the nurses and doctor scurried about for this affair.

God, I thank You for another day of life, I thank You for the blessings You've given me, for bringing my family together ... I ask that You be with me right now, protect me, guide the hands of these people, give them wisdom on my behalf ... I ask that You bring peace to Gwen, please let her know that I'm sorry ... I pray all these things in Your name, Amen.

Presumably hours later, after coming to, I lay in bed partially incoherent, groggy, and with Gwen sitting at my side, looking on.

"I'm sorry," were the first words I spoke. Gwen looked over and put her index finger to her lips.

"It's okay. Be quiet and rest." In that moment, it felt like an acceptance of an apology. I turned my view back towards the television until eventually falling asleep again.

A week passed. I was back home, back smoking, and back thinking about the rest of my life. In that time, Gwen hadn't responded to any of my text messages or phone calls. She forgave but didn't forget. She needed space to process things I supposed. And then I got the bright idea to do something really nice for her. *Maybe I could secretly pay her bills off; maybe this could ease the tension between us.* She had a car payment with the Civic, and college loans from her days at T.S.U. and P.V.

Immediately, I called my Houston attorney, asking how we could go about doing this in a legal manner, without her knowing. He suggested my foundation. We could create this anonymous fund, which would not only pay for her car and student loans, but any of her credit cards and the remaining balance of her apartment lease. We would tell her creditors and leasing office that she was the 2011 recipient of the "Single Mother of the Year," award in February. I gave him the green light, and within days we had the information necessary to start paying shit off. We set it up in a way that by the time she'd realized what happened, it would already be over and done with.

Feeling productive about life again, the weekend was approaching. For a slight moment, my male animalistic instincts thought about "M." We could go on another simple date, perhaps, dinner and a movie and maybe the Hilton? *Snap out of it nigga*. And then out of the blue, I received a phone call from Yami, possibly a sign to stay focused.

"Hey, darling, how are you?" I answered cheerfully. It'd been a few days.

"Not so good," she answered. I could tell she'd been crying by the trembling in her voice. Presumptively, I thought it something tragic, maybe the death of a loved one, her grandmother perhaps.

"What's wrong?"

"I just found out ... that I got laid off," she answered. A slight sigh of relief, but still empathetic, I offered a solution.

"Yami, don't worry about that I got you. Come take a break, and see what life in Houston could be like. I have friends at the school district. Maybe you can apply and get on. I'll help you find a place, or you could stay with me. I have three bedrooms." I went silent for her response.

"Thanks, Doug, but let me think about it."

CHANGE IN PLANS [30]

For the first time in my adult life, I understood the true meaning of duality—being this helpless hero to others, changing their lives and circumstances—while wondering *when my change was gone come?* Dr. Dobbs called the following Wednesday to inform me that although the tumor had shrunk in size and although the cancer hadn't spread from its origin, it was still present. More chemo treatments, more weeks of I.V. needles piercing my flesh and veins, and more pain. More self-pity validated by the flick of a cheap-ass, 99 cent lighter with its hypnotic flame burning the end of yet another blunt, creating an alluring orange hue for the sake of my escape.

And still, I remained trapped in this self-created prison of lies, attempting to protect the emotions of others. Gwen was right. *Man-up.*

The days and weeks seemed a blur, with no communication from either one of them. Gwen was supposed to be my refuge, my personal Jesus. And Yami ... just Yami, this new "thing," that felt so right. Eventually, my patience prevailed when late one night, she called out the blue.

"Hey," I responded. Somewhat depressed and conscious of how thirsty I sounded during our last conversation, I played nonchalant.

"Hey, how are you?" she asked. *Well, I've lost some weight, about ten pounds, my hair grows funny now ... oh, I didn't tell you, I have cancer. So I cut off all my hair and now I just noticed my skin is getting darker and I haven't told my family anything. And the one woman, who was by my side through this whole ordeal, wants nothing to do with me ... so, I'm a little fucked up right now.*

291

"I'm good, just sitting here watching some TV," I answered.
"That's cool."

"So, what's up? You still looking around?" I asked, pretending to care.

"Nah, actually, they gave me this shitty severance package. It'll hold me for a few months. I've been thinking about your offer though."

"Oh?" I replied. A jolt of enthusiasm washed over me, but I remained cool.

"So like, what's an average teacher's salary out there? Like what range?"

"It depends. I was getting … from my friends that they started off around $41,000, but with years of experience it can definitely go up. You've been teaching eight years right? You should be in the 50s," I answered.

That was a close call.

"Yeah, I'm actually in the 60s, but the way things look out here, gotta go where the money is."

"Okay, so you're saying what, you ready to make that move?" Excited than a motherfucker, I sat up from my usual couch potato posture.

"I'm seriously thinking about it. You'll help me find a place?"

I smacked my lips,"You tripping, you know that right? Y'all can stay with me, at least until you get situated."

Yet again, the thirst. However, she was more than welcome, a nice distraction from this bullshit tumor.

"I mean, we barely know each other … one date?"

"True, but if you really felt some kind a way, I don't think we'd be having this conversation. Sometimes you gotta step out on faith."

"No I appreciate it for real. It's just a big decision to make."

"Understandable, especially when I'm trying to get to know you," I responded. She laughed some.

"You trying to get to know me, huh?" she answered suspiciously.

"I don't know why you refuse to believe a guy like me could be interested in a girl, excuse me, a woman like you." I went silent waiting for her reply.

"You're a trip, but I like that. Honestly, I don't know. It's a little fast, especially since we seem to have an interest in each other." Immediately I was on Cloud 9.

We're officially in like!

"Well, just to let you know, I'm a gentleman. I won't do anything to make you feel weird. You and Jocelyn can share a room or have your own. I barely have company anyway. We can make this move about getting you back on your feet and maybe we see where things go." She went silent again. I remained silent right along with her, cognizant that too many words could damage the perfect pitch.

"So, let me talk to my mother about this. Even though she'll disagree, at least she'll know, right?" We shared a laugh. Her concern was fair enough, but I could give her a different kind of life.

After we hung up, my mind raced with possibilities about the coming days, weeks, and months. Thoughts of what lay ahead fueled my imagination; everything from hiring an interior designer to spruce up the place, to looking into private schools for Jocelyn.

Realizing this new living arrangement could be questionable, I was prepared to tell Mama about it more so than the tumor. This was my second chance at love and an instant family life.

The next day, Lamont and I decided to hit up Sullivan's to shoot shit and talk more business. The Fullbacks' idea was really sticking and worthy of more planning. So far, my financial commitments were the $500,000 for Bioko's deal, and $100,000 for Raul's gym, leaving an available budget of $400,000 for this newest venture, my million dollar cap.

"Let me go head and tell you this now before it happens ..."

"What?"

"New York is coming down. I'm a help her out a little. Her and her daughter moving in with me until she finds a place. She got laid off." Lamont kept drinking his rum and Coke like I never said anything.

"More power to you nigga," he answered. "When she coming?"

"Ain't worked that out yet. Maybe in a month though."

"Oh, okay. She pregnant?" Of course he had to ask.

"Nah nigga, not me." We laughed. "I told you ... just helping her out."

"All right, well cool, moving right along. Let's get to this business."

"Oh, and I told Gwen about the money. You should a saw that shit."

"What she do?"

"Nigga, read me my rights, clowned in the motherfucking lobby. Dude, I sat there like a bitch."

"What she say though?"

"How could I kept this from her, do I think she's a gold digger? ... especially after being there for me with my appointments and shit ... it got a little crazy for real."

Before I could realize what I'd said, thanks to a third Long Island and a half-smoked blunt on the way there, he jumped all over it.

"Appointments for what?" he asked.

"Nah, just some observation shit. The doctor asked me to bring somebody with me in case they had to put me under to run a test."

"Test for what though?" He wouldn't relent, putting me on the spot.

"It ain't nothing for real. They thought they found something. I asked her to go with me 'cause I ain't wanna freak my mama out," I answered nonchalantly. Thinking that was enough, I reached for my Long Island for another sip of ambiguity.

"Damn nigga, you be lying. What's up for real." His "read" was uncomfortable. The night wasn't meant for interrogation, but for shooting the shit, talking business, pointing out women ... light.

"It ain't nothing man. They found a tumor but it's under control—they got it under control—I'm good now, for real." His eyes grew big, he put his glass down and gave a look so intense, I had to respond. "I ain't wanna worry nobody. I didn't know if it was serious or not, that's why I ain't say nothing."

"That's some motherfucking bullshit though. Thought we were boys ... we talk about everything ... you tripping dude," was his frustrated reply.

This juggling of secrets had finally caught up and gotten out of hand. As carefree as life was supposed to be because of money, money didn't matter. My secretive way was damaging relationships left and right. In a last ditch effort to gain his sympathy and change the flow of the conversation, I revealed the whole truth.

"Man look, the tumor they found, it's cancerous." His demeanor changed. He put his hand over his mouth and just stared. It was a shitty thing to do in Sullivan's, but his rant, as genuine and heartfelt, wasn't helping my cause. These days were about escaping the truth, running towards a façade in hopes that reality and wishful thinking would somehow mesh in the middle.

"Damn, dude I'm sorry," he said. He looked over with grief in his eyes, enough to make me sympathetic.

"The good thing is, the cancer hasn't spread. The tumor shrunk with the chemotherapy treatments. We caught it early," I offered.

"Man, how your moms take the news? Nah, hold up, fuck that. How you win the motherfucking lottery, hundreds of millions of dollars, and then find out you have a fucking tumor?"

We sat there pondering the oddity of it all while the band played, the sounds filling the room, 30, 40 and 50-somethings, Black, White, Asian, Latino, dancing, lost in youthful memories to the cover band's rendition of Kool and the Gang's "Celebration." We shook our heads, and suddenly bust out laughing. We were back.

The night continued on with us scoping the room, talking our usual shit of what we'd do with the random asses we saw, but underneath, his earlier question bothered me, *how your moms take the news?* The conscious decision to spare her the devastation wasn't fair but rational, right? Shameful, I know. But as I sat on that elevated stool, pretending to be engrossed with the atmosphere, the conviction of telling her sat in the pit of my gut like a hundred pound weight. *God, when I tell my mother this news, please give her strength ... please give her peace and understanding, please give me the confidence to tell her.* My quick little prayer was arbitrary and contradictory with yet another alcoholic beverage in my hand against doctors' orders. What was I praying for, if not change itself? Right then and there, the drinking stopped.

For too long, even before the money, getting by was my M.O. Some of it was Gwen's fault, my mother's fault—their pampering ways, and my belief in the illusion of a charmed life—as broke as I was, as we were. And now, in some ways, holding on to that boyish charm to face life's randomness wasn't working any longer. Truth had finally charged me to be an adult, a real one. The blame rest squarely with me, praying when convenient, doing accordingly when absolutely necessary, but not caring deeply until caused to.

I thought about Gwen more and more, the place I'd put her in with my well-meant, ill- executed timing. Hopefully my attempt at retribution would change things, but as they say, no good deed goes unpunished. Sure enough I received a phone call from her, expecting some civility.

"Hey, Gwen."

"Doug," she replied. It was dry and humorous. Assuming she'd put the pieces together, this was either a "thank you" or a "fuck you," call.

"How are you?" I asked.

"I'm good, but let's just cut to the chase," she answered with more humor in her voice. "So I went to go pay my rent the other day, handed the check to the girl at the front office, she hands the check back and says my lease has been paid for the year. You know anything about that? Then I went online to make my car payment and some credit card payments, they've been paid off ... you know something 'bout that? Then I got an email just the other day saying thanks for the payoff of my student loans ... not sure how that happened." Listening to her rattle off detail after detail was entertaining, and by the tone of her voice, she seemed grateful, although not admitting to it. *Was this the official acceptance of my peace offering?*

"That's a blessing for real, congratulations! Who do you think did it?" I asked facetiously. She smacked her lips and I immediately laughed. "What?"

"Dude, you did this for real?" she asked, her tone high pitched and curious. The temptation to exaggerate was curbed with the relief that she was back talking to me.

"I told you, " I answered. An overwhelming feeling of calm came to the conversation, while she continued her polite voicing of disbelief, sporadically laughing, but surely grateful now.

"Thank you," she said.

She seemed humbled, understanding of my silly imperfections. This is what should've happened before asking her to do this other thing. But thankfully, Gwen and Lamont were fully aware of what they needed to know about my life, aside from her lack of knowledge about Yami.

"So you know I have to ask," she continued.

"What?" But I already knew. I was officially being called to the carpet, again.

"Have you told your mother yet?"

"No, but I will, soon. It's time."

"You want me to be there when you tell her?" Her comfortable offer was enticing, that familiar pampering that allowed me to be coddled and not face what life usually gave adults. *I got this.*

"No, I need to 'man up', remember?"

"Right, just pray Doug," she replied. *Already ahead of you, babe.*

Not sure of a first step, or a proper introduction, I called my mother one day, with random small talk, asking about the house, how's life officially living in Houston. Of course she offered nothing but positivity on everything, as expected.

We agreed that I needed to come over and check around the house. She mentioned something about a funny noise coming from the attic, since my last visit three days ago. Considering the information I was about to share, my demeanor remained upbeat and easy, not wanting her usual sympathetic overkill. Everything about my presentation had to be meticulous and methodical, from what I'd wear to what I decided to drive. She needed to know that although the news I'd share would sound dire, in spite of it all, everything was okay … if she'd only believe.

"Hey Mama, I'm on the way. I got something to show you too," I offered. My obvious tactic was distraction. I'd arrive in my shiny brand new, yellow Lamborghini, appearing carefree with Buddy in the passenger seat, the life of a millionaire. And at some point during the visit, while sitting in the living room or out back on the patio, overlooking the retention pond, I'd graciously deliver this bombshell news.

The elevator ride down was somber. The stainless steel and mirrored paneling and the 14 inch monitor to the upper right played some bland slide show of the facility offerings and ads for locals businesses. The agile suspension of the elevator car interrupted our intended destination.

Two white kids, probably tweens or early teens, got on. They both offered polite, contrived smiles, as I them. Presumably the sons of some resident in the building, they went on discussing their previous topic. The articulation and passion they displayed was refreshing, something about Ferrari not having a turbo version of one of its sports lines.

"Dude I promise you, even if there was a turbo version, it still couldn't beat a Lamborghini," one said to the other. They appeared to be brothers or at least cousins, having similar facial features, with Justin Bieber-styled brunette hair and greenish eyes.

The other fired back, "You've never even seen a Ferrari or Lamborghini in person anyway," a perfect segway for my line in this script.

"Yeah, I agree with him. A Ferrari couldn't beat my Lamborghini."

"You have a Lamborghini?" the taller of the two excitedly asked.

"Wanna see it?" I answered back, in a weird pedophilic tone. Suddenly, I was the stranger with a "Lambo." When the elevator stopped on my parking floor, I flashed the keys like the pied piper I'd temporarily become, en route to my latest $400,000 toy. For a moment, thoughts about the conversation waiting to be had between Mama and I vanished. My focus had changed to impressing these two urbanites. When we reached the car, I pulled off the covering, stuffed it in the storage compartment, hopped in with Buddy and revved it up. Their eyes glowed with every ramped up RPM, as the sound of the force coming from the exhaust set off a few car alarms. They stood there, the recipients of their own personal car show, something they hadn't expected. I waved them over to take a look inside, while 97.9 "The Box," played on the radio.

"Sir, you play for the Texans or the Rockets?" the shorter one asked. Taking a breath and choosing my words wisely, I looked at him and smiled.

"Nope."

We said our goodbyes, while the engine continued running. Another memorable moment in a line of many since becoming rich. I was proud of how I'd learn to handle random comments. Perhaps the reflection of it served me well, driving down Highway 59 on the way to see her. Instead of being the victim, I'd embrace her emotional reaction to the news, the anger and sympathy. Of course she'll remind me that she knew something was wrong all along. Just getting through this allowed me to focus back on what was most promising.

A leisurely drive, I went the speed limit, avoiding my usual grandstanding for onlookers. A much needed conversation was on my mind. *How do I say what I'm about to say without the drama? Could she just listen to me, and process it later?* Then Devin came to mind. *He should hear the news, call him.*

"Hello?" he answered.

"Hey, what you doing right now," I asked.

"Was about to go to the grocery store, what's up?"

"I'm heading to Mama's right quick. I wanna show you my new car."

"You bought another car, nigga?"

"Yeah, I'm a be there in 20 minutes. Come see."

Devious, yet necessary, the closer I got to Mama's house, my thoughts raced and an odd pain formed around the back of my neck, possibly tension. I gripped the steering wheel tighter with every plausible imagining of her reaction to the news. *God guide my words.* Honestly, Devin needed to be there in case she fainted or worse. Reaching the Sugarland exit, I called her again, to see if she wanted anything from the store.

"Hey Mama I'm just at the light. You need anything before I get there?"

"No, I'm okay. Well, I wanted something sweet, but I don't want Dr. Doug to get on my case," she answered sarcastically.

"Mama, it's okay. What do you want?" I was so agreeable that day, an obvious contrast from the usual me.

"Nah, I'm fine. I just ate a while back, don't worry about it, come on."

"You sure? It's no problem," I offered.

"It's okay, Doug. I don't need it."

"All right."

We hung up, but I made a quick stop at a convenience store for her favorite Neapolitan ice cream sandwich, and a pack of cigarillos. Afterward, I hopped back in the whip and drove slower than before, letting others cut in front, being courteous at every chance. It was pathetic. Then, I reached her house. Devin's truck was already parked in the driveway. I called him.

"Y'all come outside, I'm here." When they finally came outside, I was sitting on the front left side of the car, arms crossed, beaming with pride, a sadistic front to the reason I was really there. Mama just shook her head while Devin was obviously impressed with my latest purchase.

"The Lambo though, this shit nice, Doug ... sorry, Mama."

"What kind of car is this?" she asked, while giving Devin the side eye.

"It's a Lamborghini. Lamborghini Murcielago."

"Lamborgenie?" she asked. Devin and I started laughing. "How you say it?"

"Lam-bor-ghi-ni." I repeated.

"Oh, okay. Looks expensive too, how much you pay for this?"

"A lot," I replied.

After a few minutes more of small talk, we all retreated inside to the grand entrance of the house, highlighted by the smell of "newness" and look of luxury. Mama had her way with this blank canvas of a house, putting decorative pieces sporadically, yet perfectly placed for a warm appearance. From the marble flooring in the entry way, to the expansive size of the "great room," it was light years away from what she endured all those years.

"Y'all want something to eat? Got some fried catfish in there from last night ... mustard greens too," she went on. I handed her the bag with the ice cream sandwich, and she smiled. Devin went to the backyard with cellphone in hand making another call while Buddy followed. Lately he seemed aloof, even unavailable. I wondered what he was up to these days. Otherwise, I fixed a plate, put it in the microwave for a quick blast and sat at her massive granite counter top island.

"You get your walk in today?" I asked. One of the attractions of the neighborhood was a fitness field for residents, along with an Olympic-sized pool and park area.

"Not yet, I will. Had to clean up some. I talked to Junior the other day. He went on and on about the house," she said. Now it felt like both of us were avoiding something.

"Oh, that's good. He's okay?"

"Yeah. Junior gone be Junior," she replied.

Her new lifestyle seemed to fit her well. Her demeanor was easy, no longer the stressing of "trying to make it." The only problem now was the introduction of what I wanted to say. Devin was still outside and needed to be a part of this conversation. Mama went back into the living room, resuming one of her beloved Court TV shows. All alone in the kitchen, I suddenly thought of my father, how I could tell him anything. I imagined us going to Lake Conroe, out on his new boat with a couple of six packs, shooting the breeze. Of course, he'd offer some encouraging bullshit, appreciated nonetheless, because of his strength. He was a strong yet caring man, although unavailable.

Continuing to eat, I took pause to reflect on all that was good in that very moment. My mother wasn't living in sub-par conditions, Devin, however distant, wasn't raising his sons on a check to check basis. They would know suburban life. And Douglas Moore, the retired social studies teacher, who'd neither been married nor with children, seemed to be experiencing a rebirth, albeit vague. If I died, they'd remember me this way, not the way I use to be, a thirty-six year old teenager, self-absorbed, and appearing to give a shit most the time. They'd remember me as the son, the brother, nephew, friend, and ex-boyfriend that changed the course of their lives.

After I finished eating, I joined her in the living room, taking hold of the available chaise portion of the sofa. A stupid move, I was sure to fall asleep before having the conversation as planned.

"So Mama. everything's okay?" She turned and looked at me slightly put off by my randomness.

"I'm fine. Why you ask?" Little did she know this was my build up.

"I wanna tell you something. It's kind a hard for me to put in words, but I've been praying about it. I just want you to know I'm gonna be okay." As I spoke, Devin and Buddy finally came back in. "Hey man, perfect timing. I wanna tell y'all something right quick." Devin looked at me confused but obliging, while Buddy walked over to where I sat. Just then I heard a text notification from my cell. A creature of habit, I checked it, right in the middle of this news I'd taken so long to share. Not thinking much of who it could be, I only planned to glance at it, getting back to the moment at hand. It was Yami.

"Hey Doug…gonna call later but anyway, how does mid-March sound?" Stunned with the news, I leaned my head back, relieved with her answer.

"Uhm … Yami and her daughter are moving in with me in March."

ROOMIE [31]

My life was officially going at a speed of 200 miles an hour. The old adage, *thoughts become reality*, rang true, minus the thought of having a tumor. And honestly, I never believed that Yami would actually take me up on my offer but she did. On Monday, March 21, she and Jocelyn arrived at George Bush Intercontinental at 7 that evening. In baggage claim, they looked as though they were refugees lost in the land of Houston.

Since her arrival, two weeks old, she'd become accustomed to these wide open spaces; a southern way slowed down and appreciated with barbecue and iced tea. She enjoyed leisurely drives down Westheimer and strolls through the Galleria, and yet, we hadn't had sex. We did finally kiss though. One night while having dinner at Vic & Anthony's, a five-star restaurant downtown, the flow of the evening caused me to feel a way about her. An unexpected moment after a simple conversation about learning to forgive, we held a gaze prompting me to lean over and gently kiss her on the lips, in public mind you. We never stopped from that moment on. But then we had another milestone.

One night, after our usual blended family dinner, Yami and I remained in the kitchen while Jocelyn sat in the living room watching TV. We were playful, occasionally bumping into each other on purpose while cleaning up. At one point, she even splashed water on me after an off-color joke about her breath. Taking advantage of the moment, I went up behind her after she turned her back and started tickling her. Of course she squirmed, so I stopped. But I leaned in, kissing her neck. She never budged, and neither did my confidence. My hands grabbed her waist in the process. Her submission motivated me even more, with a full on erection flush with her ass. My hands went from her waist, to her stomach, and upwards to her breast, groping like a sex addict freed from contempt. Suddenly Jocelyn yelled, "Mom are you coming?" It broke our stride.

But later that night, after watching another one of those long, drawn out kid movies, Mommy put Jocelyn to bed, while I remained on the couch. Something about the night all started from the kitchen. When she came back, she lay beside me, and without permission or some prompt from her, I leaned in for another pronounced kiss. She assured me my decision was welcomed by caressing the back of my head. True to the moment, I lifted her shirt. I was poised to perform my signature move. She gave in. Slightly moaning, her movements accommodated my proactive judgment; I stopped and looked at her.

"Let's go to my room."

She looked at me, seeming hesitant but curious, and answered, "Okay."

We stood together, but she led the way, walking up the steps as I imagined the things to cum. The anticipation of taking off her tank top and sports bra, sliding down her plaid boy shorts and red socks for a revelation, culminated months of preparation ... it was time. When we finally reached my room it began, a sudden embrace followed by more passionate kissing, hands exploring all over while inching towards the bed. The lights never came on. Everything we did was second nature, only with the aid of faint moonlight peering through sheer curtains. She stood back, pulled off her top and lay in bed. Being conscious of my condition and recent stitches on my lower abdomen, I only pulled my T-shirt and sleep pants off. I left my tank top on. Lame.

We were finally in my room, in my bed, after two weeks of saying goodnight and walking our separate ways under the same roof. This was a breakthrough, a monumental moment in our history. Resuming my prior technique, I massaged and sucked at her breast while reaching below. Her moaning became more evident with this rhythmic multitasking. The buildup was strong, while I gently and steadily slid down her shorts and panties. *Damn, I wish the lights were on.* What I couldn't see in the dark, my hands could tell. Shaven ... clean shaven. With every lick of the tongue and tease of my fingers, her sensual stream of excited bliss continued flowing, inviting me to the other side. With a full erection, I stayed licking and sucking at her breast, attempting to get in the act when suddenly we heard knocking at my door.

"Mom…are you in there?" *What the fuck … not now honey bunny.*

"Yes, Sweetie what's wrong?" Yami asked.

"I can't sleep."

In the dark, I could see her apologetic expression. Duty called.

"Okay, honey I'm coming," she answered. "Doug, gimme a second. Be right back."

"No problem," I replied.

Oddly, I wasn't frustrated. We'd gone further than ever before, never taken such liberties with each other's bodies … progress was made. In that wee hour, continuing to lay in wait, confidently planning the next phase, I'd go straight for the gusto, no foreplay. Even the thought of it caused me to pleasure myself, thinking it would be a short wait in time. Yet the seconds turned to minutes, which turned to me falling asleep. *Can't miss what I never had. Good night, Yami.*

Surprisingly, during the first weeks of her stay, my family, especially my mother had taken a liking to her. Presumably the New York trip was necessary. We'd had dinner at Mama's a few times. Grace and Yami seemed to be forming a friendship, but most of all, my Bible-toting, Holy Ghost filled and fire-baptized mother, hadn't yet rebuked me or our living arrangement. We were shacking. Assuming she gauged my demeanor and new found happiness, she'd allow me the time and effort to figure things out. And all the while, my medical challenge remained, with another cystoscopy exam scheduled for April.

Yami commented on my weight the day she arrived, "You've been on a diet?" Sadistically, it fared well for my desired appearance. Going from a size 44 inch waist to a 36, my ascension into haute couture, 300 dollar designer jeans that fit. I was fresh to death, perhaps.

Within those first few weeks, she'd finally met my best friend. We decided to meet at Sullivan's one night while Jocelyn stayed at Mama's. Just walking in with the anticipation of Lamont's reaction was nerving. My thoughts ranged from *what'll he think?* to *will I have to check his ass for getting fly?* When we first walked in, we saw him and Dana sitting at a table near the piano. Dana spotted us and gave a wave. Lamont followed suit and rose to greet us.

"Well, well, we finally meet," he said. He offered a polite hug as did Dana, but I knew, at the first chance he got, I'd get a verdict.

Sure enough as Dana and Yami continued small talking, he turned his back to them, and flashed an "okay" sign with a wink. *Nigga approved.*

"So we've heard so much about you, Ms. Yami, all good of course. How ya' liking Houston so far?" he asked. The moment had turned into "show & tell." It was all about my shiny new friend from New York City.

"I'm actually enjoying it here … much slower than the Bronx," she offered.

Of course we all laughed in accommodation. Things were off to a nice start, while the jazz pianist for the evening resumed his post. I motioned to a waiter to place our drink order, as they continued. The mood was light, intoxicated with the urge to be ourselves, under the influence of course. But sadly, I'd forgotten to prep my good friends on what questions or topics to discuss. Dana asked, "So what did you do in New York?" Already synthesizing the possible course the conversation could take, my options were limited.

"Oh, I worked at a middle school. I'm a teacher," she replied.

"What a coincidence," Dana said.

"You teach, too?" she countered.

Say something now motherfucker.

"Dana is actually a pharmacist … for like ten years now, right?" I asked, attempting to deflect the train wreck in progress. Dana looked over confused, but Lamont knowingly smirked and shook his head. More damn secrets. "And Lamont is a probation officer for the county." Lamont looked over, nodding his head in agreement, and then posed a question.

"So what is it you do again, Doug?" he asked facetiously. Dana looked at Lamont.

"This guy is so silly, you know that. I wish I had a glass to toast this joker," I answered, pissed but deserving of his shenanigans.

The waitress finally came over and took our drink order. Another dicey situation was dodged for now, but the constant maintenance of these unnecessary lies, much less secrets, was taxing. Consciously, I refrained from my usual, opting for cranberry juice instead while Lamont took notice, sheepishly glancing at me.

"Cranberry juice, Doug?" Dana curiously asked. *I know, huh? Bummer.*

"Taking a break," I answered.

"That makes two of us," she added in her pregnant state.

Lamont looked up at the ceiling as if wanting to break his silence. I appreciated the obvious fact that he hadn't told her anything. That burden still rested with me.

"What's your usual, Doug?" Yami asked curiously.

"Long Island."

The topic needed changing once again, with the possibility of being asked *why the break?* or *how are you losing weight?* Our routine for the two weeks had been waking up at about 9 a.m. or so, taking showers, getting dressed, and going somewhere for breakfast. She never heard me mentioning a gym schedule, or saw me eating low-fat rice cakes, or drinking protein shakes. When I'd go to chemotherapy it was always masked as a business meeting, and when I returned, it was always the strain and stress of the "meeting" that gave me my weakened disposition. Some days I'd sit in the car for hours, trying to recoup from another session and keep up appearances.

"Y'all excuse me, going to the restroom," I said rising up to walk away, I needed a breather. This casually random conversation ran the risk of exposing other Doug tidbits. *Yeah by the way, Doug use to be a teacher before he won the lottery, and even though he has a cancerous tumor on his bladder, there's no need for alarm, it's shrinking.*

When I entered the restroom, I went straight to the mirror and sink, turned on the faucet, and let the lukewarm water rush through my hands, preparing to wash my face and my fear of the evening away.

Things had gone too far. Why didn't I just tell everyone that mattered to me, about the money the day it happened, about the tumor diagnosis the day it happened? What was the worst possible scenario? With all my miscalculations, it didn't change the fact that people were still owed the truth. Lamont walked in.

"You all right?" he asked.

"Yeah, man."

"Dude, I understand the money, but did you say anything about the tumor?"

I was being silly and childish. Maybe if I told her before things got deeper, she'd forgive me. Maybe she'd understand the complexities of whatever the fuck I thought I was doing.

"Man, my mama still don't even know," I answered.

Lamont voiced his disagreement by smacking his lips, as if the last cookie had been taken from the cookie jar. *Why was everyone else so sure, so confident in how to handle my business?*

"Man, at some point ..."

"I know, dude," I interrupted.

"Just saying," he replied as he continued to the urinal farther down to my left. Looking in the mirror, disgusted with the space I was in, one Long Island couldn't hurt. Breaking my own self-imposed covenant seemed a quick fix for the night.

"Fuck it," I answered, and walked out.

As I walked back to the table, the pianist played a lively tune. Around that time, the club portion of the restaurant where people watched live bands play, was about to open.

"Lamont convinced me to get a drink y'all," I lied. Yami seemed to be enjoying herself, constantly looking around the room, taking in all the sights and sounds of a Houston crowd. For simply being there with me, she earned the right to the truth. When Lamont returned, we decided to go to the back area and snatch a booth before it got too crowded as usual.

Looking at Yami, my pride swelled. *The baddest bitch in the whole damn place is with me.*

Reveling the superficial shit like her looks, my money, and what I drove made for another night of escapism. Reality could wait another day. When we sat at the booth, I immediately got back up to go to the bar.

"Hold up, man," Lamont called. Maneuvering through the brewing crowd, the band for the evening took the stage as light applause rang out to start the festivities.

"Your girl bad, dude," he spoke, while waiting at the bar for the next available bartender.

"Thanks, man," I answered. *You goddamn right.*

Yami wasn't much of a drinker. She nursed the same glass of Riesling from earlier. I, on the other hand, mentally prepared for a maximum two Long Islands, a proper buzz, sporadic dancing, and hopefully when it was all said and done, some crazy love-making.

"You said she Puerto Rican?"

"Yeah, why?"

"She look like she from the boot, them creole girls," he replied. "She gotta sister?"

"Nigga, you gotta wife." We laughed, classic Lamont.

"Man, dog, ooh, imagine y'all run into Gwen, though."

"Man, I ain't worried 'bout that. We good, that's the past."

"Yeah, but she was going to them doctor appointments with you, all that shit."

"She don't even go with me any more … ever since that day." I responded arrogantly even though I cared, but Lamont had a point. I didn't know how she'd react seeing me with another woman, after implying the intentions of rekindling something. "I'm probably more worried about my teacher friend from the party."

"The chick in the green … hair to the side?" he asked excitedly. "I knew you fucked."

"Yeah," I answered like a smug asshole. Five months ago was a world away.

"Look at Dougie Fresh," he responded, giving me a pat on the back.

The band began playing its first number, and the bartender finally approached us. "Long Island, please." The words left my lips like a secret omission, a broken promise made for the sake of my health.

Wow, I can't even take a break? It's just one drink though. Don't kill yourself. Yeah, but the tumor is in my bladder, duh.

When we got back to the booth, Yami flashed a pretty smile, distracting the small war that waged within. "You still on that Riesling, huh?" I asked.

"I'm not a heavy drinker, and you gotta drive," she answered.

She was right. Getting wasted could be a turn-off, but these ongoing charades had gotten old. *I like to drink … a lot.* Continuing on, the crowd grew along with the energy in the room. My opportunity to be lost with it dared my rationality. *I could drink three, that's it, no more than that.*

"Hey y'all, I'd like to have a toast for my friend who decided to take a chance on life and see our lovely city … welcome to Houston, Yami." We raised our glasses, clinked, and drank in her honor, the beginnings of the evening. She looked over and gave another million dollar smile, intensifying the guilt inside. *You should tell her about the tumor, soon.*

Looking around the room, the familiar scene of unfamiliar faces carelessly gyrating, either on or off beat to the cover band's rendition of Bobby Brown's, "My Prerogative," provoked me to ask her to dance. We walked to the dance floor, me beaming again, looking for onlookers to connect with. *Yeah, she's with me.* With an available opening, we took claim to a spot and began this grown-up play time, seductive teasing and grinding our way through the song. She turned out to be a pretty good dancer, and that solidified my expectation of her in bed. Before we knew it, we'd dance through four songs straight and decided to take a breather. When we reached the table, Lamont had tequila shots waiting on us. *Nah man, not tequila.* I grimaced but saved face.

"This is mine," I asked, pointing to one of the glasses. Dana and Yami laughed knowingly.

"All right, Doug, it's our turn to do a toast to Yami. Glasses up everyone," Dana offered.

We all obliged. I drank yet another potion, the cool feel and bitter taste of peer pressure in my mouth, down my throat and in my mind. *Okay, one tequila shot that's cool, no more.* Immediately after biting the lime, I sipped the rest of my Long Island like a "G," some sort of unnecessary bravado for the table. "You want another one? I got the next round," Lamont offered sarcastically.

"Nah, I'm good," I answered, my only sane moment thus far.

The night went on as usual, with the only difference being our celebrated guest. From time to time, I'd just sneak a peek at her or ask if she were okay. Lamont and Dana decided to hit the dance floor as we watched for a change.

"How long have they been married?" Yami asked.

"About seven years."

"That's nice."

It was a simple question, unworthy of investigating. I didn't think much of it. Suddenly an older gent randomly came to where we sat.

"How are you guys tonight?" he asked with a British accent. He had short-cropped white hair, with grayish looking eyes under the subdued lighting of the club, and he stood about 5'5 tall. The deep wrinkles on his face suggested a man who'd lived a pretty rough and long life. Obviously drunk, his words stammered out, only dignified by his effortless charm. "Mate, I must say, your friend here is perhaps the most beautiful woman in this room, really and my girlfriend is sitting over there," he pointed, while we laughed.

"Thank you, sir," Yami replied.

"And she's so beautiful that I am going to buy you two a drink," he continued.

"Oh, sir, thanks, you don't have to do that," I said, but he'd already turned towards the bar, stumbling a bit in the process. We looked at each other like *WTF just happened?* Moments later, while Dana and Lamont were still dancing, a waiter approached our table with a bucket of champagne and two glasses. Looking around the room for the short Brit to thank him, he was lost in a sea of rhythmic commotion. *Fuck it, it's champagne, a grape … you can do this.* I grabbed the bottle, popped the cork and poured us glasses. By that time, Dana and Lamont had come back to the table.

"We popping bottles now?" Lamont asked.

"Nah, some dude just rolled up to us and was like, 'I wanna buy you guys something to drink. You look like a nice couple.'" I looked over at Yami, sparing any awkwardness between her and Dana from the truth. Then I asked a waiter for one more glass, which he brought back a few minutes later. "Hey y'all, I'd like to make another toast for good friends," I said. We all raised our glasses, indulging the free will of the evening. So much for a promise.

An hour and a half had gone by, along with my convictions. Glass after glass, dance after dance, what turned from a reserved adult night out, became a turn up session. Lamont got the bright idea to buy another round of tequila shots, complementing the bottle we finished 45 minutes prior. Officially, I was buzzing, consciously aware of becoming drunk, and no longer giving a fuck. Yami even seemed more uninhibited. She and Dana took to the dance floor, wilding out, getting acquainted with Houston's night life. And before knowing it, I was stuck. The space I held was overbearing and uncontrolled. Perhaps the chemo treatments had lowered my tolerance. During my better days I'd still be going. Wanting to avoid the title of party pooper, I sat there, my vision slightly blurred and stamina burnt. I wanted to go home and get in bed … alone.

"You all right, dude?" Lamont asked.

"Not really, feeling kind a weird man, nauseous, I don't know."

And then it happened. I never expected anything like this in my life. Out of nowhere, my body decided to shut down, passing out from an upright position, onto the table and sliding down to the floor. Unconscious for a whole minute, Lamont said that he thought I died. After I came to, apparently I'd been lifted up and put back on the booth seat, courtesy of Lamont and some very nice patrons. It was time to go. Logistically, we decided that Lamont would drive my car home, as Dana and Yami followed. Sitting in the passenger seat embarrassed and tired, all my focus turned to Yami's thoughts of me. *What's she thinking right now?*

"How you feeling man?" Lamont asked.

"Like shit…I ain't ever passed out in my life."

"You think it's the cancer stuff? I mean like the treatments and shit?"

"Maybe. I was thinking that, too."

"Man my bad on the drinks, I thought it was all right for the night."

"I ain't tripping."

When we finally reached my place, Lamont parked the car and caught back up with Dana, as Yami waited for me in the lobby. After saying our goodbyes, Yami and I got on the elevator. She asked if I were okay on the elevator ride up, but her facial expression read something else, some other concern. When we got inside, I felt weak, uninterested in climbing stairs. I sat on the couch, while Yami came over and began undoing my shoes. Afterward, she unbuckled my pants while I unbuttoned my top. Sensing the fatigue I felt, she offered, "Wanna come to my room instead?" I answered with a nod, got up in my T-shirt and drawers and we walked to her room together in silence. I immediately laid down, ready for deep sleep and R.E.M. Yami, began undressing, this time with the lights on. Fighting the urge to doze off, I laid on my side, eyes seemingly shut, but enough to see her in her matching flesh-colored, lace panties and bra, her maintained waist line, complementing her curvy hips and abundant thighs. She looked over my way and asked, "How you feeling now?" and smiled. *Good night.*

WHAT'S DONE IN THE DARK ... [32]

Feeling well rested, the next morning I awakened to the aroma of chorizo and papas swirling the room, Yami's signature dish. My appetite sparked. I walked downstairs to find her sitting on the sofa in her favorite plaid boy shorts, red tank top, and red socks with a plate of food, watching *The Color Purple*. "Morning," I said.

"Morning. Made breakfast," she answered.

I walked into the kitchen, fixed a plate, and came back to sit beside her. Her focus was laser sharp, watching in total silence, ignoring me.

"Hey, sorry about last night. I've never passed out in my life," I offered. She turned from looking at me, nodded her head, and went back to the TV. It felt odd, even cold. *Did she care?*

We continued eating, watching the movie when all of a sudden she said, "Can I ask you something?" My heartbeat immediately raced in fear of her question, not sure of what to expect.

"Sure, what's up?" I answered, pretending to be calm and reserved.

"This morning, you were lying on your back. Your shirt was up. I saw a scar under your belly button area. It looks fresh. Did you have surgery or something?" Everything came to a screeching stop. I was at the crossroads. Do I continue lying or roll the dice? *If I tell her everything she might freak out, get mad, maybe even leave, or she empathizes with me, becomes understanding of why I withheld the truth, and we live happily ever after.*

"Well, it's a little complicated. Uh, my doctor wanted me to see a specialist a while ago. They discovered blood in my urine ..." As I spoke, she reached for the TV remote to turn the volume down,

313

devoting all her attention to my words and body language. "Long story short, they found a tumor on my bladder …"

"Do you have cancer?" she interrupted.

"The tumor is cancerous, yeah, but it hasn't spread. It shrunk with the chemotherapy treatments…"

Yami

From the moment Doug spoke those words, my heart sank. I'd been down this road before. When I was 17, my father who I loved with all my heart, died of liver cancer during my senior year. It crushed me so much that I didn't even attend my graduation ceremony. There wasn't anything anyone could say. My mother or sister, family or friends couldn't do anything. I lost a pathetic amount of weight from depression that scared everyone. Now this? I was just getting to know him, just beginning to fall. Imagining another man leaving my life like my father when he died, and Luis when he was sent to prison for a life sentence. This was too much to comprehend. Why is love fucking with me? I'd rather cut my losses now, than to see another love lost. I know it's selfish, but Jocelyn didn't deserve it either. Luis went away when she was only three and although our relationship was already on the rocks, he was still her father. She still deserved to be held by him, to feel protected by him, but to have another man come into our lives and then be stripped away in only God knows when? I don't know … it just isn't fair.

As I spoke, Yami's glance diverted from mine, seemingly shamed at what she saw. This wasn't the plan. Then she stopped looking at me all together, rather off in the distance, past me, disgusted with a fucking loser.

"When were you gonna tell me this?" she asked.

At least her tone was bearable. Gwen on the other hand deservingly railroaded me and threw me under the bus. My judgment was cloudy. I hoped some kind of way this moment could wash away, or at least be a laughable memory later on in our lives.

"I panicked a little, didn't wanna worry you, but my treatments are working …"

"That's not the point, Doug," she interrupted.

"You're right. I apologize for not telling you earlier. It was stupid. Everything just started picking up with us. I didn't wanna scare you off."

She looked back at me, directly into my soul, and then a single tear fell from her right eye, a silent pain revealed. I felt like shit all of sudden, with no possible recourse for the hurt she felt. Why am I such a pussy? Oddly, coming clean, was freeing to a degree, regardless of what was next. With my immediate family still in the dark, maybe she'd help me get through this, maybe even take the place of Gwen.

A few days later, the tension remained. Dinner time was awkward now. One night, Yami cooked and called Jocelyn to the table, and they sat by themselves while I remained upstairs avoiding the awkwardness. Jocelyn even called for me. It was a first, but I pretended not to hear. Then things took a turn for the worse ... no more "good nights" or "good mornings." I initiated them but they were not reciprocated. Only a matter of time would reveal the direction we were heading.

Sure enough, after another taxing yet promising chemo session, a long Wednesday afternoon enhanced with bad traffic, I finally reached home, and discovered an envelope taped to the door. Not being delinquent on anything, even my old bills, I found it odd, but not alarming. Entering my place, the silence was deafening. I called out to Yami a few times, but no response was given. Not giving it much thought, I figured she'd taken a taxi to the store or some other random place like she had on numerous occasions. I sat on the sofa, opened the envelope and it was a hand written letter.

> *Dear Doug,*
> *I know I've been an obvious asshole to you these last few days. It's not right, but you need to know that I felt disrespected that you wouldn't give me the courtesy of being able to make my own decision regarding your personal business. Do you remember asking me about my father, and how I didn't go into much detail about how he died? He died of cancer when I was 17. It messed me up so bad I had to see a doctor for depression. And then, I didn't tell you about Jocelyn's dad, but when I said he's "away," I really meant he's locked up in prison doing life for some bullshit he did in the streets during our younger days. That's two men out of my life, out of Jocelyn's life, and I just couldn't imagine going through that again. I really am feeling you or else I wouldn't have made this move, but I deserved to know that information, because I've*

*been through the pain of loss and I couldn't bear losing someone
else. I know you say the treatments are working and that's great,
but what if they didn't? All my family is in New York, I don't
have a support system out here like you. God forbid, if things
got worse, we'd be alone. I'm very sorry for doing things like
this, but I'll call you when I get back to New York. All my love,*
     Yami.

As bright as the day was, the room went dark, I went dark. I
was in some disturbed place where hurt and self-loathing seemed
a volatile mix for destruction. *Fuck that bitch.* I hated her for that
fucking letter taped to the door of my $4,000 a month apartment. I
hated her for the vulnerability of loving someone new and having
the courage to show it. I hated her for the encouraging words I
gave and the prospect of a life together, her and her cock-blocking
daughter. *Fuck them.* I hated her for the cowardice she displayed,
and her hypocritical rant on mine. Who the fuck was she? And
then it hit me: she was me, but stronger. She'd rather go back to
unemployment and cold weather in Alphabet City than to live a
lie in paradise. She was bigger than me. That's what I hated.

Days went by without communicating with anyone. Mama
called a few times but I ignored her calls. Devin was already in his
own world, and Lamont seemed busier with the anticipation of
their second child. I couldn't care less about much, the Bioko deal,
Raul's gym, Fullbacks, nothing. Love died and it stung, burning
any desire to be committed to anything or anybody. The irony
mushed me in the face. I never pursued Gwen. We just happened
through mutual friends who thought we'd make a nice couple.
But I consciously, of my determination and desire, pursued Yami
Conchita Orozco.

In apartment 1702, I wept for her. An embarrassing sob that
ached and stripped me of my dignity, was replaced with contempt.
The day was coming when I'd have to tell those who'd met her,
"She's gone back to New York ... it didn't work out." So many
times I wanted to unfriend her, some passive aggressive bullshit
meant to ease the pain, but who was I fooling? Some days I'd look
at her pictures, lost in the imagination of our love-making, more
irritated at the fact that it never happened. All that was left was
self-pity. My cars, status, and money, were all secondary to Yami's
exodus. I began spending more time alone, focused on the next
cystoscopy exam. "M" crossed my mind, a nice rebound play, but

the effort wasn't there. After months without any communication, I supposed she probably dismissed me. Back at square one, going to random clubs seemed a plausible choice for hitting on random chicks, but what about my soul? I had found love already.

The conviction to tell my mother before the exam lingered on, frustrating me as if coming from God. Perhaps if the results had turned negative and the tumor was finally operable, having her support and Devin's support would only be natural. At least she couldn't leave me. I decided to give her a call, with the intention of stopping by and telling her the news.

A lazy Saturday afternoon meant for sleeping in late, I found myself driving to Mama's house poised to share this information. Having had my own heart broken, I was more relatable and empathetic than before. There would be no long drawn out build up, and no guessing. I planned to be direct but affirming that the situation was under control. This time, it would only be her and I, supporting each other in the process.

When I finally reached her house, a certain calmness washed over me, a spirit of peace intended to guide the words I'd say and hopefully influence her reaction to them. She answered the door with a smile, and we hugged.

"How you doing?" she asked.

"I'm okay."

Sure enough she was in the middle of another court show, with something cooking in the oven.

"What'cha cooking?" I continued.

"Baking a cake for the neighbor. Her birthday's tomorrow," she answered.

"Oh, that's nice of you. Making friends already, huh?"

"Yeah, she's nice. She and her husband invited me to their church. I might go."

"Great," I answered, thinking of the timing for this bombshell. Then she asked.

"What's going on with you? I called a few times. You all right?"

It was now or never, or until I absolutely had to tell her. *Tell her now*. I sat down at the island, looking at the granite counter top, the intricate randomness of the design, flecks of gold sporadically placed against a pewter and gray back drop.

"Have a seat with me, Mama." She looked over with a confused smirk, but obliged. Her mood seemed too pleasant for what I had to say. "I'm so happy so see you living like this, making friends

... turning this house into a home." She kept nodding her head in agreement.

"It's definitely a blessing," she said, waving her hand in glory.

"I need to tell you something, but you gotta do the best you can to ..."

"What's wrong, Dougie?" she interrupted.

I looked at my hands, thinking of the words, even the first word ... *so unfair*. Overcome with emotion, tears welled up in my eyes, and a lump rose in my throat. I was fearful of breaking her heart. I looked in her eyes. "I have a tumor on my bladder and it's cancerous." Her facial expression immediately changed to a grimacing look intensified by the fact that her eldest son was "sick." I sat there in silence, quiet and shaken by the moment. The burden had been passed on.

She seemed at a loss for words. Shaking her head she said, "No, no ..." The tears ran down both of our faces. *This conversation was way overdue...*

She got off the stool, walked over to me and gave me the longest, tightest hug I'd had in a while. Our embrace was in remembrance of Daddy and Andre, both gone less than five years ago, so fresh in our memories, and yet a terrifying trend.

"It's gonna be all right Mama, I promise." She continued sobbing with no end in sight. Later on, after we cleaned up, we continued talking, me revealing that I'd been in treatment for some months, with another exam on Monday, and that Yami and Jocelyn had gone back to New York. She was visibly upset with me for withholding the information, but accepting of my rationale. Afterward, she offered to attend my appointment, and then I left. The only people to tell now were Devin and Grace. On the drive home, the relief of telling her gave me a euphoric surge, assuring that life was good in spite of it all. Feeling hopeful, I thought about going to Chacho's, but changed my mind. And then my cell rang. It was Gwen.

"Hey there," I answered.

"Hi, how you doing?"

"Good, your timing is impeccable," I replied.

"Why you say that?"

"I just left my mother's house. I told her."

"Good for you. How she take it?"

"She cried. Shit, we both cried," I answered.

Telling Gwen that I told my mother was a plea for reconciliation masked in small talk.

"I'm happy for you, for real."

"Thank you."

"I've been thinking about you. I'm sorry how I reacted, but I prayed for you and asked God to forgive me, and I'm asking you to forgive me," she said.

"I was wrong for real and I'm glad you called. Of course I forgive you. No hard feelings at all."

"So how's the treatments going?"

"I have another exam Monday. My mother is going."

"That's good. I'd like to come, too, if that's all right with you. It'll be nice to see your mother, and I owe it to you," she continued.

"You don't owe me, but I'd appreciate that. It won't be a problem with your job?"

"Don't worry about it. Just give me a time," she answered.

"All right ... nine, same place."

"All right, well I guess I'll see you then."

"Okay."

We hung up after saying our good byes. I was happy to know that she was still down for me, a different kind of love weathered by circumstance.

On Monday morning, after picking up Mama, we were on our way back to the medical center, back to Dr. Dobbs' office, with a new resolve. Whatever news I'd get, I was prepared. I'd made my peace with my loved ones and for that, my spirit had been refreshed.When we arrived at the lobby, Gwen was already there with a special surprise ... little Morgan.

When he saw me, his eyes lit up as mine, and he ran towards me like old times. A little emotional, I fought back the tears while hugging him.

"What's up boy, you getting big, huh?"

"Yes," he answered.

Mama and Gwen hugged too, a long overdue gathering under an odd circumstance. Devin and Grace still hadn't known of the situation, per my request to Mama. They'd get the news after today. We went on to the office and sat in the reception area, as I waited to be called to the back. When the nurse finally came to the door calling my name, that old familiar ball of nerves hit my gut again. All the nursing staff offered polite smiles, seeing I'd become a regular, and again I was asked to wait in that holding cell.

"Mr. Moore, good morning," Dr. Dobbs said as she walked into the room. She was especially chipper, a good sign perhaps.

"Hey, Doc, how are you?"

"I'm hopeful," she answered.

After more small talk and a discussion about the progress of my treatments, I was asked to change into the robbing for the exam. Afterward, I said my usual prayer of grace, before being escorted into the examination room.

Lying on the gurney, with legs spread and propped up, my eyes danced back and forth, ignoring the procedure all together. Occasionally, I'd hear Doc's voice her thoughts with a "hmm" or "okay," all in a positive tone. I couldn't imagine what she saw, only believing that it was all good. Less than ten minutes later from the insertion of the probe, we were done.

"Doug, I don't want to get your hopes up, but the tumor has shrunk considerably. I need to look at these samples, check the vitals, but this bad boy looks ready to pop out."

"You serious, Doc?" My heartbeat went into overdrive.

"This whole process is about containment. We generally don't like to operate with the fear that the tumor has left remnants behind … cells that we didn't catch. But at this stage it looks operable." I beamed. In spite of it all, Yami leaving, the weight and hair loss, I was back.

After getting dressed, I went back into the reception area where everybody waited. I flashed a smile, with Mama and Gwen smiling back in anticipation.

"What?" they asked.

"My doctor thinks that I may be ready to remove the tumor."

My mother immediately began speaking in tongues while Morgan looked at her fearfully. The amazement of this possible twist of fate was overwhelming, but I had to wait some days for her final call.

I thanked God, all that day, all that week, and the anger that filled my heart for Yami, had been replaced with the chance of a second chance. I called Lamont with the news and of course he was happy for me, but Devin needed to know the truth. I decided to call him, agreeing to stop by his place for a chat. When I pulled up to his house, his truck and Grace's new 7 series were parked in the driveway for a good afternoon wash. He looked so suburban with his cargo shorts and Lakers jersey on, laboring over Grace's car. I got out and began helping him, rinsing off the lather.

"'Sup dude? Nice whip; bout time you brought that girl a car."

"Shit, she wasn't gone stop bugging me until I did."

We shared a laugh, finished up, and went back into the house where we retreated to his Lakers man cave, with posters of Magic, Kobe, Kareem, and Shaquille placed around the room. He reached in the fridge to offer a beer, which I declined, and then he popped on the TV and took a seat in his cheesy, oversized, leather recliner.

"Damn, nigga. Is that a 70 inch screen?" I asked. His man cave was fanatical.

"Man, this HD shit is crazy. When them boys be dunking, that shit look like 3-D."

He was obviously in a mood that didn't warrant what I had to say, but again, he deserved to know. He continued on about the TV, the season, and the new car. "Man, I took that shit up to 180. I thought I was gone fly in that bitch," he continued. His breezy demeanor may not have been accepting of the news I had so I opted to ask why he seemed so distant lately.

"Man, I wanted to ask if everything's all right. You seem kind of busy all the time. I was wondering if you and Grace were okay. You okay?"

"I'm fine. It's all good."

He continued looking at the screen, but judging by his quick reply, something didn't gel, and as his "big brother," I could usually tell when he was lying.

"All right then, I'm a leave it alone," I answered. Then he looked at me, got up, and closed the door.

"Look man, don't tell Mama this, all right?"

"All right. What?"

He took a deep breath, looked up at the ceiling and began.

"Man, this chick I went to high school with, we started talking and shit before we moved here. Anyway, we fucked and shit, and now she telling me she five months pregnant, dude."

I could see the sincere fear in his eyes. It was a shock because of the fact he wasn't that type of dude. The irony of it all, his secret running concurrent with mine, was reason enough for someone to break this silly little chain of family stupidity.

"How you know for sure it's yours?" I offered.

"I don't know. We fucked twice that's it. The last time was right before we took the plane ride here. That weekend."

Considering this to be a teachable moment, I went with my gut, telling him about my situation in hopes of it giving him the courage to handle his. When I finished laying the details out, the chemotherapy, the biopsy surgery, and this last exam, he sunk into his seat, stung by all I had to say. It made his affair look like an after school special.

"Why you ain't tell me?" he asked.

"For the same exact reason you ain't tell me, Mama, or Grace … your fear of our reaction."

GRATEFUL [33]

On Tuesday, May 3, ⸱the call I'd been waiting for finally came. The exam concluded that the tumor was in fact, benign, and ready to be removed. Everybody that knew my situation rejoiced. The urge to call Yami was replaced with a quaint inbox note:

Hey, Yami, hope all is well. It's been a while since we talked. Didn't want to bother you. I'm still sorry for how things turned out, but got some good news. The tumor is benign. My surgery is on May 10, my mother's birthday, crazy right? Anyway, hope you and Jocelyn are doing ok, tell her I said hello, and please pray for me. Love you.

If I learned anything during this ordeal, most of all, it was courage. Being forthright was the only way to be at my age, a necessity for my mental health. Most of the shit I put others through was avoidable had I just trusted them without overthinking for them. It was arrogant believing my "way" was doing everyone a favor, assuming what was best, when in fact, I didn't even know what was best for myself.

With millions of dollars in the bank, my profound awakening had been the realization of a bankrupt spirit. Wealth had already been in my grasp whether stepping foot in my classroom, delivering my lessons along with lessons on life, enjoying good times with good friends and drinks with coworkers, or quaint telephone conversations with Mother. These were the jewels. Of course I was thankful to God for this sudden fortune, something that could leave a true legacy of benevolence in the world. Within the year, my charity work was beginning to take shape. We made a donation to a revitalization fund for low-income housing in Third Ward and the L.E. Moore Scholarship Fund was officially in operation.

On the day of the surgery, I sat at the edge of my bed, in reflection, blessed to be alive. The family slept over in support of the operation, while Grace and the boys would stay behind. Gwen had been such a support despite the sabbatical. Her prayers were enough. Lamont offered to come, but Dana was nine months pregnant, so I told him to chill.

At about 7:55 a.m., we were out the door, yet again to the medical center. Mama started singing an old church hymn we use to sing as kids: *"This is the day, this is the day, that the Lord has made, that the Lord has made ..."* It felt corny at first, but the feeling was undeniable. A smile came to my face and I joined in, *"I will rejoice, I will rejoice and be glad in it, and be glad in it."* Devin remained silent, but he laughed and smiled as he drove. The morning sky hadn't fully broken in. It was overcast and a grayish hue. Slightly hungry, a sausage, egg and cheese McMuffin was perfect but against the instructions of the doctor to abstain from food and drink the night before and morning of the surgery.

"After this, we should take a family trip to Paris for a couple weeks y'all." I offered. Mama seemed ecstatic over the idea while Devin mockingly replied in a cheesy French accent. Secretly, the prospect of a love interest to accompany me made the idea even better, but my family deserved this more for what I'd put them through.

"Ooh, we gotta see the Eiffel Tower," Mama commented.

"Yeah, Gracie would love that. Y'all gone be shopping and all that. Me and Doug gone go somewhere and chill, okay, Mama?"

"Whatever, we don't need y'all," she answered.

I laughed. The moment was healing me from within. We were living.

As we approached the Fannin intersection, we began singing "Happy Birthday" to her, having fun, with Devin clowning the most in his falsetto voice. When the light changed he immediately took off, not noticing the speed of a car approaching the intersection from the right. Before he could react in time, the driver careened into the side of us, T-boning the truck in the collision. We slid some feet from a side angle, windows busted, airbags deployed, my life in danger and flashing before my eyes. The driver of the white Nissan Altima hadn't paid attention to the light or either made the conscious decision to run it. Everything happened so fast, so unreal on this day of all days. My memories came in flashes, snapshots of my life: me learning to ride a bike with Dad, graduation day, my first kiss, Gwen. The moment stunned us all but hurt me most. When I looked down, shards of glass were in my lap, with the warm feel of blood running down my face, into my eyes, my vision was blurry.

Devin called to me, "Doug ... Doug, you all right?" Incoherent, spaced out, too hurt to cry, scream, yell or care, I wanted to look back at Mama but the pain of moving permeated my body.

She never said anything the whole time, except maybe faint sounds of a moan, but barely anything. After the mayhem, Devin got out the car, walked to my side, and then on to the other driver who seemed non responsive. This was seriously confusing. *Was this really the day that the Lord had in mind? Could I rejoice in this?*

A weird tingling feeling went up and down my right side, a deep pain perhaps not conscionable yet. Oddly, seconds later, from the angle in which the car stopped, in the sky, the sunlight broke through shining fiercely on my face.

Suddenly I heard my mother, "Doug ... Doug?" her weakened plea, for which I asked, "You okay?"

She didn't answer but rather, continued repeating my name. Things were serious. I sat there not quite sure how to process the moment, what life lesson to be learned. All out of positive affirmations, I stared at the sun, through the blood in my eyes, smiled at the randomness of that early Tuesday morning, said "Thank you," and closed my eyes.

ABOUT THE AUTHOR

Levi Lamont Beard, using the pen name "L. Lamont," always had a knack for writing, going back to his days at Pasadena City College in Pasadena, California, where he honed his gift through journalism and creative writing courses. Having articles published on the collegiate level further sparked the interest to write and even dabble in poetry.

After earning a Bachelors of Communications degree from Wilberforce University, he moved to Houston, Texas and embarked on a career in education. While earning his Masters in Education Administration degree from Prairie View A&M University, his first short-form play entitled, "Consequence," was published in 2007 through the University of Houston's Houston Teacher Institute, aimed at designing a creative writing curriculum through playwriting.

Besides his love for writing and composing music, his career in education has spanned 12 years, beginning with the Houston Independent School District as a middle school English teacher, and currently as a high school English teacher for the Abu Dhabi Education Council in Abu Dhabi, United Arab Emirates. He is married to Dr. Pamela D. Bilton-Beard, also an educator, for over 13 years.

www.ingramcontent.com/pod-product-compliance
Lightning Source LLC
Chambersburg PA
CBHW051334250626
47155CB00007B/2591